ALSO BY DARRYL PINCKNEY

FICTION

High Cotton

NONFICTION

Out There: Mavericks of Black Literature

Blackballed: The Black Vote and U.S. Democracy

BLACK
DEUTSCHLAND

BLACK DEUTSCHLAND

DARRYL PINCKNEY

FARRAR, STRAUS AND GIROUX   NEW YORK

Farrar, Straus and Giroux
18 West 18th Street, New York 10011

Copyright © 2016 by Darryl Pinckney
Printed in the United States of America
First edition, 2016

Library of Congress Cataloging-in-Publication Data
Pinckney, Darryl, 1953– author.
Black Deutschland / Darryl Pinckney. — First edition.
    pages   cm
    ISBN 978-0-374-11381-0 (hardcover) —
ISBN 978-0-374-71314-0 (ebook)
    1. African Americans—Germany—Berlin—Fiction.
    2. Gay men—Fiction.   I. Title.

PS3566.I516B58 2016
813'.54—dc23
                                                    2015032651

Designed by Jonathan D. Lippincott

Our books may be purchased in bulk for promotional,
educational, or business use. Please contact your local bookseller
or the Macmillan Corporate and Premium Sales Department
at 1-800-221-7945, extension 5442, or by e-mail
at MacmillanSpecialMarkets@macmillan.com.

www.fsgbooks.com
www.twitter.com/fsgbooks • www.facebook.com/fsgbooks

1 3 5 7 9 10 8 6 4 2

For James Fenton

Make sure the moon in the grotto is turned on.
—Ludwig II of Bavaria

BLACK
DEUTSCHLAND

ONE

It doesn't always start with a suitcase. Sometimes things begin with the wrong book. Berlin meant boys, Isherwood said. Fifty years after his adventures among proletarian toughs, Berlin meant white boys who wanted to atone for Germany's crimes by loving a black boy like me.

The first time I saw the Mercedes-Benz star revolving over Europa Center, West Berlin's triumphant commercial hub, I knew I was home. I had a room in a hotel near the main West Berlin station, the sort of place where burned-out hippies beat up their girlfriends. I didn't even turn on the light as I tossed in my bag. I hit the heavy-named streets, delight in my stride. You would have thought I'd arrived in Venice. But I'd read quite a bit about how the not-old-for-Europe structures of West Berlin, stripped of decoration, felt squeezed by the postwar functionalism of the here-to-replace-what-was-unremembered.

I pranced to the central shopping mall. West Berlin was the outpost of Western prosperity, the floating island of neon and pleasure deep inside Communist territory. This was its core. I'd read that after the construction of the Berlin Wall, both sides wanted to distract their populations from the border cutting through the heart of the capital. Each side created its own new city center away from the Wall. East Berlin had Alexanderplatz, dominated by the giant needle and revolving restaurant of a television tower visible for miles. West Berlin had Europa Center, a wall of steel and glass, a courtyard of shops and offices nestled beside an office tower, the only one of its kind in the city when erected in 1961. It blocked out, psychologically, the wall of mortar and wire that ran parallel, along the same north-south axis, dividing east from west.

The standing rectangle of office tower looked across the Tiergarten, a vast park that had become as quiet as No Man's Land because of its proximity to the Wall. At any hour, the Tiergarten was filled with boys, silently cruising under the cover of postwar linden or chestnut trees. The tower block was grounded in a narrow plaza. The past sat on the shoulder of everything you saw in Berlin. The ruin of a Romanesque Revival spire marked one end of the plaza, chiding the ugly modern octagon of beehive-blue glass next to it that was built as the new church and also as a memorial to the old one. Had there been traffic, it would have flowed around this plaza. There the Kurfürstendamm begins, West Berlin's show street that makes a humorless diagonal through the city, along the route Prussian kings took to their hunting lodges.

In the middle of the plaza a round fountain of big beige granite dollops is still running. My very first night in Berlin, the people hanging out around the fountain, young or just longhaired, looked like they'd met at the train station a few minutes before and had walked over to conclude unsavory transactions. Young couples, families of shoppers, and groups of moviegoers kept their distance, sitting under umbrellas at the beer, cola, and coffee tables at the other end of the plaza.

The company emblem turned in the friendly sky. Behind the red Mercedes-Benz star, perfectly in line with it as I looped back around, was a pink August sun just beginning to quit.

This was the start of the awful 1980s. I saved money from my second job, a telephone-marketing gig, for the few weeks I could afford to spend in Berlin every summer. Just before Chicago flipped out because of AIDS Terror, I was getting away, but every summer coming back too soon, broke and heartbroken over some kerchiefed bartender and feeling superior to everything about my hometown. I was leaving pieces of myself in Berlin, like a bird carrying its feathers one by one to a distant nest. In the Cold War days, Berlin was far away, a disco ball behind the Iron Curtain.

I smoked menthols on bar stools, snorted lines in paperless stalls, and threw up on corners all over the Near North Side, protected by my dream of eventual escape. Though born in Chicago, I was just passing through. Whatever had happened in the Golden Rectangle, whatever was going down on the South Side did not matter. I may have fallen apart in the city of my birth, but the city of my rebirth would see me put back together again. My real life of the happiness I deserved would begin once I got over there and stayed. What had not happened in Chicago would finally happen in Berlin, the city that owed me and loved my fantasies.

I was idiotic during my first visit to Berlin. I bought drinks three nights running for a sour-smelling old man who told me he had inherited from his father the most rare footage in Europe, twenty-seven seconds of Nijinsky dancing. Of course the film was held in a bank. He'd invite me special to see it.

"It used to be 'Aimez-vous Paree?' that the black GI ran to," my dad said, rolling slowly in his chair, up to and back from his desk. "But you and your cousin can't get enough of that 'Sprechen Sie Jive?'"

I didn't tell him that because I'd been in a bar all day I'd snored through the Berlin Philharmonic concert that my cousin had taken me to. I forgave before anyone else did the young blind prowler I had been, who drank as though Weimar culture could be got through the bottle.

After those few summers of desperate rehearsal, tourist make-believe, I was recently sober and alone in a train compartment about to be locked tight for the border crossing between the fast-driving, exhibitionist German Federal Republic and the paranoid German Democratic Republic, with its harsh fuels. I'd left Chicago behind for good. I was inordinately proud of my one-way ticket. I'd become that person I so admired, the black American expatriate.

•

Branches of the same people who are black in the valley are white on the mountain, Frederick Douglass said. The beautiful hair of the Nubian becomes frizzled as he approaches the great Sahara, he added.

•

Mad, unknowable people were hijacking planes over Europe and setting off bombs at the Frankfurt International Airport the summer I came back to West Berlin ready for adult life, willing to register with the police. My new job came with what I considered glamorous international paperwork. The address I was going to wasn't far and I could nod to the Mercedes-Benz star—I always let it know when I was back in town—as the taxi turned in the opposite direction, onto the Kurfürstendamm.

The city arched its back in the sandy heat. My cousin Cello and her husband and their four children and a nanny from Stratford-upon-Avon lived not far from the seedy Zoo Station, but their address was historic, bourgeois Berlin. The street doors were heavy polished oak, and the front staircase wide slippery oak. Their apartment had four balconies; it was an apartment that went on and on, around the whole side of the corner building, with high ceilings, even in the maid's room, where, as I discovered, Cello intended to install me.

"I tripped over my baby," Cello said when she opened the door. She bounced a shrieking brown toddler with beautiful long curls in her arms as two other gorgeous little honey-colored boys reached up and tried to tickle his toes. "Remember peanut brittle?" she asked. Her boys had big eyes.

I shrugged and Cello cupped the screaming head, turning her baby away from my raised hand. The long, sleeveless pale-blue satiny dress she wore looked like a nightgown. She had on silk stockings, in August, and glistening black-and-white saddle oxfords with rounded toes.

To me, she looked like the music she studied, mostly because of her hair. She was a throwback to our great-grandmother's locks, got from some slave master. Instead, we'd say Cherokee. Her hair came from our Indian blood. It was the only thing she had on her sister, her lack of acquaintance with the hot comb. She didn't have to suffer for white-girl-like hair. Her nap was soft. She piled her amazingly long, undulating black hair on top of her head or dismissed it over her neck with wide combs. Her attitude toward her hair was as striking as its abundance. Look, okay, I have good hair, as it used to be called in Negro America. Fine, not frizzy. But I'm not going to let it mean anything to me.

Otherwise, Cello was the color of a Snickers bar and had a large nose and lips copied from Man Ray. She was tall, one of those girls who would have been comforted by the publication of Jackie Onassis's shoe size in the *Detroit Free Press*. Her ample hips gave her her music-camp nickname, which she was instantly proud of. Men noticed her breasts. Her posture was incredible. But her eyes were too small for her face. She did not get her mother's big eyes; she got the raisins of her father's side of the family, my side. Her glasses had to make up for a lot with their style. It was because of her eyes that other women, including her mother, felt that there were other women out there prettier than Cello. That made them generous about her brilliance as a pianist. Their approval lapped at the stairs Cello ascended when in their presence, her hair in her hands, just like the illustration in an old book we had about a princess in trouble.

Cello kicked at the tricycle that, apparently, had been involved in the collision of mother and child. "Bad tricycle," she said in German. The older boys started kicking at the various toys that had turned the spacious foyer into a mess. The entrance hall framed three sets of double doors, one set of which opened onto a large salon, also chaotic from child's play. An American fire truck that the children could ride was parked under a long black piano, which seemed to have rolled to rest where it was, not wholly in the corner, blocking the way to another room. Everything in the room felt as if it had been flung there, tables and telephone books and little wooden musical pipes and tiny drums and tiny T-shirts and Beethoven scores and plastic juice cartons with built-in straws.

"Who are you?" the oldest repeated in English.

"I'm Jed." I was nervous about saying even the simplest things in German to a child, but I again asked him his name.

Once more he didn't reply, and hopped away.

"Otto!" Cello said, putting her hollering youngest on the parquet. A hefty young white girl looked out from behind a door.

"Why aren't you in the kitchen? Where's Hildegard?"

The rosy-faced brunette scooted back down the corridor, agile in stretch pants she ought not to have had on. Cello lifted her boy again.

I just so happened to have been tested while in the rehab. The reason I'd not looked up Cello the last two summers I came to Berlin was that she'd told my mom that she could not have me around her children unless I had the AIDS test. I was secretly relieved not to have her reporting Stateside about me, as if people couldn't have seen for themselves had they wanted to.

My cousin didn't have to reply to the thank-you note I sent when I got back to Chicago after my first trip to Berlin, but Cello also didn't answer when I wrote her the next year to say I was coming. She finally agreed to meet me for breakfast the day before I was scheduled to leave. I slept through our appointment. She forgave me in Chicago when she brought her three children to see her fading grandmother. Maximilian hadn't been born yet. But when I came back to Berlin that summer, I promptly disgraced myself.

Now Cello was ready to help me in my starting over. She was showing me around the apartment, though I'd been there when they moved in three years before. By the end of that visit, I was sweaty in the mirror of the bathroom I kept adjourning to. I was not good enough at anything or good-looking enough to get away with being dirty, she said then. She'd kept me at arm's length since. But Cello was good at wiping the slate clean.

"You remember where the kitchen is," she said, in German. Back in Chicago, I was her cousin, but sometimes in Berlin she'd made it clear to me that I was her second cousin, a distant family obligation from the United States, a country relation she had to do something for. The boy in her arms and his six-year-old and five-year-old brothers trailing us down the hall that let in light from two sides were hardly kin to me. Cello handed Maximilian to the nanny and walked me, her mitzvah, past a pantry, a laundry room, and a bathroom. The corridor turned right. We walked through an open door and sat side by side on the bed.

How she accumulated shawls on her way down the hall I couldn't say. She folded three or four layers of delicate stuff over her bare shoulders. Underneath us, the intricate pattern of a lovely white bed throw. Cello sprang up and ushered the children from the room, telling Otto and Konrad to join their sister and brother at the coloring table in the kitchen.

The furniture in the bedroom was on a smaller scale than what I was used to, real Biedermeier with white marble tops, the lamps dark Prussian iron. The last time I'd been in that room, there'd been only a camp bed and cartons piled on cartons. I wondered how I was going to ask Cello if I could make some room in the glass case for my own books, which would be arriving soon. I somehow had the feeling that the books had been in that case unexamined for a long time. Every space was taken up. Books were crammed on their sides. Cello didn't read books, not really. She studied scores. Her eyes flashed across bars, like a burglar looking at windows for a way in. Yet somehow she had absorbed the vibe of the most important literary works of Western culture. She would have balked to be reminded that her father had this talent.

Cello's father was my mom's first cousin. He went nuts in the civil rights movement. Her mother thought she had a singing career, which meant that Cello and her little brother and sister pretty much stayed with us. Our extended family wasn't large. There weren't many of us, because of the family members who had no siblings or children or had just lost touch, not to mention those who weren't speaking to us. Cello never could decide what to do with me. After all, I was the only person in West Berlin who'd known her when she was called Ruthanne. And I'd seen her face during one of her mother's cabaret performances in Old Town in the 1970s.

Cello was infinitely more musical than her mother. The gap between them in regard to absolutely everything about music, from degree of talent to the type of music that engaged them, was deeply painful to Cello. It was my mom who called the blind piano tuner, got Cello to lessons, and discussed her next steps with her teachers, and no one more than Cello wanted her mother to be too wrapped up in her own singing lessons and choir practice to pay much attention to Cello's day-to-day development. Cello had a life of her own elsewhere, behind the temple of the Art Institute, at the American Conservatory of Music, then on to the Chicago Musical College.

She was set apart by her destiny. She was not expected to look after her brother and sister; she was never asked to go to the store. Cello never had a child's free time or an adolescent's schedule of lassitude behind closed doors. She ate separately, later or earlier, like the poet-slave Phillis Wheatley in the home of her doting Methodist owners. Then she'd disappear upstairs. Once we'd finished, she liked to help my mom to wash up. We often had my mother's social causes in the form of women bums and female cons staying with us, but Mom didn't like for anyone else to help her do the dishes except Cello, no matter how many had been at the dinner table.

My mom was the person she talked to. Mom was the one in the family who knew the Chopin *Fantaisie-Impromptu* when she heard it and just what it would take for Cello to learn it as well as she wanted to. Cello practiced two hours a day downtown and then was driven home, where she played some more. But sometimes she sat on Mom's piano bench, not playing. She had to take out some of the music stuffed in the seat in order to get it flat. She liked to costume herself in an ankle-length pale blue taffeta gown and sit there, head bowed, hands folded in her lap, lights low.

Her gift was her sanctuary. She represented Negro Achievement, whether a National Merit scholar in high school or a finalist in the Chicago Stokowski Society competition. Negro Achievement took her out of the women's game, out of the black women's game. She renounced the pleasures other girls lived for. Like a sprinter or a dancer, she sacrificed everything to the single-minded pursuit of perfection. She was going to give up everything for her art, and because she was a black artist, people around her who didn't understand the music added, her attainments as an artist were also going to count in the freedom struggle.

No matter what the DuSable Club president handing her a modest check said, Cello never pretended that her presence at the Mozarteum was as necessary to the liberation of her people as the registration of black voters in Mississippi. I heard her tell Mom after one such ceremony that she'd managed not to laugh at the way the pastor kept referring to "J. S. Bach." "Not C.P.E.?" I didn't get it. She and my mom shared a language I didn't speak. Cello lived on a plane I could never reach. My older brother had his sports zone, which was taken very seriously, but the most anyone ever thought he'd get were two chances, high school and college, to say farewell as a varsity player. Cello got away—first to Salzburg, then to Boston, and finally to Berlin. She was the only person I knew who lived in that somewhere else I yearned for, Europe.

After all that, she did not have the public career she had prepared for, but nevertheless to the family, especially to her mother, who was afraid of her, she was like somebody famous. She was the wife of a rich white man not from where we were from and therefore not bound by our rules. That made it a stinging judgment for Cello to have returned to Chicago only once in seven years. She displayed her sleeping infant daughter and her two sons, her fulfillment, to the women's clubs, white and black, that had vied with one another to give her prizes. The children's names were not unfamiliar in Northwest Chicago, but they were rare on the South Side.

Most people assumed she'd given up her concert ambitions in order to have children. Cello never said otherwise. She never talked about the calamity of her stage fright. A long time ago, Mom had wagered that if the fat twelve-year-old pianist lost weight, she would no longer lose her presence of mind in recital. My mom devoted herself to Cello's problem and Cello responded by throwing herself into a regimen that murdered the evil twin in her head.

Cello wanted the concert stage and Mom figured out that Cello could shed the pounds holding her back if she had somewhere to treat the matter privately. Private, in this case, meant somewhere where no one knew her, which was another way of saying where there were no rowdy, hurtful black youths calling her names. That was the bond between us, the reason we only went so far with each other: the knowledge of what it had been like to be a fat black kid at a mostly white school. Mom arranged through a connection on one of her committees for Cello to have private swimming lessons at the medical school. Eat, swim, practice, eat, school, practice, eat, practice, sleep. That was why she was excused from meals with us, in order to protect her from the temptations of mashed potatoes. She ate small portions of regulated this and measured that all day long.

Her mother couldn't handle a daughter with such special needs and there were times when Cello came to stay not because things were unstable at home again, but because Mom believed that Cello had a better chance of staying on course under our roof. For plenty of obvious reasons, she binged if around her father and mother for too long. Mom would insist on taking Cello's brother and sister as well. Eat, swim, practice, eat, school, practice, and then more of the same until she made it to sleep. In every room of the house, a clinic of the self was in progress. Mom was a missionary and we, her children, were an indigenous people. She liked to feel us striving to better ourselves. Television was strictly controlled. But Cello was an altogether different story. The weight-loss program worked. It took five years, but it worked, and Cello went off to auditions that she and Mom both believed had a chance at last of going well.

•

In English, Cello, sitting next to me now, was saying that she remembered the last time I'd arrived in Berlin sober and how it took only one party for my sobriety to mean nothing. There had been chatty Japanese people with thick business cards and runny noses and then in no time there were painted Turkish boys gawking around her hallways. She exaggerated, but I was sitting on the pampered bed in the room she was letting me have for free. The wallpaper had a motif of a bird of paradise in a cage. There had been only one Turkish boy. He did wear eyeliner, a lot of it. And purple eye shadow. He'd never been in an apartment as large as hers. He meant no harm. But she'd had Dram inform me that they had to think of the children.

Cello repeated that she did not believe in new beginnings as a rule. People were who they were. People didn't change. I remembered that her sister was the one who'd had the fight with her about how not all black men were like their father, starting with my father, for instance. Cello said she was doing this for me because I had so much to prove to my poor mother. It was almost my last chance. She said she was for the first time ever impressed by something I'd done. She got up and turned off the table lamps she'd turned on when we came in. Cello's coughing fits before performances came back to wreck her life, but the weight never did.

My new beginning, she said, taking me back down her long corridor to the big salon. She said she agreed with N. I. Rosen-Montag and architects like him who were frank about what an opportunity the destruction of Berlin yet represented. Even before she'd seen my article in the *Herald Tribune*, she'd heard that he'd taken a lot of heat at a conference in Copenhagen for his jokes about the debt the German people owed to the Allied Bomber Command. He was often in the news for remarks like that. He could stir things up, get issues talked about. Talk shows and universities chased him. His influence on architecture came through his lectures, writings, and the dissemination of his exquisite drawings. His collections of poetic images sold widely in that world, though he had built hardly anything at all.

Rosen-Montag had also seen the article, in which I was scornful of those who lacked irony and Berlin cosmopolitanism, those who refused to acknowledge that by destruction Rosen-Montag meant reconstruction. I praised him for his dissent from Walter Gropius's children and the arch social vision driving much postwar architecture. I made an analogy between blacks and white liberals in the civil rights movement who couldn't give up the moral high ground and Germans who could only deal with their history by flailing themselves, but I probably didn't mean it in the way the people who patted me on the back for it took it.

Then there was a big architectural theory meeting at the University of Chicago. Rosen-Montag conceded that Gropius meant well, but he marveled at the naïveté in our surprise that the isolated, supposedly self-sufficient towers of Gropiusstadt, or Gropius City, should have become the setting for the social ills associated with low-hope life. Gropiusstadt was at the far end of Neukölln, in the south of West Berlin, hard on the guarded border, too near the East Berlin airport. The complex of fiercely utilitarian apartment houses was hard to get to by U-Bahn, I told myself. I'd never been there, though I imagined that its shopping arcade was haunted by bored, disaffected working-class youths with rotten attitudes, just the kind of pimply, loud, large boys who might need my understanding in the middle of their greasy nowhere.

Rosen-Montag didn't lecture, or really address us. He invited us into his head and we were sightseers on a retrospective tour of his disillusionment with postwar architecture in Berlin and around the world. He was dissatisfied with the modernist principles he'd grown up on, or with what had become of them, and to such an extent he had to ask what else could they have

tended toward. It had always been so, that form had to follow
function, but he'd nevertheless had many dark nights of con-
science about his German masters of the minimal, they who'd
taught him to love American grain silos and Shaker barns. He
tore at his hair and twisted his sleeves as he spoke, his wide
mouth the gateway of pressing thoughts, radical proposi-
tions. Oh, didn't the Bauhaus Archive look like a toaster and
Scharoun's Siemenstadt housing like machine-gun nests? He
pulled his shirt out of his trousers and seemed on the verge of
peeling off his clothes altogether. He said an intellectual falling-
out-of-love was no less traumatic than the extinction of a sexual fire.

Afterward, the room was hot with debate about the tenets
of urban planning and Chandigarh, the town in India designed
by Le Corbusier. An elderly avant-gardist, the one professor
from the un-esteemed Chicago outlet of the University of Illinois who still hoped for something from me and for me, cut
through the throng and introduced me to Rosen-Montag.
He'd done Rosen-Montag a favor when he was an unknown
in the United States, and Rosen-Montag had not forgotten.

I'd been sober thirty-three days and said the first thing
that came into my head. I told him that I would never go back
to the Berlin Zoo, because on my first trip to Berlin I saw an
orangutan who had been trained to wash the floor of her cage
with a bucket and a rag. They had put a mammy's red kerchief
on her head. She looked so sad, mopping and wringing. Rosen-
Montag immediately offered me a position.

Cello said it was her chance to repay my mother for everything my mother had tried to do for her. She was going to help
salvage me, she said. She was, as she said her grandmother used
to say, going to help me win the race with myself. It irritated
me when Cello attributed my mom's words to her grandfather
or grandmother, who did not like my mom. "I'm going to help
you win that race with yourself"—that was what Mom used
to say. And then she would ground me or try to make us earn

the money for what we wanted. Cello's grandmother never said things like that. Other peoples' fates, especially that of her troubled son, Cello's father, were not her concern. It would have been rude, not to mention inconvenient to her radio and television schedule, to try to make them so.

I could tell that Cello couldn't quite believe the news that I had been hired to work with Rosen-Montag on the book he was writing about his current project. I would also do a series of interviews with him as the work progressed. She was somewhat reconciled to my galling reversal of fortune, because I referred to myself as a cog in the wheel of Rosen-Montag's propaganda ministry. I kept to myself the information that Rosen-Montag happened to have been on the wagon the night we met. He liked that I'd just got out of rehab, the sort of social fact you blurt out when you just get out of rehab and don't know how to behave.

Cello moved us back to German conversation. I followed her to the front door, where I'd left my four suitcases. To get them on the plane had cost me. Now the bedroom where I'd smuggled in that painted Turkish boy was kept for Dram's mother and father when they came up to town and needed to rest after lunch, or for Dram's mother to change before a concert. Those were her sets of Brentano and Hölderlin and Heine in the bookcase. A short corridor to the side of the front door led to a small bathroom with a thin shower and, just before it, a maid's room, with a sweet window onto the inner courtyard above the narrow bed.

"Dram is pleased," Cello said, still in German. I was fairly sure she said that my having stumbled upon something interesting to do should keep me out of trouble, if I had the will not to sabotage myself. I was in no doubt that she said Dram would come at six o'clock to put the children to bed and to have dinner with us and then he would go back to the office, as he did every weeknight.

Her German was as intimidating as everything else about

her. I'd once heard a boy from Poland converse in English with a boy from Yugoslavia. It was weird to hear English used as a device, with no cultural inflections. Cello would have said that she was making me practice my German, but she was also canceling out our equality. I didn't know where she got her accent in German, but I was sure it must have been an upper-class one.

Maybe because she never felt that she could depend on her parents, Cello was not the kind of person to waste an opportunity. She always knew where she was. Her will, her application, never failed to impress adults, and her renown as an achiever made her peers a tad uncomfortable in her presence. I mean us, me. There she was, always far ahead, ahead even of my brother. The Negro Achiever was a species of secular saint. To be young, gifted and black, Nina Simone sings.

Cello knew that the Curtis Institute in Philadelphia rejected Nina Simone when she auditioned in the early 1950s. Cello said she heard that the school had long been accepting black students by the time Nina Simone applied and maybe the Curtis faculty's criticisms of the jazz legend's playing were fair. I was so shocked when she told me that.

·

I helped with the children's tea that first month, but they remained leery of me. I thought Cello must have said something to them and to the nanny about not going down the narrow hall to the maid's room anymore.

She had her narcissistic grandmother's sense of style. In a time of tundra-wide minimalism, her deep rooms were criss-crossed with sofas and colorful textiles and tables large and small and mirrors round and square and chairs thick and thin and bookshelves high and low, one concert grand, one baby grand, and an upright in the so-called nursery off the kitchen. Early instruments and ethnic instruments hung on some walls, but mostly where a drawing or photograph might have been were windows. Sunlight attended the happiness of Cello's days. Therefore the reception rooms in front had mirrors, but nothing framed, and the hallway leading to the bedrooms in the rear was bare, except for children's drawings taped up at random. Dram encouraged the eldest to put on socks and slide with him on Sunday mornings.

Cello's happiness included her status as the possessor/confuser of Dram, heir to a family manufacturing firm, Schuzburg Tools. A branch of the family had become immensely rich building Russia's railroads. Mentioned in Tolstoy, they perished with the White Army. Dram's branch of the Schuzburgs had survived because a nail was a nail, a contract a contract, a customer in the right, whether kaiser or National Socialist, NATO or African dictator. The family firm made things most people hardly thought about—hammers of every kind, nuts and bolts and screwdrivers of every size, more and more different kinds of hammers, then hundreds of varieties of electrical instruments.

Cello's large-faced, husky husband gave up his music studies after his older brother was killed in a drunken accident not far from his home on the Schlachtensee. He rolled his car backward down a little birch-spotted embankment. It hit something and flipped over and smashed him. Dram buried his brother and went to work. His father didn't ask him to come back. He just did. There was never a question that either of his two older sisters would take over after his brother's death. Dram never talked forging capacities or galvanization facilities in front of me, but I knew from Cello that under his management the company was beginning to win prizes again and that its hundreds and hundreds of employees in West Berlin and Dortmund were deeply loyal to him. I'd already seen for myself how his father hung on his every word.

More so than my father or my brother, Dram represented

to me the man who embraced with gusto his part in the life he'd made. He did not doubt he was entitled to his sense of well-being, his freedom to luxuriate in the squeals of his children, to defy his wife as her protector, to spoil her as his woman, to be indifferent to the domestic help once they'd been vetted. He stood his ground when wolfing at another man over a parking place directly in front of his building. He swung his dick widely in everything he did. Plus, he wasn't motivated by German guilt. The men in Dram's father's family married cultured women, one of whom had recent Jewish-convert blood, which had put her children at risk during the Third Reich. Then, too, it became known in the 1970s that Dram's mother had assisted people during the war who were hiding Jews and communists in the vicinity of Lake Constance.

Dram never once mentioned to his mother that the brilliant pianist he'd met when he was in graduate school was black. He told his parents that he was going back to Boston to get the woman who was to bear his children and when their taxi drove up Dram's mother did not exclaim, You're a Negro. Cello claimed that seven years later her mother-in-law had still not referred to her being black. The only thing she ever said, Cello boasted, was that her grandchildren were going to be beautiful.

Cello's little sister, Rhonda, was the family knockout. My mom taught her early to grab a leaf or slap a wall, to do something aggressive when men were behind her on a street. Mom worked hard to countermand whatever Cello's mother had told them about sex, without letting on that she considered their mother on the loose side. To her credit, Cello never saw herself as a beauty, no matter how imposing in her prim voluptuousness she had schooled herself to come off as. The fat girl lived on inside her, violent in her feelings against the rice pudding her children loved.

Dram's sister played for the company on Cello's first afternoon in Berlin. He had an upright in his apartment, but he got Cello a practice room with a good Blüthner down in Dahlem. Finally, the family was too curious and one Sunday lunch they begged her to play. This is Cello's version of events. She doesn't know why she chose a Chopin nocturne she'd never been able to master and so had never played to her own satisfaction or to anyone else's, to be honest. When she was telling me this, I noticed in a way that I enjoyed how once again Cello had inserted into a story about herself some criticism meant to show how honest with herself she was capable of being. She was hard on herself. She knew that. It was a fault. She worked on it. Cello said that when she finished the nocturne, Frau Schuzburg came up behind her and whispered to her that she would never forget what Cello was giving up to marry Dram.

To my credit, I did not give in to the bitchiness I felt toward her at that moment. I did not say, What was that? As in, What did you give up? Because I knew she meant her concert career. It never took off, I knew, because she had coughing jags in the wings before she was to sit down to play for performances or just before she was to place herself under a recording microphone. The career she'd never know whether she could have had or not. I didn't ask why Frau Schuzburg assumed Cello would be giving it up. I also refrained from asking how she had managed not to have one of her fits when playing for Dram's family.

Someone once compared her to Philippa Schuyler, the prodigy whose Harlem Renaissance father, George Schuyler, a black journalist married to a white woman, held her up as an example of biological advancement through the mixing or "invigoration" of the races. Cello never spoke to that someone again. Black girls like Mom followed Shirley Temple's career in the 1930s and 1940s and had time left over to clip stories about Philippa Schuyler and to tune in to her radio broadcasts. But at some point Schuyler decided that her friendless upbringing on raw food and tour dates had been a form of bondage and she stopped playing the piano. She joined the John Birch Society and died in a helicopter crash in Vietnam. Her mother committed suicide on the second anniversary of her death.

Cello's sister was Cello's only relative invited to her wedding on Lake Constance. Mom was very hurt by that.

.

I'd come a month early, to settle in, but really to be alone, to drift down memory's canals while the family was away. But they weren't going on holiday, after all. And so for those first thirty-one days, my beautiful August, I kept family hours. It had not been blue-black for long when I got into bed with a starchy-feeling towel and I got up when I heard the nanny whining all the way from the kitchen about the mess the children were making already.

I stayed away from Rosen-Montag's workshop. The new one was still being set up, and they weren't expecting me until September. He wasn't back in Berlin yet. I went to the new State Library. Mostly I walked the passageways, train tracks, and dead ends by the river in the old warehouse district northwest of the Reichstag, where Rosen-Montag was to realize some of his schemes about restoring our living spaces to a human scale. So much of it was off-limits and covered up, I couldn't guess what was going on.

I was also staying out of the apartment. Cello made no demands on me. She didn't want me too involved with her family. She treated me like a convalescent. She was watching me. I wish she hadn't told her mother-in-law that I was in AA, because brave Frau Schuzburg gave my hand a squeeze when they had me out to Wannsee for Sunday lunch. She was encouraging me not to end up drunk and behind the wheel.

I was staying out of the apartment so I wouldn't be smoking in their house. I was free to do so in my room with the window open. But I wanted to impress Cello—and Dram—that I was doing my part to keep clean the air that their children breathed. She'd refused to become pregnant until he quit smoking. Maybe I was also staying out of the apartment in order to be like Dram, a man who came home from work, though I'd nothing to do just yet. Cello shut herself up with the baby grand during the day, interrupting herself frequently to oversee her children's activities, and when I didn't go out, it was easy to make myself scarce because that was how we grew up. I hid in my maid's room, fortified by books and cassette tapes.

Keeping family hours took a decision out of my hands nightly. I would head around the block for a final cigarette, but come in after ten minutes. I turned my back on the city of orgies and joy. I was like someone on parole. I was frightened. I was worried enough that the clichés of the Alcoholics Anonymous Big Book were true that I found an AA meeting in English down in the suburb of Dahlem, near the U.S. army base. Soldiers bitched in country accents about their wives. It didn't matter to me that the two German women who ran the meeting acted as sponsors to the handsomest of the discontents and never let anyone else talk to them. I was afraid not to go to a meeting. Cello's "Good night" on Saturday night after I'd been to a meeting was genuinely warm, I felt. It was true that not to drink could make a drunk feel alone and lost.

When I hear recordings of Cecil Taylor live, I am once again downstairs in a West Berlin club, back in the golden age of chain smoking, drinking another glass of white wine in the free zone of staying up all night, talking out the lyric dark, and then falling still as his instrument meets the dawning light—"the brewing luminosity," Taylor called it. Memory will let in the cool scenes, the hip blowouts. However, the real truth of my summer life in Berlin was held by the plastic interior of a tacky bar. Only the year before I'd spent whole days and nights in the ChiChi Bar, a dive set back from a wide, leafy deserted street behind the plaza of Europa Center.

I'd hung out in the ChiChi since my first trip to West

Berlin. My fourth night there I let myself be picked up by a nice French girl and the night after that I successfully chatted up a boy from a small West German town. I'd shaken off the sour-smelling old man with his fake Ballets Russes act. The bar's owners, Zippi and Odell, tore up my tab for the night my last night in town. In the years following, the first thing I'd do when I got back to town was head to Europa Center. No matter what I got up to in between, I ended my holidays licking my wounds at the ChiChi. I sent Zippi and Odell amusing postcards.

There was a traditional high culture that Cello and Dram lived in and there was an alternative high culture that I was about to go to work in, but the Berlin I lived in with my soul was around the train station and the porn theaters, the cheap lights and fried-food stalls. There were also loud beer bars and serious bookstores tucked under the S-Bahn tracks. I felt at home in a bad bar that did very well. Maybe the ChiChi had been "in" in the '70s. It was listed as a gay bar in out-of-date guides, although anybody and everybody could be found there. White women scored with the black men more than the white men did. I perhaps wrongly assumed that things went on between the black men, American and African, but not counting Odell's buddies. It hardly mattered, because the real business of everyone there was to drink.

Addiction insulated the bar against fashion. There was a group of regulars who'd put in much bar time together. They were the audience for the life-changing mistakes that the ChiChi specialized in. It was a place where people experiencing a bad night strayed in to finish things off with meltdowns, blackouts, fistfights, seizures. Sex was just the messy afterthought, something to do when daylight hit.

"What time do you close here?" I asked Zippi my first night at the ChiChi.

She lifted her head from the bar. "We are never closed here."

In all of my walks when first back in Berlin as a recovering alcoholic, I never let myself go to Europa Center. If I got out at Zoo Station, I took a long, roundabout way to Cello's apartment, just to avoid going by the old smells and sights. Avoid people, places, and things, I wanted someone to say at my AA meeting in Dahlem, because I'd yet to open my mouth in that meeting. Back up in the center of town, I'd walk with my final cigarette of the day and look down the Ku'damm toward the bright intersection and the street that led up to the train station. I could feel my steps continuing. I always loved the sound of my footsteps in Berlin. The Negro in Europe.

And I knew they'd be there at the ChiChi. It was never too early for Odell to slap a wet towel on the bar and Zippi to slam the cash register. There was always a fight going on between them; there were always drinks of some kind sitting in front of them. Maybe Big Dash had come in, reeking of Indian spices. I could see them, some of whom I'd groped, quiet because it was early yet, drinking fast, their cigarette packs and fancy lighters on the bar, on their way to not needing to drink as fast, and not one of them thinking of me.

Alcohol wasn't thinking of me either. You cannot one-up someone who has dumped you, but my former love, white wine, was showing that to be not always the case. I left white wine, yet when I stood there on the Ku'damm, with the sky blue behind me and the east ahead of me end-of-summer dark, it was white wine that was over me already and in the arms of someone else.

TWO

The conquest of the earth was not a pretty thing. The splendor and misery were gone. Symbolic, unchaste Berlin was still the barracks town of Frederick the Great, but the once-teeming capital had also become a small town with a big past. You could crawl into the disfigured city as into a shell. You could treat it as either inhabited ruin or blank space. You could write your own ticket, regard the city as backdrop, a theatrical setting, and appropriate the citizens as extras for your daily dramas, your tremendous inner opera buffa.

The wintry light cast a spell. You were going to walk out the door and reinvent yourself. You were going to turn a corner and there in the neon haze would be the agent of your conversion. Or you could go around in a nervous silence for days, as if the city had been depopulated, leaving only an architecture of signs, layer upon layer, and a dialogue between vanished buildings and their replacements. A preserved fragment of the bombed-out-then-mostly-demolished Anhalter train station shot up from the hard earth to scream at a white block from the 1970s that was like the architectural equivalent of a bimbo.

"Paradise is locked and bolted. We have to make the journey

around the world to see if it is open at the back," Kleist said. Berlin hid its historical face until you slipped over there, into East Berlin, into the immensity of Unter den Linden, Apollonian Baroque and the ineptitude of Karl-Marx-Platz. I didn't try to stop myself from liking the dereliction, the forgotten pockets of buildings still so scarred by bullets that I would not have been surprised had Marlene Dietrich emerged from a doorway to sing "Black Market." Overdressed, laden with the Communist state's unconvincing currency, I found the usual racial situation reversed. These white people who spoke low like inhabitants of a ghost town were the primitives, the needy tribesmen I couldn't take back with me. The sky was a glittering frontier of fumes, creeping mists, and the Berlin Wall itself the white surf.

Back in louder, wandering West Berlin, I turned around and faced the Wall, an exhibition of found art, an explosion of graffiti, like a high school yearbook. I was told that a man was sometimes lowered in a cage from the featureless earth of No Man's Land to wash away the many-colored scrawls of slogans and hearts. I didn't believe it, though none of the graffiti went back very far, certainly not as far back as the crosses behind the Reichstag in memory of those killed trying to escape that August of 1961, when the Wall went up overnight.

The Wall made the lucky part of Berlin artificial, held its grumbling, caustic population in the jealous embrace of privilege. It was a poor city, West Berlin. The conquered city had become the subsidized city. Old Germans willing to live in encircled West Berlin received tax breaks and the young were exempt from national service. The real estate was worth nothing and there was no heavy industry to speak of, just the hundreds clocking in at Schuzburg Tools and other family companies like it. The city services were not massive. Workers of the world—clock out and spend four weeks in a spa. The only big business, it seemed, was culture. The students, filmmakers,

artists, musicians, actors, writers, and professors were the aris-
tocracy, and a foreigner, an intruder, never had to make sense.

•

I longed, as did Cello's nanny, for those times when the family was out. She and I gravitated to the balconies, in spite of
the wet and cold. We went out onto separate balconies. It was
understood. Our needs. I smoked. She ate hidden chocolates.
Neither of us had had anywhere to go on New Year's Eve. We
said when we met in the kitchen that we were exhausted from
the noisy family Christmas and didn't want to go anywhere
anyway. She was paid extra to watch the children that night
and Cello approved of my staying quiet.

Valentine's Day went unmentioned in the kitchen, but not
the Ides of March. The nanny said she didn't give a fig about
Shakespeare. All her life she'd been disgusted with the Bard.
On her nights off, she'd taken to coming in giggly from a
bar frequented by British soldiers. She was getting drunken
phone calls after ten o'clock. I knew that Cello would have
Dram speak to her before too long. I was not sorry to see her
go. She'd been good with the children, which many mothers
resent in a nanny after a while. But she wanted to trade confi-
dences with me about Cello, as though she were my equal, or
rather as if I were down there with her.

She broke down the day of her departure. Cello took the
children to their grandparents on Wannsee the night before.
Dram informed the paid-off girl that the children would not
be coming back that night, that it was best a parting scene
not be imposed on them. He assured her that Cello was at that
moment explaining to them that their au pair was going home
because her own family missed her and that they should be
happy for her.

Dram wasn't there the morning she left. I'm the one who
watched the tears erupt when she pulled her bags into the

entrance hall. Her curling iron was in its box in a plastic
bag. I made her sit down. I got her a tissue. She'd been a fool
to agree not to tell the children anything until the last minute.
I listened to her sob about how unfair it was to expect a young
person not to have a social life; how unreasonable it was to
keep the oldest out of school just to prevent him from saying
goodbye to her; how unfair it was that their mother couldn't
see they'd become attached to her. She didn't trust a reference
from Cello not to be a stab in the back. I called her a taxi. I
helped her take her bags downstairs. I hugged her. Humiliated,
she was on her way back to her previous job in the gift-wrapping
department at Marks and Spencer.

She told me to beware. She'd heard Cello and Dram having
an intense discussion about me. Obviously she didn't know
what they said, because in her ten months in Berlin she'd
learned not a word of German. But they'd repeated my name
often, she said, and not in a nice way, she didn't think.

·

N. I. Rosen-Montag had proposed the reclamation of an industrial wasteland on a bend in the River Spree, near the
housing estates of the Hansa Quarter, as a focal point of the
International Building Exhibition, or IBA, a series of meetings of architects, designers, and planners that was taking
place in West Berlin over a period of years.

Much outrage followed the announcement that Rosen-
Montag, a paper architect, had been given such pride of place,
not to mention the huge commission, the chance finally to
build. That was some time before I quit drinking and taking
drugs. By the time I joined the project, hip Berlin columnists
were gleefully relaying rumors that Rosen-Montag's small-
dwelling idea, his back-to-the-eighteenth-century-scale crusade,
was seriously behind schedule and likely to be wildly over
budget.

What made his peers quiver was the fact that he was a part of both the New Building and the Old Building sections of IBA, the sole architect to be so engaged. He could construct anew, fill in grassy gaps, and he could remake and revive old buildings, be an exponent of what the IBA director called "critical reconstruction."

The Lessing Project, Lessingsdorf, was always going to have a hard time asserting itself against the modernist parks of the Hansa Quarter, overgrown strips between broad streets by railroad tracks. The Hansa Quarter was sacred ground for modernists. A postwar model city with contributions from many international architects, it had been the star attraction of an International Building Exhibition thirty years earlier. How dare Rosen-Montag insinuate himself into the landscape. On the map, Rosen-Montag's sudden grid at a bend in the Spree looked like a Band-Aid on the raised knee of a napping Berlin.

Everything Rosen-Montag did woke up a front page in West Berlin. Perversely, he didn't establish his workshop near the site between the river and the Hansa Quarter that he was being paid an incredible sum to reimagine. Instead, his headquarters sneaked into being south of the Tiergarten, behind the deserted, decaying embassies of the Axis powers in the old diplomatic quarter. His workshop consisted of an enclosed courtyard of white gravel on which sat six corrugated steel half cylinders arranged in an allée, vintage Nissen huts got for scandalous expense from Australia.

Rosen-Montag's people translated without discussion the statement I prepared on the historic spirits that inhabit such structures and the benefit to arts groups the city-maintained space would provide after Rosen-Montag closed shop. Then, too, some French guy in the eighteenth century had proclaimed the hut as the foundation of all architecture. The generators behind the huts hummed in my ears when I lay down to sleep.

Rosen-Montag's heavily locked-up site west of the Reichstag had been photographed from above and everything below the surface had been explored. Thousands of photographs, drawings, slides, blueprints, maps, and models were stored in their own hut back in the embassy quarter. Only two of the seven structures he was working on had been completed, a disused railroad garage and an old dairy. The city had had to buy them, at inflated prices, from the absentee owners because Rosen-Montag would start at no other point in his plans. He was still haggling with the authorities about the number of square meters of government-controlled property they were going to let him express himself on.

No matter what he was asked at the inaugural press conference that I had seen a film of, Rosen-Montag in reply praised the Berlin Senate for its vision. By the time he rose from behind the bank of hostile microphones it was as though he'd come to support the embattled Senate, the defenders of culture and historical truth, rather than the Senate having boldly hired him to do Cicero knew not what.

Rosen-Montag was so good-looking and charming he could get away with anything. He set great store by his having been born on the day of Germany's unconditional surrender. It had been a bleak December day when he finally opened his workshop to journalists, but he stripped off his sweater and took questions in an overcrowded, steaming hut with his shirt unbuttoned to his belt. Aviator sunglasses crowned his head. His hair was all volume and he had a long stride and big feet. The women patrolling the huts knew where he was at all times, and no one was more alert to his movements than his wife.

She had been Rosen-Montag's assistant on a project to reinvigorate a dangerous barrio in Rio, a project abandoned after a member of his staff was shot and killed. She'd become his project manager and his second wife and she kept a cold eye on the young women who followed him everywhere with clipboards and black binders thick with his drawings, musings, shopping lists. We wore discount versions of his elegant fitted clothes—black jeans, black T-shirts, black jackets, lustrous black leather overcoats—but we looked like a United Colors of Benetton clothing ad nonetheless, because Rosen-Montag liked to lace his German and French workforce with faces from around the globe—Japanese girls, Brazilian girls, an Egyptian girl, a guy from Bhutan, me.

Rosen-Montag had no interest in men; he was not even competitive with other men, though he loved to interrogate dead great ones, Schoenberg, Schinkel, Marx. He did the thinking and sketching; apprentices of different grades turned his drawings into specs and his diagrams into models, no women among the apprentices. He also did not hire women for the heavy jobs and his wife was careful not to either. But women ran his life, girls handpicked by his wife according to undisclosed criteria. He went everywhere with an entourage; white smoke wreathed the yellow bulbs in his hut as the slender women around him picked tobacco from their tongues and debated what appointments he could cancel in his impossible schedule.

The huts were meticulously clean. No roll of tracing paper was allowed to remain where it had fallen; every scrap of foam core had to be captured. But sometimes things smelled like a poker game because of the beers mixed with the smoke. I especially loved the stink of the apprentices and architecture students in black woolen sweaters that they hadn't cleaned all winter. The two studio huts where blueprints dried and models were constructed smelled of boys' armpits and ammonia. In the narrow canteen hut, any pasta sauce and even cigarettes were overpowered by the mustiness of old Europe, the Europe that Americans got on the plane home and complained about as not taking showers every day.

Women's scents dominated my hut. Women's voices answered the phones, their German, French, and English requests and explanations a counter hum to the generator outside, directly behind me. I sat in the rear, facing the well toward the door. I had a wobbly white plastic desk and an overly designed chair with a thin seat. The press girl who was too busy for chitchat had a larger, steady desk to my left. I had to stand if I wanted to look out the dormer window on my right. Once, I saw an assistant in high-heeled black boots stagger over the gravel to clutch after a page of vellum sweeping away from her. Across from the window, two fax machines spat unpredictably, and when they did I thought of a particularly crazy person talking to himself in fits and starts in front of the once-proud Ida B. Wells Homes back in Chicago. Mostly, I read, hiding, I thought, how inadequate my German was for the job, though presumably it was not why I was there.

I hadn't made friends at the workshop. Young Germans spoke English because of rock music, movies, and educational policies in the American and British sectors. But they returned my wave at five o'clock as though they were too exhausted for any more translation. I was the only one to quit at that hour and I did not come in on weekends, when the real life of the workshop got going. I'd come in on Monday and hear what had been decided, or finished, or that Rosen-Montag had drawn for six hours straight. The only music permitted conformed to his tastes, things that his arm could move well to.

I was missing out on evening action at the workshop because I was getting home in time for dinner with Cello and her family. I was missing out because I was going to the AA meeting on Saturdays down in Dahlem, stepping onto the bright orange underground train with a ticket, my days of daring to ride without a ticket over. A couple of black noncommissioned officers from the meeting invited me to play pool, but I was in an agony sitting there, looking stupid in their married quarters rec room, not knowing how to play, and they got tired of remembering to include me in the conversation. When they learned that I didn't work for any U.S. outfit, they didn't know what to say to me. They did not understand my job. I didn't much either.

Rosen-Montag shook my hand when he at last returned to Berlin, but I had yet to have a one-on-one or a walking meeting with him, which he said our work would grow from. Each month I gave his wife a bundle of texts, the higher blather about themes I knew Rosen-Montag to be interested in, and she would report back in a week or so that I was to keep going, that my attack on the assumption that government-subsidized housing projects were permanent features of the urban landscape was exactly what he wanted to say. She handed me a slip, which I handed to a girl with hair so henna-rinsed it was magenta, and the girl had me sign a register, and then she slid across her sturdy metal table a white envelope with my name on it, an envelope swelling with fresh West German marks. Jed Goodfinch. Adult life was working out.

I had lunch alone, walking through the cold drizzle to a small Greek restaurant presided over by a hairy waiter, in the vicinity of the Anhalter station's memorial fragment and the Gropius Building, a lovely Renaissance-style palace designed in the nineteenth century by the Bauhaus founder's uncle. Or was he his great-uncle? It had been derelict since the war, its mosaic and tile decoration long since stolen, pried off the walls and on sale from antique dealers around the continent. Once a museum, recently restored, the Gropius Building was much admired, though it had no purpose anymore, like many prewar public spaces in Berlin. It was fun to trespass, to roam its staircases and darkened rooms. The sound my heels made jazzed me and brought out guards or assistant curators reluctant to correct a black American with International Building Exhibition identification. A mere street of cobblestones separated the Gropius Building from the Berlin Wall that followed its right angles.

Sometimes I brought intriguing volumes about urban design to the canteen hut, but I still finished my sausage sitting by myself. I hadn't made my pilgrimage to the Schinkel Pavilion on the edge of the grounds of the Charlottenburg Palace since I'd been back in Berlin. I used to visit the idealized little house on the palace grounds in order to brood in front of a gloomy Caspar David Friedrich landscape. But my soulful moments at this shrine had been as made up as the Gothic ruin in the white mist he laid on so thickly.

There was no reason for anyone to go to the part of town the workshop was in, unless it was to attend a big party in one of the empty buildings the city couldn't think of what to do with. After autumn expired and it was too cold for soulful walks that didn't wake up my soul, I began to spend a fortune on taxis and turned in the receipts. I did not have new friends or the new feelings I wanted to have in Berlin, but I was doing what black expatriates in Europe had a harder time doing than getting people to go to lunch with them: I was earning a living.

·

"Could Schubert do anything besides modulate?" Cello moaned. "And then he puts in a repeat. Just goes on and on. It's kind of hard to take. The *Trout Quintet*. It's the most overplayed chamber piece on the planet. It's a great piece, but that doesn't mean it's not overplayed."

She grabbed her head at the thought of the concert she'd just endured. She leaned against the cabinet, her way of not having to sit down with me while doing enough to get debriefed on what I was up to. She said she was impressed by my sobriety, my seriousness. She said she'd been sure I would look up the drunks and disco trash that I used to hang with. English signaled that Cello, my fellow African American, was in an off-the-record mood with me. She congratulated me on

the first anniversary of my sobriety. I didn't care. I wasn't thinking about white wine anymore.

Usually my conservations with Cello were brief because
they were in German. She and Dram took me at my word that
I wanted them to correct my grammar. I wished they hadn't
taken me at my word when I offered a token room and board.
But Cello was in favor of my adult life; Mom said Dad was
relieved I could pay my way. They fed me dinner and Cello's
resentful Russian maid gave my bathroom the most cursory
cleaning, but still they made her do it. I stayed caught up with
the phone bill as well.

Cello unplugged her phones during the day, anyway, when
she was deep into something like one of the Liszt *Transcen-
dental Études*, which, were she to be honest with herself, she
said, was slightly beyond her in the first place. If she really
couldn't concentrate, or if a passage was really upsetting her,
she'd throw on a coat and rush off with her satchel to
Dahlem, where she kept the practice room Dram had got for
her years before.

I had to use the phone in her study, when it was plugged
in. It was the nearest to my maid's room. When the call was
for me, she had a way of knocking on my door, escorting
me back into her study, handing me the receiver, and then
withdrawing—far off to the kitchen—or retreating, closing
the doors of her inner room with the Bösendorfer. The call
was seldom for me. Mom did not like to have to make conversation with Cello. Dram did not believe in separate phone
lines for husband and wife.

Cello was telling me that the hideous-looking church at
Europa Center actually had pretty good programs of Bach
cantatas. Then the phone rang. It was well after ten o'clock.
Dram had gone to their bedroom as soon as they'd returned
from the concert. The new nanny, from somewhere in Kent,
had turned the heat up unacceptably. Cello told me in German

that the call was for me. She was on her way out the door, but I motioned her back. She moved when she heard me address Rosen-Montag. My German fell apart as we negotiated in simple sentences where we were going to meet.

In the meantime, a bomb went off in a disco over in Schöneberg frequented by American soldiers, especially black guys. Hundreds of people were injured, among them scores of American personnel. Mom and Dad phoned to make sure I'd not gone disco dancing at a straight club that night. A sergeant and a Turkish girl were killed. Real life.

•

I was too happy for any of it to have been real. To my astonishment, when I contacted the black noncom officers from the AA meeting near the American base in Dahlem, they agreed to get Rosen-Montag's name onto the VIP list, which hadn't existed before I called, for a memorial that their group of black servicemen had arranged on its own. It happened to fall on the day an infantryman in a coma was to receive the Purple Heart. There were prayers in an auditorium provided by the Free University and a Gospel duet that didn't need amplification.

The United States had bombed Tripoli and the press that showed up wanted to make something of the black support for taking the fight to terrorist regimes. Cello showed up, too, in a wide-brimmed black hat over one of her moire night-gowns about to fall from her candy-smooth shoulders under a gleaming Mata Hari jacket. She said many people they knew had come down to Dahlem for the memorial. People who would not have gone to an event associated with the U.S. Army, never mind in support of U.S. policy, felt that they could come in honor of the victims of the bombing, because this memorial was known to be black-organized. Odell once told me that a president of the German Federal Republic went to Africa in the early sixties and began his speech, "Ladies and Gentlemen, dear Negroes . . ."

The servicemen's wives cut looks at Rosen-Montag's wife and assistants, all in black. Photographers had noticed them as well and were whirring away. It looked like a fashion shoot trying to be provocative, sleek dominatrix boots and U.S. servicemen in uniform. Rosen-Montag asked which of them had friends who'd been hurt and took up his position behind them, his wife by his side. Rosen-Montag didn't move in his seat the whole time. He paid strict attention to the proceedings. He knew how to be a white guy deferring to black authority, he who believed the poor as well as the rich should have beauty and high design in the home. It was an angry crowd, but not everyone hated the same thing or the same people while the duet sang of sacrifice.

In Berlin, I only saw U.S. soldiers at AA meetings or on the street when they were out of uniform, but you could spot them. I'd never been to the American PX. Détente prevailed, and the U.S. presence was supposed to be low-key. Maybe that was about to change again, to go back to when prayers were said in the hope that the United States have power in a city people claimed Hitler never trusted. I liked the suburban grammar-school-looking America House, Amerika Haus, a sort of club, help desk, and library with a lecture program, not far from the newspaper stands around the Zoo Station. I once went in just to sit, but I left when I saw Cello already doing that in the lobby, dozing down the pages of *Time* magazine, her canvas grocery bags helter-skelter around her.

It fell to me after the memorial to introduce black to white, American to German, Cello to Rosen-Montag's wife. When Rosen-Montag talked to you, even to men, he concentrated fiercely, totally, on you. He was so into what you were saying, increasing so dramatically in size as he revved up to answer you, that when he focused his attention on someone

or something else, your world was cast back into darkness. He
turned to his wife and suddenly Cello was the most noticeable
figure in the crowd. Two photographers took aim at her from
the steps below.

A number of people from the Lessing workshop waited on
the sidewalk. They'd been unable to get in. The afternoon was
brilliant. Spring had come while we mourned, a typical Berlin
incongruity. Black guys gathered around me as the brother
who could put them in with these females. The press girl was
in no time smoking with the black soldiers. I heard Rosen-
Montag say that the charred Roxy Palace in Schöneberg
where La Belle Disco had been looked like his childhood. He
was from Hamburg. Cello said it also looked like hers and
she was from Chicago.

∎

We were behind her grandparents' six-bedroom house on South
Parkway. Her grandmother did her best to keep us from coming over, and to keep us out of the house when we did. It was
old and dark with wood passages I longed to explore. I hated
her grandmother for not letting us look around ever.

Cello, Ruthanne, was then twelve years old and I was seven.
A ten-year-old boy she liked had me pinned against a bush.

"Taste it."

"No." I pushed away the stick on which was speared a little
clump of something with grass mixed in.

"Go on, you know you want to."

Cello held her dockyard-rope braids and my older brother
and her little brother and sister watched, transfixed. Dogs in
the alley and cars at the corner sounded very close.

The cute boy whacked the clump up against my chin. It felt
sticky.

"What is it?"

"Chicken doo."
Everyone ran, but I couldn't.

■

"Your cousin is talented? What an extraordinary family you must come from," Rosen-Montag said on the banks of the Spree, the sun pouring over his hair and shoulders. He liked what I'd said about Frank Lloyd Wright's Robie House. He spoke only English to me and therefore so did the rest of the workshop. Now that he'd been seen talking to me, and I'd followed him with his assistants in a second car to construction sites, people who'd previously not bothered to talk to me talked to me.

Something was up. Even I could feel it. His siege was about to be radically modified, if not lifted. Rosen-Montag was seldom in his hut. He had more meetings with officials in government offices and more meetings in other countries with art commissioners. The fax machines chanted less often, the press girl made more phone calls than she received. There were fewer people around. Berlin had gone to his openings and groundbreaking ceremonies, had taken notes at his news conferences and lectures, but I heard remarks in the canteen, in English, pointedly, that now Berlin was laughing because the governing mayor had declined to attend a screening of a documentary about Rosen-Montag at an ultrahip cinema in Schöneberg. He'd had enough. Not even the architect's name was really his name, it was a feeble joke, an alternative paper said up front.

Rosen-Montag's wife gave her time to what was going on at the railroad garage and the dairy. Machinery worked away in the dirt between them. Anyone who was anyone had his or her own hard hat and passes to get by security on Lessingstrasse at the river site. Rosen-Montag's wife made a big deal at morning meetings of whom she was sending to do what at Lessingsdorf. Those in his entourage who previously had paraded around as though they were indispensable looked nervous in the canteen hut. Some smoked behind Rosen-Montag's hut, because they didn't want anyone to see that Rosen-Montag's wife hadn't taken them along to key meetings with structural engineers.

Rosen-Montag wanted to return to small Berlin—chamber structures, as he called them. He wanted people to stay home and watch public events on monitors. Television created community. Human beings wanted to live in cities, but city spaces did not have to be Roman. Population did not have to aggregate. Life without a Crystal Palace or a Coliseum need not be a hardship, he said. He opposed the giganticism of what he called classical Modernism. He wanted to move from the beehive or anthill model of human dwelling to what he called the pod, or leaf and branch model. He was the enemy of population density.

A part of his mission was to bring "the old corridor street" back to Berlin, to create a system of narrow passages and pedestrian and bicycle ways and footbridges connecting West Berlin's districts as though they were still villages in orbit around the capital. Rosen-Montag was a champion of reconstruction and the renovation of what exists, a new trend in Western urban policy.

He was against town planning, but he had to execute a plan that called for the instant filling in of his grid rather than development over time. As far as I could tell from one structure that had been finished, what he had going in Lessingsdorf was a dazzling series of stripped, echoing, nineteenth-century brick-vaulted halls. The laying out of the grid went on in a numbing blare of motors.

They said that it was unusual for Rosen-Montag to lose his temper with his own people, but nobody roared more that spring about the false utopia of solar panels than he did. Not that he was even using any. Sometimes he overheard what kids were talking about and went after them. He was especially touchy because he had been forced to abandon a projected encampment of sparkling Buckminster Fuller–type geodesic domes in the next block, his gesture at the radically hybrid.

One Friday I saw a hunk under a yellow hard hat doing battle with the boss over something banal like air ducts. The whole area looked like a science fiction excavation site. Deep pits crisscrossed the sandy terrain and inside them ran large, bright pink and blue pipes having to do with the modernization of heating systems in the city. Rosen-Montag and the hardhat were bellowing at each other across ditches.

It was German opera; the master and the assistant were thunderous gods. Rosen-Montag tore at his own cowboy shirt and his sunglasses added to his menace, but the yellow hardhat, dressed in a wife beater, stood his ground, his triceps slick. Rosen-Montag in his fury began to kick sand. Even his wife stopped what she was doing to marvel at his tantrum. Assistants eased toward him. The pointed toe of his black cowboy boot was powdered white. The hardhat coolly walked off into the shade of a warehouse.

When I found a reason to follow him and offered a menthol that he declined because he rolled his own cigarettes, I learned that his name was Manfred. He said in English that Rosen-Montag may have been a well-fucked dog once upon a time, but at forty-one he was already an idiot. He flipped open a lighter. His hands were not steady.

Manfred drove a jerking Deux Chevaux. I went to a corner pub with him in Schöneberg, near his place. He had quite a few beers and railed about the Bitburg visit. He came from a navy family in Kiel, submarine commanders who attacked convoys. He cursed his grandfather and he cursed the president of the

United States. He was as handsome as Burt Lancaster in 1948.
I had so much coffee, I walked the streets.

•

"Wagner is a cheap whore who stole everything from Haydn,"
Cello finished from her end of the table and dusted the extra
pepper from her hands. I could keep up with some of what she
was saying.

She was Rosen-Montag's dream date. I had to sit back as the
two of them enjoyed the fluffiness of their wit. I found out
things I did not know about him. He hated being at the Institute for Advanced Study at Princeton because its architecture
made him feel he could never get cozy in his bones. The out-
doors oppressed every interior. Yet he adored the work of Ludwig Leo, which was usually hidden in trees, behind some
park, his startling little buildings, a lifeguards' training station or a pump house dotted around West Berlin. They fell
from outer space. They fell off an unidentified flying object,
he said.

It had thrown me a little when Cello repeated that she wasn't
asking me to invite the Rosen-Montags to dinner, she was
telling me when they were coming. She and Dram hardly ever
had anyone over, apart from Dram's parents, spinster sisters,
and a merry pair of married television actors with a child Otto's
age. He liked to watch their video of *The Magic Flute* as often
as Otto did.

They didn't know anyone, she claimed, and yet she and
Dram had a social life outside the home that she hushed up
about around me. She made his secretary do everything. Dram
knew rising Social Democrat politicians in West Berlin from
the time when they had been university leaders of Maoist cells
that issued communiqués as their contribution to world revolution. Dram and Cello hated to leave the children, but sometimes they felt obligated to attend dinners for international

artists appearing at the Philharmonic or for elder statesmen receiving honors at the Free University. And there were any number of Schuzburg Tool occasions, but within the firm, very private.

Once I got through the first anniversary of my sobriety, she passed on to me the invitations she received to gallery openings and poetry readings. Cello was a woman people in certain circles wanted to meet. "West Berlin is a village," she liked to say. But I had no idea how she had managed to land a couple so in demand internationally. It was the kind of information Cello lived to withhold. My pride would not let me inquire.

Dram had done the cooking, free to be German, because Cello had more than enough discipline to resist the most mocking sauce. I was so pleased when I understood something said in the general conversation that in my brain I lay down on the rug with my understanding and so missed the next part of the conversation. This was German for adults.

"No one knows the tuning Beethoven was used to. We don't know how they tuned E-flat against G-flat. Only certain voicings will work in distant keys. Or else it will sound out of tune. He avoided certain tones in some keys. Like you wouldn't put garlic with celery," Cello said to me in English in the kitchen, a translation of what she had said to Rosen-Montag, seated on her right, of course. I was to her left. She handed me a huge wooden board of revolting cheese to take back to the dining room, far, far away.

"When it comes to spatial matters, all humans are Euclideans," Rosen-Montag declared. I recognized the language of his manifestos. He got a ribbing from his dinner companions, but the candlelight made them tender. The balcony doors were thrown open to a civilized Berlin evening. I was the only one not drinking. What else Rosen-Montag was telling a free and skeptical Berlin about Euclid, I couldn't say. I once saw a news clip of a British pop star being interviewed at Cannes.

He answered in English, but with a thick French accent. He sounded like Inspector Clouseau. I could tell he thought he would be speaking French any minute; he was on that runway to instant capability, the liftoff of immediate expertise.

It looks very bad in the X-ray, I'd say to the doctor. No matter the situation, I had to be one of the experts. When I drank, I could talk wind velocity with smudged, drained firemen. I entered into any scene where life put me, an expert, a veteran, an old China hand, regardless of what it was about. When not drinking, I disappeared into the cushions.

To pay me for Rosen-Montag, so to speak, Cello offered the director of a scholarly institute underwritten by Dram's father. I made a stab at explaining in English how much I agreed with Rosen-Montag's low opinion of Riverside, Illinois, Frederick Law Olmsted's suburb outside Chicago. Cute curving streets, hickory-filled spaces, gables, gingerbread. But the director was desperate to turn to Rosen-Montag's wife, who was bewitching Dram, or she could pretend she was, because he had such good manners. When the table got up and resettled in the great salon for coffee, she acted like she'd never heard of the Farnsworth House by Mies van der Rohe, and the director took my place beside her.

Rosen-Montag had been a machinist and carpenter in his radical youth. He and Dram talked welding for a while, a word I knew well enough. I noticed that Dram touched Cello whenever she flowed by, checking to see that she was having a good time. Her amazing hair was all over the place, let out for the evening, flying around her head and mouth, making her look like Ophelia drowning, when all she was doing was just standing there. They took turns going to look in on the sleeping children.

Smokers predominated and Cello ordered each of us to select a balcony. I was at last alone with Hayden Birge, a composer, a guy my age she always said I should meet, the other black

American gay guy at the dinner, whom she'd seated at the opposite end of the table, far away. I'd seen him struggling down
there with the director's well-bred but incurious wife, a corner
that was not going well but that Dram couldn't do much about,
because Rosen-Montag's wife would not let him leave her.
The director had glanced up at his wife in her failure to get
Rosen-Montag to look at her. I'd smiled at her, both of us left
out of what Rosen-Montag was telling Cello, but she hadn't
reacted.

Hayden was very cute. I liked him right away. He smelled
wonderful, and his burgundy linen loved his lean body. A native of Brooklyn who'd gone through Juilliard, he was looking
for funding for his latest piece, *In a Country Garden Counting
Tiles on an Adjacent Roof*, a three-hour work for unaccompa-
nied chorus singing motets in the Bruckner style. I couldn't
tell how serious he was about anything he said and he wasn't
going to help me out. He had beautiful cherry lips, a beautiful
smile.

I noticed that he looked down to the balcony where Cello
and Rosen-Montag were laughing in full view of every satellite in the Clarke Belt. Hayden had been waiting for it. Rosen-
Montag's wife gave in and took her demitasse out to join them.
Hayden's smile at me got wider. It was as though he'd just
taught me something. I imagined Rosen-Montag's entourage
waiting in the street below, like a team of horses.

Hayden slapped my wrist and called me "child." He told
me that clearly I needed to get out and he would chaperone me
gladly. I knew he was going to tell Cello the next day that he
was right, I was definitely not his type, but we could be friends.
He loved Scharoun's Philharmonic Hall. It looked to him like
Noah's Ark. He loved Berlin, he said, and no matter where
he worked, he considered it his base. He stabbed out most of
his cigarette and rolled his eyes about Samuel Barber, whom
I'd just discovered. The slow movement of the Barber quartet,

live or recorded, was played at every memorial he went to in New York lately. The *Adagio for Strings* was almost a reason not to go to New York.

I think when we came in Rosen-Montag was saying that twenty-two thousand miles into space is private property. Dram called us to order and said that everyone in Berlin was thinking of the ill winds from the Ukraine. How could parents not be in despair. Europe had been at peace for more than forty years and that was a miracle. Few in his profession had done as much as Herr Rosen-Montag, he said, to goad us into thinking of our future in the language of the green earth. I laughed a little bit after everyone else.

"Remember Franz Josef Strauss"—Cello quickly explained to me in English that he was a right-wing Bavarian politician— "and his 'Better a Cold Warrior than a Warm Brother,' an attack on gay people and an endorsement of a nuclear world." Dram gestured in the direction of Hayden and me, the two black men in the room. Cello was simultaneously translating in my ear and Dram was saying, to a dinner party, that it was a time to express solidarity with the Russians as fellow Europeans. If Chernobyl taught us anything, it was that we were interconnected. Rosen-Montag clapped the heartiest of all. Dram held out his hand to Cello, but she shook her head and blew him a kiss and stayed with us, applauding him.

Cello was dressed in a fantastic array of light apron over stitched bodice over red silk slip, her legs in silver fishnet and her feet in black kid slippers. Dram, however, undressed for dinner. He created in the kitchen and left the devastation to their cleaning lady, who'd been an anesthesiologist back in Yekaterinburg. She'd been a wreck for days. Because Dram made pitching in seem like an upper-class trait, I pretended not to notice that no one helped me either to clear or to serve after the first platters and bowls had been carried festively to the table. I did service, from the chilled consommé to that fraternity-sock cheese. It didn't matter, just as not drinking white wine with them or not being Hayden's type didn't matter.

·

I hollered that he opposed the placement of buildings in relation to nature instead of in relation to themselves and the streets. Manfred yelled back that he threw a bug down in the dirt of the Mark Brandenburg and told us to pick it up. I sometimes wondered what the lights of West Berlin must have looked like at night from the surrounding East Bloc—dark villages of the Mark Brandenburg, the old state and ancestral seat of the long-deposed Hohenzollerns.

The band on the ground floor of the Gropius Building was so loud we had to climb high to get away from it. Manfred said that a party at the abandoned Hamburg station would have been cooler. It was the first sandstone terminal to be built in Berlin. He had taken me into the black pit of the dead structure, but what sounded like bats made me uneasy. He held my wrist as he led the way back out.

He was taking the stairs two at a time. He said that it was completely okay by him that, to Rosen-Montag, Thomas Jefferson was the inventor of the street grid and not the author of the United States Declaration of Independence. He slammed his empty plastic cup and it popped back up at him. "Death to tyrants."

I told him about Sally Hemings, the slave mistress to Jefferson the slaveholder and the half sister of his dead wife.

Manfred said Rosen-Montag also fucked his slaves. It was the only thing he knew about the Romans.

There was an uncrowded bar on the third floor and nothing on the walls, so people were smoking. They were smoking all over Berlin. The winters in Berlin smelled of coal and the horrible gasoline of East Germany. Coal went away in the spring, leaving the smell of tobacco to get stronger. East Bloc cigarettes and cigars were as noxious as its fuel. The stench was vital enough to float across the border. I told snippy Americans who backed away from my breath that I'd moved to Europe just to smoke. As far as all those people in the cafés, restaurants, bars, discos, kitchens, beer gardens, and offices of Berlin were concerned, Marlene's eyes were still fluttering as she got lit up, Emil Jannings's cheeks were sunken as he pulled on a torpedo-shaped cigar, and Zarah Leander had dangling from her mouth a long white tube of tobacco in need of a match.

Manfred ventured that I smoked Reynos because I knew that Europeans rarely bummed menthols. Furthermore, he added, black people loved the taste of menthol. He waited. I laughed. He was happy. He'd been able to say it and do me the courtesy of maybe expecting manful indignation in response to his having taken liberties with my culture. "Jed, *Mann.*" He gave my wrist a hard squeeze.

When I came back from my voyage to the men's room, some stacked but not-pretty American girl had taken my seat. He'd studied in America for four years. I heard him tell her, "Had Byron lived, he would have gone to teach in America. He was thinking of America. He certainly would have made a lecture tour. And he would have been prosecuted for sexual harassment. Possibly of little boys."

Right there in the museum, someone passed me a nasty-tasting joint, the flavor of burning human hair.

The American bunny wanted to dance. She identified the blaring sound as a country-western spoof, "The Other Sofa Comes on Friday." I ignored her look when they got up and I followed them. A girl was always going to want to save him. She was short.

When we wedged our way downstairs, Manfred murmured into my neck that he preferred to go somewhere quiet than to stay on at Rosen-Montag's ego-insane party. The American chick could not believe that her lusciousness had not moved him. I was to look for Cello, but even she in slippers from Damascus didn't matter. We left what Manfred said was a double funeral. Rosen-Montag's reputation would be nowhere soon and the Gropius Building had been so successful at hosting temporary exhibitions that it was to become a permanent space for traveling shows.

That I had had what in AA would qualify as a "slip," because of that joint, also didn't matter. Manfred pressed my knee in the taxi. We went back to his neighborhood pub and discussed German history. Moonlight changes the shape of a river, Twain said.

•

Dram said that he taught Cello to drive in the empty, cracked streets of the old diplomatic quarter and they probably conceived Otto in a squelchy expanse somewhere between the sealed Japanese and Italian embassies. It was very uncharacteristic of him to say such a thing. We were taking garbage down the circular back stairs to be recycled.

I'd been lying to Cello about attending AA meetings and the next Saturday, when I said I was going to the American soldiers' meeting down in Dahlem, I went to a straight-porn cinema instead, and was fascinated to observe Rosen-Montag a few rows ahead of me and off to my right. He held a beer and was smiling up at the dubbed hijinks. The blonde next to him looked just like the blonde getting hammered in the film, except she clearly wasn't getting what she wanted and wasn't willing to fake anything.

She turned toward Rosen-Montag in her seat and whined something, smoothing a strand of hair behind her ear. Her nails were incredibly long and vulgar and unhygienic looking. She had a terrifically angry nose. But Rosen-Montag was ignoring her, smiling at the tit dunes up on the screen. Then the beer dived out of his fingers and the blonde threw her legs over his lap. Rosen-Montag looked back over his shoulder, as though for a waiter, and didn't see me. I thought I detected glassine excitement in the size of his pupils, even at that distance.

The story of Saint Paul in Rome is the story of a major party killer. I came up from the downstairs porn theater and lit another cigarette. The smoke blew me in the direction of the Europa Center. I had not had a drink in more than a year, but I was twenty-eight years old and I had not been naked with another human being in an even longer time than I'd not had a drink.

THREE

In 1934 a composer's widow comes in secret to dangerous Berlin in order to fulfill her dying daughter's last wish. She must abduct the young Ethiopian prince, whose presence they have heard is magic. She must rescue him from the Nazis, who have him under arrest in the cellar of the Crown Prince Palace. They have hidden him away from the sound of music. When he hears music, he dances, and when he dances, he enchants, he brings peace, ends war.

The composer's widow sings an old Gypsy folk song that lulls its hearers to sleep. With the help of the Berlin envoys of Haile Selassie, she smuggles the prince from the palace. The child is frightened and inadvertently gives them away. The composer's widow betrays the emperor's emissaries and outruns them, as well as the Nazis, to the Austrian border. But the story about the little prince is untrue. He is no dancer, no gentle creature. She soothes the prince to sleep with Gypsy song. He is agitated when he wakes. She gets him to the bedside of her daughter. The little white girl is happy to have the royal golliwog to entertain her. The little black boy, however, is far from happy. He isn't full of magic; he's a prince.

The prince goes on a rampage around the isolated villa. He

throws objects, smashes windows, swings the cat by its tail. He eludes capture. The composer's widow sings the old Gypsy folk song and it puts him to sleep. But if she stops singing, he wakes up and flies at her. It is a curse. Other pieces of music will not pacify him. She must sing the Gypsy song over and over. While singing, she writes a note for her daughter to take to the gamekeeper. She carries the prince into the woods so that her daughter can wake. The little girl wakes, sees the note on her pillow, and crawls to the gamekeeper's cottage.

The gamekeeper finds the exhausted composer's widow and the sleeping prince in the woods. The gamekeeper has come with Gypsies he's paid to sing. They put the little prince in a cage and stop singing. He rages as they carry him to jail. After Germany annexes Austria, the euthanasia laws of the Nazi regime come into effect and the little prince is taken away to a concentration camp.

·

Hayden Birge wanted to call the opera he was supposed to be writing *Freaking Black*, but Cello didn't like the title. He said it was based on a strange story his favorite teacher, a dear old queen, had told him about Alma Mahler's purchase of an Ethiopian prodigy to entertain her daughter, who was dying of polio. The boy played beautifully, but he was seriously disturbed: whenever he wasn't playing, he exhibited disgusting antisocial behavior, shitting over everything. Hayden said that Cello's libretto was not what he had been expecting.

To me, her libretto sounded like children's theater, and I detested both folklore and children's theater. Hayden said its plot problems were the least of it. He said he had had in mind a libretto of utter craziness, like those letters in which Mozart tells the people he loves to shit so much in their beds that their beds explode. Cello feared they would appear to be ripping off *Amadeus*.

Hayden had had a success two years before with a concert performance of a chamber opera that he said was about uptight Europe—*Lully's Toe*. The right people in West Berlin saw it and it got written about. Cello phoned a Swiss foundation that paid his musicians. Then she persuaded the director of her father-in-law's institute to donate its stage. The institute hadn't been behind the piece until the first night, when it was clear that people liked it. Once Hayden had introduced the sextet and soprano and countertenor and reminded the Germans that they could laugh, they did. But Hayden's program note was positively ghoulish about how fatally infected Lully's toe got after he smashed it with a heavy stick he was using to beat time. Hayden said that in the piece he went overboard on the things about Europe that the inability to keep time and the crushed toe were metaphors for.

Somehow, after that, Cello began to think of herself as his collaborator, he said. He didn't say anything about her access to funds and institutes and city politicians, her cachet as a Berlin personality, the retired black American artist married to Schuzburg Tools. We were having lunch in Café Einstein, near Nollendorfplatz, Herr Issyvoo's old stomping ground, and I would have wagered that some of its cultured clientele had heard of Cello. It felt as though Hayden and I were meeting in secret, because he had asked me not to tell her of our appointment.

I wanted to ingratiate myself to him. I liked the conspiratorial atmosphere, but I couldn't think what would be the equivalent of nylons in our exchange. When he complained about Cello's tendency to rewrite his music, he ended by laughing it off, saying that she was just headstrong, and rubbing his sinewy neck.

He said he didn't mind if I smoked, but he wouldn't. I emptied two sugar packets into my cup. He only smoked after dinner. No wonder my skin was the way it was and his was perfect. He never used cologne; what beguiled was his wonderful

Bond Street soap. His gray cashmere sweater was fragrant. His shoes were Italian, a brand I'd never heard of. He confessed to a weakness for clothes. He was a gay guy who got the boys he went after. I could tell. He did his hunting late at night, in clothes I never saw, among boys loaded with attitude and shirtless in autumn.

Stravinsky had three face-lifts, Hayden said. He said that Cello couldn't bring herself to write about a black person shitting on Europe. It was going to be a problem, he said. Maybe Rimsky-Korsakov could set what she'd written, but he couldn't. He said he thought better of letting me read her libretto because it was bad enough that he had even told me about their collaboration. She'd not mentioned it to me.

•

Cello and I were communicating mostly through the occasional phone message she left on my tiny bed. Rosen-Montag's people called more often than Chicago. I hadn't been around for dinner in a long time, and the one Sunday lunch out in Wannsee that I'd gone to over the summer had been a torment because I was missing a date with Manfred. When I told Hayden about Manfred, he said, "For who can make straight what God hath made a 'mo."

I'd only told him because I hadn't wanted to go back to Cello with the latest. She'd said nothing when I told her that there was an assistant architect working with me on the Lessing Project who was beginning to mean a great deal to me. We cared about each other, I said. Cello gave me no opening. She looked straight ahead. Two of her children played in the back seat of the Mercedes. She did not want me to discuss boys around them, I decided.

When Manfred accused himself of being lazy, of not having the self-respect to resign, I would tell him that that wasn't true. "There's a difference between troubled and lazy."

He didn't let me talk to him about what his trouble might be, which was why I ended up laying out to Hayden the facts of an afternoon when the trees in Berlin's squares and along its boulevards were still full.

I'd left Manfred in his corner pub, seething as usual about the German fascist past. The next day he picked me up for our excursion to the radio tower and racetrack constructed in the 1920s dressed in the jeans and shirt he'd had on the night before. An American beauty was smiling up from the passenger seat of his Deux Chevaux. I stood there, a homo with a picnic lunch from Kaufhaus des Westens, "KaDeWe," the woolly mammoth of a department store not far from Europa Center.

.

Mom used to say, "You have to kid yourself. How else do you keep going? That's always been my motto: keep kidding yourself."

.

I kept the ChiChi to myself. It was not a threat to my adult life. It was my time off, my skip through the looking glass, the boys' club where in my head I scored all night, gently moving the poet's thigh, that second thigh, and that left leg.

The loveliness of autumn in Berlin could not penetrate the ChiChi's door. Behind it the atmosphere was like that of a ship far from land. Travelers tired of one another's company, the regulars remembered that they'd bought me drinks every summer when I ran out of money. To them, I had arrived via helicopter, bringing supplies, more troops, the USO, or something. I bought everyone in the bar a drink my first night back. I paid off Big Dash's tab. I wanted to wash after he smothered me in a humid embrace.

The windows of the ChiChi were painted over and then completely obscured by the haphazard decoration: a mass of tiny Christmas lights, the wires stapled to the walls; plastic ferns and plastic ivy everywhere on nails, hung with dozens of mutilated garden elves, some just torsos with dusty knives still in them. There were some good things from Odell's collection of music posters and walls of postcards from servicemen and refugees and former barmaids who hadn't forgotten the help and home Zippi and Odell had given them in cold, indifferent Berlin. The place looked like the inside of a shoebox of secrets. It was so swathed and coated and coded, no one ever knew what time it was outside. Nights passed unseen.

The dark toilets were beyond the ebony dance floor. The red kitchen was behind the green bar; the racks of green and brown and clear bottles and glasses looked over the bar at the crazy windows. Small round red tables were placed under the windows and along the remaining wall space. You took a seat and maybe someone interesting would join you.

I was always going to be in Zippi's good books, I felt, because I found postcards from the turn of the twentieth century, racist cartoons, images of grinning black clowns over words such as "I haven't seen you in a coon's age." I had a whole wall to myself of these sociable postcards that laughed at black people. It was behind the bar, off to the side of Zippi's cash register. She admitted that Odell had to explain them to her. She put the wine bottle back without comment when I held up my hands and ordered a cola.

I'd come back on a good night, but then I had to stay away until the next fat envelope of cash was pushed toward me across the magenta-headed girl's metal table in the office hut. I had to lie low again after another insane night of throwing money around in the ChiChi. Big Dash and some of the other black guys lined up along the bar raised glasses and cheered me, The Party. I didn't tell them I'd stopped drinking and they apparently hadn't noticed the colas and water with gas, no ice.

Big Dash was oblivious, unaware that he smelled of the
restaurant where he washed dishes, not caring that two for-
eigners, Italians, deep into whatever they were talking about,
were not in the least charmed by his 2:00 a.m. Bessie Smith
impersonation. When really high, he'd lean on the bar and
sway and sing stupidly. "Does he hold your head down . . . till
you can't breathe . . . Does he grab your head and wish you had
a ponytail . . ." He thought he had a black diva's power. What
voice he ever had he'd destroyed a long time ago.

Odell could be depended on to walk over and turn up the
music on the deluxe cassette player on its own shelf below the
glasses and bottles. Odell usually played funk until midnight
and jazz until dawn. He controlled the selections and the volume. The mood in the ChiChi was sometimes determined by
how Odell was feeling, what he wanted to hear. Everything
came back to what was the latest in his stormy marriage to Zippi,
and often, to prove a point, he'd throw himself into some
aspect of the business, whether designing a new ad or ordering a new outside lamp, but always at a weird hour. A store-
room between the two toilets held a number of previously
ordered and uninstalled improvements. The new piece of equipment wouldn't be what he'd wanted or right for their look and
he'd send it back, eventually.

He did everything for the business, for the ChiChi. He
washed the bar every morning, mopping around the dozing
and the drugged up. It was theirs, his and Zippi's; it kept them
us-against-the-world, however much they battled each other
on a slow night. I felt that they stayed understaffed in order to
keep themselves up to their necks. Odell had been in the army,
stationed forever in Giessen. One year he didn't re-up, but the
cops back in Los Angeles were making life too hard for black
men. He missed not having to worry about them, a feeling he'd
never got tired of in Europe. He came back to Berlin to take
pictures. He was drawn into his own pictures, like an anthro-
pologist. He stayed.

I knew that much from his conversation about politics. He and the man I had right away taken to be his new dealer went on for some time in Black Power fashion. I thought it was risky for someone who was a dealer to go by the name of Bags. My height, but twice my girth, dark-skinned Bags had a shaved, shiny head. The tattoo on his left forearm was very evolved. Everything about him made me uncomfortable, as though I knew that one day I'd be questioned about him under oath. He, too, was ex-military. Bags would have the latest unemployment figures for black men his age in the States. When guys in their circle talked about going back, he would point to black unemployment. "They don't want us."

•

The authentic mattered to Odell, wherever he came across it, and he liked Big Dash, didn't seem to notice anything off-putting about the man. They went back a ways, but I didn't know anything more. I was not in their circle. My place was over by Zippi and her cash register. I was her regular, much as I longed to be one of Odell's, a masterpiece of muscle bundles. But she claimed me, and she commented a great deal in between glances on what her man was probably getting up to with his buddies over there.

She'd appeal to Big Dash to tell her what was going on, but as queenie as he was in the muumuu-like roominess of his unpleasant shirts, he would not sell out a man to his woman. Though a gay guy, he was not a "girlfriend."

"If I'm going to be dealing with Odell when he's in this kind of mood," he said by way of accepting my offer of a drink.

Zippi signaled to me. She told me that that was enough. Big Dash could barely stand as it was. I mustn't treat him anymore. They were taking care of him, keeping him up to a certain amount of alcohol per day, but no more.

"Oh no, she's not talking about my business tonight," Big

Dash pleaded with the ceiling just as we both turned to look at him.

I thought that Zippi was also looking out for me, letting me know that I didn't have to keep up the grandiose level of generosity. It was okay for The Party to be over. I was permanent, a regular, not leaving on a jet plane. But more than anything, she wanted Big Dash to be able to walk, because she spoke to Odell through him for much of the night. To bring lemons, to get the glasses their one busboy forgot. A mediator was supposed to prevent either one of them from misreading the tone of the other, a thing they never did by themselves, whether in English or German, as far as I could tell.

"You've burned your hand."

"Well, you know my hand. It's like a wall."

And yet at some point in the evening, because of the game of Chinese whispers they played through Big Dash, one or the other would explode.

Zippi avoided my questions about how they met, saying only that they had both been with other people and it was complicated. They'd been together eleven years. I couldn't tell how old she was. I suspected she was probably older than Odell, who had not been sent back to Nam because of his skill with engines, someone whispered. He remained on the base in Germany. They said Zippi had broken with her mother over her black lover. The one time I pretended to be so drunk I could ask about the gossip, she hunched her shoulders and swiped at her adorable black bangs, as if to say, "You know how it is."

She paid me the compliment of speaking to me in cryptic expressions, half phrases, sighs, as if I, too, understood the helplessness of her kind of love for Odell, that hip-film total surrender to his animal presence that her bearing told me she experienced daily, a submission, a sexual drowning that was the secret of existence. I was going to be excluded from the mystery for the rest of my life, AIDS promised.

"That son of a bitch owes me one hundred and twenty marks. He promised," Big Dash complained suddenly into his fists on the bar.

"The amount of farting that must go on in your brain," someone, a "brother," yelled at him after a while.

Everyone was performing, because of the new element I'd introduced, so I thought. Manfred wanted to sit at the bar and the whole joint scoped him, so I imagined, talking to Bags about something called *foti seng* that elephants ate.

Bags said that for years he didn't know fresh asparagus and didn't know that eating asparagus made your urine smell. He thought the urinal where he was standing needed cleaning or that his towels were going moldy. He didn't know until his woman at the time told him. He said he thought she would save him, but she was too busy removing the asbestos in buildings that went up in the city during the construction boom to have any love left over for him.

"Six hundred and thirteen ways to go nuts," Big Dash said, arms raised in exhortation of the bottles behind the bar. "Vectors of existence," he pronounced, hissing like a black preacher.

Bags went over to investigate a possible customer, and Big Dash rolled along the bar in our direction, stopping far from Odell, who usually stayed where he could also keep an eye on the kitchen door. The ChiChi's snack menu was erratic, even with a microwave back there.

"Why don't you walk on my back for a good half an hour." Big Dash's breath could have stopped a dog race.

"Okay, pal." Burt Lancaster stuck his nose into his tall glass.

"No, tread on me. For real."

I'd wanted to show Zippi what complicated was; I'd wanted to show off Manfred, and Cello's end-of-the-week business trip to Zurich removed her as a threat to my playacting. Dram was more than happy for Manfred to be mine. They got on well because of their leftist pasts and their consequent mistrust of the left. The nanny from Kent made bangers and mash of the most elegant sort. Dram didn't go back to the office, but then Cello had called to say good night to the children later than expected.

One of Dram's husky sisters had set up a Ping-Pong table in the smaller salon. After the nanny and then Dram had left us, Manfred and I played. The to-and-fro with him eased me into a light-footed condition he moved to end quickly, gently. He simply laid his paddle aside and suggested we head toward his pub in Schöneberg. I proposed the ChiChi instead, one of those crazy places that gave rise to the very Berlin expression Big Fun.

He turned down his sleeves before we headed inside. Once acclimated to the smoky dark, he'd been powerfully relieved— it was clear—to find himself in a sort of black vets' bar and not the auntie bar he'd braced himself for. His formal manner toward Zippi was his way of saying that he could make himself at home among my black brethren.

Odell's jazz tape got him going in a near monologue about Dexter Gordon in Denmark. Sometimes there was more English speaking going on in the ChiChi than German. We didn't often get to hear how really fluent Odell was. He rewound the tape so that they could go over this or that fine point. Manfred said he'd have to go because he had to get his car home. But one of Bags's customers sent him a U.S. Army–style boilermaker.

Manfred rolled a cigarette, dropped the shot glass in the beer, and took his boilermaker around Big Dash's ass. He was down at Odell's end of the bar, with Dexter Gordon, and in a flash of her scarf Bags's German customer joined them. Zippi made me another coffee. Their coffeemaker was like a miniature vending machine. A button caused the milk to pour into the cup with the coffee. I lit a cigarette and gave Zippi a look that said things were complicated. But her look as she placed the saucer on the bar and rested her hands on either side of it said that actually things weren't that complicated.

Sure enough, Manfred bowed to Zippi and gave my neck a massage with one paw. All of Bags's cheaply dressed but attractive customer swayed as Manfred held the door for her and her scarf and saluted Odell once more.

Zippi marched down to Odell's end of the bar and had words with him. He took his time changing the music and taking over down by her end. As he came toward the cash register, I moved to the other side of the bar in the opposite direction and followed Zippi through the door to the kitchen, where she was walking toward the spliff Bags and the busboy were sharing. She held it out to me and I drew in the smoke.

•

Manfred pressed my left hand flat between his hands and said that I had a Balzac thing going with coffee. I couldn't help myself. I didn't know Balzac had died of caffeine poisoning. I didn't know that Balzac believed in ghosts. I was never going to know how fat it was, but to sit with him, to receive Manfred's thoughts, to be impressed by his expressiveness made me happy. I didn't know that Balzac was masturbating under the cloak in Rodin's statue.

He told me of the best date he'd ever had. A girl who'd torn off his clothes made him drive from Greenwich Village to L.L. Bean in Freeport, Maine. They stopped in New Hampshire to buy booze. She just stuck her hands down his pants and they were off. They did it five times their first time. He loved her, but she was bulimic, and he could not get along with her mother. Manfred was both touched and embarrassed that I cried.

Yet I no longer accepted rides in his Deux Chevaux from the Lessingsdorf site, his yellow hard hat flung onto the back seat with the mess of his life. All roads he took led to his pub in Schöneberg. Instead, I had those soulful walks at last, in the brisk late autumn air, the waning light turning even nearby figures into silhouettes. I went into the Tiergarten, in a way that I would not have dared to enter Chicago's Midway at the same hour. I emerged at the Great Star, Der Grosser Stern, a large traffic circle around a several-story monument finished with cannons captured from the French after the fall of Sedan in 1872. I took the long way around and dived back into the landscape of wet branches in the evening streetlights.

I ignored the boys not giving me a second look and made my way to the workshop, a forgotten encampment, with so many inside the Nissen huts unsure of what to do next, how to proceed. Women ran Rosen-Montag's life until he broke out for however long he chose to, reminding them whose court it was. When he was away, and had refused to allow his wife to accompany him, his wife was impossible, sick with rage at the staff in the huts, sick with rage toward the contractors at the different sites, and sick with the unexpressed. Manfred had heard that three firms of builders were about to be dismissed. Everyone was staying out of everyone else's way, it felt like to me, as though not to be noticed was a way to keep your job.

But I came on stronger than ever. I swaggered. Rosen-Montag's wife even sent me to brief American journalists in her place. I requested Manfred specifically. He was acute about Rosen-Montag's models. I didn't let it get to me that I couldn't introduce him to the anxious women around the huts; they'd been on the project far longer than I had. Yes, we know each other, a pretty girl would say, in German all of a sudden, with nothing further to add, she smiling, Manfred smiling, both looking at me and not at each other.

From the workshop huts I walked south, out of my way, in order then to go west along the Landwehr Canal. It was a long way to Europa Center and the ChiChi from there, but I always got to where I was going. The ChiChi was my café, my Dôme, my Deux Magots, my Blaue Reiter hangout.

I committed myself anew to the warrior architect who'd brought me back to Berlin. I believed that my articles helped protect him. I compared Rosen-Montag's architecture to the filmmaking process. I said his few buildings that had been realized and his planned ones that we knew about were scripted, crafted, languorous and deliberate, casual and controlled, and I dared anyone to ask what that meant. Each building was a self-portrait, I said for no reason whatsoever, intimate, personal, and I concluded with something about his having achieved an organic pace in the development of his ideas since he was the first non-Japanese to win the coveted Hotta Prize in 1970, which launched his international career. I wrote seated at the bar, across from Zippi's cash register and the coffee machine.

"All men are pyromaniacs. I'm a pyromaniac," Bags said. "All men are."

Zippi didn't look up from the cocktail menu she was proofreading.

The prices being high meant that everything at the ChiChi had to be a little drawn out.

"All men are pyromaniacs," Bags repeated. He'd decided that he could wait to tell his old lady that his girlfriend was pregnant.

"They're not printing any more money."

I wasn't drinking, but I was sitting up half the night in a bar again.

Odell had a side business in copper scrap. He moved it at strange hours. I drove with Bags in a borrowed truck to a muddy garage in dark Moabit. I did the unloading. My shoes would not recover. Bags asked me to wait until we were back at the ChiChi before I lit up. Berlin was not New Jersey, but he didn't want to take any chances, two black men in a passed-around truck. I ignored him. Bags turned a corner, pulled over by a brick wall, and leaned against his door. Even after I'd put it out, he kept looking at me, sure. He looked down at his crotch and then back at me and then out his window at the silent street.

Twice Bags asked me if I was telling the truth about having been tested. It was hard not to be offended when someone whose crotch you'd been doubled over, someone you'd been wordlessly intimate with, used words on you like they were a form of bug spray.

The laws of physics applied to bar babble. My talk was liquid filling up the volume it found to flow into. If I didn't have a strong enough opinion, I presented an occasion for others in the bar to occupy empty parts. I didn't want to be taken over, but I couldn't help myself. I met Bags in the kitchen, for transaction purposes. For Zippi, I mixed the hash with non-menthol tobacco. Manfred never again joined me at the ChiChi. He didn't see how cooled out I was after a toke, but at least I was not white wine's bitch.

•

No fact ever killed off a myth, they say. Cello was boiling eggs. She gave herself time before she answered me. She was humming the last section of the D-Major Toccata and it made her happy. It was youthful and robust. Dram had heard her read through it and she'd decided to learn it for him. I was surprised that Cello needed her Dahlem practice room for Bach, but she said she wanted to have it down by the time Dram got back from Dortmund. Though my room was close to the front door and far from their bedroom, Dram knew how late I was getting in and said so, on Cello's instructions, I assumed.

Cello had last seen the Rosen-Montags at the Gropius Building circus, from what I could tell. You had to be careful with Cello; she was so socially cagey. But I knew when she and Dram had gone out to dinners and I guessed that she would not have been able to resist telling me she'd seen my boss. I thought I hid successfully my glee that I was sitting on something Cello wanted: N. I. Rosen-Montag. I stored up bones to toss at her when we crossed paths. I was very casual and calm, deep in my thoughts as usual about my terribly interesting job and the visionary it put me in contact with. I was not drinking, yet I was an expert on something, the boss. I admired him, but I knew his limitations.

I'd explain that Rosen-Montag was the sort of man who remembered everything people said to him, but he didn't realize that that was because people tended to say the same things to him all the time. I offered that Rosen-Montag had the mood swings of a dictator, killing people off one minute, sentimental about them the next. Of course a lot of what he said in meetings had to do with his extravagant regret that he hurt so many. I could tell that I sort of got to Cello, because one afternoon she said rapidly, almost angrily, that sometimes when people misbehaved they believed they were following the dictates of genius, when, in fact, it was just another relapse. She was always telling me that I was getting above myself, and at the time I assumed that that was what she meant.

"He's awful. All liver, no brains," Manfred said again, downcast by the terribly familiar phenomenon of having watched someone he respected blossom into an asshole.

I had no trouble seeing the justice of Manfred's criticisms when we discussed Rosen-Montag over cigarettes by the Hansa warehouse slated to become a children's clinic. But it was just as easy for me to go to the ChiChi to embroider my paragraphs on his work with yet more sincere and irresponsible language. I liked telling Dram that I'd been out late again with Manfred, even though it was untrue.

Rosen-Montag certainly blew Dram's no-phone-calls-after-ten o'clock rule. My master's women would summon me back among the phantoms of the workshop, in the hum with his drawings and notes in English and German. I would leave and look for Bags and sit with Zippi while Odell's buddies discussed fugitives of the revolution who had come back from Algiers ten years earlier. The ChiChi was one place where Rosen-Montag couldn't find me. Odell hung up the curtain in front of the entrance, so that when fools rushed in, the damp didn't sneak in behind them.

"You can't get good pussy in North Africa. That's why they all come back. Nothing but boy ass and camel grease and if you see a pretty girl she is somebody's sister and if you touch her you die," Big Dash boomed.

•

Hayden came to the Nissen hut workshop and walked with me to the bad Greek restaurant. The weather was turning fast. When he saw the restaurant, he refused "to lunch" in a lichen-lined hole and took me in a taxi to an empty, expensive hotel restaurant near the Zoo. He said he didn't know what to do. His soft, luxurious trench-coat collar was turned up spy-style. Cello had come back from her Swiss gold mine, but she was being coy about whether Hayden's agent would see a contract and he needed to ask someone about an advance against his commission.

"Brancusi was a cross-dresser and a racist," Hayden said over a shrimp cocktail that reminded me of the iceberg lettuce at Sunday lunches at O'Hare in my childhood.

The doctor would ask me what I was doing and I would be honest with him. I was practicing having cheekbones. The Almost Ran have round heads, never long ones. There are sometimes a lot of us in the choir.

Hayden was saying that he doubted whether Cello even told her money people about his piece, she was so intent on her libretto. She said she submitted the tape he'd made of a sketch, but he had no way of knowing what that meant.

"Plenty of women smart enough to be bitches make up their minds not to be."

He exhaled. He put out the cigarette it was way too early for. He didn't have to tell me that he didn't believe in her opera, strapped as he was. But he wouldn't let me be catty about the number of pianos Cello had, for all the good they did her. He said he was leaving to substitute for a friend at the last minute on a conductor's job in Stuttgart. I picked up the check.

He said that I would learn that every artist in Berlin had a messed-up project, something life-defining on hold, something bringing him back, not letting him go.

In those days in West Berlin, restaurants and bars would phone to taxi ranks. You didn't have to go to them. Not only that, the taxi driver would park and come inside and ask the maître d' or the bartender for you by name.

Our tall driver that afternoon had a glossy black, curly beard and a thin hoop in his left earlobe. You knew his pubic hair looked exactly like his beard. He cool-jogged ahead to get the door for Hayden, the loose buckles on his thick-soled black boots tinkling. But Hayden walked by him, around to the passenger side up front, and came to rest.

I said I would walk. I said that where I was going was just around the corner, but nobody in Berlin was paying attention. I heard a door close, but I didn't look back to see if the driver was running around to get the other door.

•

"You're wise even when you're flying a kite." The things my dad said sounded like quotes or wise sayings. "These are pancake days." But they weren't, somehow. "You're a pool of sanity in a sea of cologne. One doesn't mind being either." He was a black man who wore a bow tie and was never mistaken for a Black Muslim.

•

I was the most adroit negotiator since Lord Carrington had been in Zimbabwe. There was a chance Cello might introduce

Hayden to her elderly Hungarian princess who had the Swiss-based foundation that helped American composers working in Europe.

"She's so old she's nostalgic for the Ottoman Empire," Cello said in English.

"Miss Thing, you need to get out more."

Cello despised camp. She was annoyed with me for taking her to meet with Hayden and when I first proposed that she discuss their problems with him when he got back to Berlin, the look on her face said that she would never forgive him for letting me in on her business.

"Stanley Dell tried to write a Jungian interpretation of Uncle Remus. I was thinking we could use that," Hayden said.

I was impressed by Hayden. He wasn't nervous, wasn't in the least apologetic for who he was, was not cowed by her. She was wearing a couple of strong faces at that lunch. First, she looked down at him from a great height. Then she looked around at the Café Einstein, horrified, as though she'd been kidnapped and had only just regained consciousness and didn't know entirely where she was. After a while, she'd go back to glaring at Hayden.

Hayden really tried to get on with her. "What you said after the reading meant a lot. And it helped." They'd known each other for a while, I was thinking. "And it meant a lot that you even turned up." He'd managed to organize on his own a read-through, with twelve singers, of some of his ambitious choral piece.

"When a man is desperate for a compliment, it is the same as shooting a horse," Cello said in German and looked up at the wall, as if noticing something really interesting about the play of light on it that we just wouldn't get so why point it out to us.

"I know we said we'd work on the opera," Hayden continued in real person's English.

"Your music sounded different, perhaps because a musician could learn it," Cello persisted, *auf Deutsch*. She held her green tea with both hands and lifted the warm cup to her forehead.

"An idea has to speak to me. I have to hear something."

"Ever been fucked by a bottom?" Her English came out angry. She brought the cup down. "A guy trying to prove he's straight? It's no fun."

Hayden waved goodbye to Cello's unforgettable hood of beautiful hair. Across Berlin, old videos and new songs were continuing in the usual venues. I thought his piece was wonderful. I was impressed with myself for being on his side and thrilled that Cello was not.

"Thank God the spirit of Chinese capitalism makes them willing to serve another drunken customer," Hayden was saying some hours later. He said he was glad I didn't mind that he was drinking for me as well.

I thought that, finally, I was going to hit the town with Hayden Birge. But at some surprising point he hugged me and walked away. In honor of his hurt, and my having been almost Grade A, I did not double back to the ChiChi.

I spent the weekend hanging out with Manfred and a braless blonde oncologist originally from Leipzig. She kept him on the move—three museum exhibitions, two movies—and cooked every meal. I understood her German. He'd come get me at her insistence. Manfred was the white boy I wanted to bring home to my black parents. Dram didn't mind his calls and Manfred returned me well before curfew. He wasn't drinking, at least not in front of me. I didn't say anything to him about it. I didn't have any coffee for two days. As a result, I slept twelve hours after I left him. When I woke, the sheets were soaked with the sweat of withdrawal.

I ran into Hayden in the large newsstand across from Zoo Station. He was subletting his place and taking a contract conducting in Wales for a while, just until he could get his shit back together. There was always one day in Berlin when darkness came faster than you were ready for it to. Rainy, icy winter had jumped down on you, throwing its low clouds across the bottom of the world.

◼

"We don't have a drummer here tonight, but we do have a hit list," Cello's father said to *The Price Is Right* on television.

◼

Cello did not flee from me, but she had little to say to me or to anyone else when I was around. One of the reasons I liked Dram was that he maintained a sense of proportion about everything. He'd studied to be a scholar of music and had given it up to take his place in business. He did not confuse the two. Because he'd studied creativity, he did not consider businessmen as creative as artists.

His part was to be the bass line, the steady support that could be counted on without question. The flights were for Cello to make. She was his wild, unpredictable music. So, too, her kooky friends and relations. But only up to a point. He did not play when it came to his family. Therefore he had to speak to me immediately when their Soviet-certified doctor cleaning lady turned over to him the little fold-up of cocaine she found on the floor behind my toilet. He for one did not want to see a repeat of what had happened to me four years before. He didn't want Cello to have to live through the fear again.

He wanted me to know that this was his decision alone, as head of his family and the protector of his children. He had not consulted Cello. She had been an ally of my good health, he said in English. I'd been living with them a long time, he continued in German. Perhaps a change was in order for us all.

The hashish from Bags never lasted long enough for me to bring any back to their place and though I knew he also had cocaine, I stayed away from it. Cello couldn't face me, in a tired rather than sheepish or censorious way. As disappointed in me as she was, I had a suspicion that she knew something about where the drugs might have come from that she wasn't telling. I did not question her. I was too amazed by this slice of real life. The moral upper hand was mine to study, homeless though I was. I wrote a long note of thanks addressed to them both.

Cello phoned me at my Nissen hut and said that I had a concubine's mentality, but she didn't understand why. She said my mother had lied to me all my life about my being good-looking and I should spend just enough time in front of a mirror to see myself as the world saw me. I was not my brother and never would be. It was hard to strike back at Cello because she went on for so long, and by the time she spat out one sequence of hurtful remarks I'd changed my mind about saying what I thought I had to say, because the rule was that Cello and I only went so far with each other. It's just that the demarcation of what was considered "far" had shifted considerably into my territory.

I didn't tell her about N. I. Rosen-Montag's great plans for me. Cello had merely shrugged when I'd suggested they have the Rosen-Montags to dinner again. I guessed at the time that that meant she'd already tried and it hadn't worked out. I was pleased that I had enjoyed the times when Cello had had to show an I'm-glad-for-you face when we met by her study door and I gave her the briefest of rundowns on how busy the builder of a city was keeping me.

I decided not to tell her about a conversation I'd had that afternoon with none other than Susan Sontag. I'd come across Sontag in Cello's favorite record store in Europa Center, a large two-floor operation filled with classical music that Cello seldom bought. She agonized over new recordings, as though they were a kind of betrayal. I looked across the aisle and told Sontag that I'd heard her speak back in my hometown. She'd been a freshman at the University of Chicago when she was sixteen. I'd not expected a grin. She said she was glad she never became a teacher.

I told her I had moved to West Berlin for good and was never going home again. She told me home was where my books were. I told her that I had some books in Berlin, some were in my parents' house, but most were in storage. There I was, in the fraternity of Americans Abroad, talking to this famous woman with the white streak in her hair. She said Twain called Berlin the German Chicago because it, too, was always in a state of becoming. She inclined her head and walked off when she sensed that other shoppers had realized she was approachable.

•

I didn't just move away from Charlottenburg, from downtown West Berlin. I stopped watching TV, West German soap operas, American thrillers on the Armed Forces Network, and perplexing costume dramas on East German stations. I'd been kicked out, a laugh riot at the ChiChi, a rite of passage in becoming a true citizen of West Berlin. The mail didn't come and Berlin was happy. A man with icy raindrops on his thick mustache was repairing the façade of the Hotel Kempinski. I smiled; he didn't. That did not have to mean bad news.

I didn't see Cello the night I left. Much earlier, across the courtyard, I could hear her calling her children into bed with her. Dram waited before he went back to the office, doing dictation on a portable machine. He shook hands with Manfred and grabbed a suitcase. Manfred manfully took two more of them. He didn't humiliate me when Dram wished us good luck as though he thought we were together. Manfred said we might as well deal with the boxes of books. They left no room for me in the car. I followed in a taxi.

There I was in Schöneberg, on a futon on Manfred's floor. It worked out because mostly he stayed over at his oncologist's. He wasn't drinking. I fingered his shirts in his absence but did nothing too creepy. The hot-water heater worked in the shower, but I wore a sweater and two pairs of socks under the duvet. I looked up over my boxes at the weak courtyard lamps trapped in the black of his wet, streaked window. A Liberty Bell, a gift from the people of the United States, slept in the tower of the city hall.

When he was around, he would yank my arms down toward the floor and stress how cool it was to have me staying with him. I was not in the way, *Mann*. To be pulled down like that meant that my head would bang against his shoulder, uncoordinated as I was. I listened to him close his book and turn off the light and cough. Though I was the goat in the stable that lets the stallion sleep, I couldn't help it. I thought maybe I could rig my dreams. I tried to drift into sleep holding on to the image of us united and running the ChiChi.

FOUR

The first city to be mentioned in the Bible was built by an outcast. Poor Cain. The Lord rejected his harvest offering and then told him it was his own fault. How smug Abel must have been, but we mustn't blame the victim. After all, that mark Cain negotiated from the Lord saved his life while Abel's flock grieved for the touch of its dead master.

Cain was a fugitive, but as the son of Adam and Eve he was simply acting out the family tradition of exile. His wife, that roadside convenience, probably endured many a night of listening to Cain's guilty tears and then many a morning of his loathing because she had witnessed his tears. Somehow he pulled himself together, and east of Eden, in the land of Nod, he founded a city, which he named for his son, Enoch.

Perhaps by the time Enoch grew up he was completely bored with his father's neurotic, repetitive story of how harshly the Lord had used him. There, over the sputtering lamp and the darkening wine, was Cain, becoming morbidly self-pitying as he trotted out his old grievances and regrets. Perhaps Enoch and his mother exchanged a look, and one of them would say, My look at the time. We must to bed. And then they would abscond from the company of the anguished man.

I like to think that in this new city Cain found friends who welcomed his talk. Maybe some among them were true friends, but how could the founder of a city ever be sure people received him because they liked him. Perhaps it didn't matter to Cain. An audience was an audience. Theoretically, the inhabitants of this city had to be his relations. If not, then they were phantoms, figments of Cain's imagination. Hallucination was another family tradition. His parents believed in their conversations with a serpent.

•

The Chicago I grew up in was full of people who could not get away. They couldn't cash checks; they couldn't buy tickets out of town. State Street was Stuck Street. People without gas money went to work on State Street. They ate government cheese for lunch. The Dan Ryan Expressway slammed through property that had slipped from family hands before the Great Depression.

Liquor stores, beauty shops, check-cashing joints, gas stations, and tambourine Pentecostal churches in former drugstores made it impossible for me to understand what had been so fabled about Bronzeville. There were a couple of corners, but most everything was boarded up. My dad couldn't get over the loss of the Regal, his favorite theater, the place with the balcony where he became a man, and Mom said she was tired of debating whether the Taylor projects could ever be cleaned up.

The South Side had been the scene of bitter anti-urban renewal meetings. The people, as represented by Mom, lost. She minded the high-rises we couldn't see, those finished in the late sixties, so much so that she wouldn't drive downtown with us to look at the Marina Towers or the Hancock building as they went up, the kind of Sunday excursions Dad liked to propose, almost as a joke. He liked to drive under the post office.

While he read the *Hyde Park Herald*, Mom sat defiantly with *Voices*. She and her white friends at the Unitarian church defended themselves against the charge that Hyde Park wasn't just an integrated neighborhood, it was where white and black united to keep out the poor. The University of Chicago did what it felt it had to in order to house faculty in the neighborhood, to prevent the whole shebang from going to the dogs. I never particularly wanted to live in a spanking new apartment tower like Dr. Robert Hartley's, but I wished we owned one of the cubic E Houses the university had bulldozed into place around itself in the early 1960s, especially after I learned who I. M. Pei was.

Root Square, as my mother succeeded in having East Ogden Square renamed, hidden by maples and elms, was a small, old pocket not far from Mom's friends. My earliest humiliations at bat took place around the corner in Nicholas Park. Everywhere you met the smiling unreality of the neo-Gothic university. Mom said Dad wanted us to live where we could safely walk to school and come home for lunch.

We never took public transportation when I was growing up. After we left home, my brother, Solomon, and I had to hurt Dad's and Mom's feelings to make them stop taking us to the airport and picking us up from the airport. In the end, Solomon wouldn't give them the details of his flights, which sent Mom up the wall because her days were nothing if not schedules. She suffered, wondering what had happened to me, until she heard the trunk of the taxi. Solomon clearly believed I owed him on this one and I went along with him and wouldn't let Dad drive me. Solomon rented a car when he landed. He and I seldom visited at the same time.

Our house always looked as though it were playing dumb. The front garden died under the steps up to the front door and after a lifetime of costly and impractical schemes for it from one of Mom's crazies after another, Dad declared it his territory and instituted no-nonsense, low-maintenance conifers, evergreen bushes and hedges that shielded the house. It was so unassuming it could have been a movie set held up by a giant T square in the back. But the narrow limestone façade hid what a warren it was. A couple of Mom's crazies were usually lining up their shoes compulsively on the third floor. Mom gave shelter only to women, not that some of them weren't as scary as any man. Cello was often ensconced on the third floor, too, in the room in the front, the sacred presence, the personification, however unwilling, of racial uplift through art.

My brother and I and Cello's siblings had the second floor, each to his or her own cell. My brother and I were never bunk-bed pals. We had our own rooms. Mom and Dad's bedroom was also on the second floor, but maybe because there was only one bathroom per floor, they spent a lot of their time in their basement domain, in his den, her office, and the back room where Dad worked on his planes and Mom painted placards. The closets everywhere were packed with boxes of labeled rocks or the minutes of forgotten social betterment ventures or 78-rpm records. Mom had the carpet removed on what she from time to time called the parlor floor. She put her beloved piano on sheets of acoustic-boosting tiles. We'd been there as long as anyone.

The flat-roofed, three-story houses of tiny Root Square wanted to scoot over some blocks and huddle under the El to get out of the rain. Once, I saw Dad look around when he was putting Cello's father in the car and I could tell that in his head he was urging the old-timers to hold on. Two white "yuppie" couples, as the white Sunday supplements called them, had gone around the square trying to interest people in a new home-owners' association. Mom suspected that they were checking to see who was their sort of black person, the kind that would fit in to the gatherings they were planning.

As a child, I knew that my parents were kind of laughed at,

but people respected them. Mom was built like a fire hydrant and though Dad was tall, his caboose was enormous. Dad was wild about sports, but neither he nor Mom was athletic. They walked like two bears in love. They couldn't dance. Neither wore clothes well. Everything Dad had was dark gray and Mom stayed in dark green from season to season. They both had short hair, in order not to have to do much to it and, in Mom's case, in order not to be accused of having "good hair." Dad's name was on the roster of a few black clubs, but that was because loyal friends had insisted. Once a Kappa, always a Kappa. Some remembered the *Eagle* in its better days. Mom wasn't in any black women's club and the Quakerism of her college pacifism meant that her committees in later years were mostly white.

Dad was an only child. His father died when he was young, of a heart attack on the train where he worked as a porter. My grandmother was a schoolteacher who ended up making paintings of photographs she liked in *National Geographic*. I remembered her on the third floor for a while. Then I hated going to see her in the nursing home. Her canvases were strung up around the back porch like the flags of all nations. Because Mom's father's family hated her mother, Mom grew up as an only child. I once accused Mom and Dad of having me just so Solomon wouldn't be an only child.

I didn't always feel that I belonged to the three of them, the walnut sitting with almonds. Because I was darker than my brother and my parents, to my way of thinking, had I been able to put shame into words back then, they had an expectation of acceptance I was denied. They would always look like decent people, the right sort of black people, whereas I had to talk for a few minutes before white people decided not to throw me out of wherever I was. Cello wasn't light-skinned either, but she'd been a prodigy all her life. Her soft yet regal manner opened every door.

Mom wrung her hands when she saw me. I knew I looked terrible, a walking, sebaceous coffee bean. Cello had not reported me, but Mom and Dad knew I had moved out before I left Berlin. Mom concluded that Cello and I had had a disagreement of some kind, but she wasn't going to push me about it. This would not have been the first time something had blown up between us. I'd been there awhile, as Dram said, and that was enough of an explanation. That Cello had kept quiet about the cocaine put me back in the sleuth mood, but there was nothing I could do about it. Mom studied me enough as it was. They used to be so close, Mom and Cello.

Dad had his own sheen on. Climactic tournaments in the sports he followed were only weeks away. Every year he parked Cello's father, Ralston Jr., in a chair in front of the TV and kept up a running commentary on the games. Sometimes Solomon was in town and Dad had someone who answered and argued. Plus, I could tell as soon as I stepped inside the house: there were no crazies in residence. Dad was a different man when he'd had Mom to himself for a spell. He was outgoing and funny and put syrup smiles on the pancakes he should not have been eating.

•

In 1934, the Shay brothers, Ralston and Reginald, founded *The American Eagle*, and for a while there, in the late 1940s and early 1950s, it was a serious competitor in the weekly black newspaper market. It had an opera column, record reviews, poetry reviews, a very popular medical advice bureau, and a religion reporter who had an inadvertently entertaining way with the latest Baptist scandals. Its pages were open to a number of local cartoonists. The real star was Uncle Ralston himself, my mother's uncle, who doubled as the sports reporter.

It had not been as easy to get back to the Alabama State Normal School as they had thought. Why the Shay brothers could never go back, they didn't want anyone to find out, Cello's grandfather liked to say. But that was a bit of make-believe, tough-dude publicity. My dad said that the Shay brothers worked one summer at a resort hotel in Wisconsin in order to earn their school fees, but they lost all their money to hustlers in Chicago. Their father told them not to come back to Alabama and they didn't.

The *Eagle* appealed to obsessives among Chicago's black residents, and given how crowded and rough that big place was, there were thousands of people who found something in the paper they could lose themselves in. Uncle Ralston analyzed first basemen and heavyweights, black and white, with such contrariness that he incited readers in Chicago and in other cities where the *Eagle* was distributed to send denunciations, which he printed unedited—except for obscenities—under the title "Letters to the Dunderhead." He made a bad call early on as to Jackie Robinson's potential.

The *Eagle* reprinted odd facts from old almanacs: "Did you know that in 1910 . . ." Its news stories were mere notices compared with its features. But then the *Eagle* treated Bible sales meetings and barbers' conventions as news stories. Because it was not a daily, it did not waste more time than necessary on the weighty questions of the moment. People searched its columns for mention of themselves. The paper was full of names, lists, memberships, reunions, prayers for the sick and the shut-in, who had gone to which bridge tournament, who had been licensed by which state authority, and what benevolent lodge had met where.

Uncle Ralston liked to say that they starved for the first ten years at ten cents a copy and then the war saved them. But they had made it to safety before then, when they got their own Goss press and the newspaper could come flying off the rack folded and cut. The investment was his wife's. Her family's insurance company had begun in the murky areas I read about in Urban Studies classes, among slick blacks who, for worthless stock in burial societies, took nickels from Southern blacks come North for jobs. The *Eagle* had white visitors during World War II because the army noticed that the paper printed letters about the treatment of black soldiers in Southern states where their training camps were located, most of the letters from members of the soldiers' families.

The bullying by the army did little to enhance Uncle Ralston's reputation after the war. He had some profile in the National Negro Chamber of Commerce. He was a Republican, officially, convinced that his support was important to Congressman De Priest, and the *Eagle* had ignored the New Deal in its pages while loving the post office as management training ground for Negroes. Uncle Ralston sometimes blamed his refusal to sell war bonds as the reason he could never get on the boards of the Wabash Avenue YMCA or Provident Hospital. He'd rejected membership in the Negro Newspaper Publishers Association at first, but he joined up after the war, when the House Un-American Activities Committee was interested in everybody and he needed cover.

He had a business on the South Side, but he was not popular, his position among blacks not secure. He said the snobs in the Forty Club looked down on him because he came from Alabama. He was jealous of the black leaders on Truman's commission to desegregate the military, Mom said, as if anyone would have called on him for such a thing. Uncle Ralston did not become a Democrat until Rockefeller lost his party to Goldwater's crazies. There were stories about his wife's family that Mom liked to tell, about their having been in the policy or numbers game as much as the insurance business. She said that Uncle Ralston met Cello's grandmother when the Shay brothers worked as bookies for Cello's grandmother's father.

"Keep the Panthers out of our schools," Uncle Ralston said, looking at Mom. He told her she was a hypocrite for joining the National Housing Conference. "What's wrong with your house?"

My mother was Betty Shay, Reginald's daughter, and she married my father, Alfred Goodfinch, the newspaper's young treasurer. Ralston Jr., vice president, was his best friend, mostly because everyone said so. They spent a lot of time together in the office, each in his world, not talking much. Ralston Jr. was the black nationalist casualty in the family, showing up everywhere with secondhand bean pies and pamphlets. Dad kept his distance from the struggle, though he was no self-hating black guy or fastidious conservative who somehow wanted to limit his exposure to other black people. He was on the side of historical justice, he just had no appetite for confrontation, whether it be on the streets or in the committee room.

It was 1966 when the Pennsylvania Railroad failed and Uncle Ralston went to Ghana to fetch Ralston Jr., Cello's father. He must have realized on the plane back just how whacked his son was. It was his third big mental episode in two years. Ralston Jr. was going to miss out. He'd gone off the deep end and was going to miss out on the enormous changes heralded by the Great Society. Uncle Ralston believed in Lyndon Baines Johnson as a white man who had seen the light. But his son had fallen out with his own reason just when it was his turn to be lifted up by federal programs and low-interest business loans and the Negro vote.

The *Eagle* froze, culturally, that summer Uncle Ralston went to Africa for the first and last time. He resisted change in any part of the newspaper thereafter. By 1968 the news stories and columns said first, "Afro-American," then superhistorical "Aframerican," and finally "black," in spite of Uncle Ralston's objections. For a year, he'd refused to give his permission to switch to something more in accord with the times. Then they just went ahead without his permission.

Bit by bit, the managing editor dared to go over the publisher's weary head. Dad, acting vice president, went upstairs to the office in the two-story tower on the right to inform Uncle Ralston of what had already been done. If a thing had been decided for business purposes, then Uncle Ralston could accept it. After all, he'd lived through some dicey times that required him to eat compromise every day, he pointed out. Dad therefore presented change as business, as something about which the paper had no choice. But what was wrong with the *Eagle* had been a problem for some time. The old crew was either dead or retired and they couldn't be replaced for what the *Eagle* could pay.

There were mutterings outside, in the community, wherever that was, that Uncle Ralston was an Uncle Tom, a relic of bygone ward politics. He wasn't. He was as much of a race man as my withdrawn, private dad. But he sat out the militant years not because he didn't understand the anger, but because the revolution had taken his son, so he believed. One day his suave heir had tailor's bills and met white politicians at the Palmer House, and the next he was in denim overalls, flying to Ghana in search of his pre-industrial-age, natural soul.

The women were the grunts of the revolution, the ones who didn't miss the meetings, who put away the chairs and made the calls and bought the coffee and kept the minutes. Mom was a self-declared enemy of the Blues. "Everything is allowed, because I'm feeling bad." She wasn't a big fan of Gospel either. We seldom went to church anyway. Mom would show up at different churches and colleges for Handel at Christmas and Bach at Easter. She said she worked with so many pastors during the week that she needed rest from them on the weekend. But she liked priests, the guitar-playing sort. No tunes of the counterrevolution there.

Mom's mother had come up from Georgia and picketed Woolworth's in 1930. She got pregnant and didn't go back to Atlanta to teach music. Mom's parents got married once her father's divorce became final, but her cousins back in their teaching positions at Morris Brown College had always been a little "funny" about her, Mom said, and they were not close. Her father's family, the Shays, particularly Cello's grandmother, gave her the feeling of being picked up with a pair of tongs.

Mom's father's children by his first wife blamed his decline into drink on her mother. They would never have anything to do with my mother. They went out of their way to be rude to her at his grave. The minister asked the widows to compose themselves in the presence of death. Mom's mother, Lucille, bridge player and comrade to white leftists, wore white gloves, yet she was the brawling kind. There was no estate to fight over. Reginald's bankruptcy hadn't even been a drama. It was just a legal declaration of what had been so for a long time.

Lucille—Champ, her friends called her—rotund, puffing, carried the odd survival supply in her purse, like a flashlight or a thermal blanket that could fold down into the size of a deck of cards. "What I have to have is a heel. I never leave the house under five feet six." Her wig looked like a helmet of steel wool, something that could cut. Mom seldom saw her; we never experienced her as a grandmother. I was fat, but Champ couldn't keep her eyes off my brother. Some Laboratory High School girls stopped bickering over Solomon when our grandmother showed them the .22 she'd brought along to his graduation.

She started ringing doorbells in her huge building at upsetting hours, showing neighbors her .22 and letting them know she had their backs. When Mom decided that her mother couldn't live alone anymore, she had to drug her to trick her into the nursing home. Mom asked Dad to remove the illegal handguns under the kitchen sink and in Champ's night table. Solomon said her place smelled like a human barnyard. There were dead mice in the oven. She had gone downhill right along with the famed Rosenwald Apartments where Mom grew up.

Mom kept a picture of her mother outside the Grand Terrace Ballroom on VE Day. She believed in music in the schools. Mom said her mother had been proud of knowing the legendary teacher and violinist at the DuSable School, Captain Diet. Through him, Mom had had first-rate music teachers. Champ gave Mom that.

.

"I always thought 'Negro' very distinguished," Dad said. Solomon got up from the table. "Negro Spiritual, Negro historian."

"Ne-gro, Ne-gro," Cello's little brother Ronald and sister Rhonda chanted.

"'I am a black woman the music of my song some sweet arpeggio of tears is written in a minor key,'" Mom recited.

"'And I can be heard humming it in the middle of the night,'" Cello continued from nearby. She had been going to a hairdresser Mom disapproved of, someone who worked from a chair in her apartment bathroom. She'd styled Cello's unbelievable hair into balls and loops tied up in heavy gold thread. She looked like she was wearing a queen bee's egg sac.

It was perfectly okay to stare at Cello when she came back from her unauthorized hairdresser. Mom was hoping to pressure her into returning to the fold, the shop that was also a policy parlor, not far from the *Eagle*, where she'd been going for years. Otherwise, we were forbidden to manifest our giddy responses to Cello's experiments with her looks. That would add to her self-consciousness about her new life as a beautiful young slimmed-down pianist who'd impressed a jury with her playing of the *Appassionata*. Cello's new, maybe still shaky confidence showed up in how many of Mom's rules and Dad's maxims she didn't want to follow or believe anymore.

"And I can be heard humming in the night," Mom said.

"What?"

"The poem. Mari Evans. The line is, 'And I can be heard humming in the night.' And don't say 'what.' Darling?"

Both Cello and Dad answered.

"And since when did you stop being my brown baby?" Dad said behind Mom's chair. In those days, he went back to the *Eagle* after dinner.

I was enamored of Cello and spied on her a great deal when I was a boy and she a teenager. I knew absolutely that she used to crack the door to the basement and stick her hair in, even if I didn't understand what it was that she was trying to catch the sound of.

•

Nobody could kick me out of Berlin, I told myself. I had not flunked out. No construction went on in the winter months, I told the ChiChi. Incredibly, Rosen-Montag was attending to two projects in Japan. I was just taking a break. I had to. Rosen-Montag's wife informed me that I would no longer receive wads of West German marks every four weeks. Instead, I would be paid from chapter to chapter, invoice to invoice— meaning, irregularly. I never asked about the faces no longer around the Nissen huts. Anyone not involved in site construction or Rosen-Montag's next projects was expendable, the canteen gossip said. My German had improved. Stray bits of information seeped into my understanding unbidden.

To celebrate my departure, Manfred himself prepared an onion tart. His blue-eyed oncologist brought a horrible, giant cookie of the season. I got to sleep, but a part of me must have been listening for it. She tried to keep it down when Manfred brought her to orgasm in the middle of the night. I could hear his balls slapping her ecstatic behind.

My campaign for an adult life was not over. I had merely withdrawn to winter quarters. Some mornings it was so cold in Chicago the pavement burned the soles of my feet even in my Doc Martens. Mom and Dad had so much stuff in the garage the car wouldn't fit. I went out in the mornings to scrape the ice from Dad's windshield. I wanted him to see how together I was, mundane things included. My Berlin books were in those boxes under Manfred's front-room window, I liked telling myself. The rest were back with me, in my room in my father's house, because I could no longer afford the storage bill across town.

I was working for the process server of a lawyer friend of Dad's while revising chapters that Rosen-Montag's wife had decided were not headed in the right direction. The editorial committee of Rosen-Montag's foundation recommended that more emphasis be put on getting his points across through his illustrations. I was stunned to hear from such a body. My chapters were in danger of being reduced to captions unless I could come up with something.

Dad had an office at home, in his basement den, and another at the Cracker Jack plant, an accountancy side job, and his main one in the *Eagle* building and printing plant off Wabash, near Forty-Third, in its own dead-end pocket of parking lot. One of the former dairies in the neighborhood, the *Eagle* building was sometimes mistaken for a hamburger joint because of its bright Art Deco front of white purple-bordered tiles, with two-story towers at either end. Only the front of the plant was decorated. The rest stretched toward a far alley, a wide, flat one-story structure of industrial brown and unreconstructed factory windows.

The public walked into a bleak, dusty reception area. Behind the listless secretary, a wall shielded the open-floorplan mysteries of the editorial process. A thicker wall farther back did nothing to block noise from the presses in the rear. The staircase up to Uncle Ralston's domain was crooked. Dad and Ralston Jr. were shut up in the tower opposite, their stairs precarious with boxes there was no room for elsewhere. Nobody was ever worried about inspections. From the men's room between editorial and press you could see across empty lots to the orange of the tin-drum fires of a homeless encampment two blocks away. Arguments on the rear wooden fire escapes could be sudden and violent.

The whole neighborhood was a hazard, from the boarded-up buildings to the people fighting and sleeping with the trash on the green island of Garfield Boulevard. Dad's office had stacks of papers and books and clippings, and boxes held rocks and minerals and philosopher's stones and model airplane kits, the sophisticated kind, the kind you didn't have to share with children, the expensive ones that really flew, operated by remote controls. His office was the perfect place for him to get away from Mom's crazies, the sad cases that Mom was always trying to help.

In the 1970s, when I worked menial jobs at the newspaper in the summers, there were advertisements from local black businesses—hair creams, hair straighteners, mom-and-pop restaurants, an independent black drugstore convenience chain, funeral parlors, a car dealership, a guitar and drum store, an African clothing design firm, a Third World–oriented travel agency that didn't last long, a couple of motels, fraternal organizations, father-and-son sports events, sorority clothing drives. But I thought of the paper as a rickety operation, because the ads were for what most everyone my age could see was the obsolete, aging, segregated-Negro market.

The jingling of the typesetting machine, the viscosity of the squid-black ink, and the clack of the ancient press never won me over. I hated journalism and politics and preachers. But at least when I was a sullen teenager the phones rang convincingly. By the time I left for Berlin for good, there weren't that many political and city offices where Uncle Ralston could get a call through. His stories were hardly local anymore anyway. The struggle for copy had been resolved by depending on syndicates of sensational urban crime. The classified sections had shrunk. Meanwhile, Ralston Jr. had put a stop to what would be Cello's mother's last attempt to get away by having a really spectacular breakdown that culminated in his streaking naked across the parking lot at the Black Star Funeral Home.

Mom's father drank up his share of the newspaper and their other ventures. That's no doubt why Uncle Ralston couldn't really deal with me. In his mind I smelled and walked like his brother probably used to after five o'clock and often as early as three. Cello sometimes liked to remember, ever so casually, that her side of the family still owned everything while mine had become her grandfather's employees. She liked to draw attention to the differences between us in what she called the psychological terms of blackness.

Dad sometimes referred to Uncle Ralston as Old Man Shay or Old Man Ralston, but it never caught on at the plant or in the family. He was just Uncle Ralston, even to Cello and her sister. His outer-galaxy hopes of becoming a great patriarch of a black Chicago dynasty clan he transferred to the back of his young grandson, Ronald, and to my brother, Solomon. He just wanted to freeze-dry his son, the phone calls from some white underling at the State Department had been so humiliating. It had taken Uncle Ralston a year to decide to go get Ralston Jr. from Ghana. It was a big deal, like a spy mission. At the time, I celebrated Ralston Jr. in my nine-year-old head for being far, far away. When I grew up, I was going to live on the moon and shine its light into Solomon's face whenever he tried to sleep.

Nobody could kick me out of Berlin, but I was back where I'd started, alone in my room in Chicago, at my desk, as if still making up incompletes, handing in late term papers, unfree when those who had not messed up in their classes were enjoying what I had not earned. I did not go by the *Eagle*, and Dad had not encouraged me to say hello to anyone. Because there was no one upstairs with me, they let me smoke in my room. The house was redolent of Mr. Clean and Pine-Sol anyway. Mom had time on her hands. She never had a cleaning lady.

Growing up, I didn't use the ground floor of the house unless I was alone. I ran away after meals—we all did, except for Cello and Mom. When a crazy was staying with us, she might go to the living room after dinner, expecting television or company. But she learned to disappear. Cello played very loudly. Her scales pursued us up the stairs and into our cells. The hour was selfish, but Mom rejoiced in the technique that produced the sound. Then Cello was gone. When Solomon went off to college next, I realized how little he'd been around, how quiet he was in general. My turn was coming, but my prospects as a Negro Achiever were narrowing every semester.

I was alone in my room most of the time but seldom alone in the house. Ronald and Rhonda had elaborate board games going on his bedroom floor at all times. It never occurred to me to touch Dad's alcohol in the kitchen cabinet. I also didn't turn on the TV. When Mom was out at something like her class in First Aid for Activists and Dad was at the *Eagle*, I liked to have doughnuts and hot chocolate in the living room, surrounded by old books on Napoleon. I never went to the basement when I was alone in the house. I never told on Cello or Solomon for going down there when Mom and Dad weren't around.

One time I struggled into Cello's blue taffeta, turned on the living room record player, and opened the front door for a winter lip-sync concert. Mom and Cello did not pay as much attention to vocal music. Making my first move, I ripped the dress. I put everything back, but my crime was soon discovered. I knew enough not to admit that I'd had it on. I was just being destructive, angry with Cello.

I could feel Lake Michigan. You could feel all of the Great Lakes and their conspiracies of ice crystals and surface winds.

I used to disobey and make my way to the edge to watch the kids who dared to climb out onto the ice chunks piled up in the frozen rim of the lake. In North America, winter was not dreary, as it was in Northern Europe near the pillaged Baltic. It was big and wild and eventful with storms that looked around for somebody to kill.

•

I took a bus to a meeting, in order not to be in my room. The bus was heated and so was the side room of the Episcopal church where I was pretty sure I would meet no one I knew.

"My name is Jed and I'm an alcoholic and drug addict."

"Hi, Jed."

"I have ninety days back."

I was rewarded with applause.

"I haven't spoken in a meeting since I got out of rehab almost two years ago. I just thought I should. That's all I got." That's how the soldiers at the AA meeting in Dahlem would sign off. They'd stop talking and rock in their chairs, unable to make eye contact with anyone after admitting that they'd gone ballistic on the playground or placed a bet with their pay or put in for a transfer.

I had a dream about taking drugs, not about drinking. I was back again with a crazy of Mom's who a few years before had stolen the Christmas money from one of the shelters that Mom took an interest in, not far from the tracks. Mom believed in trusting her crazies, in treating them like adults. She was not discouraged by how seldom that worked out. This woman's getting out of control, her daring to, was my fault. Mom's first rule was no drugs in the shelter or anywhere where she was and I knew that this crazy was using, because I let her fix me up with my first speedball.

It was easy to rent a respectable person's curtain-shrouded living room for a few hours in order to consume drugs in private. The host was usually hovering around, himself or herself an addict. I insisted on watching as Mom's crazy opened the packet containing the new needle. Sometimes I remember that I have no right to be alive. She must have cooked up the heroin and cocaine while we were sitting there, but I have blocked that out. I couldn't look when she found my vein.

It was to be my last speedball. I held on until the effects wore off. I knew that I would never try that again. It was too powerful. I would not have cared had our host's fourth-floor apartment caught fire. That astonishing apathy in the head, that indifference about the body was dangerous. I couldn't wait to get back across the line, to go back to being an aluminum-foil-carrying cokehead in sawdust bars for gay losers. But for this woman, her new connect was the jam and when she at last turned up at the shelter, moving in slow motion, everyone but Mom knew that she was back at it.

Cello's sister, Rhonda, was visiting, in from her own life of Negro Achievement as the lone black woman accepted into the neurobiology department at Johns Hopkins. In spite of everything, she came back to check on their mother from time to time, to listen to her wail that "that spook" had ruined her life. Rhonda said that Sister Speedball was obviously wasted and she reminded Mom that she, Mom, believed in the greater good. The shelter was a place where battered women came to feel safe, sometimes bringing their children and the few toys they'd grabbed.

Mom asked the woman for her keys. Unfortunately, she was what Dad called "street," someone, so he believed, who would never get away from finding the bottom the most comfortable place to live. How many from Wendell Phillips High had given up before they were beaten, he'd ask. "She's real tissue on the heel." She'd made copies of the keys her first day as third custodian, one of those jobs Mom invented in order to give some parolee a break.

When we met by chance in the laundrymat on the wrong side of Washington Park, where her connect's runners could be found, Sister Speedball was talkative, waiting for them to come back with her shit. She explained that she'd got some guy to help her boost the shelter's two televisions, the typewriter, and the electric can opener, but they couldn't figure out how to get to the stuff with people around all the time. So they dropped that plan. She figured it was best not to use her keys, anyway. Instead, she let herself into the shelter late one night and jimmied the front office and then broke open the desk that held the strongbox of considerable Christmas cash.

Sister Speedball could brag to me because she had something pretty big on me. My mother blamed herself because she hadn't kept the funds in the bank. Miss Speedball laughed, as if to say she'd got over on that social worker and she didn't care that I knew it.

The runner was back. Lady Speedball got in his car. The laundrymat seemed to heat up, though nearly empty, a few dryers going. The connect himself, the semi–big man, was outside. He wanted everyone to see him ordering runners around. He wasn't going to last long. Yet I took my turn speaking to the blood who whispered to him. As revenge on this sad junky, I copped more than her usual dose. I showed them to her when she came back. I wouldn't let her have the bags until she had sex with me.

I could not say, "I'm going to fuck you," or "Give me some pussy." I said, "Take off your clothes first, bitch." She was a mess to look at, scarred, sagging, and puffy all at once, at forty years old. I hadn't thought this through sufficiently.

She eased herself up onto the filthy sink in the laundrymat bathroom. "Why do I get myself into these situations?"

That was my line, but it was this woman who'd said it. I was amazed she even knew a word like "situations." Her claim to be a victim got me hard. She was merely in a hurry to do the drugs she had. Up close, that pachyderm's ear between her thighs raised alarm. Moreover, there was no mistaking the semen leaking from her folds. She had been in negotiations with her runner. I called the whole thing off and gave her the bags, wishing her an overdose.

The low point of my drug life was not the speedball, and not those few minutes in the laundrymat bathroom. It was afterward, knowing what Dad and Mom thought of guys like me in our neighborhood. I forgot my dry cleaning and didn't go back for it. Two of Mom's other crazies had seen the junky thief woman with free amounts of cash. I kept quiet. I wanted to get to Berlin, the chance to be another me.

In my dream, I have boned a clean version of this junky silly and we are doing powdery lines of cocaine on a glass coffee table. However, I am not soaring from the cocaine; instead, I am slumped over and jerking like Manfred's car, as after a speedball. She is about to cut off my tongue with a pair of secateurs, but as she leans in—I wake up, greatly relieved it was a dream.

Someone at the back of the meeting was talking about her Resentment Issues, a young white girl, a redhead in a lot of knitted layers. She did not look out of place among the older black workers, but then no one looks out of place at an AA meeting. I thought about getting up to wash my hands, but dozed off instead. It was so snug, even with the lights turned back up for "sharing" after the speaker, the "qualifier," had finished. A few old guys were asleep. I turned over under the covers, safe in my father's house, with Mom downstairs trying to decide if she really believed that grapefruit juice caused baldness, as she had read in the latest issue of her alternative medicine newsletter.

•

In the more than ninety days since I pulled up in the taxi and saw Dad and Mom at the front door, I had dried out. Dad had brought Ralston Jr. over on Christmas Eve, as usual. But that was it. Things were so quiet all over town. I did not go to my dive bars in the Loop or my sober coffeehouses in New Town. I did not cruise anyone, not even white boys sitting with college hockey bags in Union Station. I went about my business and then went back to my parents' house. They saw no one; I saw no one. I liked the way snow lowered the city's decibel level.

I walked past the homeless and did not take off my glove in order to dig into my pocket for an inflationary dollar. I stayed away from the laundrymats and bars on Garfield that had always been in my peripheral vision, whether I was using or not. And I stayed far away from the upstairs of the German-run student pizza parlor in the neighborhood where I first learned to score weed. I was going to unattractive neighborhoods, waiting with soggy envelopes of court papers in front of super-locked doors and windowless last-known addresses. I stayed wrapped up, hooded, silent. It was too cold to smoke outside for long, but I didn't shirk from assignments. I stood on the train back to the Fifty-Fifth Street station in Hyde Park.

I worked on Rosen-Montag's pages, shuffled through photographs and drawings, making sure Mom and Dad saw them when I came to the dinner table. But Rosen-Montag's people had let me know that they were printing the book in Italy. Apparently he'd sat down and rewritten every page placed before him. Then an editor I'd not heard from earlier announced that they would keep my page about Mary Cassatt's murals for the Chicago World's Fair, something irrelevant I'd thrown in for fun because it showed women laboring together. Otherwise, my sentences on various subjects had become blocks of text to help fill up a page or add to the design. Most of what I'd done wasn't used even as captions for the numerous illustrations. The cost of the printing was what occupied everyone. I thought about confiding this to Dad, as if to bond with him over a work problem.

I sometimes thought Dad would have preferred that I had not told them about my alcohol and drug problems, at least not all of them. I hadn't. But I could believe that he wished I had gone away someplace, cleaned up, and come back without mentioning anything. Ralston Jr. couldn't help himself. I could have. Instead, I'd introduced this story into Dad's life. It hadn't remained confined to the magazines he read. I pulled it out of the newsprint and set it walking around his house. This was what I had become to him, an embodiment of a social problem, the old slander of what black men were like, and I took his conversation, no matter the subject, to be in the end about the stuff he wished I hadn't told them.

It was their job not to forget, his tone let me know. It was one thing to be a lost youth who drank and quite another to be a black drug user. One night Dad brought up a new law, the Anti-Drug Abuse Act, which had taken effect just before the holidays. I would get five years in prison for having even small amounts of "the crack" in my pockets. That is, if the police searched me. Dad was being brave, facing my past, schooling me on the new American reality.

"The crack" and I had not met. The speedball had been warning enough to me about seeking the big bang. It was altitude I looked for, sustained flight. But every drug I'd ever tried I had done so without thought, in an instant, so I wasn't going to let myself think I could not fall that way, too. This law offended me, as did Dad's approval of it. I would escape. Because my future was in Berlin, my future had not in my mind been criminalized.

Social policy made for unpredictable temperatures between Mom and Dad. The movement of history influenced their union, the way the stars unsettled the fates of others. Dad held that the law helped Chicago's first black mayor by taking the responsibility for the War on Crimes from his shoulders. The mayor and his police force were obliged to enforce federal law. But Mom interpreted policy according to how it affected people she knew or could see. A lot of her crazies were plain gone, among the disappeared, methadone survivors who'd bent over and eaten the ground somewhere.

The threat of "the crack" was a ways off, in the boarded-up streets of Woodlawn and Englewood, streets where dead branches speared through burned-out box springs that had not yet been collected by the Department of Sanitation. But it was still Mayor Daley's police force, not Harold Washington's. Mom refused to wear the blue ribbons of the War Against Crime Week sponsored by the police department; she wouldn't keep the porch light burning, in spite of what radio and TV said the black community was doing.

It wasn't like Mom not to have any sympathy for the cop they'd found burned up in the trunk of a car a while back, and just because that man they chased from Cabrini-Green to the railroad tracks out on Western Avenue had a record didn't mean that the cops were justified in shooting him. Dad countered that he had stolen a car and kidnapped a girl and brandished a gun at the squad car in pursuit so what else were the police going to do other than what the police tended to do in the first place. Mom said that was her point.

I said that Uncle Ralston would call a meeting in order to draft a statement of support for the police department's Office of Professional Standards. Mom said Uncle Ralston would call a meeting about the need to establish a commission to investigate why petrified dog shit, those white turds, were no longer to be seen on our city's streets. Uncle Ralston came to his office at the *Eagle* every day, but he didn't say much, Dad said.

The *Eagle* had always been on the side of the Chicago police, even during the infamous Democratic Convention, when Dad physically restrained Mom, tackled her in order to keep her from reaching the front door. Solomon had jumped on Dad's back, screaming that he was hurting Mom. That was when

Mom gave up and stayed home. We'd never seen Dad like that. Rhonda came out of her hiding place and sat with him. Ronald found excuses to be around Solomon. Mom hugged Cello and me and cried at the reports of teargassed demonstrators. She might have had friends among them. Dad said again that her place was with her children, in one piece.

The *Eagle* had also been on the side of the cops when the gangs took over everything soon after the riots. Dad got some friends from the university police to escort Mom around town when there was a possibility that a grand jury might call her to testify in the case of a gang leader who'd stolen the money nobody could believe the federal government had granted him for youth training programs. But the *Eagle* got nothing back from the police, or even from the mayor's office of the time. Nothing happened when the *Eagle* championed the elderly; nothing happened when the *Eagle* criticized black youth.

"There's nothing morally wrong with sulking," I heard Dad tell Mom. She hit him, lightly, and the debate was over. He was her comfort. Her shelters for battered women had closed; so much had been rolled back, defunded. Mom's crazies weren't family, but they were her philosophy.

Dad was happiest when taking care of Mom, she who took care of the known world. She let him remove her calendars, her schedules, from the refrigerator and from inside the front hall closet. I didn't go down to the basement to look at the calendars over her desk. The house was devoid of activity. Usually Mom would be on the phone, arranging a ride for an elderly person, looking around for a juvenile defender, advising a fledgling women's group on how to apply for grants, willing to sit on hold with Cook County agencies. At the same time, there'd be someone trying to work off a loan by repairing the furnace he knew nothing about or someone repaying a favor by washing windows he was too worn out to do properly.

Her fellow committeewomen came and went throughout the day, soldiers for the Coleman Report. Around teatime, chubby white clergymen of a certain age or scrawny movement types would drop in. Now, as if overnight, there was none of that. Dad would come in early and sit with Mom. They liked to say that they first saw each other as small children at the 1933 World's Fair and they never forgot. She'd get up and make dinner for us. I noticed that I talked more as the weeks went by. I stressed the importance of Rosen-Montag's ideas to urban policy around the globe. Mom listened, but she didn't know what to say. I'd given a made-up full description of what my life at Cello's had been like. Mom listened, but didn't answer.

Mom used to shed tears of pride over André Watts. She was confused when Cello turned seventeen and confessed that Watts didn't send her the way he did Mom. They'd always been as one on such matters. Mom slowly went back to playing after Cello was gone. It had been years. She wasn't ashamed of being rusty, she said. She did a little at a time. Dad said he could have exploded with pride the first time he came home and realized that it was Mom at the piano. Now he would go so far as to suggest a piece she might want to play for him, but she would hug her shoulders and look away. They were together a lot in their basement.

I knew that if Solomon had seen Mom taking pills, he would have asked questions. Instead, I let her sit with Dad and his games, leaning against him on the sofa, not reading. It really frightened me when I saw her race out to the front steps one frigid evening in order to cool her body down. Dad was up and after her. He caught her and fanned her with his *U.S. News & World Report* until she stopped wrestling and his magazine fell apart. Only other people seemed to find that kind of love.

•

I couldn't believe that Mrs. Williams was alive. She'd been flunky to Cello's grandmother since Cello's grandmother got married. Mrs. Williams cooked for her, ironed for her, and at the end watched episode after episode of *The Love Boat* with her. Cello's grandmother had not left her a penny, but Uncle Ralston—Dad, really, signing Uncle Ralston's checks—looked after her. If Uncle Ralston had mistresses, then Cello's grandmother had Mrs. Williams.

"Loretta Shay wanted to be Miss Anne so badly," Mom said. She didn't like to explain "black" things to her white friends. They would just have to catch on somehow that black women called white women Miss Anne, the way black men called white men Mr. Charlie. "Bossing that Williams woman made her feel like Miss Anne. Beulah, peel me a grape."

Nobody had cozy stories about Mrs. Williams. She didn't bake. She didn't care about the rest of the family. She didn't even look after Ralston Jr. She sided with the neglectful Loretta Shay. They both ignored him. Who knew that "Mrs." Williams had a son of her own, brought up by her parents in Alabama, and maybe he was an illegitimate cousin—or half brother—to Ralston Jr. Now here was that son's son, in our living room, clearly suffering from AIDS, brought over by Mrs. Williams to play for Mom.

I could see my stricken smile on Mom's face and I knew that Dad, in the kitchen mixing drinks, was wearing the same expression of being totally bugged out by our guests. My raisinette eyes were huge with the effort not to stare at dark oblongs the size of leeches on Clark's neck and hands.

Dad returned with a tray. Mrs. Williams was disappointed. She hadn't expected iced tea.

"How long have you been diagnosed?" I heard Mom ask, awkwardly, for her, who ordinarily dived in with no compunction, needing to get somebody's story in the first twenty minutes of acquaintance.

"What do you mean?"

Silver bangles nearly slipped from his bony hands. He strung together popular tunes, the sort of music Mom had nothing to do with. His last job had been on a cruise ship out of Florida.

The pitcher of iced tea was for Mom. Dad decided we could all have some. Mrs. Williams said that that was a new one on her, iced tea in Chicago in February. I thought Dad wanted to tell the smiling skull that we had no room-temperature water. Mom hadn't been able to say thank you when Clark finished playing. He went back to his seat. We smiled some more. Dad came back with a jelly glass of water.

Dad and Mom had inherited many chairs and tables, but nothing about the conglomeration was designed. Our house was storage space, a pack-rat outpost. One side of the hallway, between the living room and the kitchen, was lined with ribcage-high shelves of oversize illustrated books about black American history, Africa, television, the stockyards, and baseball, along with an encyclopedia from the year Solomon was born and a set from the year I was born. On the other side of the hallway were seven unmatched side chairs. We were the lobby of a bygone rooming house or the waiting room of some settlement charity.

"It's so interesting here," Clark cooed. My eyes had been following his.

Mom used a stepladder to dust the iconostasis of reproductions that my paternal grandmother had liked to razor from books and then frame. She vandalized volume after volume in that fashion. We had her small paintings of waterfalls and atolls in lots of places, as well as framed posters from Black Expos over the years. The plants were plastic.

Mom's acoustic floor tiles were more than twenty years old. Three of the same kind of standing lamps grouped beside her piano, the mahogany companion that broke her young solitude. It had been her mother's purchase. My grandfather's creditors carted off everything, I'd always heard, but Champ would have murdered anyone who tried to take the Steinway. I like to think she knew how much Mom loved it.

"Have you read all these books?" Clark asked Dad.

"Now, your buddy Ralston there was a reading fool," Mrs. Williams began. "I don't care for this," she said, replacing the glass of iced tea on its coaster. "All that reading you all were trying to make people do stuffed up his head. His rag head burned clean through. I wish we could put something in this." She shivered.

"We tried to shoot that chicken before the egg boiled, I'll not argue with you there," Dad said. He wouldn't look at the glass she raised and peered into and put back down. He knew how to wait people out.

I ran to call them a taxi. It took forever to come. Mom did have an old Christmas present she'd not delivered to Mrs. Williams, a plastic container of decorative soaps. She could send her off with something. Mom took Clark's right hand, lesions and all, into both of hers and said that the gift of music meant that we would never lose hope completely.

"I can dig that."

Dad clapped Mrs. Williams's shoulders after he helped her on with her coat. He handed Clark his gear item by item and slapped him heartily on the back. It was a test. I shook hands. But we didn't come down the steps with Mrs. Williams. They picked their way, though there was no ice or snow. I'd read plenty of articles, but I washed my hands anyway. I saw the jelly glass in the kitchen trash. That freed me to take Windex to Mom's piano keys.

When I was first back, Mom was going to let me talk, when I was ready, about the friend in Berlin I'd moved in with. But after Mrs. Willliams's visit, she wrung her hands, tormented that that wasting away and denial could be my future. They'd seen a TV movie the summer before about a son coming home to tell his family he has AIDS.

I looked down at lamb chops. We were eating later than usual. Mom had called Solomon. She was in that kind of mood, Dad's pleading eyes said.

"These are pancake days," I said.

Dad filled the sink and Mom pushed him aside and plunged her face into the ice and water.

•

I was little. I heard Mom telling Dad about it. He had not gone with her to the airport to welcome home Uncle Ralston and Ralston Jr., Dad's sedated and unsteady best friend. Dad said he'd gone to the United Center and followed what Chicago's new team had accomplished in the Western Division just so he could have something to say to him.

The trip back from Africa had done more than just exhaust Uncle Ralston. Rest was not the answer, from the look of him, Mom was saying. There was that tone in her voice that I would come to know well, a tone that said how deeply engaged in the problem of this human being she was—not in this human being's problems, but in the problem that this individual's life represented, what this particular life meant. In this instance, the long trip back from Africa in the company of his mad son had taken something out of Uncle Ralston that would never be put back.

Mom meant something different from the utter fatigue she and Dad experienced after getting back from our turn at the lake cabin nobody loved or the forgiveness she meted out after that last attempt to take the five of us children somewhere cultural. As with everything I overheard as a child, I didn't understand until much later what I had managed not to forget of what came my way. I never thought of Uncle Ralston as walking around with a hole, but then one day he'd come down to the editorial room to see if anybody was there, and finding only me—which was the same in his view as no one being there—he'd gone back up to his office. The sun went right through him and hit the floor. I remembered what Mom had said about the part of him that would never be put back.

To have met Mrs. Williams's grandson rekindled in me

that panic I was ashamed of. But I was crawling all over myself. I decided to fish in the virus-free Mattachine generation. I took an action, as they say in AA. I could tell that the grizzly guy in the meeting at the Episcopal church liked me. Twenty years my senior, he saved a seat for me. I let him get me water, too. I wasn't interested in what he said in the meetings, but he'd been stationed at an ordnance ammunitions depot near Bamberg in the early 1960s and had spent some time around the university in Erlangen.

"Segregation was a way of life. Something we expected," he said over his black coffee. "Major Schuler was fairly decent," he continued after a while in his blown-fuse drawl. "Fräuleins who only associated with whites avoided you." I had asked him what Germany had been like for him. He stopped talking again. The ease of the silences was a pleasant surprise.

Another surprise about this older man was that he lived so far out. I found a pay phone. Dad didn't know what to say. "A friend from the meeting . . ." They'd heard so many of my concoctions. They couldn't help it, the only place they trusted me to be safe was under their roof, in front of their eyes. In the beginning, they took my interest in Berlin as an extension of a school project—and Cello was there. But then they appeared to understand when I spoke about the need to start over. I didn't talk about it as getting away. I suppose I didn't want to know what they really thought of it.

He breathed heavily into his collar as he drove. He took me to a short-stay motel out in Aurora. You can't offer anyone anything, so you get to it. He hadn't had it in a while either. His sperm was very warm, as if his scrotum had a thermostat. He'd been sober eight years, he said again, and was separated from his wife, not divorced. I wouldn't let him drive me home. I took the West-Northwest back downtown. I wouldn't give him Mom and Dad's number.

He'd taken classes somewhere when he was stationed over there, but he was mysterious about Erlangen, after all. "Asians coming from Korea and Vietnam associated with you." He brought me a present, an old but pristine textbook, *A First German Course for Science Students*. He translated: "Air is a body. The bottle looks empty, but it is full of air." He snapped the book shut and handed it to me. I thought of the way he made the condom snap when he got up and pulled it from his dick. I agreed to go back to the lopsided motel. "A friend from the meeting . . ."

He tried to sell me on Bebop. Charlie Parker gave me an anxiety attack. I returned his precious tapes to him. He presented me with a copy of Harvey W. Zorbaugh's *The Gold Coast and the Slum*. It was slightly bowed. He'd underlined "A nondescript community may be interesting, of course, but it will not be restful and will not be satisfying merely as an object of contemplation." I said that my mother had the book in her sociology shelves.

I found it impossible to think. He could make the chewing gum between his corner teeth snap and crackle. Or click like fingernail clippers. He'd quit smoking eight years ago, when he went off painkillers for the last time. He said I looked healthy. He wanted to phone me from his job at UPS, though he couldn't tell his AA sponsor about us yet. He said I needed a sponsor. He wouldn't kiss me. Because of him, I wasn't the desperate size queen I had been, but I stopped going to the Episcopal church meeting. He had grandchildren photos in his wallet. My parents didn't.

•

"Now we must put our finer feelings to bed as the great task of sleep devolves upon us," Dad laughed on the stairs.

"Sleep for America," I heard Mom say.

In the book of my heart, pages keep falling out, many of them marked "Mom and Dad."

•

Manfred said again he was sorry he'd not answered my letter.
I phoned rather than not hear from him. I told him that what
was considered cold in Berlin was nothing. He'd had winters
in Boston, which were, indeed, nothing compared to one
winter he failed to last out in Minnesota, he reminded me.

•

Line 1, the subway from Zoo Station to Kreuzberg—then the
Turkish quarter close to the Wall—left its tunnel and became
an elevated train by the time it reached Hallesches Tor,
more Isherwood territory, but nothing like it had been before
the war, given how much of it had been bombed and rebuilt.
Sometimes in Berlin, at the right time of day, the bleak apartment towers that I could see from the train at the raised platform of Hallesches Tor would make me think of Chicago, that
dog growling at me as I walked along but unable to get at
me through the fence.

Then one morning when the cold was letting up and I had
a briefcase full of summonses to hit people with, it was my
being on the El that made me remember Line 1. I began to
think of the kebab stands downstairs at Moritzplatz, the next
elevated stop. Not far away were the really hip gay clubs, the
Kreuzberg I wished I'd gone to with Hayden. He said once that
he loved nothing more than that first spring night when everyone in Kreuzberg was out, even grandmothers. He ran up
and down Oranienstrasse, from performance cabaret to New
Wave club, stopping in between to sit outside with friends at the
anarchist cafés or in the squares noisy with Turkish men. He
raced from one possible story to another, and fell asleep wherever he was.

As an American in West Berlin, I did not think about the
law. I was above it, a camp follower of the occupier. The law
was a historical subject—Berlin as the bureaucratic center of
crimes against humanity, scene of the Congo Conference,

scene of the Wannsee Conference. When I saw someone with white hair, I wanted to accuse: What were you thinking? You're sitting around the dinner table and your ambition is to overrun France and kill the Jews?

Like Odell, I wanted to live where authority had little interest in black men. Checkpoint Charlie, a border station for Americans between West and East Berlin, a gray arena of mortar passages, electric gates, and tin sheds, was a terrifying place, but back in West Berlin I probably could have got away with petting a policeman on his head. A wave of homesickness came over me, right there on the El, within sight of meatpacking plants, making me wonderfully ill.

FIVE

You tried to stay in Berlin, to hang on to your life there, like greenhorns in the films about riding broncos and steers. You got thrown from time to time, you fell clean off, you slipped and you slid and got pelted by sharp blows as you stumbled back to your corner. It was not the most open of states of mind, and you needed your head to be wide-open.

Nights in West Berlin, the involuntary island, that petri dish of romantic radicalism, were strenuous because they never ended. In the cordoned-off city, it was time that could be manipulated, either stretched or discounted. Space was limited, the square meters were finite, if not all in use, and the broadest thoroughfare had to change its name, dissolve into a park, or turn back on itself. To repeat yourself was a pleasant option.

West Berlin had none of the frantic, last-call activity around four in the morning of major American cities. There was no equivalent to that sinking feeling that came over you in a pub in London when the landlord called, "Time, gentlemen." The bar stools were not hauled up, the doors not bolted. Nobody was hunting for an obscure after-hours joint or passing the hat for a taxi ride to some heard-of place on the edge. The empty streets were ours; they belonged to the young. That was how we knew we were young. Iggy Pop said that there were no children in Berlin and everybody laughed because his observation revealed what time he got up—after children had gone to bed. They called it the Berlin Effect.

It was the Wall that kept alive Berlin's fame and pride as a dangerous city. You needed to find a way to get back into the mix of Berlin. It was okay to take time out, to go someplace where you could make fast money or get over a failure of some kind, but if you didn't come right back, then you risked not getting back at all.

Dietrich sang about still having a suitcase in Berlin for a reason. She had to threaten herself. That suitcase was a saddle, but life was not a rodeo. It was a buffalo scramble. You stampeded, mane stormy, tearing up the ground, bellowing opposition, freedom.

.

I paid homage to the Mercedes-Benz star and crossed the plaza toward the ChiChi. I'd missed the smog, but I had stored-up, Dad-derived basketball remarks. I used the names Dave Corzine, Michael Jordan, and Scottie Pippen in one sentence; I said the Bulls were at last in sync on offense and defense.

Odell leaned back on the bar. "Listen to Chi-Town."

"Full of the bull and the woad," Big Dash said, doing a Hawaiian dance with himself.

Beyond him the miniature Christmas bulbs strung around the walls blinked and twinkled. What a place to worry about acceptance—but the black guys talking to Odell were session musicians who'd been working in Europe for a while now, one of them said the last time I tried to engage him in conversation, two years or more before. They laughed at Big Dash's jokes, but not at mine. They remembered me drunk. Across from them at a table, two German women I used to get smashed with checked their compacts and called out to Zippi for another round.

Odell's buddies sometimes avoided newspapers in order to enjoy a game from the States that they were to watch a day or two later. I thought I was talking to guys who might as well have been living in Upper Saxony when it came to being up on the latest in the NBA back in the States. I forgot that they all knew someone with access to AFN. They didn't want my praise of the communication skills between Chicago's players. They were also for the Lakers. Expatriates, not chauvinists, they were as interested in the Rugby World Cup as they were in the NBA finals.

My trove of Chicago basketball remarks had little value in the international marketplace of sports. Yet I refused to exit Odell's orbit. I'd waited for Bags, stepped into the kitchen with him and Zippi, bought him a drink, but I would not get lost. Zippi was back down by her cash register, arms folded. Even barricaded inside the ChiChi, I could feel that a clear spring night in Berlin was about to happen, that the downtown streets were gleaming with what West Berliners considered traffic. Cars had been controversial in the winter because of the smog attack. But now people could breathe again. Working mothers were stopping at the butcher's; divorced men were hurrying home to telescopes; lights in big apartments were going on.

I'd missed it, not shared in a Berlin winter of hardship, the high-pressure system of Central Europe. Odell's guys drew closer together and left the rest of the bar out. The music got a little louder. More German women entered, staff of some kind from a nearby discount department store, ChiChi regulars getting their weekend binge going a day early. I waited until no one could hear me. I asked Bags if I was talking to a new daddy.

He said the woman he lived with didn't care that he'd got another woman pregnant so long as he stayed where he was, with her. He had a son and daughter back in the States, he said. They were teenagers. Where they lived people had only one reason to want a handgun. "A motherfucking rifle won't motherfucking fit in your glove compartment." He pressed his nozzle of fingers against my temple.

·

To continue the celebration of the second anniversary of my not having had a glass of white wine, I was prepared to burn off more of what I'd got from Bags. Manfred put my glass of water before me and pointed at the little rectangle of hashish I'd unwrapped.

"Irma is against stuff," he said in German.

I put it away. "Here progress has come to die," I repeated, in German.

If Venice was a museum of the Renaissance, then Berlin was the museum of Modernism. "*Na, ja, Mensch*," Manfred finished.

I was familiar with his rap and enjoyed the feeling as I listened to him that I could comprehend a complex argument in another language. Manfred once took me down to Free University to sit in on a lecture given by Klaus Heinrich, a philosopher and a cult figure among students in West Berlin. After *der Herr Professor* said good afternoon in German, I understood not a single word of what he went on to say for over an hour. I didn't even hear conjunctions—and, or—I was so stunned by the isolation my ignorance had pitched me into.

After I left for Chicago, Manfred carried my books down to his storage cubicle in the cellar. There were various plants around his apartment, signs of the blonde oncologist's presence in his life. I took the first opportunity to get out of their way. Her greeting when I got back had been warm, but clearly Manfred was under orders to let me make my own arrangements for dinner. He offered to take me with him in the mornings and bring me back to Schöneberg in the evenings and that was going to be enough.

To get out of their way, I let one of the girls at Rosen-Montag's Nissen enclave put me in touch with a lesbian friend who was looking for a roommate. The futon I borrowed from Manfred filled the tiny room. I spent my life there crawling around on it. But the place was not far from Manfred's. He could keep an eye on me, he said. I reminded him that he was a year younger than me. He said he was the one who defended his older siblings with his fists against their asshole father. The bony lesbian whose roomie I'd become fretted that I was too uptight an American for her liberated lifestyle, symbolized by her having painted her walls bloodred and taken the door off the bathroom.

In spite of himself, Manfred was protective of Lessingsdorf, Rosen-Montag's mad partial grid, his intersections of illusory and real places. Manfred cared about how things turned out. Lessingsdorf was being billed as "The Interrogation of a City." Rosen-Montag's foundation people loved it. Everyone loved it except Rosen-Montag. He hated everything; his vision was being betrayed at every corner. He and his wife and principal engineers would bluster at one another in the cold. Rosen-Montag would storm off, disappear, sometimes for hours, or whole nights. For some reason, his famous cool was gone. Manfred loved the long hours, the unreasonable demands on the workforce to meet deadlines. People were going crazy. Not since the Olympic Stadium, I joked to Manfred. It was notorious. He didn't laugh.

I'd missed the smog and I'd missed out on the bonding that went on among the workers of the Lessing Project in the desperate winter months. Manfred was still going to look out for me, the unsuspecting American adrift in the unrepentant Fatherland, but he was busier than ever. No matter what he said about Rosen-Montag, he saw himself as poisonously German in his sense of duty.

As I lit a menthol cigarette, Manfred scooted away a little

and continued, saying that Rudolf Hess defined a leader as someone who can't empathize with other human beings. I was trying not to translate, not to hunt for English words. I wanted to be in the German. But Manfred was talking about Rosen-Montag's problems with a design review board, and annoyed with my smile of pleasure, as though he'd sung "The Miller Songs" for me alone, he switched to English. "The chief difference between the engineer and the artist is the technical function, which is much stronger than the artistic one."

Manfred tried to impress me with the bureaucratic destroyer lumbering in our direction. That Rosen-Montag had been summoned for review at this stage was very political, he said. Several such boards had approved his plans over a period of years. They would not be his friends; they would answer to the Senate. Its business would not be announced. The project was to be examined behind closed doors.

Manfred was rationing his cigarettes. He refused to cheat. We weren't having coffee, because it made him want to smoke. Irma was sensitive to the smell. She would never cease reacting to a childhood spent in the GDR, he'd said when we first talked about her. He pushed open the window onto spring and dusted his hands. Soot lay everywhere in Berlin.

Though it was not as fat as previous ones, I had an envelope of West German marks. I was in Manfred's kitchen, made neat by his girlfriend. He was glad I lived in his neighborhood, however much it irked him that I said people liked to predict Rosen-Montag's downfall. It didn't matter that I waited until she was dead to the world before I visited the lesbian's toilet-for-the-emancipated. Reinstalled in West Berlin, I again left the world of facts.

•

It was a book-launch presentation, but it felt like a tribunal. I could taste in my cigarette behind Rosen-Montag's hut the atmosphere of trial, of my having to justify my presence in the Lessing Project. Even Manfred was taken aback that my meaningless launch had been put on the schedule of Rosen-Montag's overawed and therefore troublesome foundation board.

Rosen-Montag's assistants brought in men in suits and women in sensible heels, their hairdos human colors. But their necks strained toward seats around the conference table as though on leashes. We had no idea why they should listen to me on the subject of what architects call the aesthetic utterance through the art of space. No one had opened the red folders containing my text, but then they'd only just got them, and they hadn't come with coffee.

Rosen-Montag's wife introduced me in English and I began. After a while, I could tell that I was failing to make much of an impression on the dozen people around the table, but at least I was getting by, as usual, getting away with it, as always, because no one cared. I was a diversion, a black American on the project. The largest print run for the huge illustrated book was in English, however.

"These photographs speak of imperium," Rosen-Montag interrupted, in English.

Mom and Dad had a tattered bound book of souvenir portfolios of the great international exhibition held in Chicago in the Gilded Age. I must have looked at this warped book when very young, because Mom said the brown crayon attempts at boxes around the Beaux Arts domes and fountains in some of the photographs were mine. It contained black-and-white views of the White City, the fantasy town of neoclassical pavilions erected beside Lake Michigan.

"They have nothing to do with my work," Rosen-Montag said, running his hand through his lion hair.

The Columbian Exposition opened in 1893 to mark the four hundredth anniversary of the European discovery of what they called the New World. Every territory and each state in the Union sent exhibits. Dozens of countries built exhibition halls made from steel, staff, and plaster. A Hawaiian volcano of electric lava stood next to Old Vienna. The furs in the Russia pavilion were for sale and so were the Krupp cannons in the German Hall. There was a Women's Building and a Horticultural Building, an Electrical Building and a Manufactures and Liberal Arts Building with a mile-long arcade under its roof.

I clicked the button that changed the images Manfred had helped me to assemble on the carousel. He'd done most of the figuring-out that got the grainy pages of the borrowed book turned into slides. He'd wished me luck and gone off to fight with East Berlin state company representatives about a shipment of gravel and concrete. I looked at faces that had quickly made themselves replicas of Rosen-Montag's face. By the time I completed the circuit around the long table, I'd caught a chill.

I wanted to tell them to study the derby-headed, darkly dressed masses in Mom and Dad's old book. Against the vanilla of the pillars and parapets, the arches and façades, the tiny figures looked like fallen music notes. "In the environs of the White City, there was nothing left to wish for." Chicago aspired to put on for the world a show of magnificence, but very few of the fairy palaces were built to survive a Chicago winter. There was nothing permanent about them.

"I understand absolutely nothing," Rosen-Montag pleaded in German to his entourage standing behind him.

I kept talking, as though I were a recording. I talked to the tops of heads. As soon as I said that Bismarck considered international exhibitions a necessary evil, I saw all too clearly that I had taken the wrong approach. I only meant to say that Rosen-Montag's project would be what a future generation looked back on and wished itself into. I never considered that I might be implying Lessingsdorf was as impermanent as the Chicago Exposition. It was the scene of new inventions and new styles and the Lessing Project offered the same, I'd planned on saying.

"Who has extended to the Bismarck this invitation,"

Rosen-Montag demanded of his wife. I began to see what Manfred had tried to convince me of. As if daring anyone to try to shake him up and hold him accountable, Rosen-Montag was on the offensive with everyone, wherever he went, about everything. He was unhappy. He showed it to everyone. People redoubled their efforts to please him.

My German entered the space like a variety of squirrel rare in the city. I rifled through the Manfred raps in my head and tried to give his views about how in Berlin there was a tendency to build horizontally, along a west-east axis, instead of a north-south one. I turned from side to side. We had internalized the Wall. Uneasy laughter among the assistants made me think I'd said that we had eaten the Wall.

I tried to attack the skyline of my hometown, a gray specter on the water when viewed from shores of the South Side. I said something about phallic architecture, or thought I had, and got somewhat more relaxed laughs. The truth was that I never minded the skyline. But I wasn't interested in the questions tall buildings asked. I was happy on the seventh floor around the atrium of the old Sante Fe Building. Mom and Dad's dating stories were about places like Grand Central. He kissed her hand the day they tore it down.

Rosen-Montag maybe felt pity when I tried to speak on their level, in their language. I went 1930s Hollywood Negro. I was smiling and perspiring. I was moments away from tap-dancing. I swam back to English and the beauty of decentralization.

I clicked the carousel to the image of a divided screen: on the left side, a panoramic black-and-white view of the Chicago Exposition taken from what was called the Spectatorium; on the right, a colorful, touched-up aerial view of Lessingsdorf that Manfred had taken from the runway rooftop of one of the apartment blocks in the Hansa Quarter.

I said that Berlin's 750th anniversary was a time to remind ourselves that the city's history need not be dominated by the legacy of Nazi devastation. I said it was not true that East and West Berlin were two forms of government yet one city in spirit. Rosen-Montag stopped fidgeting. He'd been stroking the skin inside his shirt. He asked for a coffee. He liked departure from the conventional rhetoric of the celebrations.

Rosen-Montag said evenly in English that Paul Goodman, a prophet of decentralization, had left his world a far better place than Bismarck had his, but what was he to do with Paul Goodman at this stage.

I had nowhere to go with it. A phrase from Brecht-Weill launched into my head. O moon of Alabama. I almost sang it to Rosen-Montag because I had nothing else.

The people in the Chicago photo must have known they were at something special. But we could not see any women, and all the men were white. The important division was the border between what we had been and what we were becoming.

"To call for decentralization away from utopian centers moves no one, and not the German people, that is certain." Rosen-Montag was asking me what this meant and I had no idea.

"Turn to the River," I said to the hut, ditching the remainder of my presentation. "In this is the meaning of the Lessing Project. Water is the life of Berlin."

My use of a project mantra, Turn to the River, calmed Rosen-Montag somewhat. His coffee came, borne by a willowy French girl with coal-dark eyes. He had the power to ornament his life with such creatures. The conference table asked for coffee, its mood a little deflated. There would be no sacrifice, but allowances had to be made for the black American, Rosen-Montag's experiment, much as the eighteenth-century court of the Prince and Princess of Brunswick had to put up with their royal highnesses' determination to send a black man, Anton Wilhelm Amo, to university to study theology in order to prove that a black man could study theology.

Throughout history, water has meant communication, I

went on. There was still no wooden dock for the pleasure boat
that was to take passengers from Lessingsdorf to the lakes in
the west. I said Rosen-Montag was the first architect working
in West Berlin in a long time to dream along a north-south axis.
I got a sigh from him.

Manfred had heard that Rosen-Montag was furious that
the opening of the Lessing Project was not the inaugural event
of that season's 750th anniversary celebrations. I clicked to the
final images in the carousel of the Chicago Exposition as seen
from Lake Michigan and then one of Rosen-Montag's project
as seen from the river. It looked its best from that view. It
looked most real from that angle as well. Perception has a destiny, Emerson said.

Suddenly the table was talking generally. They were trying
to come up with a summary of what I meant. I was so tense
that I didn't notice I was understanding their language, I was
just understanding. I was at last living in the moment, as AA
urged me to. Because my remarks had been obscure and in-
conclusive, so were the comments of the foundation people
concerning Rosen-Montag's book. But then, it existed. They
didn't have to have a critical opinion. They just had to hope it
sold. It didn't matter that nobody understood what I'd been
trying to say about the book, since I'd not had time to mention it during my talk.

Outside the hut, people going by avoided me. I smoked and
separated sounds. O moon of Alabama, we now must say goodbye. By the end of the day I had been reorganized. I'd already
found two tiny desks pushed alongside mine for the entourage
girls who were members of a new publications team that had
been put in place while I was in Chicago. Later, I telephoned
Manfred from his pub, but he wouldn't meet me even when I
told him that the lesbian had asked me to move out.

They'd kept driving in East Berlin when the authorities in
West Berlin tried to empty the streets for two days back in

February. Factories in East Germany did not close. People were going to work by car all over northern Germany, therefore what was the point of further inconveniencing West Berlin, Manfred said every sane person had tried to say.

•

One building of the Chicago Exposition was still in use. It was not on what had been the actual fairground, but it was near Jackson Park. I wanted to go there. Dad said, "That's Jackson Park down the street, Jedediah." I was twelve years old and I did not know where I lived.

•

The press girl was not going to survive the debacle of the afternoon's architecture tour bus. First, there were not enough places. Manfred snatched my pass. He walked up behind the press girl and slapped the pass against her stomach. She did not turn around, but her hand took over from his as he spoke into her ear. She was facing several important personages who had been promised seats for Rosen-Montag's lecture in the field on contemporary architecture in West Berlin.

The sun was out in the west, but it was drizzling in the Tiergarten. Manfred ushered me out of the office hut and shoved me ahead of him onto the gravel.

"Have you rescued me from the Order Police?" I said.

"Shove dynamite into red baboon asses," he said.

I liked it when Manfred took the training wheels off his German and spoke angrily in his northern accent. But he could tell when I'd missed something. That I wasn't following, that I was just being admiring, frustrated him, even bored him. I was not as smart as he thought.

He asked me to remember how critical Rosen-Montag was of most new architecture in West Berlin. Moreover, his passengers would be admirers of the immensely popular director of

IBA, the International Building Exhibition, whom Rosen-Montag had been attacking in recent interviews. "Wrong bus, Rosa Parks," Manfred said in English and pulled open the canteen hut door.

It was true that Rosen-Montag didn't like much in the way of recent work. But Berlin would agree with many of his judgments. The Social Science Center complex designed by James Stirling got nicknamed Birthday Cake because of its most distinctive feature: a layered half-moon building. The rounded side faced the street, the pink middle floor sandwiched between a pale blue ground floor and a pale blue top floor. "And they have murdered a wonderful old building to make room. They beat it to death with sledgehammers," Rosen-Montag said to me at our only private meeting. Yet he had once loved Stirling.

He could still speak well of Bruno Taut and Hans Scharoun, but then they were dead. He had some sympathy for their reform movement. That didn't stop him from misbehaving at the opening of Scharoun's long-delayed chamber music hall at the Kulturzentrum, that tiny area of library, museums, and concert halls tucked under where the Berlin Wall turned east, cutting through Potsdamerplatz, once one of the busiest squares in Europe. And while I was amused that there was a U-Bahn stop called Uncle Tom's Cabin, he thought Taut's sprawling housing estate down there a laugh riot of the misguided in materials and design.

Mostly he mourned the decay of the New Objectivity he'd been made by. He didn't like a building in Kreuzberg that was a highly praised part of the IBA. To him, Bonjour Tristesse, as the curved apartment house on a poor street was called, resembled a diesel engine about to run him over.

Manfred said again that I didn't want to be anywhere near the blame-thrower Rosen-Montag's people would strap on after such a public relations miscalculation. He was grubby from inspecting cargo on the river. The canteen was more crowded than I'd ever seen it. He parked me by a noisy wall.

Manfred had a type: the most attractive woman in the room. He barreled steadily past any man to reach the smile he hoped to create in her face. He put his weight into his step. Girls vibrated along with the floorboards at his approach. If they weren't free, he did not press, but in his stories about the open American road, the spoken-for were the ones who went after him hardest.

I could see that he had our coffees but that he was taking his time rolling a cigarette, taking up a lot of counter space to do it. Then I saw a long-limbed woman, the kind he liked, draw next to him. She spoke. He handed her the cigarette and lit it for her. Then she was following him to my wall. He went back for the third coffee, leaving this new silky blonde and me to establish in declarative English our connections to Rosen-Montag. She didn't have one. She was an expert in stucco restoration. She'd come from Warsaw for the IBA. She'd heard about the bus tour. She was probably wearing her best business suit.

Manfred inserted a chair between her silkiness and the next guy at our back table. He said the architects and journalists were bound to stone Rosen-Montag, that the bus probably wouldn't make it as far as the National Gallery by Mies. The Culture Center was not easy to get to, broken off from the rest of the city. I could tell he wanted to ask her how she got permission to travel to West Berlin.

He cupped his hands around his GI's lighter. He looked up quickly. An uncool guy would have grinned. She hadn't time to disguise her gaze. His expression remained friendly while he placed a proprietary boot against the leg of her chair and slouched a bit, opening his thighs. He held his coffee cup and his cigarette in the same hand. She waited, unembarrassed.

I was seeing what she was seeing and I'd seen all he'd

needed to. She was a beautiful woman. She was much older than we were, poised and vulnerable. It was as though Ingrid Bergman as Anastasia had left her Technicolor court to rendezvous with Burt Lancaster in black-and-white.

The smoke was criminal. Manfred asked in formal German, a contrast to his posture, what she thought of the accelerated construction going on in East Berlin. I only caught the first part of what he said, but I could supply the rest. In preparation for its 750th anniversary, East Berlin had been knocking itself out. New apartment buildings were going up daringly close to the Wall and the medieval quarter had been worked over, the bricks that could be seen repointed. The East could not let itself be upstaged by the West.

Her long answer came with elegant movements of her hands. I couldn't see her face anymore, she had turned toward him completely, but I could see that he wanted her to see his eyes roam happily over her face. He just held the cigarette, as if forgetting to smoke, and then stabbed it out in his saucer. He folded his hands. After a while he twitched his nose, his cute trick, and reached for the cigarette she was neglecting.

Guys were supposed to understand. He'd stopped paying attention to me as soon as she arrived. I ceased to exist. He was focused on her. I didn't have to take it personally. He'd blocked out everyone else as well. It was important to him that she saw that and believed him. I was watching, but anyone could. The noise gave them the privacy they needed to let talking become sitting there, a waiting for him.

Remnants of the Red Army Faction had attacked a U.S. Army train in retaliation for one of its members receiving a life sentence for the execution of a businessman ten years earlier, during the young leftist terror of the "German Autumn." Berlin recalled with incredulity the bombings, courtroom shootings, and safe houses, the violence that they said came out of the anti–Vietnam War movement. But it was the Nazis Manfred talked about. They were still the biggest story in town, bigger even than the Russians stationed in the loneliness of East Berlin's outskirts. Manfred stepped to the side when he stood, and she did not look back as she went ahead of him.

Albert Speer, Hitler's architect, who was my age when he was hired, said that in 1938, when he showed his father, also an architect, the model of a transformed Berlin, Germania, capital of the Thousand-Year Reich, the colossal dome of the Great Hall and the swollen neoclassicism of the Arch of Triumph and the Palace of the Führer, his father said, "You've all gone completely crazy." I'd seen the Pergamon Altar over in East Berlin that Speer claimed as his inspiration. Manfred had never been to the East.

•

I stayed on the city bus past the ChiChi. I got off not far from Savignyplatz and walked back in the direction of Bahnhof Zoo. I saw that *The Threepenny Opera* was still playing in the big theater along the way and I decided to see it. I was in Berlin, in the grip of a stupid situation. How had I not noticed before that this work was about fools getting what they deserved.

Hayden Birge was reserved at intermission. I stopped wagging my tail and climbed down off his leg. A thick-necked boy beside him excused himself to go to the men's room. Hayden relaxed. He said I would not believe the number of gymnasts from around the world who were in Berlin and in need of consolation. The muscular, compact Austrian had been knocked out in the early rounds of the international competition that was taking place down at the huge Deutschlandhalle.

I told him I'd left Cello's place, but I did not mention the cocaine. Though of course I'd been to Europa Center and the ChiChi, I said for effect that I was taking a risk showing myself in Charlottenburg. He said what everyone else said, that I'd lived on Cello for more than a year. Sure it was a big apartment, but not only did Cello need her space, so did I, and I had to accept that. He was so unfazed by my news, I didn't ask if he'd seen her. He barely answered when I asked how long he'd been back in town. His Tyrolean returned. Hayden again became as smooth and alert as a leopard. He fluttered fingers at me. He and his date headed back to their seats, Hayden lavishing his succulent smile on the boy. He hadn't bothered to say we should get together or that he'd call.

I hadn't much sympathy for Brecht/Weill's Jenny. The lesbian back in Schöneberg was anxious to get me out. She and her new girlfriend took lengthy baths together by scented candlelight. I stayed out of the apartment for as long as I could, walking and walking, learning once more to enjoy the company of my old friends, my footsteps. I was again keeping away from the ChiChi, now that Zippi had become the middleman between Bags and me. The last time I scooted down to him at the bar, he thumbed me back in her direction. She collected the money from me as well.

Hitler promulgated a law that if you were not already blond, you couldn't dye your hair, Manfred told me. After *The Threepenny Opera*, I prepared to take myself by foot across town. In front of a late restaurant, comfortable people were having suppers of white asparagus and white wine under soft garden lights. I was not Invisible, I was that worse thing, Unwanted, a sign badly written and stuck with masking tape on my back. I was wearing the wrong thing. I went out anyway, to Kreuzberg, by taxi, left alone in a corner in every gay bar I entered.

•

A freshly shaven Manfred was in his car on my corner in the morning. He wanted to take me on another tour behind the meters of trompe l'oeil murals of row houses in Lessingsdorf that were to be either raised up into place or unveiled on existing surfaces.

"It will be 'Burn, Baby, Burn' when the whole village is up," Manfred laughed, a cigarette in his fist on the wheel. For some reason, he saw the whole thing as provocative. He said he confessed to Irma that he could not cope with the opening of the Lessing Project and the rationing of his cigarette intake at the same time. She wanted to burn his clothes.

I wanted to stay in Schöneberg, near Manfred and the cooled-out Saturday market in the church square, but Schöneberg didn't want me. I answered ads in the back of a community newspaper. The ads were from women who said when I called that they were looking for women. Two were curious to see what an American guy might look like as a roomie, but the interviews didn't go well. I didn't get to say much. Of course the gender-empowered of Schöneberg were not racist.

Manfred seemed to know more about fresco-secco pigments than he had the day before. But guys understood: his business was his, not mine. He parked on the street next to the front gate and I heard him running on the gravel.

I choked on air when Rosen-Montag's wife suddenly banged the car's hood.

"Where were you."

She gave the door another bang with her fist and rejoined her husband's assistants. They let her go first through the gate. I was hoping she wouldn't cancel the talk I was to give in a week's time at a nearby hotel, which was an architectural curiosity because it used the remains of the entrance of a bombed hotel as its doorway.

Every week the project hierarchy seemed to intensify. Manfred jumped back into his car with new site passes and threw the engine into gear. The press girl had not been fired. It was too close to the opening for the kinds of scandal Rosen-Montag's people did not want. What scandal they wanted, they got, and on camera. To start with, a number of academics had been filmed as they were given the news, along with sugary croissants, that there were too many passengers for the bus. They had excluded those most likely to have fits of self-importance.

Apparently Rosen-Montag had not disappointed either. The camera was also rolling when the lecture bus made its first stop, at an intersection of canal and rather unattractive apartments. They stood next to a carnival with a Ferris wheel. The press girl told Manfred that Rosen-Montag said he had nothing to say about these apartments. He said he was not from the Porto School and did not make bunkers for the poor. He imagined city homes of individual character. The problem was that followers of Portugal's distinguished architects, regarded as the beginning of the Porto School, were on the bus.

Manfred liked for his car to be seen outside a nondescript restaurant abutting the elevated train tracks that had refused to sell to the Lessing Project or join in with its spirit of urban reclamation. There were two score of artisans and electricians, apprentices and street cleaners working frantically on the other side of Lessingstrasse, behind the high wooden fence. But where we stood was fringe West Berlin, weeds in the useless concrete, anarchist graffiti on the sides of the S-Bahn tracks.

Manfred said I'd been rejected as a roommate either because I was not a student or because I'd indicated that after the 750th anniversary celebrations my employment would be precarious.

It was the worst thing, this hopeless thing. It was going to be the worst thing, his happiness for you when you met someone who didn't compare. I said I'd been cruising in the Tiergarten. Show me the way to the next pretty boy. For we must die.

He asked if I'd been safe, but he was glad to hear I'd been bad, because he'd not been able to imagine as a man how I could stand to be celibate. My eyes strafed the Khyber Pass of his chest. At least we had never talked about it. I never let discussion of the impossibility of the relationship I wanted with him take the place of the relationship I could not have with him.

We were standing in the restaurant parking lot with cups in our hands. We let the whine of saws and the smell of wood and metal at high temperatures from across the tracks distract us for a while. Manfred squinted at the towers in the trees and said that Rosen-Montag had ended the shorter-than-expected lecture tour with a chant: "Tear down the Hansa Quarter." The Hansa Quarter and I were born the same year.

■

"Pancake days is happifying days." There was a Colored Folks' Day or Negro Jubilee Day at the Chicago World's Fair in August 1893. It was put on after considerable protests from blacks. Indians were part of the World's Fair, if only as trophies, humbled Gauls. But there was no mention of slavery. Frederick Douglass pointed out that there was no mention of the progress black people had made since slavery either. Because of the insult of the World's Fair's indifference to black Americans, they were urged to boycott what some were calling Watermelon Day.

Sissieretta Jones, the greatest black soprano of the day, had been scheduled to appear on Colored Folks' Day in *Scenes from Uncle Tom's Cabin*, an opera in which Uncle Tom was to be burned alive. It started out with everyone believing in his own promises. It ended up a confidence game. The producers didn't have an opera to stage, though they sold tickets.

Sissieretta Jones arrived weeks later, sang "Ocean Thou Mighty Monster," and then got out of town with the money. Some people came just to see her gown. Her costumes were sculpted creations, as Beaux Arts as the pavilions. She could handle a long train and she liked to finish her satin front with every jewel she owned, every medal she'd ever been awarded, dozens of sewn or draped pieces. Stagehands were honored to carry her into place before the curtain rose. She shimmered and glistened in the sidelights. Then she breathed.

I thought about the car wrecks I'd been in, my amazement at being thrown around, at being caught up in the old story of action and reaction, impersonal unless you believed in the gods, in their antipathy. Less than a year earlier I'd announced to the ChiChi that I'd taken Jackie O as my Higher Power because Mrs. Onassis never gave an interview. She knew how to keep things to herself. I was sorry I'd been flip. To be speechless was an expression of powerlessness, not pride.

I'd had another flop. Six people came to my hotel talk about Faner Hall at Southern Illinois University in Carbondale, Illinois. Nobody came from the IBA or the Lessing Project except for Manfred and Irma. I'd tried to strike an unbothered tone. But I couldn't pull it off in a dusty side room that had once been part of something bigger. I was too proud of my interpretation of the gigantic Southern Illinois University classroom building to call off the talk to many empty ballroom chairs.

Faner Hall was a betrayal of the deconstructed building because the steel and concrete so plain on the outside protected a maze inside. Famously, people got lost in it. Twenty minutes was the most the eight of us—a janitor waited by the light switch—could manage. Manfred said he couldn't follow what I was trying to say about Louis Kahn and that a visual component would have helped because Faner Hall was unknown in Germany. And once you'd walked through the white, green, and red ruined arch leading to the Hotel Stuttgarter Hof, you'd had that Berlin experience, too.

The May Day riots in Kreuzberg on the part of labor unions and anarchist youth would have been another Berlin experience, but in my belief in mistakes and punishments, I went back to the AA meeting in Dahlem instead. I didn't come from a black family that prayed. Jesus was not in our closets. I went to Dahlem to protest. My Berlin dream was floating on the river. Either I sat still or there was no in-between. I was on the verge of having one of those AA breakdowns, but something held me back. It was shaming enough that Odell's session buddies probably remembered my Ethel Merman imitation from my drinking days. Big Dash did. I couldn't let myself lose it in front of the two black American noncom officers who were still coming to this Saturday evening meeting.

They nodded in unison; I nodded in return. That was somehow enough. Their solidarity with me restored me. This would forever mark out my generation of black expatriates—we exchanged silent greetings on the streets and in the cafés of Europe, even when young black American corporate lawyers living in Cheyne Walk or on Tverskaya-Yamskaya Street no longer wanted to have any idea why we would. But that night the presence in the AA meeting of two black soldiers urged me to compose myself.

Berlin did not see me weep for myself and repaid my adherence to its code with news of a room for rent down in Friedenau, almost the end of the U-Bahn line. An acquaintance of Irma's had wall-to-wall blue carpet throughout his apartment. My shoes were to remain on a mat outside the front door, but I deposited them in a plastic bag at the threshold and took them to my peaceful room, where two windows looked out onto a shady street of small parked cars. My new landlord was from East Germany and spoke no English. I could of course use the bath and the toilet, but the rest of the apartment, including the kitchen, was not part of the deal.

I made myself useful, doing errands at Rosen-Montag's wife's command. In the company of a roadie in between jobs, I delivered to bookshops and institutions around West Berlin stock of Rosen-Montag's book, the very work I was supposedly an editor of, and his books of drawings and blueprints

concerning the Lessing Project. I missed my books and started
to buy new ones. I walked through Lessingsdorf a little at a
time and then took the subway from the Hansa Quarter station to the Zoo Station. There I had half a pizza. Then I went
back down to Friedenau. In a matter of days I had a routine,
just as AA advised. Long before dark, I raised the drawbridge
between me and life as it was being led around me.

But my landlord was an usher at the Philharmonic Hall. Once
persuaded that our tenant arrangement was okay, he got me
into concerts. Sometimes, when the lights went down, I slept.
I no longer accepted my shame about having done so. I was at
home in the city, I insisted to myself. Then sometimes it was
true what musicians said, that a live performance could teach
you something about how a work was constructed. Music could
do more than relieve your solitude or comfort you. It took you
on a journey and made you a part of something beautiful.

One night in June, the crown of Scharoun's hall was golden
in its spotlights. The Wall, the twelve-foot-high continuous
concrete barrier that split Potsdamerplatz into two identical,
empty sides, was right behind us, bright on one side, dark on
the other. The happy audience of the pianist Peter Serkin overtook demonstrators giddy from waging what they thought of
as battle with the riot police. The U.S. president had spoken
in front of the Reichstag that afternoon, the top of the Brandenburg Gate visible behind him. Young Berlin had been protest-
ing his presence all day long, marching through the Tiergarten,
chanting by the Wall.

A couple stopped to light up, praising the power of Serkin's
introspective Beethoven Opus 109, and five or six rubber-
headed Reagans thundered past us, running for the cover of the
trees and the safety of back courtyards beyond them. I could
see black police vans on the other side of the church square
and teams of policemen in tight black gear holding back dark
German shepherds. Not the everyday police in green jackets.
Someone threw a bottle. It didn't seem like the police wanted

to play anymore. They were no longer giving chase to the slogan shouters in Halloween masks.

I ambled into the dark of the Kulturzentrum. The laughing hair made me look. They were impossible to miss, sitting on the wide white steps leading up to the Fine Arts Museum. I was passing too near Cello and Rosen-Montag.

"You must hear this," Rosen-Montag said in English, without preamble, as though I'd just come back into a room. He stood and lit his cigarette. I had mine. Cello remained seated, though she looked as if she were slaloming in place.

Cello said in German that when Peter Serkin's father, Rudolf Serkin, made his debut in 1921, he played the fifth *Brandenburg*. He then asked Adolf Busch what he should play as an encore. The *Goldberg Variations*, the violinist who would be his father-in-law said. "So Serkin did. All thirty. Busch had been joking. When Serkin finished, six people were left in the hall: Adolf and Frieda Busch and Mr. and Mrs. Artur Schnabel and Mr. and Mrs. Albert Einstein."

"You understand? Tell him your idea for 'Tunes over the Water,'" Rosen-Montag said to her.

We smoked as Cello leaned farther back on her hands and faced the heavens, her enormous, firm breasts settling back down. She explained that barges of musicians on the Spree would serenade Lessingsdorf at its opening. There could be a competition. Mom would have said that she was wearing an excuse for a sleeveless pink dress.

Their eyes were wet with tears. Rosen-Montag had been bouncing on the balls of his long feet the whole time and Cello's mounds of brown dough rolled with her laughter. More of her hair was twining its way around her throat. We finished our cigarettes and Rosen-Montag waved me off and sat beside Cello's tresses. I didn't really want to kiss her on the cheeks, but I wanted to be sure and needed to get close enough to inspect her pupils. She sat up and hugged her elbows, as she used to as a teenager.

"West Berlin is a very small town," I heard Cello say in German as I walked away. The seats in Scharoun's Philharmonic Hall went down toward the stage. It was not the kind of place where anyone's head got in your way. Nevertheless, what a story Cello's and Rosen-Montag's hair was going to make for the people who'd been near them while Serkin played softly, arctic clear and softly.

•

"Use value is a fiction created by exchange value," Cello's father, Ralston Jr., once said, patting my shoulder. "May the funk be with you always."

•

The seven hundred and fifty specially invited guests about whom Rosen-Montag was ambivalent wandered around his shining garage that had been sectioned into multilevel open office spaces; his vaulted dairy; and his airily reconstructed workers' houses on a green square. And everyone was utterly charmed by the giant panels that filled Rosen-Montag's grid. Trompe l'oeil after trompe l'oeil showed the arches and long French windows of elegant, affordable houses that might be there someday. The renovations around the Gendarmenmarkt in East Berlin were only slightly more real, I heard someone say. His painted houses should have given off a retrograde quality, but what he planned in brick seemed as airy as any glass box.

The late-June sky admired itself in the river and Lessingsdorf was a hit. It was an urban playground, a carnival, a peep show, a hall of mirrors. It offered West Berlin the sort of party the city adored. Shirley Bassey and an unafraid brass section were what people we didn't know also wanted. That party went on, very well dressed, among Rosen-Montag's elegant, happy-making imaginings. No one knew how he pulled these things off. They were giant magic tricks. His simple constructions and meters of bright paintings on canvas mounted on wood had a way of feeling like time travel.

There was no music on the water. But Rosen-Montag had won his fight to have reflective sheeting line the opposite bank of the Spree. Meanwhile, the crowd in Lessingsdorf was so sophisticated, either in black tie or black punk or black chic, there was so much middle-aged magenta hair and youthful blue hair that people didn't want to be middle-brow and say the obvious—Potemkin Village—as they walked around the narrow streets of movie-set lighting and deep gutters and vaulted brick ceilings intended to speak to the brick passage-ways and courtyards of the serene School of the Arts campus at the end of the bus line outside Havana, Cuba.

No one had to be told not to leave a glass or a napkin on the sidewalk. This was a German party, after all. Not even the anarchist youth who'd been allowed to crash would litter. Rosen-Montag would not permit bins or cylinders, though codes required them. They lay under colorful plastic in the middle of one of those blocks. There were, however, terra-cotta urns all over the place, filled with sand where people plunged in their cigarettes. They marked Rosen-Montag's progress as he moved around on the opening night of his creation, a reenactment of a Belle Epoque pleasure garden, a combination of fantasy and license, more than a twentieth-century revision of the eighteenth-century style.

It was clear I'd not seen Cello a week ago, though she must have known or been known to some in the concert audience, that gorgeous black American woman married to a distinguished patron of the city's music. To her credit, she looked me dead in the eye. She wore new glasses, ultrahip frames from Milan. She took them off for me to admire. Her eyes were turned-off burners. I offered to take her and Dram over to Rosen-Montag and his wife to say hello. They'd said hello to the Rosen-Montags and to the governing mayor and his wife at the same time, but they thanked me for offering to be of service. Dram made a somewhat ironic bow. I'd forgot that his father tended to know the residents of Bellevue, the nearby Berlin home of the president of West Germany.

But his congratulations on the success of the Lessing Project were sincere. I could tell. He even found something to say about the book. The trick was to let Dram and Cello stream away before I had to talk about where I was living or they had to ask what I planned to do next. Their retreat was framed by forced perspective into gardens and side paths that did not exist. People looked back at Cello after she'd gone by, trying to name which diva or tennis star's girlfriend she was.

I finally found Manfred and Irma in one of the large white marquees set up on the approach to the Hansa Bridge. He was pulling her arms down toward the floor, making her head bounce a few steps. He was telling her that nothing was finished, that he still had work to survey. He saw me and let her go. He went on with what he was saying, his normal accent full on.

Irma held up her hands, as if to say, No further explanation required. He reasoned with her, an unlit cigarette in his fist. She was to enjoy the party while he went around to see what tasks he would face in the morning, when the work was to continue. He said he had to find that person from the Office for Metropolitan Architecture.

He kissed her hair and muttered for me to look after her. She wiped her eyes with her hands and sat. I pulled up alongside her, both of us looking at the slit where he'd stalked out. Sometimes you have to overcome your fear of saying the obvious.

•

By her old age, Sissieretta Jones had run out of money. She sold her houses. She sold her jewels and her medals, one by one, then in lots.

·

To kill a buffalo bull you must first cut off its tail when it is at full speed. Cello's hair smelled of smoke. Maybe I was losing my sense of smell, but I detected smoke on her breath.

"Where have you been?"

Her practice room, she said.

Anyone could see that she had been crying. She was nearly an hour late. I wasn't alone in the hut and was glad of it. They were packing up the enclave for Rosen-Montag's archives. The billboard advertisements along the perimeter from corporate partners that Rosen-Montag had had his final preopening tantrum about were going up. The show was over for us now that the public was lining up to see his futurist village of good taste.

I guided Cello to the same empty restaurant in the hotel near the Zoo Station that Hayden had taken me to. Her driving was a worry. Rosen-Montag famously bunked off the day after his openings. Even before the party, it was clear that his wife was relieved to be getting him out of town.

Cello admitted to nothing, confided nothing. I asked her no questions. Maybe she hadn't washed her face and hair since the Lessingsdorf opening the week before. Maybe she just stared at her children in their baths. Perhaps Dram was in Dortmund again. Manfully, I ordered for us both, and she spooned carrot soup and tear spit for a while. Through me she was reaching out to my mother in this, her woman's hurt. She was squeezing Mom's hand, not mine.

It had been the worst day. I was in awe of my discretion with Cello, but I took it as a consequence of the shock I'd had. Manfred had also got out of town, in a matter of days.

The family of a girl in Rosen-Montag's entourage had a small *Schloss*, a little palace, in West Germany that needed extensive work on its wiring, plumbing, and interior decoration. He needed a break from Irma's flowers, Manfred said. He brought up his backpack from his storage cubicle. He wanted to give me things, but I'd nowhere to put them. He threw out his furniture and Irma's plants. He dumped as much as he could, quickly. We loaded his boxes and lamps in a moving van run by former junkies. We took my boxes up to his empty apartment. I would have to do something with them soon.

I had several coffees and he several beers at his pub in farewell. He controlled our hug in the dawn's early light, holding my neck down on the edge of his shoulder so I couldn't kiss his cheek, in case I was tempted. His crotch was an insulting distance.

I'd not slept and I ate more french fries and swilled more coffee as Cello lost herself to her heartbreak in the blessed desertion of the hotel restaurant. The one waiter stood far away. I wondered if we looked like a story about black deportation. Instead, we were a story of when there is no one else to turn to, when you did not want to be alone, alone in Europe though you were, when music of any kind would be only a prelude to suicide, alone and black as you were.

One of Odell's session musician friends, Afer, once explained to me how he fled his Johannesburg township the night rumor reached his uncle that the security police were coming for him. He spent a long time in the Cameroons, trying to find a school in the West that would take him. He had a chance to go to East Berlin. From there, he crossed over. There had been nothing to stop him. He was not a Third World guest worker living in a concrete tower in one of the outlying districts of East Berlin. Once across the border, once in West Berlin, you ask for asylum. His case had been pending for a while, then got settled in his favor. His story was real, whereas my story sounded to me like an imitation of others I'd read.

I don't know what told me that Cello was "holding," though

she would not have understood what the word meant in that context had I asked her. I made her give me the cocaine she had on her. I went to the toilet and flushed it. She'd needed someone to take from her this last remembrance. That was why she was eating and sobbing. She was crashing; I was crashing. I was a fellow addict, someone you ask to watch over you when you're in withdrawal, when you're facing cold turkey, when you don't want anyone in normal life to see you. I made up my mind to abandon Manfred's futon on my next move.

I ordered ice cream and Cello laughed at last. What got to me was that Manfred must have been planning, not merely contemplating, his exit for some time and he'd not told me. Irma didn't want to see me, because she believed I'd known all along. I had no idea that Rosen-Montag's entourage included a countess. Manfred had made arrangements to give up his place, to redirect his mail, and behind my back as well as Irma's. I didn't want to feel "left," as he'd left her. On the other hand, I was obscurely flattered, obscurely turned on to have a share in his strange fashion of forsaking.

"He loved the flashlight more than he did the hearth," Dad said of guys he'd heard had left their wives.

I thought of the time I flapped around inside a car as it rolled over into a ditch. It was eerie, the disconnect between knowing what was happening and not being able to do anything about it, that having to go through with what was happening, unable to do anything about it.

You couldn't get away from your own authorship fast enough; you couldn't run from the deed fast enough; you couldn't wait to be the white-haired person decades later, full of regret when the intrepid young journalist tracks you down.

Cello was drained and my stomach was taut and round. I used to wait outside her door on our third floor when she

cried from shame because of the madness of her father, how
public his mania liked to make itself. Then there was her
mother, proud of her nightclub engagement at a hotel over
in Hammond, Indiana. I'd just wanted to sit with her, to
keep her company, the only thing you can offer someone in
misery.

Aunt Jemima was hired to cook pancakes and tell stories at the
Chicago Exposition. Her booth was a giant flour barrel. They
said she made more than a million instant pancakes at the fair
that one summer. Buttons featured her image, the fat, shiny-
cheeked, big-eyed black woman in a kerchief: "I'se in town,
honey." They called her the most famous colored woman in
the world.

Aunt Jemima liked to run her mouth, but black people
didn't like her, because she told stories about how happy she'd
been on the plantation. In one story, she cooked such delicious
pancakes she saved her master's life. The Yankees decided to
spare her master; or the Yankees were so enjoying their pancakes he had time to sneak away. Cello's father couldn't remember which.

Ralston Jr. told us that Aunt Jemima never made any money
from that pancake recipe. He was dressed in pajamas. It was
Christmas Eve. He fell asleep. Rhonda got Cello to come downstairs then. We argued over whether Aunt Jemima had been a
real person. Cello and I didn't want to believe it, even after
Dad and Mom had stepped in, dispensers of the facts.

Because I was fat, kids in the school corridor who'd never
seen Mom chanted behind me, "Ain't yo mama on the pancake box?"

I was going to random AA meetings in German. Dram had come to Schöneberg to help fetch boxes of books and take them back to their cellar. I was not following my books to Charlottenburg. Yet through Cello's intervention I got out of Friedenau before I ran out of the money to pay for my room of blue carpet. A friend of theirs, a professor of North American Studies, had been kicked out by his wife of three decades. He had a new place near the university in Dahlem, with a cheap room he thought suitable for a graduate student type. He liked that I cleaned up in the kitchen. He sat and talked. He was a specialist in the hideous Francis Parkman and called things by Indian—Native American—names. Hashish was "shongsasha."

I cleaned a lot, while he complained to his estranged wife's answering machine that she had not thought about what he was to do with his laundry. He called his friends and saw them often. He talked so much about his marriage and separation it drove me to my first heterosexual incident in some time.

He accompanied me to the Waldbühne, filled with indignation that his wife had got their adult daughter on her side. I'd wanted it to be one of those magical nights of music asking for my forget-yourself attention. The glitter Jessye Norman wore soared upward, answered by the stars. The birds quieted and the dark pulsed with love for her. Deep, deep. But it was as though my landlord professor had not been listening, had been instead watching for the concert's end so he could pick up where he left off, right along with the mosquitoes, so many bouncing above the grass they looked like the tips of reeds.

His English was idiomatic, fluent, and he had to use all of it on me. I saw her check me out in the crowd of people filtering through the tunnel away from the band shell hidden in the forest. I'd been hurrying, to get away from my landlord professor's circular analysis of his family dynamic. She'd kept up with us, this bold girl in worn-down flat shoes. She was trying to attract me, not him. Since Manfred's going, I had been drifting about, as useless as Telstar. I suddenly veered onto her side. She had a strong odor and dark hair. It took my landlord professor a moment to register what was going on. Then he increased his pace ahead and away. Guys understood.

I bought condoms at a gas station. I lifted the heavy sack of all my pointless, fruitless pining and bore down on her, the sweet, lonely Polish loading dock. Nothing is mysterious to a seaman, they say, unless it be the sea itself. I didn't keep our next appointment and she had no phone.

·

One Saturday, I left the AA meeting in Dahlem early and went to one of those free Bach concerts in the ugly modern church at Europa Center. The musicians were visiting students, but it was another place where I could escape my landlord professor and myself.

Cello and Dram were both there. I was sure they'd wandered in on impulse. We got up and went outside at the same time. Cello shook off the bad experience, swinging her hair back and forth and making animal sounds. Dram lit up. They were young again. I was nostalgic for that sad, drifting feeling of a few weeks earlier. Money, the expatriate's enemy, was ending my days with the frightened professor, he who was so unprepared for bachelor life. But I could see where his wife and his daughter might think his conversation a poor return for waiting on him hand and foot.

They'd maybe had something to drink, Cello and Dram. They'd maybe had one of those where-are-we-now conversations, without either being irrevocably honest. Dram stepped on his cigarette. "Okay, he decided he is straight," he said in English, as if Manfred had come to his senses. Cello lightly cupped my chin. Dram got behind me and said over my shoulder that I was not to give up hope. Cello took my hands, backed up, and let go.

Dram doubled back to thank me for being there for Cello during her recent cancer scare, but he'd been so unable to guess what was up with his wife that he wished I had told him she was consulting a specialist in Switzerland, someone his family did not know. Cello, swinging her arms and her hair, stayed off in the distance as he told me what she evidently had had no trouble getting him to believe. Dram said her music foundation had never before had so many meetings, so he'd been concerned. He knew that something was up. He tapped my shoulder and caught up with Cello. Dram and Cello pulled on each other as they walked hand in hand across the plaza toward the Ku'damm, their children, and home.

Their atmosphere of hearts still beating gave me permission to be friends again with the ChiChi. I was not feeling at all vulnerable to the promises, the lies of white wine. But in one of those addict's crazy minutes, as soon as I saw Bags, I asked if he had any coke. He handled the heavy side of his business himself. Hash put me to sleep and Berlin asked for a brother to be somewhat awake, I explained. He called me Cuz.

The streets had been busy ever since I got back. Small parades and street fairs and demonstrations and ceremonies and bands and protests. There were official and unofficial festivities marking the city's birthday. Lessingsdorf had been one of those parties for the intelligentsia, for the arty, for what Manfred called the schicki-micki. I paid no attention when I heard the honking outside. It just sounded very loud. The ChiChi usually muffled most of the city noise, what little found its way behind Europa Center.

A regular who was leaving came back immediately and spoke to Odell. His body language alerted Zippi, who came flying. Odell ordered her to stay put, no cops. His buddies were with him. If Bags and Big Dash were among them, then

I was going to be as well. I was in no mood to stay behind with the girls.

I recognized Afer, the guy from South Africa with the ancient name, who had been granted asylum. I saw blood on his forehead as he lurched toward the curb. He went down. He'd been hit so quickly, I thought somebody had thrown something at him. I didn't realize he'd been socked again by a burly man who jumped into a small car of other burly men holding small flags.

Odell's buddies stormed the car and cut it off. Big Dash was rocking the vehicle by its door handle. Three or four languages accompanied the assault. The burly passenger rammed his door against Big Dash, and Bags pulled the passenger from the car. We set on him. The other burly East Europeans—Bulgarians, Odell said later—were out and swinging metal pipe.

Bags went down and I jumped on an East European's back. It was not like the movies. To be kicked in the stomach by a goat could not be much worse than an East European elbow. Moreover, he spun, and I with him. The law of physics predicted my flight over the hood of a parked car. I banged my head going down on the other side. I saw spots.

" 'Fly me to the moon,' " Big Dash sang to an East European. The big white dude paused and Big Dash kicked his attacker hard in the nuts.

It was a black-white, African-American-African-Slav melee. Afer lay unconscious and Big Dash was on his knees, blood overflowing his mouth, his lower lip a fountain. Two men had Odell, whose free arm punched at the ribs of an assailant. Two session men grunted with an East European, and Bags had the fifth man from the tiny car. It was like the movies. He slammed his forehead down on the man's nose. The huge man lay between parked cars. I rolled over and raised myself onto his throat. I was not dead. He kicked. I was not a eunuch. I let go. I struck before I got up. His teeth cut my knuckles.

Bags palmed me five, drew his fingers along mine, and ended with a snap of his fingers.

It was over, except for Zippi shrieking that she'd called the police. Afer was back among us, surrounded by women. Odell motioned for the session musicians to slip away as the sirens neared. The East Europeans sat with their backs against their tiny car, panting, touching their bruises. Odell flipped a couple of pipes into nearby bushes. I didn't see Big Dash get up and leave. Hours later he came back, stitched up and drinking through a straw.

The West Berlin police were no different from police anywhere in their dislike of paperwork. They were answering drunken calls about football violence and minor-league anger all over town. That we were Americans, black Americans, made them even less willing to pursue the matter. They made it clear that if they detained the East Europeans, then they would take us in as well. In the end, Afer wouldn't go with the ambulance. The medics asked him questions in German and English, then left, removing their rubber gloves. I saw the dread in the policemen's faces when Afer produced his documents. They did not want to have met up with him.

Our documents were in order. Odell wanted the police to come in to see how much in German order the bar and everything about it was. They'd handed our passports or cards or registrations back to us, the Americans, without comment. Bags had expired, laminated army ID. But he'd refused to get lost. He was an American. The police were deferential to Zippi. I did not know until that night that she was an Israeli. I also think I learned that she and Odell weren't married and that she was the sole owner of the bar.

Show us the way to the next whiskey bar. Bruised and sore, I felt wonderful, connected, thoroughly in Berlin. Bags knew a painter with a storage closet on Moritzplatz, in Kreuzberg, an oval at the bottom of a dead-end street leading up to the Wall. It was quiet and Turkish. Mice ate at canvases during the night. They didn't bother me, spread out on Manfred's futon. I had been the kind of guy who freaked at the way they flicked along your peripheral vision, that something extra in the room. But I'd become badass.

SIX

He said it was because his friends pulled a white priest from a car and beat him for five minutes. He said just one three-minute regulation round was a very long time when you were being hit. He said it was because he and his friends surrounded a bus and terrified everyone on board with the Confederate war cry. Mostly that day, he rebel-yelled through the trees, running so fast in his new red high-tops that he overtook the black demonstrators to his right who were being chased by white teens like him.

He said it was because he belonged. He'd been on South Sixty-Third Street when the high school students from up in Belmont-Cragin wouldn't let the demonstrators go beyond that point. He said it was because it was their turn in the streets. He'd been in Marquette Park when white citizens of Chicago threw bottles and rocks at the colored people taking cover behind the line of police. A friend sat on his shoulders in order to see over the helmets.

He'd been behind the line of smoke inside the park when the mood among them turned. He said that when the police finally charged, people ran in every direction, and therefore so did he and his friends. Their battle plan fell apart. The thud of police boots terrified him, he said.

He was with people he didn't know by this point, he said.
Fear had darkened everything around him. They happened
on a group of five women. He had not expected anyone to hit a
woman. A white guy caught one of the white women with a
simple cross. He said she was lifted off her feet, almost parallel
to the ground. The other women threw their bodies on top of
the fallen body of their friend. They prayed, he said. The guy
who hit the white woman hollered "Go home" over his shoulder as his gang sprinted into the tree line toward a golf course.

•

I had come back to Chicago to help out Dad, I told myself. I'd
come to lend support to Mom. Uncle Ralston and the *Eagle*
had failed. Dad got the so-called board to call in the receivers
over Uncle Ralston's head. Everything Uncle Ralston had was
being readied for the lawyers. I'd been helping out for far longer
than I had anticipated.

Two bald janitors from the *Eagle* wheezed and I said that I
would shift the files and microfilm to their final resting place
in the room that used to be Cello's privy chamber. We shook
hands. Their smiles contained a great deal of precious metal.
They rocked back downstairs, last paychecks signed by Dad in
their pockets.

I'd had a summer of lying low. Bags invited me to his old
lady's place in Schöneberg and I watched them drink. The
suffering of hanging out in a Schöneberg that Manfred had
dumped wasn't helped by the speedy coke I got from Bags. I
was glad when I had to admit that I didn't have the money.
He would have turned me on anyway, but his old lady was on
his case about loose business practices. He hung out in more
than one bar or café, but the ChiChi was most like home to
him. He didn't understand my need to stay away from it for
certain periods, precisely because I could so easily convince
myself that the ChiChi was home.

I'd been dropped officially from Rosen-Montag's Japan plans before the summer started. I visited the inland docks and the closed Art Deco swimming pools and the unused subway stations that had interested Manfred. There was nothing I was yet willing to do about the feeling. One day I went to East Berlin and sat. I used the border crossing at the train station on Friedrichstrasse and felt myself in my private movie. I sat in the Lustgarten, where young Nazis had burned cartloads of books. I sat in a youth club in the basement of the Ratskeller, trying to overhear a man who had something to do with the building's restoration talk to a group of expressionless students.

I had to show myself that I could manage homelessness, the short-term renting and long-range crashing. I could improvise, I could jump on what circumstances offered. I could do it not as a falling apart, but as a getting it together.

Because Bags's painter friend wasn't paying for his storage space, nobody brought up the matter of my paying anyone either. Consequently, I had enough money to eat rice and drink Turkish coffee for a while. Coke was for others; travel was for others. I mentioned my thirtieth birthday to no one. Then one fine day I did not have the money to feel part of the West Berlin daydream of My home is the sea / My friends are the stars / Over Rio and Shanghai.

•

It was easy to be sober in Chicago. Mom continued to phone Cello, because of the *Eagle*'s demise, though I knew Cello cared less than her mother or my brother about the newspaper. But it had been a long time since talk came easily between them. One afternoon Mom was electric with the news that she and Cello had discussed how hard the Grieg Concerto used to be for her and how she could almost breeze through it now. Mom no longer hid the row of medicines she took in the mornings.

Cello never referred to how often she and her little sister and brother had been dropped off at our house at the last minute or how often my father had gone to pick them up, to give them some stability, as Mom called it, while their parents went through their latest drama. Then came the night of the big fire and she didn't really leave again until she went to the conservatory.

She'd found her way back to Mom, even if I sometimes suspected that she felt toward my parents the loyalty a sovereign lady restored to her throne might have for the folk who protected her in her exile. Her feelings toward my parents she kept on a channel completely separate from her feelings toward me. I was keeping her secrets, and she'd helped me out, but I was not rewarded with a new intimacy. It didn't matter, compared with the sense of power I now felt in my relationship with Cello.

Before, it had been okay to owe her because she owed Mom. But now she owed me and I could do the grown-up thing, the male relative thing: I could forget it, call us even. I'd looked out for her, in my way. I thought I was so butch, suddenly needed by the first black winner of the Stokowski Society competition, she who hardly ever needed me before or cared. It was my turn to be cool about her, and therefore as cool as she.

I was impressed with myself. I was not hinting that I was keeping the lid on something big: Cello was an Ibsen play in blackface. To lie and to keep my own secrets had been the chief strategy of my life, but complete discretion for someone else's sake was a new experience of maturity for me.

I ventured again to Mom that I'd been emotionally ambushed when that friend who had given me sanctuary in his place took a job in West Germany. Mom's tone said she understood that I'd tell her about Manfred when I was ready. But it was she who was putting me off. As a subject, my private life was not reliably housebroken. If I could just not bring Berlin inside, not after she'd gone to the trouble of washing and waxing the difficult, messed-up floors of that part of the house.

Dad told Mom to leave me alone, every man had to stand on his own after a point. It was not unusual that he was home in the middle of the day. He could disappear into his basement for hours. But the back porch and halls were lined with boxes from the *Eagle*. There were more junk chairs than ever in the living room. Then the phone rang. Mom picked up in her basement office.

We heard her cry out. She bumped into Dad as he ran down to her. They panted back up together and turned on the television. Reporters stood in the rain in front of Northwestern Memorial. The tears were already coming down for Chicago's first black mayor. A press spokesman was saying that Harold Washington had been pronounced dead. He'd had a heart attack at his desk that morning. The phone rang again. Dad pressed Mom into a chair and went to answer.

I'd grown up seeing Mom wipe her face in front of the television, or while she was on the phone, or over a tissue-thin newspaper or a blue letter that folded back up to be its own envelope. In my memory, my dad is in the kitchen, pouring her a glass of water, trying to think of something else to do for her, brought low by news of another assassination, in Jackson, in Birmingham, in Dallas, in New York City, in Memphis, in Orangeburg, in Los Angeles, in Kent, in Munich, in Beirut, in Port Elizabeth, or blocks away, over on troubled Madison Street.

•

I was eight years old going on nine and Uncle Ralston was bringing Cello's father back from Ghana. Dad fed us catfish sandwiches, but Cello ate tuna from the can without a trace of mayonnaise or a crumb of saltine cracker anywhere. My father took the five of us with him to Holy Cross Hospital after he got the call from Mom. Dr. King and the protestors had been trapped by white mobs at certain points during the day. She'd gone on the march against Dad's wishes.

We found Mom and her nuns. They had short hair instead of habits and they wore pants. They were sitting with a white boy, a high school student, who was shaking his head and saying that that was the last time he was going to use violence. We'd missed it. The hospital emergency room mixed the wrong kind of whites with blacks. "Take a bath while you're here," some white guy snarled at Mom, and Mom's white boy raced over and slapped the guy's face sideways. But we'd missed it. Dad was so put out he wouldn't speak. I was planning to wish again for superpowers when I blew out the candles on my birthday cake in less than two weeks.

I got to ride in the back of the nuns' station wagon with the distressed white boy from the North Side. He tried to smile at me, but his heart was heavy. He said at least three times that it would be fine to let him out at the corner. Solomon had white friends in his scout troop and at school. He said in sports you just did, if the other guy was good enough. Mom had white friends. Cello didn't talk to anyone, but had I friends, they would have been everyone, too.

That summer Martin Luther King was trying to persuade white Realtors to open all-white neighborhoods like Chicago Lawn or Gage Park to black homeowners. Any time we heard Mom and Dad argue about Martin Luther King we got nervous. Mom and Dad explained things. Dad explained them again, taking back what Mom had said. I never understood, not until much later. One of the surprises of growing up was finding out what things had been about.

That night, Mom wanted to prove that it was not dangerous out there; she was willing to take just me along for the ride, a Friday-night treat. But it was dangerous. South Kedzie Avenue was blocked off behind the whipping lights of patrol cars. Mayor Daley's most loyal whites were shocked by what they'd done, the smell of tires burning in the night heat. We left the hospital, looking back, Dad after us, pulling at Mom's belt, confused, Mom and Dad hitting each other's arms, nuns running alongside, ineffectual, everything noise, bright lights, and sirens as we left Dad behind.

There was what I thought happened and what Mom and Dad told me later. The nun driving knew how to take backstreets. She ran stop signs and some lights. Because they had a kid in the car, they hoped they wouldn't look like protestors, Mom admitted. The year before, a white woman from Detroit, a mother, had been murdered in Alabama for driving blacks home after a march. Infamous Selma.

When we pulled up that night we could hear Cello at the piano. We were expected to go to bed. Dad was waiting at the front door with Soloman. Cello's brother and sister were already upstairs. We'd missed *Hogan's Heroes* on TV, so the day was over for them. They were used to plans falling through, those two. Cello shepherded Solomon and me toward the stairs, a sign of her new maturity. Adults needed to talk, especially the ones in their right minds. I'd not been afraid, not once that night.

Dad said that every friend he had on the university police force was looking for Mom. He said they were burning the clergy in their cars. But Mom and Dad didn't have an argument. I remember that Mom thanked him. She reminded him that she'd let him go to Sam Cooke's funeral and now they were even. She said that afternoon they had parked on Halsted and never got anywhere near the back of the march. They met up with waves of red-faced Americans running amok. Mom said they looked like they played pinochle, not bridge. Mom and Dad both laughed, in the middle of the emergency sounds still going in my head. Cello led me on.

The suburb of Cicero, Illinois, kicked Reverend King so hard it made Mahalia Jackson groan. Mom didn't like her, but everybody knew that Reverend King adored her as the song of trial. Mom told me years later that she had, indeed, piled on top of the knocked-down nun with the other sisters to protect her that night in Marquette Park, but she hadn't shouted prayers to anyone.

•

On the day of Harold Washington's funeral, we met by the front door, dressed in a kind of mourning, for the mayor, for the black family-owned newspaper that would not have been able to cover the story of the fallen black hero. It had been a while since our house had been a gathering place at such a time. Something like church platters of carrots, celery, deviled eggs, and ham and cheese slices between miniature buns had been placed around the living room, dining room, and on top of the hall bookshelf. The church-platter fairies turned out to be two arthritic, trembling secretaries, the last of Shay Holdings, Inc.

They talked at the same time, but not about the same thing. They were right behind Mom as she retreated to the kitchen. One was telling Mom that she would never forget her winter as a returning graduate student in Detroit. The snowplows were out every morning. Wayne State was practically stranded behind the walls of snow the plows had built up. The other was asking over her, like a descant line, if Aunt Gloria, Ruthanne's mother, had ever made that album of Christmas songs she was always talking about, because she could use gift ideas.

The doorbell rang, admitting former newspaper staff members. Word had got around. Before too long, the living room seemed full of old heads examining the trays in Dad's and Mom's hands. Maybe I didn't comprehend or stop to consider what the end of the *Eagle* might mean to them, but these people did, elderly vendors, retired machinists.

The doorbell kept ringing, bringing in movement types, Unitarian church types, grandmothers who'd got off night shifts that morning, University of Chicago sociology contacts, more people who used to work at the *Eagle*, neighbors, black or white, though some of them, blacks included, wanted to call the square East Ogden again.

Of the many women over the years whom Mom had made phone calls to jails for or loaned money to, few stayed in touch or went back to school. This did not mean that they had not turned their lives around, wherever they were, Mom sometimes said. Dad let her believe what she wanted when it came to her crazies. He didn't argue. Mom moved on to greet an old colleague from the National Welfare Rights Organization. Two former crazies in front of me didn't look as though they were doing that great, but that was no reason for the old secretaries to pretend the crazies had not said hello and that it was a sad day. Shay Holdings, Inc.'s last servants walked out of the kitchen rather than be compromised socially by the formerly homeless.

"Good soldier, where is thy switchblade?" I heard Dad say to a priest from St. Thomas the Apostle up the street. Dad wore a black armband and a red bow tie. Mom had fixed to the back of her head a fractured fascinator of small artificial cream-colored roses.

The television in the living room, the only one in the house, had been going nonstop since Harold Washington's heart failed him. He was a good man, ahead of his time, the television repeated, the professional mourner among us. I heard Shay Holdings, Inc., say that she couldn't hack the cold November rain or the downtown crowds, and that she was glad to pay her respects without having to mess with a service, while the other secretary topped her with her gratitude that she had found all of her recipes in a big Christmas box, when for the longest time she just assumed she'd lost them with her other things that time her basement flooded.

They were hanging out by the hall bookshelf, glancing into the living room where denture-rattling Uncle Ralston sat with a mute Ralston Jr. and a low-moaning Aunt Gloria. Everyone was in the kitchen or the dining room, Mom and Dad, too, so as not to have to navigate that triangle of family weirdness.

I looked at Cello's father, sitting in his fantastic absence of mind. His first breakdown wasn't called that, but the second, in 1964, was impossible to explain away. He became manic over Dizzy Gillespie's campaign for the presidency. They brought him home, almost hog-tied. Cello was twelve. Before she ever had a date, he'd been brought back from Africa, and then he starved himself in an adaptation of Dick Gregory's diet. In those days, he carried around chess pawns that he'd press into our palms. We'd hand his secrets over to Dad.

"Who they?" a former crazy asked of me in the hall outside the living room.

"When the going gets rough, make pancakes," I heard Dad chime somewhere.

•

"Happy trails. Put it there."

"Jed."

He slow-motion punched my Pillsbury Doughboy middle. "Jed."

He didn't tell me his name, but I knew his name because he came to see Mom a lot in the days following the riot.

The white boy backed Dad up in his not letting Mom go to any more demonstrations that summer. Dad said it was bad enough that there were psycho nurse killers loose in the city. As if to make it up to her, the white boy let Mom convert his feelings into an eyewitness account of a white riot by one of the rioters who had repented of his ways and joined the very movement he had attacked. He spoke roughly; she put it down cleaned up. He understood quickly that that was how things were done.

I sat around and watched them, my legs swinging from the chair. He lasted two weeks in the movement. He confessed that his people didn't know about his open letter in the *Eagle*, a colored newspaper, and they didn't want him in parts of town he didn't know after dark, even at his age. He'd not told his people enough about what he pretended was the church group he'd become interested in. I'd somehow won my own copy of that issue of the *Eagle*, though I did not understand what the trouble was about. I couldn't believe he'd been one of the whites throwing cherry bombs at our cars. I couldn't take my eyes off him.

I'd come across the yellowed copy of his letter from the summer of 1966 in the bottom of the last box in my closet. I started to ask Mom what had become of him, but I didn't want to learn that she'd found his name on the Vietnam War Memorial in Washington, D.C., which Dad had refused to visit with her.

•

Dad said, "Crow is my least favorite food. It's even worse when taken with the recommended slices of humble pie." He was telling the story of how Mom believed in Harold Washington from the get-go, while he thought the poor man would just lose and lose.

Mom raced into the living room, as though getting away from someone in the hall. She looked over at Aunt Gloria, who still had her head in her hands, the straps of her black patent leather purse wrapped like reins around her hand. The priest pushed through us and sat beside Aunt Gloria, comforting her. We could pretend that the triangle of family weirdness was a vigil for coalition politics in Chicago.

The television's prayers had let up and we'd come to a political history part of the broadcast. Uncle Ralston tried to raise himself from his chair, his teeth knocking. I didn't know if he thought to welcome us into the living room or if he was going to attack the television. I was sure I saw Ralston Jr. clock exactly where his father was.

"The negrificity of these proceedings." Uncle Ralston found his feet. "I object."

"I know." Ralston Jr. leaned over. "Chubby Checker and Cassius Clay are the same man. Muhammad Ali is somebody else."

Dad put a tray of raw celery and carrots in Uncle Ralston's shaking hands and pushed him back toward the chair. Miniature carrots jumped like Mexican beans in an old-fashioned arcade game. I couldn't believe that that was Dad. Ralston Jr. swerved away with a grin when his father landed back in the chair with a fart.

"Excuse me," Dad said and stuck a carrot between Uncle Ralston's porcelain incisors.

Uncle Ralston would never retire or sell up or invest in anything new. His black suits got shiny with age. When people came to Dad with a plan they wanted him to run by Uncle Ralston, Dad had a way of getting them mired in the muck, remembering how magnificent Texas Instruments had been and how much he admired the company for getting out of oil and in with the government over the whole semiconductor thing. He knew there was no point telling Uncle Ralston anything radical, he who let a chance to get in on the Seaway National Bank go by.

Uncle Ralston did not want women at business meetings, though middle-aged and older black women comprised most of his company at its death. The *Eagle* had shrunk, and women ran Uncle Ralston's subsidiary Bible and religious printing businesses. Dad said that the properties owned by Shay Holdings, Inc., including black nursing homes, a medical supply company, and soul food restaurants southeast of the defunct stockyards, didn't exactly lose money, but they didn't make enough to keep the newspaper going. It was over. Uncle Ralston was holding the baby carrot like a candle and blinking up at Dad.

"One day we will all get away to that better place." Mrs. Williams was in the hall, much to my surprise. She entered the living room followed by a thickset man with processed hair. I looked around for Mom.

The thickset man was already working the room, saying, "What's happening, brother man," handing out his attorney business card, and telling the women that women were the healers in the black community at times like these, the conjure doctors, the root workers. It was impossible to squeeze his hand, to get the advantage over him in a handshake. I could tell he liked to be the one to let the other guy go. He wore gold rings on both hands, a gold watch on one thick wrist, a gold ID bracelet on the other. His clothes weren't cheap, but they were inner-city threads, brands popular among blacks, like Cole Haan shoes. They were appropriately gray. His hair smelled like James Brown's music.

The attorney settled on an arm of Uncle Ralston's chair, took the vegetables from him, and handed the tray to one of the elderly secretaries, who, like me, was inspecting the only plausible man in the room.

Mrs. Williams came over to me, beaming. "I see you, your nose all up in the air, you sissy," she whispered. She was smiling away, lightly touching my sleeve. "God's judgment is upon my grandson as it will land upon you one day, for we are made Hebrew Israelites, not punks."

"Fifty-fifty box," Uncle Ralston began, pointing at Aunt Gloria.

"No, no, no, no," we heard as Aunt Gloria accelerated in heels across Mom's tricky parquet and raised her purse against Uncle Ralston. She didn't get to him. The attorney intercepted her easily and scooped her with evident pleasure against his double-breasted wool. "Hold," he called, as if his voice came from his massive thighs. The priest waited for Aunt Gloria to release the purse into his hands. Mrs. Williams tried to take over Aunt Gloria, but the attorney was not letting go.

"My understanding is that he was alone," someone said in the crowd that didn't know whether to keep looking or to act like nothing untoward was happening. "Anything could have gone on in the mayor's office, for all we know."

"I'm hip. One side door, one injection."

The television coverage moved into interviews with stricken associates of the departed mayor. Bottles and flasks and plastic cups that did not belong to the house came out of raincoats and handbags as people who loved Mom and Dad but knew they didn't know how to party got louder. Uncle Ralston craned around, looking for Aunt Gloria perhaps. She was with the attorney in an arrangement of chairs, and Dad had moved Ralston Jr. out of harm's way by a window. He, too, wore a black suit. Mrs. Williams darted off to get in on some Johnnie Walker.

In a flash, it had become impossible to remain sober in Chicago. I felt the need for an AA sponsor and was humbled that I couldn't recall the name of the guy who'd volunteered to act as mine when I got out of rehab thirty months before.

.

After I had dropped out of the University of Illinois, Cello told me that my real problem was that I did not believe myself to be good enough. Her advice was that I set my sights lower, in all things, like checking the National Achievement box, a separate category for Negroes on the National Merit exam that was judged by a lower standard and was therefore an attainable prize for black students like me, who were psychologically disadvantaged. Cello had not got over her Bicentennial Concert Disaster of the year before and she never would.

I just looked at the telephone receiver, believing, as I did then, in the poetry of my impending nervous breakdown.

To go nuts had been my plan for what to do once I had dropped out of school. But when I wasn't hearing the voices that flocked into Ralston Jr.'s head during his breakdowns, and forgetting to eat or getting lost on the El or acting out in abandoned downtown blocks by the new library didn't bring to my synapses the traffic of psychosis, I couldn't think what to do other than to drink even more.

I was soon going to run out of money and in that state I stayed with successive unsuspecting someones. I was usually asked to seek shelter elsewhere once it had become clear to my helper in my crisis that I would continue to drink up everything alcoholic that came into the house. I knew I was putting off having to go home to face my parents, the son and daughter of graduates of black colleges in the traditional anti-black South.

"Remember, they have to take us now, but they don't have to keep us," Mom said hopefully when she and Dad left me at the brick-everywhere university in Champaign, Illinois, three years before.

My first year I spent my extra money on drinking; my second year I spent my tuition on drinking and the university notified Dad that I'd failed to register. He flew down the same day and made it to the bursar's office. He took me out to dinner and I got drunk. He stayed in a motel and said the next morning that it was okay that I could not get over to say goodbye. I didn't have a car.

He never scolded me for what I'd wasted. My dad said that one of the worst feelings in the world was that of not knowing what was one's calling, one's path. He said he knew people laughed, but he never doubted that accountancy had been right for him. He hoped I'd find mine soon. Until I did, not knowing what to do with one's life was worse than not having a woman or a family to love.

I was surprised by his coherence and moved by his leniency, so much so that I continued to drink in town and to fall behind in my classes. I filled out the withdrawal documents in a fog of being tired and broke, unable to make up the work for the term, unable to do my laundry because I didn't have quarters, didn't have the energy to carry that enormous bag to the basement, and I didn't care. My tab had been cut off at the bar downtown where I drank underage.

The disgust my parents felt at my coming home a dropout was too much for me to handle. When the nervous break-down didn't come and the locked liquor cabinet turned out to be unlocked and empty of everything except flat tonic, I called an old flame and met her at a black bar where an overweight white girl might expect some action. We got completely drunk. She paid. I could hear her laughter as her taxi lurched out of the parking lot.

I got in the car borrowed from my brother, his army-green Mercury Coupe, his beloved Tank. I thought of how my father had taught me one day at the *Eagle* to tip my cap to the ladies. I was such a hit. The memory brought me to tears. I started up my brother's Tank, roared out of the parking lot, and within three minutes had careened off a post and flipped the car over beside a disused brown railroad track, the giant warehouse into which it had once run long gone.

I remember saying to myself in a British accent, "I'm all right." The car was on its left side. I could see that the win-dows were either broken by the impact or scratched by the gravel the car had slid across. I was in my seat belt. The radio was going. "Aha," I said, still in Bunbury's voice, and pressed the window button. The left one cracked horribly and I pulled myself up quickly, away from bouncing glass pieces. But the window on the right had gone down. I unbuckled and reached up. I hoisted myself up and fell over the side, jumping back from contact with the hot underbelly of the vehicle. I got to my feet. No one was around.

I went three blocks before I saw a convenience store. I said in a heavy Bunbury-British accent to the black man behind the Plexiglas shield, "I say, I've had an accident." Incredibly, I had no injuries.

I never saw the tow truck. I was gone from the scene before

it arrived. The police dropped me at the hospital, perplexed by my bright British accent. Dad and Solomon picked me up. Mom waited at home with something new in her eyes. The crazies staying with us had sat up with her. Dad fixed things with a judge. The car had been hit while parked in the lot of the Sweet End Tavern, the insurance story said. I missed most of the aftermath. I slept through it. I slept for two days. Mom was worried that I might have a concussion. When at last I woke, they were standing over me. Solomon asked if I was all right.

I cried, which spoiled things. They went away, except for Mom. But here my brother had been looking as though someone had shot the dog we'd never had and the first thing out of his mouth was to ask if I was okay. When Cello went into how much he disliked me, I remembered that about him and held on to it, as they say.

After that, I pulled myself together for a while, so much so that Solomon asked me to cease my hysterically punctual payments. The debt kept us more in touch than he wanted to be. Dad stopped talking to me pretty much and Mom nattered in order to cover up her disappointment.

.

"The fun never sets," Dad said as he passed by. He had never been the sort of black guy who could get people laughing by remembering neck bones and rice in the Second Ward. "There is life after Sears, Roebuck." He was acting as though he were glad-handing his way around a crowded room, but what he was doing was revolving from the kitchen through the dining room to the living room and back, clapping the same dozen people on the back and saying anything that seemed jolly, spirit-keeping.

The need to smoke had reduced the number of mourners. The house had quieted down considerably. Aunt Gloria had been in the bathroom for some time. Ralston Jr.'s pockets were full of baby carrots. I was sure that he was counting between carrots, timing each one. The television was on still, but nobody paid attention, loud as it was. Mom was in earnest conversation with the priest. We didn't notice that Solomon had let himself in.

"You arranged for the pilot, I presume," Ralston Jr. said.

Uncle Ralston was up, tottering toward Solomon, as out of it as his damaged son. "Take me to North Carolina this instant." The old dictator making demands before he'd accept exile.

But my brother had Mom hanging on to his shoulders and Dad fastened to his ribs. I was in a sports bar with Solomon when Harold Washington was first elected.

"Never gave the time of day." Mrs. Williams must have been eighty, at least, someone who could remember big floods down South and weevils in the cotton and the day the Armistice was signed. Yet she was a display totem of mascara and lipstick and red nail polish and jangling bangles, her grandson's, the late Clark's, perhaps, as she stumbled from chair to chair in Uncle Ralston's direction. For some reason, I thought of Manfred's car.

"Solomon, you've been drinking," Mom said.

"Oh, you think you can smack me?" Mrs. Williams and Uncle Ralston rocked back and forth at each other, unsteady, furious, moist-mouthed, and unable to strike.

"I had brunch with my fiancée and her parents downtown. Francesca's parents had their car drop me off." Solomon had to disengage himself from Dad's look at Mom—and hers right back at him.

Mom was happier than anyone when after four years Solomon broke up with that Vietnamese chick and her Pentecostal family in San Francisco. Maybe he was still a registered Republican, but at least he didn't accept Christ as his personal savior anymore. He didn't share his dating life with me, but obviously this was the first Mom and Dad had heard of someone named Francesca.

Because Solomon was away on athletic camp scholarships every summer, he never put in his time at the newspaper. Yet Uncle Ralston would run stories about Solomon's class in Fortran for gifted high school students at the Illinois Institute of Technology, his picture bigger than any he ever printed of his granddaughter Cello. Uncle Ralston would make a toast at office lunches, the rambling contents of which could touch on the idea that one day all-star Solomon would take up the chair as editor, but clearly just as a way of introducing himself to the city before he embarked on a political career.

It wasn't just Uncle Ralston and Mom's gun-happy mother who were in love with Solomon. He was everybody's shining black prince. Cello's brother, Ronald, was almost tragic in his worship. Cello certainly approved of him as a relation. He had always been welcome in her biography. But now that I felt like a stronger candidate for her index, I was determined to be different with my brother. I was going to pour down the drain behavior brewed in envy and low self-esteem.

Solomon and I never had the talk, the scene where the older brother says that he always sort of figured his pain-in-the-ass little brother was, well, that way, because of those lame comics and how scared he was of water or balls of any kind aimed at him. But the talk with Mom and Dad had gone so badly, to my lasting astonishment, I decided not to have any more talks with anyone for a while. "I heard," Solomon said at the time, and nothing else.

Mrs. Williams was trying to keep her balance as she traced the air in front of her like someone wielding a razor. "You such a big fool, you do not believe we landed on the moon."

Dad himself had pulled Uncle Ralston's editorial denouncing as a hoax the Apollo 11 landing in the Sea of Tranquility. But Uncle Ralston forced him to print the thing the next week.

Dad often said that that was the turning point, the summer of 1969. Anyone any good on the *Eagle* began to leave after that.

The priest turned off the television and announced that he was going to find some music. I was excited that Solomon drew me to him, out of Mrs. Williams's path.

"Francesca is perfect. We both grew up in the Windy City and had to meet in the City by the Bay."

He squeezed my right bicep and I heard myself giggle and felt my teeth show. I saw Mom and Dad put their arms around each other at the sight of their eldest showing affection for his little brother. They acted as if he were ten years older than me. Behind them, I could see the attorney and Aunt Gloria in the same pose, but their eyes were closed. Their heads touched. Uncle Ralston and Mrs. Williams paddle-wheeled at each other. They both missed. They went past each other, as in a jousting competition.

Mrs. Williams was the lucky one, falling facedown into an easy chair, while on the other side of the room people sprang out of the way and several chairs went down sideways with Uncle Ralston like bowling pins.

"Hammer time!" Ralston Jr. screamed from the windowsill. "It's hammer time!"

I felt Solomon's arm around my neck and thought I heard applause. "You okay? You're being careful? Good. Listen up, you have to help us out here, Jeddo. The truth is, Francesca and I are married already. How do I tell Mom we pulled a no-wedding on everybody. Francesca's father and mother weren't there either. The last four hours have been real Sidney Poitier, blood. You don't still do that Katharine Hepburn routine you used to do? I hope not."

•

The summer of Cello's Bicentennial Disaster, I saw Aunt Gloria get into Uncle Ralston's Cadillac behind the *Eagle*. She had on a very big wig and I saw a box of Kleenex go onto the dashboard. Out of nowhere Uncle Ralston gave her the back of his hand. When he had both hands back on the wheel, she was still leaning back against the seat, her hand over her mouth and nose. I could see the sequins of her nightclub-act dress. She reached for the Kleenex and Uncle Ralston backed up his car.

I went upstairs to tell Dad and on the way to his office I told three or four people what I had seen. They knew to run.

"Loose lips are torpedoes in your own waters." Dad told me never to make Uncle Ralston's business my business. I pointed out to him that he had. He said the trick was to let people think you had. He gave me the manly task of changing the bottle in the watercooler.

•

The year Cello got married on Lake Constance, I was mugged on my circuitous way back from class, in Greektown, of all places. My bag was taken, and with it my paper on eighteenth-century monument sculpture by Rysbrack. It was not "my" paper. I'd bought it for an outrageous sum. A few weeks later I dropped out of college for the second time. Drunk, I again called Cello long-distance in Berlin. She said that she wished she knew what to tell me. She said she was going to call Mom and hung up. She didn't call Mom.

"Mooch," Solomon said when I had to come home again.

"Minnie the Moocher, to you," I answered.

"And a Big Zero."

"Hot time hoochie-coochie, to you."

"You are nothing."

I began to sing "The Wreck of the Jedediah Goodfinch."

I was on the floor, gasping, holding my stomach. My brother had rammed a fist into my gut and the fall had knocked the wind out of me. He taught me that to complete a victory an army will march through the night without rations.

Successful people, people good at life, can look ahead; they've been looking ahead all their lives, even at summer camp. They knew the next school year was coming and their bodies were getting ready for it, while yours was just goofing off and drinking sugar. People say live in the moment, but the moment was the only thing I was good at. I could make the moment last, stretch it out for days, years, my whole life.

•

"Married and moving house from one coast to the other. This is certainly something to toss around in the salad bowl of the mind," Dad said in the kitchen. Mom sat. I looked at Solomon's feet. The paramedics were gone. Mom began to cry.

•

Cello was sixteen when she moved in pretty much for good. Her siblings were ten and nine; my brother was thirteen. School was nuts; the country was on the brink. Mom's Hyde Park white people were terrified, but they didn't want to say so in front of her. I was about to be eleven and West Chicago was on TV and in flames. People were afraid to go anywhere. The mayor had given the cops shoot-to-kill orders.

Martin Luther King had been murdered, but it was open season on us, Dad said. Nobody was hiding anything from anybody. We watched television with the lights on in every room of the house. One of Mom's crazies, an alcoholic seamstress, sat with us, crying. When Solomon opened our door to check out the square, Dad yanked him back inside.

It was mine, the fear that night, the kind of being afraid you get when your protectors are themselves frightened. The policemen weren't lining up to protect marchers. They were killing black people left and right, we heard. These weren't marchers. Dad was on the phone to the caretakers at the *Eagle* building, trying to find out what was happening over there. People called with reports of gunfire.

King's assassination was the first big thing I remembered. Odell's crew at the ChiChi talked about JFK's assassination as the first or only time that they saw their fathers cry. But the night of King's murder was the first and only time I saw Dad tempted to what I believe was racial violence. The caretakers from the *Eagle* stopped by. Mom and Dad argued. The guys outside honked. He wasn't risking his person for principle; he was protecting family property. My father went out, into the looting and the Molotov cocktails and rumors of snipers.

A carload of black men in a big, late-model Buick, they got stopped, but not by the cops. By gang leaders, who said they had the situation in their territory under control. I listened from the stairs. Cello, Solomon, Mom's crazy, and a priest who had dared to creep over sat up with Mom. Supposedly he was trapped with us because of the curfew. It was the first big thing I understood and didn't want to: my Dad had been sent home.

The pictures of smoking rubble the next day were bewildering. I couldn't believe that I had to go to school. We were not allowed to go anywhere else. The newspaper's caretakers came all the way over to drive us the three blocks. They never told Cello and her brother and sister that their father made his wife, his parents, their janitor, and Mrs. Williams hide with him in their basement. Ralston Jr.'s obsession with air-raid shelters began that night. His own mother asked him to move out.

I cried when King was killed, because Mom, Cello, Rhonda, and that priest cried so much. The seamstress staying with us also bawled, turning her thirty-day AA coin over in her hands. I was scared out of my head, but it was also an intense experience to let go, to insinuate myself into their grief, to release into the air my sadness as a musty kid teased at school. I sensed that day that my misery was closer to the alcoholic seamstress's than it was to Mom's.

A few years later two commuter trains on the Illinois Central collided outside a station downtown and I understood for the first time the flinty shock of death. A family friend who made what he called antique furniture was among those killed. I didn't cry, I was so amazed by the discovery. Dad thought I had grown up. I wasn't paying attention at the funeral. The open casket didn't faze me. I was fixed on the realization that life was serious; it offered no do-overs. You don't get up from play and head home wondering what happened to the fireflies of childhood.

•

The *Eagle* hadn't had any fifty-year anniversary celebrations and its closure three years later was a story only in the black press, down at the bottom of the fifth or sixth page in other black newspapers around the country. EAGLE GROUNDED, one generous former competitor announced.

Uncle Ralston was being kept overnight for observation. Shay Holdings took a limping Mrs. Williams away in disgrace. Dad was driving Ralston Jr. and Aunt Gloria back to the house on South Parkway. One of the caretakers lived with them, but something else would have to be done with the inmates after the house, the rented-out condo in North Carolina, and the closed-up lake cabin in Wisconsin were sold.

Solomon was with Dad, who was taking him back to his hotel. That he and Francesca were staying in a hotel prompted Mom to pull the plug on her day and go down to the basement. She understood that they weren't staying with Francesca's parents on North Lake Shore Drive either, but she preferred to talk about it in the morning. She looked forward to meeting her daughter-in-law in the morning. If she met Francesca's parents in the morning, then that would be fine, too. For her to leave before the last of her guests said something. Solomon looked troubled as Mom gathered up a volume of her Bach Preludes and Fugues that had fallen under a chair.

After a while, I had on one of Dad's precious Dinah Washington albums. I was probably going to have an interview for a job as a consultant on a local public television program about Scott Joplin at the Chicago Fair. The producer had worked part-time as a starving teenager at the *Eagle*. Dad got him off the streets. He gave me his card.

"Want to dance?" I asked the attorney. He was sexy enough for me to risk Dad's sniffing the air when he got back. Now that Mom was downstairs, we were smoking the attorney's herb in the living room. He didn't take away the flame he held for me. I blew smoke and thanked him. This was just the kind of situation I would have got myself into in my drinking days.

"No, my man, but knock yourself out. Do your thing, you know." He loose-walked with the joint to the kitchen, where the women were maybe not young, but they were real.

I tried to flirt with the middle-aged priest. He turned off the record player. This was exactly the sort of thing I would have woken up ashamed over in my drinking days.

·

"You look like a panda, Alfred," I once heard Uncle Ralston say to Dad when Mom was coming back from canvassing outside the steelyards. "Like a lovesick panda booted out of China."

·

A reason for me to take drugs was not to dream, or not to remember my dreams. Stoned, I slept, the livid theater of the unconscious blacked out. Sober, I dreamed of getting stoned. In the dream, I say "Happy trails" to Zippi early in the morning and board the plane to Amsterdam with paper sacks for hand luggage, stoned and seeing spots. De Quincey said that a man who dreams of oxen will dream of oxen even when on opium.

·

If Dad noticed anything funny smelling when he got back, it wasn't as important as getting to their basement hideaway to check on Mom. He left it to me to take care of the people sitting around the dining room and kitchen tables, debating in which direction our black political future lay.

I stared at Manfred's old telephone number written in that portfolio of photographs from the Chicago Fair. One night in his Schöneberg pub he'd also given me the number of his sister in Bremen. I managed to keep control of myself at what would have been five in the morning for her, though the attorney was the last to leave. The woman he helped into her coat had plush honkers pressed against her sweater and her skirt rode a hippo-huge behind. He stomped around the walls of Jericho, letting the city of her black tights know just what was what.

Hotel Berlin was on late, a Hollywood melodrama made at the close of World War II about the end of the war on the Nazi side of things. Generals, refugees, resistance fighters, whores, and spies run around the hotel corridors and suites, scheming and lying. "Haven't you told him he must commit suicide?"

SEVEN

Some days only the admiration of the whole world will do, but the world just isn't giving it. She said that they didn't make propaganda; they made entertainment. She said some of us may not have heard of Conrad Veidt, but he was the most famous Nazi actor and he'd been a leftist Jewish sympathizer before that. She said that even though the Party knew that most of her circle had been arrested, she kept her job at Ufa until she was called up. They were sending everybody to the Eastern Front. That was in 1943. She was twenty-eight years old and handsome. She said she never lied about her age and she said what she did about having been a handsome young man, because none of the films she had bit parts in survived.

She said it was important for her to talk to the young. When she was born, her father already had been lost on his Western Front. She was a wraith, but still young and handsome when her war ended. She put on her first pair of nylons for a Soviet officer. He brought her a phonograph. They danced to big-band swing. Then one night she waited, into the morning. She never saw him again or found out what had happened to him. She didn't have a photograph of him. But she had tucked away in a *Schrank* one scratched record that he had loved.

The young thought that she was old when they got their war, which was technically somebody else's war, though America tried to make Vietnam everybody's war, she said. She did not feel old. Perhaps it was her pearls. She was proud of them, the young. They stood up and asked their parents about her war. She said that once you learned something about it, you wanted to know more. She said she would never get to the end of it herself. It just continued. There was no relief from what you could learn once you started. She didn't like the feeling of people trying to put the war behind them. She said some people hadn't forgiven Marlene or Elisabeth for leaving Germany.

She said she was not born an aristocrat, like Marianne Hoppe, the darling of Aryan cinema who used her standing with Hitler to protect Jews and gays and Communists in the theater. But she was happy to live in a land where literature was taken seriously. She said she baptized herself when the new Germany was born. When the old Germany was being thrown out, she picked up a name from the debris, vintage Louis XIV stuff. She tried it on and liked it. And she loved the letters of Charlotte von der Pfalz, the unhappy wife of Monsieur, Louis XIV's auntie brother.

She said that film had lost its importance. Forty years after the war, film was escape and there were no big problems that were completely unheard-of before. Her old gang was dead, dead to the world, in bed, any bed, lost in barbiturate confusion, but when she floated through Wertheim's, giving off a strong scent of violets, she found it an agreeable sensation to be on her own and not needing to shoplift. In West Berlin, she could live by day, in the open, unafraid, in love with the five-mark pieces in her pouch. She said it was a struggle for her to give any one of them up.

·

Cello sped again through the part of Bach's A-Minor English Suite that she remembered Mom loved. Hayden's Tyrolean farm boy said "Oh wow" as her fingers flew back down the keys. Suddenly her demonstration was over. Father Paul, as Hayden called his twenty-year-old gymnast, knew he'd blown the mood for her, made her self-conscious. "No, go on, please." He got up to block her path. "I am sorry," he said in English.

Dark hair tapped his face when she darted past his incredible shoulder. He bent backward and his eyes went wide. "Oh wow," he said. She was so fast, her hair was a force become visible in pursuit of her. She was amazing to look at; something about her held your attention. I had to admit I was proud of her. I was also feeling a little sorry for her, as I'm sure Hayden was, too. She couldn't bear her own talent.

She called out in German that she was just looking in on the children and she'd send the nanny back with the tray. We were having tea with our gay friends, she'd said that morning, also in German. It would be during naptime and before Dram came home to kiss his children.

He wouldn't hear of taking money from me for letting me crash in my old maid's room. I'd joked to Solomon and Francesca about the mice in my painter's storage closet in Kreuzberg, wanting to seem the cool black expatriate to my brother, black corporate lawyer turned trader of futures now wed to the contemporary art curator who looked like a Raphael. But he got up immediately and made a big deal to Mom and Dad that I'd been living in a storage bin. It made me tear up, my butchness fled, until I saw that Dad had looked away.

Mom in turn informed Cello and then put me on the line.

"You should have told us you were a German poet," Cello said in German. Fortunately, the difference in time zones and the needs of her children made the conversation entirely practical.

It was still cold, but I had made it back to the Mercedes-Benz star and the sound of my footsteps in new patent leather boots.

Nobody at the ChiChi had seen Bags for a while, but I

didn't ask Zippi where she got the yellow, rocklike hash we were smoking in the kitchen. I asked her for a job as suddenly as I'd accepted the joint from her. "Which one of these guys do you want me to chop to make space for you?" she said, indicating with the spliff the day bartender finishing his shift and the busboy/microwave operator. I realized that it was the first time she'd spoken to me in German. She was a completely different person, a harder, older woman than the gamine with the adorable bangs who sympathized in English.

I wasn't worried. Berlin rewarded my faith. I turned up at Manfred's pub and found Afer there. Through him I found my new address. It was going to be spring someday, and after the children had been put to bed, Dram and I smoked cigarettes together on the front terrace on the other side of the largest piano. I liked the chill in the air. Cello sat with us, draped in shawls, a cup of hot water and lemon on a little table.

They were impressed that I was doing something they considered utterly Berlin. We were reconciled all around, and we didn't refer to the Russian doctor cleaning lady, who had decided that I wasn't there. She didn't clean the maid's room or its bathroom because they were not in use as far as she was concerned. I got my own towels.

Cello thought it a good omen that I would be moved out by the third anniversary of my having got sober. The tea I waited for with Hayden and Father Paul, frisky as a ram, was my celebration. Hayden was saying that Michelangelo worked for the Borgias, even though they were criminals. The nanny was still in the kitchen. We couldn't hear anything from the back of the vast apartment. Father Paul gave Hayden a quick kiss, then another. I got up, as discreet as Michael York as Brian in *Cabaret*, and went out onto the front terrace to smoke again. Gas came out of the Zippo lighter I'd stolen from Manfred and I told myself that I felt high.

The day was colorless, the street depressed under uninterrupted cloud. I could hear plates being stacked in the schnitzel restaurant across the street. A heavy front door closed somewhere to my right. In the other direction, the Kurfürstendamm was rehearsing, "You are on your own. Burt Lancaster doesn't live here anymore."

███

The legend in the downtown dive where I spent most of my drinking time in Chicago was that it occupied the site of what had been one of the last whorehouses in town where a black man could buy a white woman.

I didn't believe it, or that there had been such an area as Little Cheyenne. The madam had a parallel business in venereal disease treatment, giving mercury oil applications and sarsaparilla baths, I was told. A lot of deaths in the neighborhood went unrecorded the summer Scott Joplin played at the Chicago World's Fair. This information came to me from a short-order cook I met at the new library. Fat, eloquent, and dark, an Irish American drunk, he and I went on costly binges together in his flophouse. I still don't know how I got away from him.

███

Potsdamerplatz was a sandy nowhere, blond and chalky in the sunrise of the north. We were riding the side of the earth that was getting higher, hanging out over bowls of coffee at a long wooden table, like farmers. The commune I'd been accepted into on Afer's recommendation was several hundred meters from the Wall, but you could see it and one of the guard towers when you looked east from the old wagon doors. Near to it, a sort of phantom Wall, an unfinished elevated electric train track, ran for some time and then stopped abruptly, as if it had suddenly realized its pointlessness. We sat down when birds I couldn't name and forgot every day to ask about flew over the Wall in the morning and again in the evening as they went back to the East.

The building, a former factory, stood on Theodor Loh-mann Ecke. Empty lots bordered it on three sides, but a blank wall, made up of the sides of prewar working-class apartment houses, abutted the empty lots. Ahead of us, by itself, out there in front, like the bull of the herd, getting ready to face the Wall, was a blackened building with a short tower. It had been a brewery before the war. It was the last building on Potsdamer-platz. Everything else around it had been bombed, the ranges of brick and dust carted away by the famous rubble women, the women of Berlin who after the war cleaned up the wreck-age of their own infatuation with uniforms.

At my interview, the twenty-one members of Co-operative One-Fifteen-Nineteen, or the January Initiative, as founding committee people also sometimes referred to it, weren't con-cerned about my politics or lack of a coherent philosophy as I alternated between tense verbal blocks in English and borrowed German disquisitional phrases. To them—the seventeen white members of the Co-op, that is—the color of my skin was my radical politics. The four black and brown members questioned me closely in English. Afer in particular seemed angry that I was ignorant of the lies that the Voice of South Africa and the British prime minister were spreading about his country.

I may not have had much Marxist theory or an opinion about the wisdom of the Spartacist uprising of 1919, but the whole house got that, like most American queers in West Berlin, I was in love with Weimar culture. I'd given Dram's name as a refer-ence, but they stressed that they hadn't asked for any references, that that was not how the decision process worked with them. It wasn't clear to me why Afer was taking so much trouble to help me. I didn't want to be his political project. But we had been in a street battle together and that meant something where he came from.

In my ignorance I thought at first that the existence of the *Spartacus International Gay Guide* was why the Co-op 1-15-19, Co-op J.I., avoided calling itself Spartakusbund or anything like it when the original ten people squatted in the large derelict building in 1980. But then I learned that the name Spartacus was more than taken. Every Trotskyite group used it.

I had the morning shift in the Café Rosa. To avoid a house meeting discussion about the white apron with wraparound strings that I'd bought myself in spite of its connotations of bourgeois service, I stopped wearing it. The commune also ran a bookstore, and a performance space, ZFB, initials for what translated loosely into the Time of Fossil Fuel. Jobs in these departments, so to speak, came only with seniority.

Lotte von der Pfalz, as he, she, called herself, was always standing at the door when I opened up. She liked to be the first customer, the first to get the fresh coffee. She was quiet for the first half hour, too. Then she talked all morning, patting her thin pageboy lightly when she thought she'd said something especially good. She said that *Leda and the Swan* had been Hitler's favorite painting, so it, like Wagner, should be forbidden. After all, Mendelssohn had been banned during the war. She carried petitions, wads of pages of what she wanted suppressed in peacetime. Pretzels, the Eurovision Song Contest, henna rinses, miniature dog breeds, Gottfried Benn.

I tried to call her Madame at first, but she really didn't like that.

"I am Lotte, simple, Jed, my old friend."

I was suspicious of white people who boasted that they treated everyone the same, that they did not see color. Then, too, she was proud of her mezzo purr. She would not retouch her lips in public and wore androgynous black orthopedic nun pensioner shoes. Unfortunately, the violet cloud around the print dress that she came in with turned brown after a while or wore off. She told me that the University of Chicago library got its start as a collection imported from a book dealer in

Berlin, thousands and thousands of books at one time. I said that that was the American way and thought of the books I was having sent from Chicago, to be reunited soon with the boxes from Cello's cellar.

■

Solomon's dark-eyed bride said she couldn't figure out why Frederick Douglass's first wife never learned to read or to write. She was on the plantation he'd escaped from and he got her out, so he must have cared for her, she said. But he married his second wife, his white secretary who was twenty years younger than he, only months after his first wife's death. Didn't he try to bring this new wife to the Chicago World's Fair, only to be prevented by the black Haitian government that didn't want its official black representative photographed with his white wife? Francesca remembered her American Studies classes. She wasn't pregnant. She and Solomon got hitched on impulse.

Solomon didn't dare go over to his wife. He moved closer to Dad by the sink and they were both just not going to notice what was happening, if anything. I was in the refrigerator door, though we were headed out soon for lunch at Francesca's parents' club.

Mom said that Anna Murray Douglass's parents were slaves, but she'd been born free and that she met Douglass when they were both working around the Baltimore docks. She knew him when he was still calling himself Bailey. She followed him to Philadelphia on her own. They were married for more than forty years and had five children. True, she stayed in the kitchen when company came. Two years after she died, he married his devoted secretary. Her family, abolitionist friends of Douglass's, stopped speaking to her. His children resented her.

Mom said most men don't know how to live on their own,

especially not busy ones, never mind a great man in public life, a great black man in the nineteenth century. Douglass was a staunch advocate of women's suffrage, Mom said. Francesca said she knew that. Mom said that Douglass hadn't done anything wrong. He just fell in love again after his wife died. That's not doing anything wrong. Francesca burst into tears. Mom didn't mammy-comfort white girls, not even her daughter-in-law. She just kept telling her from her side of the table that it was all right, she was going to be fine, it was all right.

The European football championships would be on in a week and Odell got the big television nobody knew he'd been longing for. Zippi called me a kibbutznik and asked too casually how often Bags came to see Afer. I'd not seen Bags. Zippi looked up from soapy glass water and smoothed her bangs. Her wet hand shook. I didn't look away. But we were different with each other in German. Something else was going on. I'd not sent a postcard this time. I lied and said I was not smoking stuff.

I had been going to the AA meetings in Dahlem again. I nodded to the steadfast black noncoms; one of them even dapped my fist with his fist once. I wasn't drinking. I felt nothing going past glasses of white wine on restaurant terrace tables. But every Saturday when I got back to the Co-op, I joined Afer's faction in the Café Rosa's kitchen for long discussions—the Co-op's relation to the Autonomen movement, why capitalism needs racism, how to be more Green—over soft, pliable, very black hash.

There seemed to be some agreement among the members who had survived the bloodletting of a couple of years before that they would not talk about the purge that led to the arrival

of several newcomers. I picked up from Afer that the younger
Bio-Anarcho element finally outnumbered the Red Army Faction sympathizers and their tired, bony dogs. On certain days
the floorboards on certain scrubbed floors still gave off a faint
odor of pet urine.

The bookstore concentrated on ecology and antinuclear
literature, with a small Africa, South America, and Caribbean
section that reflected an early victory in committee of the
women who opposed female circumcision in Africa over those
who said Westerners ought to leave native beliefs and practices
alone. They just expanded their shelves from there, along the
lines of problems in what was then called the developing world.
Long-term Co-op members said openly, to our faces, that they'd
asked Yao and Afer to recruit among their circles in Berlin those
most likely to be bio-sympathetic, though they were far too
with-it to call us black men. To bring in soul brothers was a
way of beefing up the male presence without antagonizing the
considerable feminist faction in the house.

Cats led mammal life in the dark courtyard and weedy lots
beyond the kitchen doors. The Co-op had been negotiating
with the absent owners of one lot. They wanted a vegetable
garden. They had worked out a deal with a pensioner for his
Schrebergärten way on the other side of town, on the way to
Tegel. Named for the man who preached the therapeutic value
of every man working his allotment of land, *Schrebergärtens*
flourished around the city.

Every Co-op member not on permanent garden duty had to
work in the garden on alternate weekends. The Co-op's arrangement with the pensioner had been guaranteed by recent federal
legislation. When the garden came up in house meetings, I
realized that a fissure existed between those members who were
relieved to be legal about some things and those who rejected
permission from the state for anything the Co-op did.

I hated working in the potato patch and I hated that

the hundred square meters the Co-op leased were so near Lessingsdorf—now into its second summer as a must-see for hip visitors to the unreal city about which the hardest thing was getting there. I found it vaguely humiliating to farm in the city. I was told that the Lustgarten over in East Berlin in front of the Old Museum had first been a potato field for a vegetable then brand new to the city. And so what, I said to myself in the June sun. That was three hundred sad years ago. I stopped bitching in my head when a couple of guys took off their T-shirts, but I thought for sure I would leave this commune by winter. I couldn't face duty in the café coal bin.

The Co-op was not a dorm, nor was it Fräulein Schroeder's rooming house. I learned that right away. It was not cool to drop in on anybody. You didn't walk up to a door and knock. You were invited up to someone's room or rooms. Until then, you met the other members in the kitchen meetings or in the corridors, on the stairs or in the bookshop at more meetings, and, most sociably, in the Café Rosa. I became the dishwasher for the afternoon shift and, apronless, drenched, I was usually so tired by dinnertime that I fell asleep after cleaning up the kitchen on my floor.

I lived at the top of the house, the fifth floor, with the lowest ceilings, as did a light-skinned Afro-German guy and a dark-skinned Bangladeshi guy. Two very young white couples who had been members for little more than a year each had a room. A room with a small stove and sink had been rigged up at the other end. Afer and his girlfriend had their own kitchen and the biggest apartment on the floor.

I had a shower, but my toilet was in the hall. I cleaned it before I used it and then again right after I used it. My windows faced the rear, the solid plaster back and sides of the apartment houses around us. I couldn't name the trees or the wildflowers growing in the lots. I got my own cube of refrigerator from a store off Potsdamerstrasse and carried it to my room on my back. But the thing the American in me could not get over was that I had a coal stove for heat. No radiators. Winter was a long ways off; who knew where I'd be.

Of course the women I thought were lesbian were not. I understood soon enough that I was the only queer in the Co-op.

■

The week before Cello's graduation from the conservatory, her father bought an old safe for all the cash he had on him, and a lot he didn't, from white mobsters in the Shore Drive Motel, because he had become convinced that Scott Joplin's lost ragtime opera was inside it and he was loudly desperate to present the score to his daughter. I never talked to Cello about her parents. Somehow you just couldn't do that to her, no matter what. "She may be a monster, Jeddie, but remember she's our monster," Mom explained to me early on.

■

It was my party. Cello's sister, Rhonda, was in town, doing a quick tour of northern European cities as part of her present to herself for having got her doctorate, plus a postdoc position. Cello held herself away from the peeling walls as she made her way upstairs to inspect my room. She wouldn't touch the walls on the way down either. Her hair appeared to coax her, to push her along. Around her sister, Rhonda wore her hair tightly braided or rolled up completely.

They'd heard of the architect's collective in the brewery, so elegant in front of us in the darkening dust. For some reason, Cello had assumed that that was the community I was joining. "I see, you're a hippie now, in your continuing late adolescence." She asked if this situation was the healthiest for me. "I can smell patchouli and something else."

I laid out a big table on the sidewalk in front of the café. It was important to keep the cousins away from the people I did hash with, but rather than not have my brothers on the fifth floor join us I begged them not to let on to my family that I smoked stuff. They did not need to be told. There were lots of things we were all getting away from, no matter where we started out, Lucky said, glad to talk English with Germans for a change.

He'd walked to Europe, almost. His family dug up the gold they had buried and sent him off. He, the eldest, was their big chance. He'd come thousands of miles, by trains to Pakistan and a flight to Turkey. It took him two years to get into Greece. An Egyptian arranged to smuggle him across the Hungarian border. Lucky had no papers. He washed dishes in a restaurant in Charlottenburg, for questionable Russians. He sent home as much money as he could to the saline-drenched farm back in Bangladesh.

Dram was not some liberal who couldn't face things. He put his hand on Lucky's shoulder and in the silence went back to his *bouletten*, or meatballs, a Berlin thing. Cello sat back in her chair when he ordered them. The café also offered a flavorless tofu dish. The rest of us were having meatballs, and the men and Rhonda were drinking tall white beers. I saw Manfred's fingers around a shaft. But in his absence, the passion could not be fed; it was dying of inanition. Hayden and Father Paul fell in with the party and they ordered tall white beers when they finally showed up, both in tight jeans.

The Co-op made Dram nostalgic for his student days—the bicycles in the entrance hall, the bookstore still open, the half-assed murals on the stairs. He relished his trip back in time, talking to Afer about the ANC's future. It was Mandela's seventieth birthday. A bomb went off somewhere in South Africa every day; grenades and land mines killed white policemen or black guerrillas every week. Afer was in a state, the anger of not being home and not trusting the Communist Party there making him extreme in some of his predictions. I was pretty sure Afer's girlfriend used to be Bags's piece on the side who got pregnant—his slide, as the jazz musicians called their mistresses.

Co-op members raised their glasses to us from the bar inside and from another table out front. We watched a Frisbee game on the second floor of the old brewery. It was like one of those old-fashioned stage sets of *La Bohème* that showed house life floor by floor. They had a good time over there, those architects. In the chilled-out Potsdamerplatz milieu, I did not consider it racializing to wait tables or to wash dishes at the Café Rosa.

No one helped me clear the plates. It was my party. "Remember, I come from a long line of house slaves," Cello swore their grandmother had said to her on her deathbed. "I pass this knowledge of me on to you."

I seemed to remember that Cello's grandmother couldn't talk at the end. I'd wanted to ask Bags why his girlfriend didn't just have an abortion, but I never did.

We were the younger generation, but we behaved as a faction within the house. We may have been the children's table, keeping company with some terrified kids who'd come with their confused mothers or grandmothers for the night, but we appealed to Mom as a chairman. To lobby her in the morning worked best. You could get things out of Mom if you waited for her in the hall when she was shuffling papers, on her way to remind someone when was her appointment down at Medicaid and she'd better leave now and she had to take that nasty bag with her.

Dad was refuge. We could not go down to his den, but when he surfaced we could sit with him and his newspapers in the kitchen. The strict rule was silence. We were never with him for very long. We stopped looking for him when we got older. Mom didn't like Solomon listening to rock on his earphones when Cello practiced, but Dad told her she had to let the point go; their son wasn't a little boy anymore.

■

"I can't believe I'm having strudel down the street from the Berlin Wall," Rhonda laughed. "This is wild," she continued, dipping her spoon into a muff of cream.

The woman who baked was one of the original squatters. Afer said that she could be a problem. I already got in house meetings that she was assertive at the wrong moments, obstructionist because of some principle of anarcho-purist living that meant continued discomfort for the house as a whole. But she baked so divinely that Cello was impatient for the water to boil and Dram picked up a random spoon and scooped from his sister-in-law's plate.

Yao shot him a look. I could tell he was attracted to Rhonda. It excited him that she, so lovely, had a doctorate. He had spent some time studying in the U.K. He claimed to be at work in absentia on his dissertation, about how excessive acid-tripping among workers adversely affected the Japanese shipbuilding industry in the 1970s and British automobile manufacturing in the same period. He hadn't been back to Ghana in years. I doubted he'd left West Berlin in ages either. He was a quiet man, stateless, older than he looked. He said probably more sharply than he meant to that the border guards still shot and killed people trying to escape from East Berlin.

My new part of town was not easy to get to, which was why they always drove to the Philharmonic, Dram said. Yao had been pleased to lend me a squeaky bicycle and I was embarrassed when Dram walked in wheeling a new silver Schwinn.

He said I couldn't be part of the Autonomen if I did not have a bicycle. Cello said she hated cyclists and that there was a great deal of Bicycle Fascism in West Berlin. They'd come by U-Bahn with it as far as they could and walked the rest of the way, leaving the car in Charlottenburg so that they could have a good time among the Far-Out Far Left, as Dram phrased it in English.

"You are a hard man," Afer told him.

After meatballs, we had to go into the gallery, the hallway outside the bookstore, to look at the cheap shirts Yao splattered with paint in his spare time. They were for sale. He worked "black," or off the books, in a nearby laundry. He was very good in the garden and was so put off by my fear of the soil that I got over it that first Saturday of weeding. Cello was more interested in the bulletin board.

Hayden and Father Paul didn't come inside with us. Hayden was having a smoky talk with Uwe, the sweet-looking Afro-German boy from the fifth floor who hung out more with the young German couples than he did with us, the other black guys. "The thing about our time is that later has arrived, we're in it now, later is here." Father Paul's English was not keeping up. "What do you think accounts for the interest in preppy-dom?" Hayden answered his own question. "The decline and fall of the West." He and Father Paul were due to leave for the Tyrol for the summer in a few days' time.

Rhonda treated the shirt she'd been given like a dishrag and at the same time scrunched her nose at the cigarettes, even outside. Dram accepted another beer and lit up anyway. He watched Uwe prepare a spliff while Hayden held forth. Lucky shrugged in answer to my look of dismay. Rhonda shook her head when Uwe offered it to her first. Except for Afer, we all declined. Yao excused himself.

I was safe in the divided city and Uwe insisted to Hayden that he was treated as a German in the United States, though

I was pretty sure that even after he opened his mouth he was still a light-skinned black to most Americans. If he was an African in Germany, which he was nowhere else on earth, then he was at least a foreigner in both countries, maybe everywhere he went, except West Berlin, haven of mongrels.

He sucked on his joint and said that he was at home nowhere, for which he blamed his parents. He blamed his parents for being strangers to each other after making him, and for being strangers to him. He blamed his father for abandoning his mother when his tour of duty was up at the end of the 1960s, causing her many years of starting each morning with shots of whiskey. He blamed his mother for letting her family ignore them all his life, for letting him leave school in order to discover the land where his father lived, and for his father turning out to be a stupid fuck in the middle of the Los Angeles ghetto.

Everyone was quiet. Cello wouldn't look at Rhonda, but she let Dram reach down the back of her chair for her hair. I put my hand sympathetically on Uwe's back as I inched by with cups. He leaned far forward in response. Hayden gave me an Oops look, his arms soon to be around superbly formed Father Paul.

Dad whistled while he worked over schedules of deductibles. Mom did not like to make too much of a fuss about the holidays. Her crazies were usually depressed at that time of year and we ourselves didn't much want to get together with family. Uncle Ralston's dynastic fantasies of a clan celebrating in style were thwarted by Aunt Loretta's inability to countenance guests, not to mention his own obnoxiousness.

"You don't want to die for something," I heard Ralston Jr. say to Dad one Christmas Eve. "I have a bus schedule to El Salvador. I want to die. In Eliot, it's Greek. I want to die. What's the difference between doing and being? The difference is infinite."

Hayden had kept Father Paul waiting to go until the last minute, not wanting to miss what he knew would happen between Uwe and Doctor Rhonda. I could hear her down the hall getting pounded. Elsewhere, Afer's girlfriend shouted Afer's praises. Loud, thumping reggae was going in the young Germans' rooms, to which I had not been invited. Yao and Lucky hadn't come back from their first-Saturday-of-the-month ritual, a visit to a one-story slot machine/porn cabinets/whorehouse establishment on Potsdamerstrasse, next to a used-car dealership. Dram had taken a melancholy Cello home, his love for her burning in his eyes. Everyone in Berlin was getting laid, except me.

I didn't have any hash. I could make out a couple going at it in a lit bedroom in the brewery across the dark. Nobody ever had any trouble asking me to cover for them on Sunday mornings doing whatever, because to them, I was very acceptable as the nonpracticing kind of 'mo. They only needed for me to be black. I could see them when I came downstairs on Sunday mornings to open up for someone, a couple asleep on the floor under a duvet by the sofa, the door ajar, or a couple half naked and drowsily postcoital at a kitchen table.

"The cat's here."

"I know. It's very moving."

Berlin was full of people who hated you for what they'd told you, Lotte said. We were alone all morning in the café, she and I.

Lotte said that 1934 had been a very bad year for queers, maybe the worst since Oscar Wilde's conviction.

I couldn't forget Rock Hudson's face. Saintly and shriveled, he talked cheerfully, but the lost-eyelashes look would not suit him. A big man had climbed from this sick man's side and loped off to an all-night diner, never to return. He'd been dead three years, but the ravaged face flashed behind that of every cute boy I cut a desperate look at, even in faraway Berlin.

•

"I have a journey, sir, shortly to go," Big Dash said. "But I'm waiting for that lost-looking dude down there to hit the can and I'll join him."

Zippi opened the big rectangle of aluminum foil and swept her bangs at the sight of the soft, moist black hash. It was coming into Europe again, I explained in German. Afghani chieftains and Russian officers had worked things out, I said, though I'd no idea where I got that news.

A football game was on TV. Odell let out a cowboy yelp. I didn't have to lie either. I'd not seen Bags, I said in English. Regulars along the bar made what they thought were coyote sounds. Zippi said in German that I could tell Afer this didn't make up for things. I let her look away first. The hash was a gift from me, but I didn't volunteer that I purchased it from Afer's girlfriend and I didn't follow Zippi into the kitchen either.

I was a big boy now. I got a white wine from Odell and took it to a thin older woman I used to put them away with. She'd had a few glasses already. We laughed at how my German had advanced. Was I reading in German the German literature I liked so much, she wanted to know. I was flattered that she remembered that I liked Heinrich Mann. Two hours later my joker was wrapped and I was balling her. To stay interested I had to pretend I was commanding her with that fat one of Manfred's I'd never seen.

•

My thing for this German dude was still very much alive. I slowed and looked up when I cycled past the building where his betrayed oncologist worked. I took to parking across from the Nissen huts. Even at a distance I could tell that the enclave looked and felt nothing like the militantly organized and clean encampment Rosen-Montag had insisted that it be every day. It wasn't clear what the site was being used for now. On the other side of the Tiergarten, I wasn't yet ready to go as far as Lessingsdorf. I turned back at the Academy of Arts.

I had a theory. The feelings for Manfred that I carried around Berlin changed in emphasis depending on my mode of transportation. On foot, my thoughts about him were sorrowful; by subway and train the images of our times together were fractured and comic; in a taxi or on a bus I was passive, the weak one, someone not in charge; but by bicycle I experienced gratitude in having enjoyed his company, acceptance that as an ideal he belonged to German history and as a man to himself, not to me, and maybe not even to his countess, taking the Rilke view of patrons in castles.

I cycled as far as the Schlachtensee. Every family on the banks of the lake was a nudist colony. Buck-naked fathers climbed trees and dived and grandmothers wiped the mouths of cherubs, the loose flesh of their grandmotherly arms sagging beside breasts content to have done their job, retired, and gone to sleep above their cascades of flesh.

The sun was going to be out for a good while yet. I was in a rowboat. Experimentally, I removed my sneakers and socks. My shirt came off next. I rowed farther into the lake. My skin was slippery from the effort and the sun. My trousers and underwear I got rid of in a single motion. I lay down in the rowboat, knees above me. It was too much on my eyes, even with clip-on shades. I sat up. I did that German thing. I looked at my navel. I noted mostly the absence of definition around it. I did the boy thing next, deliciously.

"Jed, *Mann*," Manfred might have said, pulling on my arms. He got excited when I took to something characteristic of Berlin: *bouletten*, George Grosz, controlling the line I was standing in at the cinema, his reckless parking, too much cake on Sunday, hatred of authority, exhibitionism. "How cool is that then," he'd say.

I was willing to masquerade as him on the sheets again, but my former partner in white wine didn't want me. Everything she said to me under her breath in the ChiChi was humiliating. I was, like every black man in the free city, a hustler when it came to white women. She nodded in Odell's direction. If I couldn't get what I wanted from her I'd discard her. True, I admitted. If she wanted that, she would hire from the bar one of the talented, skillful musicians, she said. She pushed away the glass of wine I'd brought her and called for one she'd pay for herself. I should have given her my black man's Who-are-you-kidding look, but I doubted at that moment that I had one.

After that, the time I would have given to the ChiChi went instead to piles of dishes and miles of bike lanes. I didn't want to lie to Zippi even if I wasn't coming around. I didn't like my gentleman's debt to Afer's girlfriend. When I asked Afer if he'd seen Bags, he said he'd gone to see his family in America. But he was coming back. He rushed over it, like a salesman covering up something defective about the product. Afer wasn't good at intrigue. He had a way of letting on that he was involved in something, keeping big secrets. But he tricked me. I hadn't expected him to understand when I quit smoking dope.

Lotte was at her table in the window one morning and we saw five guys from the architects' collective rush around from the front of the building to their cars. They had blueprints rolled up under their arms and waved big notebooks. They ran like the Keystone Kops, like they were having a good time. Lotte said it was a circulated fact that since the Cold War, German architects on both sides of the Iron Curtain were expected to spy for their governments.

I put off having a coffee that day and fell asleep without

having had any. I didn't take a break while on café duty the next day and fell into bed without having had a cigarette. It was going to be easier to ride the bicycle, I told myself. I couldn't stop sweating. I ignored the content and Technicolor of my recurring dreams.

In my intense and bewildering nakedness in the head, I phoned my mother from the café. Nothing was wrong, I said. But I'd wanted to say I was sorry. I would never forget that I'd made my rehab experience as shameful for Mom and Dad as I could. Inmates have more power than their visiting families. I could range freely over that prairie of memory where childhood incidents lay unburied, and in their guilt as creators of an addict they were obliged to render unto me hides of truth. I'd always known that her politics put Mom on the defensive as a mother. That I had denounced in the rehab her social activism as a species of child neglect explained why she had stayed in the public rooms of her feelings with me ever since. I could say I was sorry and she could say that I mustn't dwell on such things, but she dodged me, and my covert pleas. I felt it all the more now that Cello was back in with her.

She was excited about Dad's surprise: he himself had got them tickets for practically every performance of the Ravinia Festival. She was going to have Mozart and Frederica von Stade and Brahms and the Chicago Symphony all summer long. She said that our conversation reminded her that there was something she wanted to tell Cello and she hung up. It was no consolation that Solomon was now perhaps also wondering how long it would be before Mom was her real self with him again.

◼

"You can start a riot by having a black ass on the wrong beach," Ralston Jr. said when the paramedics took Uncle Ralston away.

"By having your black ass on the wrong one. Ask Carl. Ask Loraine. Your brown black ass."

■

In Berlin, when one door closed, another opened. I'd heard of her, but hadn't met her. Everyone at the house meeting was excited to have Alma back, except for the house leader's partner. The house leader and his woman were the only Co-op members with children. He used to be with Alma. They met when she got hurt at the first squatters' riots in Berlin eight years before. He still liked her. His woman fumed and baked in the main Co-op kitchen. I let myself imagine Zippi wet for Odell all day long.

Afer wanted my vote to change the name of the bookstore from Librairie Rosa to Bookshop Dulcie September, in honor of the South African freedom fighter assassinated in Paris two months earlier. I voted with the Old Guard, convinced by the argument that the name, Librairie Rosa, was already established.

Afer told me off in the café. "You are a brother of the undescended testicle type."

Alma heard this and decided that we were dear friends. She said she hadn't wanted to change the bookstore or café name because Rosa Luxemburg was her girl. Alma was an anarchist from Romansch country high up in Switzerland. She was scheduled to sing its folk songs at ZFB and we were to pass the hat. She wouldn't allow a fixed admission price for this music. She would leave again in the fall to tour. You thought of clear mountain streams when you looked into her light brown eyes and when she smiled. She wore boxy jackets and Chinese pants and brightly patterned headbands, because she couldn't manage her shortish brown hair. Her skin glowed.

Alma told me that she found my reference to *Cabaret* silly, but not a serious offense. To her, Sally Bowles was amoral. Plus, she did not like show biz and if anyone sounded like show biz it was Liza with a Z. "You have heartbreak for Judy Garland, too? *Ach so.* A friend of Dorothy. I know this expression. To frighten the bones of each song." She said she'd rather smoke than gain weight.

I told her about AA and Cello. Alma had heard of Schuz-burg Tools, but not of Cello. She told me about the time a black woman had knocked on her door in the mountains and said in French that her car had broken down. Alma had a phone and she knew the one boy in that area who ran a garage. It would take him a day to get up there. They walked to the black woman's car and walked back with her groceries and cooked together. The black woman stayed overnight and left in the morning. Alma never said to her that she had recognized her. The black woman never said that she was Nina Simone.

"But this is Berlin. You and Lotte came here for the same reason. To be gay."

Alma said she'd seen me checking out the men at the house meeting. She said we were going to have a problem because we had the same taste: anybody.

Lotte was at her round wooden table late, slurring as she coached Uwe for a part he'd got in a Kreuzberg play about the Night of the Long Knives, the June dawn in 1934 when Hitler started shooting gay men high in the party hierarchy, the brown-shirts who'd helped him to power. I left them and cycled down to the AA meeting in Dahlem. I liked most how light the sky was on my way back as I rang my smug, high-pitched bell at unsuspecting pedestrians and took on the cars curving through the Bundesplatz, cars unhampered by any speed limit, because this was West Berlin.

One Sunday I cycled to Wannsee. I said nothing to Cello and Dram about not smoking, because smoking was out of the question at Dram's parents' house anyway. Frau Schuzburg passed behind her son and said he was wearing too much scent. Her grandchildren were intelligent and well-mannered and good-looking. I remembered that when Konrad was three, he could count forever in three languages. "Timbuc-one, Timbuc-two, Timbuc-three," his performance in English began. He knew he was funny, even at that age.

Because of Dram, the Schuzburgs, of all people, had some regard for the squatters' movement. It was better to bring a house back to life than to let it crumble, innocent victim of the past. For them, the project of rebuilding Berlin was far from complete. They said squats should be brought into the system, too. The only time I heard Herr Schuzburg oppose Dram was over Dram's belief that West Berlin should be declared an international city, either to govern itself or to be governed by several nations.

Exhausted and stuffed, I rode the S-Bahn sitting with my Schwinn back up to town. I got out in the heart of Charlottenburg and walked my bike. A his-and-her leather-clad couple not feeling the heat watched their small dog keep up beside me and stop at the same bookstore table that I did under the arches of the train tracks. They smiled; I smiled. I had no problems in West Berlin, the retirement community of the '68 generation, as Dram described the city.

I walked to a gay bar on the other side of the Ku'damm, next door to the Department Store of the West, KaDeWe. "Ka-DaVey," I'd learned to say. Nice Berlin closed up early on Sundays, the department store, the ice-cream chains along the Ku'damm, the apparel shops that smelled of middle-aged women's perfumes, but not the bars. The gay bar was chatty and tipsy. I was pretty sure it was in this bar that I'd ordered Prosecco with a scoop of lemon sorbet, because I'd heard that that was what Cecil Taylor liked to drink.

There were other places around Berlin where I'd done worse, places I didn't remember until I happened into a bathroom stall. I sipped my water. My bicycle was looking back at me from the street. I smiled to myself. A thin bearded bald guy at the other end of the crowded bar smiled gold-toothed in my direction. "Leaving so soon?" the twin who was probably his boyfriend asked in English as I went toward the exit. I unlocked my bicycle and wished blessings on their backs.

Back at the Café Rosa, marveling at how remade I felt, I nearly collided with one of the architects who'd come in to buy a bottle of red wine. We were closed, but they'd let him in. He was supposed to have been home an hour ago, but he got lost in the discussion Afer, Yao, Alma, and some others were having. The Berlin Effect. The architect departed. I got into what was left over and was tough on Afer, which he said he appreciated because being interrogated helped him to hone his thinking. We were strenuously self-conscious, everybody sitting around, ready to get down with history in case it came that way again.

•

And then comes that thing, out of the blue, a someone into you, and he really did come out of one of those long drawn-out late-summer afternoons, long after lunch and hours before sunset. I was sitting with Alma on the steps of the Reichstag, between the black and brown columns that showed bullet holes from the battle for the capital in the spring of 1945. The last tour bus had departed. In those days, the Reichstag had no dome. It had a tourist travel shop, as one of the memorials, the ruins of history that could be visited, posed against, silently questioned. It had no convincing day-to-day function, like most old government buildings of that kind in West Berlin. And if not a symbol, then yet more disused, underused scenery for the endless hanging out that life in West Berlin was. We sat and talked about our plan to put Lotte von der Pfalz onstage, laughing about funding fantasies, shaking our heads to the music of the football game taking place in the Platz der Republik, the dusty, worn-down, unkempt, big grassy square in front of the burned Reichstag.

The players ran from left to right and from right to left ceaselessly in the late-summer heat, the sky cheering them on, the white soccer ball bounding surprising distances all of a sudden before being pursued once again in the white dust of the open square. They charged, the two teams of African players, so many black men in one place in public in Berlin, and half of them half undressed, charging from our right to our left, the sunlight rolling over their dark muscles, their flowing, changing, elongating bodies. They ran without fear, they ran with their voices, they ran without worries about eczema or ichthyosis, they charged from my left to my right without Vaseline on their knees or heels, of that I was sure. They had no skin disorders to confuse their blackness with, they had only their glistening selves, as brown as the banks of those rivers in the Cameroons Duallo would prove so tender about.

He and three others ended up on the steps near us. They wanted water. Alma had cigarettes and could answer in French. I slitted my eyes toward the west and then up in the direction of Lessingsdorf. Now and then she would update me on the subject under discussion and I would say I know, I know, like I had been following, like I understood more French than I could speak. He was pretty quiet, and he was the prettiest of them, slender, with a full mouth, the high cheekbones of all my dreams, and eyes I'd never thought about, large, dark, and not clear.

One of them got up and dusted himself off. Duallo stepped over into my line of vision. His two remaining comrades filled his space, stepping closer to Alma; the duel between them for her that would last only a couple of hours had begun. Some friends from the pitch called to them and they sang back, and they clearly weren't rejoining the game, which had just stopped, for some reason I didn't know. One man with legs reminiscent of a caliper stood over the stilled football. The teams talked on, in French, in Wolof, Duallo told me later, slapping themselves, kicking in the dust, hands on hips, several sitting, hands behind them.

Duallo moved us from my inhibited German to his freer English and sat beside me. I could have fainted a million times. He smelled like Aunt Loretta's cold cream in her dish in front of the mirror on her tiny vanity table as it was in 1966. Here I was, in Berlin, and he smelled like a boy's crime I had forgotten. There was a spot on Aunt Loretta's silk scarf. It could only have got there from some unauthorized someone having violated the house and been at her vanity table. It's true, I'd crept upstairs and I'd run her scarf around me, and it's true, I'd rubbed her cold cream from the open jar on my hands, and then smelled orange blossom, but I had lied about it when first questioned, until Mom, the Grim Extractor, arrived and the truth fled to her side.

And if I didn't pick up my end soon or come up with something to say, I was going to lose him. He'd put his shirt back on, flipping it together. Buttoning it up. Like the shutting of an altarpiece. The molded, packed, ribbony upward thrust of his torso was veiled by a much-washed faded gray shirt decorated with little white fish all leaping in the same direction. The orange blossom thrill of being so close to his chest turned into fear and depression that he wasn't gay, certain knowledge that I was way out of my sexual league, when he stood up and I took in how beautifully formed he was. He hadn't seemed that tall in the distance or when stretched out on the steps. Maybe it was his long neck. His head tilted down toward me. His mysterious eyes looked across my shoulder in the direction of Alma and his two friends when she suggested we drive to Potsdamerplatz in the rusted VW van one of them had.

Crammed together, talk was general, and I didn't have to

say anything. I just had to be there. Duallo had got in front
with the driver. Alma and Contestant Number 1 and I were in
the windowless back, comfortable on the carpet amid a mish-
mash of boxes and buckets and mops. Somehow we ended up
not at the Co-op, but on Oranienstrasse, at a table on the street,
crowded with alternative types and Turks, headscarves and
safety pins and U.S. Army camouflage fatigues marching by.
Alma put her chin in her hand and looked at the passing scene
as the two contestants rolled into the colloquial French phase
of their duel over her. It was an argument about music maybe,
she whispered. Musicians, she shrugged, and had some German
conversation with the girl behind us about the state of the
women's bathroom in this café.

Duallo turned from the argument and explained that musical loyalties were intense in West Africa. I said I'd never been
there. He was three when he first went out there, he said. No,
he was born in France. He was French, he said. His mother was
from Mali, but she was French, he said. His father was from
Paris. His father's mother had come from the German Cameroons to Paris in the late 1920s. There she met his grandfather,
an African nobleman whose title the French government recognized. He died before the war. His grandfather never married his grandmother. His father had had a rough time during
the war. Duallo's father had gone to his father's country in the
1960s, but he did not feel welcomed there by his father's family. He went back to a life on the fringes of the capital, in the
art and film scenes, an unhappy black Frenchman in Paris. Having several children had not cheered him up. Duallo said he
came to Berlin to get away from his father's bitterness.

He was beautiful and he was exotic and he rested a hand
on my back in front of everyone as he got up to go to the toilet.
Alma let both contestants know that Contestant Number 2 had
lost when she turned with the cigarette he'd given her and
asked Contestant Number 1 for a light. I paid the bill. Duallo

returned. He was twenty years old. That part of town, Kreuzberg 36, had contempt for big tippers. It was not the custom,
but I didn't care about seeming a bourgeois American. A leftist alternative-scene German working in a tiny döner kebab café
was probably the only kind of white person who did see me as
bourgeois. Contestant Number 2 had gone obtuse on the sidewalk and wasn't getting lost. I kissed Alma quickly and Duallo
was endearingly correct in his rapid farewell to his friends.
Night was still a long ways off.

I could have punched us through the red boxes for tickets,
but I didn't. We rode without paying, on the watch for con-
ductors, from Kottbüser Tor to Bahnhof Zoo, and there had
currywurst from a stand on a corner, laughing at the lingerie
and sex display windows in the tacky main street. He proposed
that from there we walk to Potsdamerplatz. He sang four of
his songs along the way. He explained that he believed in positive
messages. The songs were in Bambara, his maternal grandmother's tongue. I was so relieved. His sweet voice was nervous. As we walked, one of those lapis evening skies in Berlin
surrounded us. I was thirty years old for a week or so more,
but that night I was his age. Hip-person years are the opposite
of cat years, which in turn are nowhere near what gay years are
like. I would too soon admit to myself that I might not be able
to be what Duallo was looking for at twenty years old, but
that night extraordinary courage came out in alliance with
Vesuvian desire.

·

I was in my grove, my bed, and Duallo was in my arms again
when we heard over the radio news of the terrible fire in Lisbon. I kissed him and, incredibly, he was still the someone
kissing me back. It was time to step up and send that ball, my
life, hurtling through space toward the goal. I'd turned thirty-
one. I was not his age. I was going to act grown up and look

out for him. In the terrifying beginnings of the worldwide AIDS epidemic, Berlin had kept its Isherwood promises to me.

He was beautiful and black, which made me feel that I had one-upped those white boys who had no interest in me. "You're as vain as Isabella d'Este," Cello had said back in the bad years, "and all in the same lost cause. There's no there where you are." I was too pleased to mind the comparison. My difficult, gifted European cousin who never read anything herself had not considered that I, Negro Underachiever, might know who Isabella d'Este was. Keep coming back, I would learn to chant with the black noncom officers at the end of the AA meetings in Dahlem. It works if you work it.

EIGHT

The witness, an English wine merchant who would owe his life to black slaves, said in his letter that at about three minutes after nine o'clock in the morning, on the first of November, 1755, the earth began to shake. It was All Saints' Day, his twenty-sixth birthday, and he was opening a bureau in the very bedchamber where he'd been born. He knew immediately what it was, recollecting the fate of Caleo in the Spanish West Indies. He ran upstairs and was soon hanging on to a window from the outside. Tall houses collapsed into narrow streets. He thought he saw all of Lisbon sinking.

He woke deep in rubble. Dust had turned the morning dark. He used his good hand to clear out his mouth. His body had been badly crushed. A German merchant thought his people—meaning, his slaves—could get them to the Terreiro de Paco, a large square before the king's palace. Two servants—a euphemism for the enslaved—carried him in a chair down a steep hill while a third servant walked ahead with a torch.

He could hear voices begging for help. He saw dead bodies in the church doorways and lighted candles on the high altars. People loaded themselves with crucifixes and saints, surrendering to the Day of Judgment. They tormented the dying, he said. Though he'd lived in Lisbon his whole life, he feared what the Portuguese would do to an English heretic. All the while, fires slowly spread, driven by the gentle wind.

They took refuge in the square, between the king's palace and the customshouse. The rumbling he heard beneath him was not more earthquake, but the river undermining the cellars of the palace. A gunpowder depot blew up. When the fires approached from one direction, the Blacks carried him to safety and laid him on bundles and when fires threatened their new position, the Blacks again conveyed him to a safe spot. The night was fine and clear and ablaze. The witness suddenly calls servants "the Blacks" in his letter, as if danger let him see his rescuers in a more human shape.

Mules on fire galloped over people running from the flames. Just when he was expecting the sort of death he most dreaded, the wind suddenly abated and the fire burning upright made no further progress. An Irishwoman gave him watermelon while soldiers plundered the houses that still stood and robbed people huddled with what they had left. The German merchant made his farewells and joined those trying to escape by water.

The injured Englishman said in his letter that he tried to buy a place in the boat of another Englishman, but the gentleman told him that most likely there would be only enough room for his family. The Englishman asked if the gentleman's black servants were reckoned part of his family, and if not would he permit him to employ one of them to try to get a boat for him. The gentleman answered that he was welcome to send his servant wherever he pleased.

He sent a Black Boy to the waterside, promising to pay all the money he had. The Black Boy returned and told him he had arranged for a place that would cost half his money. Another Black Boy offered to help and the two carried him to a large boat full of people and laid him on a board in the middle of it. A priest trod on his lame leg. The watermen called him a heretic and the Blacks devils. They were put ashore at the edge of the city. They'd risked their lives for him. He paid them half of the gold he had. He hid in the countryside. Because so many were starving, he ate in secret. He made it to a ship and set sail at the end of November.

Thomas Chase's house didn't fall. It stood in a street called Pedras Negras, on a hill leading up to the castle. He soon returned to Lisbon and died three decades later, in the bedchamber where he was born. Death in every shape had become familiar to his eye, he said. Those not killed by falling stones during the earthquake were burned by fire; those who escaped fire drowned in the river or the harbor.

The fires in Lisbon burned for a week. Fresh troops pressed survivors into service to bury the dead, who were decomposing in the streets by the thousands.

•

I liked his Éditions Gallimard around my room, the soft, matte covers, especially the books only he and I would be into. Or so we liked to say, those books that offered glimpses of black people in the history of the continent. Like my footsteps, they approved of me, the black lover in Europe. And thou shall bring forth black Epaphus, Aeschylus said. I didn't know what that meant or remember where I'd got it from, though it was the kind of thing that Irish American drunk I used to binge with would say. I liked the way Duallo liked me for saying it, the way he moved closer to me on the street.

Back at the *Eagle*, Ralston Jr. used as references the popular histories of the nutty old journalist J. A. Rogers—*World's Greatest Men of African Descent* or *100 Amazing Facts about the Negro*. Rogers believed that one of Beethoven's grandfathers was black and one of President Harding's grandfathers as well. I remembered amazing facts from these works—

Alexander the Great had a black general, Clitus Niger, mentioned in Plutarch, for instance. I'd not studied Latin. Duallo had. But I knew about Joannes Latino, the slave in sixteenth-century Granada who ignored the Muslim uprisings around him and wrote Latin verse in praise of chinless Hapsburgs.

I was his first, he said. I believed he'd not had an open thing with a man before, because he was upset to have been shy when we passed Alma and Contestant Number 1 on the Co-op stairs one morning. Parma had a black saint, I told him. I held back telling him that one day I planned to search the back corridors of Rome's museums for that Bronzino portrait of Alessandro de' Medici, the son of Pope Clement VII by a black woman. What if he already didn't want to come with me?

He never asked for anything. He would incline his head and lower his eyes in acknowledgment of dinner or a movie, but the age difference and my being American made my taking the lead right for us. I noticed fairly soon that he wore the same pair of shoes whenever we met. I took him to a whacked-out Kreuzberg 61 designer with blue hair and studs, her back courtyard studio smelling of leather. He wouldn't really look at anything. But then days later I saw his glances at elegant men's shops on the Ku'damm down by the Schaubühne, that temple of German drama that Erich Mendelsohn had designed in the 1920s as a bowling alley or cinema—I forgot which, in Duallo's presence.

He didn't mind my telling him facts about what we were walking by that anyone could look up. He knew six languages, but we lived in English, because Duallo was interested in black American music. He made sure to have some information to share in return, something that could not be looked up, because it was about him, his life, the inside of him. He explained what he was like, guilelessly, a Jesuit-taught youth carrying an armload of character traits and offering them to me arrow by arrow. He enjoyed clothes, because he also loved music and to dance. He loved to dance, because he worked very hard. My patent leather boots were corny. I went back to my Doc Martens.

Duallo disappeared every now and then into his African student/African exile world and I understood that I could not follow. I never picked him up at the Techno Institut, but I saw his meal card. He gave me to understand that great things were expected of him. Perhaps I imagined that Yao avoided us. But Duallo met Contestant Number 1 and Alma in a Neukölln world of black men employed below their education, near Hasenheide Park, I heard from her—her being a white girl was another story, she said.

I failed at not minding how long she would go on with Duallo in French. I was even jealous of the Bambara phrases he sang under Alma's lyrical folksongs and zither. His orange scent, a cream that his mother mixed for him, slowly filled the space. No wonder he was getting looks—and me, too, the kind that said that if Duallo could be with me then he could be with the guy daring to cruise him right in front of me.

I didn't take him to the ChiChi, or to any gay bar, for that matter. Dad had refused to buy me the watch I wanted for my eighteenth birthday, on the grounds that it was too showy. "Don't parade your mule in front of people who don't have hamburger." Maybe I didn't know how to defend what was mine, because I'd never had anything. I'd lived my life camping out in other people's stories, waiting for my own to begin, but unable to get out of the great head and into my actual.

I was happiest when Duallo and I were alone, in some bad café after a museum visit, at the movies in seats I'd insist he choose, in the back of the crowd at street concerts, in my room on the fifth floor. Alma had gone on her tour—she wondered if I permitted myself to be free enough inside to understand what folklore was—but she left Duallo her James Brown record with "Funky Drummer" on it that he could really groove to.

•

Dad was the secret of my persuasiveness as a man in love. Because he had taken care of me, I could in turn protect Duallo in the American style. I was one of the few members of the Co-op who did not have an outside job. The young Germans also didn't have a slave—the slang for "job" that Odell and Bags had liked to use because it came to them from Malcolm X. But I didn't play guitar with my case open in Europa Center either.

Some members of the Co-op had been to Lessingsdorf. I didn't talk about having worked for Rosen-Montag, because that was my defeat at the gates of international cool. I'd been near glory and the she-goddess had flung me into the pits. I climbed out and stepped off into an act that was more my stride. In Cello's small village, there were many mansions.

I said I was working on a script for a documentary back in Chicago. Nobody would have cared had I told the truth: I didn't get that TV job. But I already had a job. Alma said that for thousands like us in West Berlin, that was the point—to figure out why we were in West Berlin.

Two days after Harold Washington's funeral, Dad said he would explain things to Ronald, who would explain them to his sisters, but now he was talking to Solomon and me. He and Mom had made plans for our graduate education and for our getting married and for our having kids of our own, and if we did have kids someday, and he hoped that Solomon and Francesca would, then we would learn that it's a waste of effort to try to attach a timetable to your kids' lives once they'd got seats on that rocket ship out of the nest.

All he knew was that yeast rose. He was going to go ahead and give Solomon his wedding gift and although marriage was not going to be my hangman's card he was going to go ahead and let me have the equivalent, because it could not have been easy for me to go back to school a third time and ride it out.

He told Solomon that he and Francesca didn't need her father, not only because he had brought up his son to take care of his family, but also because he hadn't been treasurer of Shay Holdings, Inc., for thirty years just for Uncle Ralston's sake. He said that he'd promised Mom that what her father had allowed to happen to her and her mother he never would. He told me not to sell myself out over there, not to let myself get taken. I still had to be a man, the head coach of a team.

My black expatriate's footsteps along the verges of Autonomen culture in West Berlin had been made possible by the vengeance of my father and his power of attorney. Cello in particular was thrilled. She referred to her parents as buried alive. Dad loaded Uncle Ralston and Ralston Jr. with drugs and parked them in two different locked-down facilities. He and Mom drove a resigned Aunt Gloria to a convent in Wisconsin. Dad cut Mrs. Williams loose without another cent, prying her out of a house Shay Holdings owned. He said she was what public assistance was for. Mom made no objections. Dad was cutting us loose, too, and Mom coped by pretending that he wasn't.

I gave Duallo a portable CD player, the latest fashion. It fit snugly into his book bag. Another thing that had changed since Rock Hudson's death was the exchange rate between the dollar and the deutschmark. Americans didn't win the lottery anymore. But where Duallo and I lay was the ancient world. I grew a beard and rolled him over once more.

·

Louis Armstrong's new tailor asked him if he dressed left or right. Armstrong told him to leave room on both sides. "I like for it to swang."

·

Because of Duallo, I walked through doors chest-first. I was no longer a eunuch to my fellow Co-op members. They made mistakes with him right off, I could tell. One girl tried to get over on him, as a pretty girl who got annoyed when the wrong sort of boy was gay. Gay was okay, so long as it wasn't someone whom she wanted to like girls, her. She would sit with him at the café bar and make her thirteenth apology in English and German if she had said something the other day when they were speaking that offended him. It's just that the flies on the eyes of the children she saw in that refugee camp would stay in her mind forever. I counted the number of times she stroked his bare arm. I thought of Zippi slamming saucers around. This girl turned up the volume. The girl was booming. She boomed at Duallo, but it waved over him.

The Co-op offered freedom because West Berlin was the back of beyond, where we'd come to live unmonitored, in a place suitable to people either not in a position to judge or those who had made it their cause to judge our judgers. But they, the white people, I almost observed to Alma when she was still around, assumed that Duallo needed their help just because he wasn't white, wasn't German. His engineering student visa was always a surprise to them, a bit like Uwe's German.

But unlike Uwe, Duallo wasn't touchy about being patronized. He figured it was their problem, not his, their assumptions of what his story would be, their slowness to comprehend a black Frenchman. I was so ginger around him; he never felt that from me. To be black in most places was to be on the touchy side. I didn't challenge him. He considered me a patient listener. I didn't understand everything, but I never tired of looking at him, of having him shower and shower, he pleased to be clean, perched in the window ledge, worrying in that young way about his future.

These should have been pancake days. But once I wasn't unnerved anymore that he would take up with some girl in the house and move on, I was sure that a secret sweetheart waited for him back in Saint-Denis or a handsome German engineer

fluent in both Wolof and French would show him a bone bigger than mine. I couldn't relax. His future was in France whenever he talked about it. He was my first real thing, too.

•

In my dream, I am in a sanatorium, attended by Mrs. Williams.
I have come to stop smoking, but she is pouring white wine
from a glossy white pitcher into a delicate glass. My hands are
tied. She has my shoes. She motions with her head toward the
open door. Someone is behind the door, but I am forbidden
to say his name. Cigarette burns appear on the sheet and I
wake up.

•

It was mid-October and Berlin life was hurrying back inside
when the sun went down. On Saturday nights, we turned the
Café Rosa into a cinema. The house vote to do so had been
unanimous, mostly because our equipment and screen were
hot, black market. Some of us still "liberated" things from
stores. Plus, ZFB was in a leaky, damp phase.

Pabst's *Westfront 1918* had been followed by Sembène's
Black Girl, which we'd obtained thanks to a name in Paris that
Duallo provided. Now we were packing them in with *RoboCop*,
and Afer made a big display of being uneasy about where our
copy came from. Guys in the back had to sit on tables.

The joy of Cello's trust account had made us almost like
family, but I'd not expected her to call me at the Café Rosa
from time to time, or for her to say yes when I explained that
I couldn't come to dinner because of our Saturday Night at
the Movies program and would she like to come to Co-op J.I.,
"Koh-op Hah-ee," instead. She and Dram had been so busy,
they'd not seen *RoboCop*, and he really liked *Soldier of Orange*,
she reported back.

It wasn't the ten extra marks I would have to put in for

Hayden and Father Paul that I resented. These would be my guests, I'd made sure with the house leader's partner, because Cello tended to sail past ticket takers and sign-in tables. But I didn't like it when I compared myself to Hayden after his season in the mountains, his butt yet more rounded and smooth, as if made by Canova.

Supposedly they'd met before, but she ignored my quick Uwe, Afer, Yao, Duallo, Lucky thing, and marched off to the bar to demand a glass of red wine, Lucky's name hanging from the biblical shawl that crossed her hair like a bridge over a dark river. Dram sauntered in her direction. He called loudly for a coffee. Though he conquered her every time, I wondered if each time he wasn't sure he would, and if that was the secret.

I did a Lotte von der Pfalz, Cello Schuzburg, Dram Schuzburg thing, standing nowhere near any of them. Lotte's arm shot out and Dram walked over and lightly took her hand. She blushed. Cello didn't budge from the bar. Dram called. Cello wheeled around, a starting-over smile along with her. Introductions were not really a Berlin thing. Our bar wine was supposedly foul, but nobody turned it down.

"She made him drive," Hayden whispered. "The ride over was tense, child. Ravel wore makeup," he continued, studying Lotte, who'd made sure she'd had a nap. "Blue eyeliner." He and Father Paul were respectful when I offered Lotte their names, but they sat at a table ahead of her.

I'd said my black housemates' names fast, so fast I'd messed up the German for Cello, Hayden, Paul, Dram, you remember my friends Uwe, Afer, Yao, Duallo, and this is Lucky. I said all these names fast, trying to hide his in there, but Hayden, like one of Hemingway's hunters, spotted him in the brush, nibbling at Mother Earth.

I got us chairs chest-first, but my face was too shiny. I moved around too fast and when I slowed myself down, I no doubt looked like someone who wasn't at home in his body telling himself to slow down. I was saying the names of other Co-op members and Cello graciously acknowledged them as she and Dram took seats at the front center table.

"Jed, my friend," Lotte said. I'd forgot her white wine. Her table had filled up with people whose orders I'd not taken.

I knew that I was in danger of sitting on it and squashing it to death. He was next to me during the film, equatorial and fruity, squirming in his seat. His body was alive and strong. It was special, like holding a child and sensing in your being as another human that the child is moving, a person is newly alive, warmth up against warmth.

Dram laughed his head off at *RoboCop*, but I couldn't have passed an exam on what the film was about. I kept quiet during the discussion afterward. Dram scooted his chair closer to Cello, got up, and pushed Lotte's chair into our rearranged circle. He wasn't smoking.

"You're not smoking," he said to me in German.

That was why everything was happening too fast. A cigarette was a magic wand. It had the power to make time stand still. The problem was that cigarettes betrayed you to your end. They got bored and put their arms down. You were used up and time began again, even faster. Cigarettes took cynical payment. They put you on the rack and killed you, ended that life that hadn't moved past the first chapter of *Confessions of Zeno*.

And the problem with love was that it made you feel bad most of the time. I'd spent the whole film not paying attention to it, sitting in the smokeless shadows—a close house vote restricted smoking until after the film—wondering just what was the vibe or the meaning of the first awkward thing that had happened between Duallo and me.

I got hung up over the question of laundry. In Berlin, it was not simple. I did it on alternate Saturdays, when I was not on duty at the *Schrebergärten*. About half the Co-op members had washing machines, usually tiny un-American appliances that had ridiculous vacuum-hose-like attachments for the sink. The rest of the house had made arrangements to use these machines. Except for the fifth floor. No one had a machine and as far as I could tell no one had an arrangement in the house with anyone who did. I'd not inherited Alma's arrangements either. Intimacy was a funny thing in a German commune. They did not want someone else's dirty laundry. But they hung their clean laundry from windows and across landings and around the courtyard, like we were some neorealist Italian film set.

Afer's girlfriend collected his laundry and returned it, brought it upstairs to the fifth floor. The more Duallo stayed with me, the more of his things he left for the convenience of having them there.

I washed his things along with mine and they were in the drawer that was becoming his. I didn't mention it; neither did he. This was the first week he'd spent every night with me. And so he was with me in the late afternoon when I carried the bag to the rare laundrymat far down Potsdamerstrasse, past the used-car lot and the Spiel Kino/casino whorehouse. I dumped everything in, his things, too. I hardly think he realized where we were.

He was talking about Afrika Bambaataa again. He had the latest album on his portable CD player. It had earphones. Two prostitutes smoked, old enough to be made to do their own laundry again, I thought. Had I not had a shift at the Café Rosa already and were I not facing an extra shift because of the film, maybe I would have acted my age and not been suddenly unwilling to accept him acting his.

When at long last I had a pile of hot clothes on the table, I tapped him on the shoulder. He took out an earbud. I walked back to the table and patted a pile of clothes, indicating that he was to help me fold. He eventually came over and stood there, earbud and CD player in his hands.

"Mann, komm schon."

It took him a while to put the CD player down safely and store the earphones. Then he picked up a T-shirt, one of mine, and looked at it. He set it down again and folded it in half, like a napkin. We were alone. He picked up another T-shirt. I was nearly finished. I was tired, but I knew we had to climb out of this. I would have to carry him up on my back and throw him over the side of the crater of misunderstanding. I'd offended the aristocrat in him.

"Merci."

He said nothing and picked up his CD player. I'd offended the boyfriend in him as well. He was not my girlfriend. He did not perform tricks.

•

The Oracle of Delphi was obviously a black woman, Solomon said, because she couldn't keep her opinions to herself. But then the Sphinx was a black woman, too. "We can't win."

And even if the Field Museum hadn't said so, Mom said, he ought not to forget that Tutankhamun's grandmother, Queen Tiyi, came from the Sudan.

"Teach, sister," the resident crazy of the moment said and left to get a good seat. The petition to Mom had succeeded that Cello's practicing be curtailed on the night that *The Carol Burnett Show* was on.

Ronald and Rhonda were upstairs putting on pajamas, but Dad had to make apologies to Mom for not checking to see who was around before he spoke. How could Cello, suddenly in the hall, not have heard Dad remind Mom that the Queen of the Matamba had been known to speak to Ralston Jr. from the seventeenth century, so she had better watch it or else she, too, might wake up in a church with a hammer in her hand and fragments of a Jesus at her feet.

Dad stole out the door for the *Eagle.*

Cello was telling me what she'd discussed with Mom about the Toccata, Adagio, and Fugue, how Bach's original opening two bars have a single line, and Busoni adds alternating octaves. He starts with an octave in the left hand and a single note in the right hand and then an octave in the right hand and a single note in the left hand and they alternate and it's not as easy to play as it sounds, this being Bach.

"Nothing like a sweat after a good Bach," Dram said in English.

I treasured the look that Duallo and I exchanged, like a couple. Wasn't that a weird thing for him to say?

"Music that has independent voices is a challenge," Dram went on. "That is why pianists are intense." His hand sought his wife's hair. "It is because of the multivoiced music that they play."

"I thought Busoni's Bach arrangements had gone out of fashion," Cello said in German to Hayden.

"Composers like his own compositions," the African American composer answered the African American pianist, in German.

"Interested in Bach arrangements from the unfashionable period," Cello said. Hayden appeared to understand what she meant by the unfashionable period.

"Schoenberg's *St. Anne* is intense," Dram said in English, looking at Afer and the others in our big circle. "Over the top at all times. The orchestra sounds giant, giant."

"E-flat Major and there's a glockenspiel," Hayden said in peacekeeping English.

Nobody was smoking. Nothing felt fun, though Duallo sat within smelling distance.

"In the middle of World War One, in Chicago, because he had renounced the eating of meat, Nijinsky's wife left him," Lotte said, in very slow English. She appealed to us one by one.

"He wanted to go back to Russia and live in a commune of no women."

People laughed and went back to talking about the film, wanting to start this part of the evening over.

"Did you see him dance?" Father Paul asked in German. He'd given up on English and understood surprisingly little of the film.

"How did you guess that I grew up in a mental asylum." Lotte had reverted to her Berlinisch.

Lucky did not know who Nijinsky was and said so.

Father Paul stood and made a rapid turn on the front of one foot. Duallo got up, and together they pirouetted twice. The café applauded and I was proud and nervous. I do not know how I knew that Hayden was miffed that I was sitting there as big chested and proprietary as he was. He'd seen where Duallo had been all night—next to me. Maybe I could pull this off, after all, though Hayden knew I'd cheated and was screwing above my sex grade.

•

Cello said she was thinking of going to Budapest for Bartók's state funeral. She confessed to me that she'd hired two German women to wash her hair, like the women in myth around that loom. She had the nicely pliable English nanny take Maximilian out for the afternoon. They went to a boutique with plenty of Agnès B. "She doesn't take him to Karstadt." While they were out, the German women would come, the boss one spilling over with "Gnaediges Frau, gnaediges Frau." They massaged and patted her burden. It took hours to treat and comb, dry and brush.

I called Cello from the café on her birthday. Mom had got up early to phone her. They'd ended up laughing about Mom's one-man protest against street artist Zeno's mural in the Fifty-Fifth Street underpass, the same week Cello had a major competition. To Mom, people's art was a social misdemeanor. Cello remembered when Mom had tried to stop Regents Park, that high-rise complex, and Dad ran home to get his chain cutters. Mom lectured Dad so hard the cops didn't arrest her. They said they could see he had his hands full. Cello said she asked Mom why her meetings in Zurich with the Hungarian countess could not be as important to her as Dram's design meetings in Dortmund were to him.

To my credit, I did not tell Cello that it was not too late for her to become an institution builder. She knew that I knew about her and her siblings, but she did not inquire about us, because, knowing Cello as I did, her not letting herself know anything about us kept her from feeling that Dad had perhaps cheated her, that I was hanging out on what was perhaps something that had been gouged out of hers.

It hit me then that Cello had taken me up this time because it excited her to be around someone who knew what she could not as a well-bred girl refer to. She'd worn her tenth wedding anniversary necklace, gold inlaid with tin, only once, and the occasion had been safely in West Germany, in Stuttgart. But Cello did go so far as to say to me that she'd often experienced the tedium of white people who thought all black people were poor until the day before yesterday. I wondered if she dared to say such things to Dram. Somehow I thought not. Bewitched as he was, he nevertheless knew an heiress when he danced with one. As Dram and Afer reviewed the situation in South Africa, with contributions from Yao, Cello couldn't hide an expression that I hoped the father of her children was unaware of.

"Never worry about how tough the run is going to be if you can work every problem in the book," Dad used to say.

Lotte told us that in 1937 the SS estimated that there were two million cute boys in the Third Reich.

•

The coolest thing I had ever done had been not to tell Cello about Duallo. She was irked that I thought myself so fly. Maybe I could pull this off, after all. Yet I did not enjoy the derisive looks Hayden cut at Cello, who had been a long time getting the message, she was so used to me being alone.

"But wasn't he with Rhonda?" she whispered as Uwe followed Lotte to the door and gave him a warm get-home-safely. Uwe's play was awful, but he'd made his stage debut. Dram patted me on the shoulder when I whisked away the chair Lotte had vacated.

My back hurt, not from carrying trays of dirty cups and sloppy beer glasses, but from trying to read lips. Any chance I got, I stupidly cruised by wherever Duallo was, just to connect with him, I told myself, when in fact it was to say to whomsoever to him cometh that the nectar in question was mine.

Father Paul was complaining to Duallo that he was tired of commuting back and forth. He had family and his studies in Austria, but Hayden would not look for work in Vienna. I convinced myself that Duallo wasn't following his German.

Hayden jumped on him, snarling that nobody in Austria was ever going to give a black man the position someone of his caliber and experience deserved. Father Paul put his hands in his lap. His love was hurt.

I made coffee. The café was noisy. Wooden chairs scraped the unpolished floorboards. The house leader bawled for two beers and two coffees; the area where I worked was slippery. Co-op members had a good time ripping further the remnants of leaflets and old posters glued to the bumpy walls.

Hayden asked me to phone for a taxi. He wouldn't dream of taking Dram away from his political philosophy and shook hands with Yao, Afer, Lucky, the house leader, Uwe, Dram, and Duallo. He threaded through the configuration of tables to kiss Cello and me, too. Father Paul was like a feather on his palm.

Hayden had seen in the paper that Lessingsdorf was being

disassembled, the trompe l'oeil pulled down. There was some controversy over the workers' houses and warehouse offices and until the disputes were resolved they were likely to remain unoccupied, an addition to the unused in West Berlin, but not exactly real estate that had no value either. I couldn't see Cello's face.

Stagnation had changed the occupied city, the house leader proposed to Dram. Stagnation on both sides of the border, the house leader's partner, the incredible baker, added. Reforms wouldn't save either side. Their two tired children stood around her, gnawing on the only sweet buns she let them have per weekend. I never translated for Duallo. Fortunately, he'd not asked me to. He said his classes were very, very hard.

Another Co-op member said he wanted to go back to the question of which was the occupied city, East or West Berlin. He propped open the front door as he spoke. The air became colder, but not less smoky. The lights in the café flickered now and then.

For me, it had been an emotionally unsatisfying evening ever since Duallo and Father Paul hugged goodbye. And it wasn't over. I regretted that I'd not paid attention to the film. At least I would have had that self-respecting experience. I got more orders for coffee and beer and red wine. Duallo came behind the bar to help me, his eyes that I could not read full on me.

•

Triumphs are much harder to get over than disasters. Uwe had his golden brown hand in his blue pouch of golden brown tobacco and rolled one for Duallo. I failed not to mind that he could have one cigarette per month. He could smoke at a party and not get hooked. He was that way about alcohol, too. I just couldn't understand how he could leave half his glass of wine, and his first one at that.

I couldn't tell if I was really in love or if I was just relieved to have someone, to have joined the living. Maybe the rain wasn't really more poignant since he'd come into my life and I was just acting but not admitting it. We had gone swimming one Sunday in the summer. He said his father had a friend from his film days and through him he'd had some holidays on Cap Nègre until his father's depression caused him to lose interest in his son, who was by no means his first. But at least he learned to swim. He liked tennis. He almost met Yannick Noah. McEnroe said he was more scared of Noah's hair than his tennis.

When we were out cycling, it was Duallo's juju beckoning me, I told myself. I let him have the Schwinn. We came to the point where I had a hard time keeping up on Yao's old brown contraption, something Anne Frank's father would have had. To head back in, because of me, was more embarrassing than how badly I played tennis, after all the training on the bike I'd subjected myself to. The next time I rattled by a display window of bicycles, I stopped.

I did not think about how I looked to him when I watched him play football again in the Platz der Republik. It was Duallo who told me that the reason the Reichstag had no function was that everyone had promised the Russians it would remain unused. He ran and time stood still and if I did not forget everything, hugging my knees on the porch of the Reichstag, I at least forgot myself. The Berlin Effect. I never met his teammates, and Contestant Number 1 left us alone where the Nazis set fire to the Weimar Republic. That was the last time I'd see him play. I think I knew that afternoon that I would one day say to myself about him that I saw him play twice, the first time and the last.

Yet I had to cover up from myself my hurt when he mentioned that he played other football matches, over in Neukölln and in Kreuzberg on the Saturdays when I was digging in the ground in the *Schrebergärten*. I'd been with him in that very square in Kreuzberg one evening. The Wall ran along the far end of Mariannenplatz. You could see a church spire and roof on the other side, over in East Berlin. Someone had painted the church front, what the Wall blocked, on the side facing south, or the Western sector.

The park was in use in every corner, families took their time packing up plastic baskets, and everything around us was purple in the twilight. Children of a mystical hue came laughing through the dusty grass, chased by papa. The scarf on his daughter's head seemed so unfair, and Duallo said so. He looked back and said her scarf did not appear to be slowing her down.

We wandered for some time. He was demonstrating with his hands different nautical knots. I made it a point of honor not to interrogate him about where he'd been and whom he'd seen, but maybe my not wanting to know was not honorable, because what he did tell me made me think of how much of his life I was shut out from. Even after he'd begun spending every night with me, I was not at ease about us.

•

Cello was telling Uwe that it would be one thing to work with Lotte von der Pfalz on a piece about the Nazi times, but she knew the black American poet he'd referred to who was living in West Berlin, a second-generation Beat figure, and her advice to Uwe would be to stay clear of him. She'd let Duallo and Uwe smoke near her. Uwe wanted to write a performance piece about race, being mixed race.

No, it was not that that black American poet was a bad man, she said, getting up to take Dram's cigarette from him to smoke herself—he kissed her—it was that he was second-rate, which was worse. Those were precisely the people to avoid in Berlin, Cello said. They were in hip Berlin because in what was actually a village they could have the careers they could not have in New York or Los Angeles or London. She switched to English. They were never-was performance artists, never-to-finish-dissertation affirmative-action parasites.

She lived by the social philosophy that if you heard what she'd said about you, then you were meant to or you wanted to, and at least she wasn't ignoring you. I'd no worries about keeping my cool with her, but not for the first time what I really felt was sorry for her. The family love only money could buy turned out to be a rental. The meter flipped fast on Cello's moods anyway.

But what was it to her that I was bedding a beautiful young man. That was proving more than enough to freak me out. I missed Zippi; I missed Alma; I missed having a friend, being one of the guys, having a gang to tell me to stay strong. I'd never understood why Cello had never really wanted that with me. I thought of unnerving Solomon with a sober phone call. AA teaches us to go back and say we're sorry to people we did messed-up things to when we were out of our minds. We were to write them letters. Apart from Mom, and only kind of, I'd made amends to no one back in Chicago. That hadn't worked. Perhaps just talking with wise old Lotte in the morning would suffice.

I was not smoking and it bothered me that the times Duallo wasn't with me felt like breaks between rounds, chances to take out the mouth guard, to pant, squirt water over my face, plan my next moves. I could not relax into my love, though he spent hours in the dark with me, and I was proud fighting the mildew in the bath in housing I wouldn't have thought nearly as cool back in Chicago.

•

Duallo had replaced the bicycle I'd given him with a racing machine he liked and taken it to school. I was back on my

Schwinn, in front of the Nissen hut enclave. Multiple chains held the gates fast; plants had got into the gravel. Rosen-Montag's glass carriage lights had been removed from above the doors. Instead, bare bulbs hung from wires that looped from hut to hut. In a few years it would look like something left over from the war.

I went on, past the Academy of Arts and one of the easiest structures to make fun of in West Berlin, the House of the Cultures of the World. I pumped toward the Spree and up to Lessingsdorf, feeling cold and sorry I hadn't worn gloves or made more of my opportunity with Rosen-Montag. The public entrance had been obliterated. I rode beside the S-Bahn tracks and turned off on a road once bumpy with trucks. Now my tires rolled on the hash-smooth black asphalt, specified by Rosen-Montag.

I could hear different rhythms, a smacking onto the pavement somewhere, a crunching of wood sound, something hydraulic. I should have known what those machines were. I realized I was riding toward what had been a great wall of trompe l'oeil depicting the backs of narrow houses and arched passages. The magic city had become a high tin fence. There was no one to call out to at the wire gate. This was a parking lot. I nearly fell over the handlebars to get a better angle, but I'd never seen another like Manfred's Deux Chevaux in Berlin. The right fender was dark blue, but I couldn't see the left one, which, to be Manfred's car, had to be green with a big white splotch.

No one was there and beyond the next fence was noise, so why call out. I couldn't say if I'd missed him. Maybe I just wanted to show off the bohemian life I'd made for myself in his absence. Maybe it had been a relief to have him gone, yanked out. I'd never yelled in my life. Dad didn't yell when he watched a game. He pulled his hands apart and bit his lip. Solomon beat his fist into his palm. I'd never yelled when I'd come. "I didn't came for a week," a blond soldier once said in the AA meeting down in Dahlem.

It was too cold to wait and see if that was his car, too pet Negro to wait for him. Straight guys aren't trying to hurt your feelings, they're just not thinking about you in that way. I'd pedaled to the Landwehrkanal by the time I concluded that Manfred was not searching for himself; but I was, or, rather, the American abroad, I was supposed to be.

One of my favorite buildings in Berlin stood along the north side of the Landwehrkanal, Emil Fahrenkamp's beautiful Shell House, with its waved exterior. From west to east it stepped down in waves of glass and treated stone, from ten storys to five storys. It had been white in 1932, the books said, but had turned the color of the gray stuff in my soap dish, my soap dish before I met Duallo.

The trees could have offered shade, had it been that kind of day, but we were fast revolving away from the sun. These would not have been the trees that had witnessed anything. Everything back then got used for fuel. What waterway wasn't also a grave. It was the seventieth anniversary of the Weimar Republic, proclaimed at the Reichstag on November 9, 1918, after the signing of the Armistice.

Two hours later, Karl Liebknecht proclaimed a Socialist Republic from the balcony of the Kaiser's Stadtschloss, which in those days was down the street from the Reichstag. The East Germans demolished the palace in 1950, except for the sandstone balcony, which was preserved and then enclosed by a dull government building of East Bloc bureaucratic vastness.

The Wall cut off the Reichstag from the nearby Brandenburg Gate, built as the western end of Unter den Linden, the boulevard of palaces, embassies, and a little Greek temple by Schinkel that fascinated everyone. From the Reichstag you could see over the Wall to passages of Doric columns and the four-horse chariot that topped the gate. The Wall cut through what had been Pariserplatz, right in front of the gate, and stopped you from getting near it.

You couldn't approach the Brandenburg Gate from the east either. The tourist hit a barrier where Unter den Linden terminated as paved expanse, Soviet-style. Hitler fans were given no chance to get near where the Chancellory and the bunker had been. In the West, you could press up against the Wall and hump it. But in East Berlin, a wall guarded the Wall. Between the two walls lay heavily patrolled grassy strips where apartment buildings had been, and the windows people are jumping from in the black-and-white films of August 1961.

I remembered Cello's sister, Rhonda, impressed that she was so close to the big, bad Berlin Wall, and I understood. But Berlin was not a Cold War story for me, terrified at the border though I was. It was Liebknecht supporting the workers' general strike, as I learned in the Co-op bookstore. They lost and Weimar culture was born.

The Freikorps came for Liebknecht and brave Rosa Luxemburg. One account in German of what was done to her at the Eden Hotel I was glad I was not able to finish. On January 15, 1919, they were taken to the Landwehrkanal, where they were shot and their bodies thrown into the water. Hers wasn't found for months. And here I was, cruising by the very spot on the bridge, maybe.

Manfred had argued that the Weimar Republic was the reason people lost faith in the Weimar Republic. "Jed, *Mann*, who ordered the murders of Liebknecht and Red Lady Luxemburg?"

My books had come. Consequently, I'd not read a newspaper, not so much as the *Herald Tribune*. It was days after the story was published that I saw Rosen-Montag's photograph in *Die Tageszeitung*—"Die Taz, bitte," as I, an insider, liked to hear myself say before my footsteps took off. His head was big and the story was small, because several key players I'd never heard of hadn't much to say about his foundation chairman's threat to sue the city.

.

And they were ordered to make bricks, and each one to write his name upon his brick. Twelve wouldn't get with the program and one of them wouldn't go along with their escape plan, saying that wild animals might as well be in the mountains for all the good running from the city would do. And when Nimrod's people came to throw him into the limekiln, an earthquake happened. Fire consumed everyone around him but left him unmolested.

■

The summer after I graduated from high school, I was in the 57th Street Bookstore. I couldn't have been accepted into the University of Chicago, but I was pretending to myself, and maybe to others, that I was an incoming freshman. I recognized the title, *The Torture Doctor.* Someone at the *Eagle* lost her copy of the bestseller about an evil pharmacist who picked up women at the Columbian Exposition and killed them. Cello's father hadn't had an episode in a while, but I guessed that he had purloined it. When I realized what the book that Ralston Jr. had was about, I told Dad.

He didn't answer when I said, so grown up, that this was not what that man should be studying. Was it true the FBI asked Cello's father to wear a wire, taking advantage of someone known to be off his rocker? I couldn't blame Aunt Gloria, I said, for trying to get away from that nut job, even though that Jewish steelyard owner over there in Indiana was married.

Instead, Dad laid hold of me. My father seized me and twisted my wrist as he squeezed me in the direction of his office door. He was so hot and filled with blood he couldn't risk speech. He didn't slam the door. He closed it. After he pushed me into the corridor. That was his head that he leaned for some time against the opaque glass.

The evil pharmacist took his unsuspecting women to his combination office/hotel in Englewood. He'd used different builders in order to hide his overall design. He locked his victims in soundproof rooms that had no windows and gassed them. He sent the bodies down a chute to the basement and reduced them to skeletons, which he then sold to medical schools. They don't know how many he killed, maybe two hundred, but not all in Chicago.

Numbers of people who came to the World's Fair never went home. They disappeared, started over somewhere else.

■

Dram came to see me at the café. I had a friend. He bowed slightly toward Lotte and then sat at the bar. I didn't mind if he smoked and it went without saying that I would not tell Cello of our conversation. No one else was around. He said he wanted to explain the sudden cancellation of their American Thanksgiving. She found a reason every Thanksgiving to cancel her plan to gather up strays like me. Cello had made him get rid of the nanny. I put more paraffin into the café stove to get the coals roaring.

"She accused me of having a thing with her." In English, we were family. "Now she accuses me of having had a thing *for* her." He swirled the dregs of his cup and swallowed quickly. "That I wanted to." He went to the door with his cigarette and peered out at the yellow street. It was cold. He came back. His coat collar was trimmed in black velvet. His ties that he was so indifferent to were silk, gifts from his wife or his mother, her friends, his sisters, the women in his office.

Lotte adjusted her ears under her thin pageboy. Otherwise, she knew how to sit absolutely still for the camera.

Dram said he didn't have to tell me his position or the

company's on taking advantage of women in his employ. But
the young lady's family rode with the West Kent Hunt and she
wanted to be a chef. "Stupidly, I fucked her. I am the cliché."
Dragon amounts of smoke rushed from his nostrils.

"Lie."

"You have seen her. I am fucking her at present. We meet
at my sister's apartment now that she is at Berkeley."

"Continue to lie to her," I said in German.

So be it, I said to myself, and that night explained to Duallo
that I had a Chicago-related work appointment I'd nearly forgot. I changed my clothes to make it look good and went to
stake out Manfred's pub in Schöneberg. He didn't come, but
Bags did.

•

"Don't turn it loose, because it's a motherfucker," James
Brown instructed the band.

•

A lot of people were in the city to get lost. "I've been away,
cocksucker," Bags said. He was hooded up, as for a polar ex-
pedition.

I knew what that meant. I just wanted to know where and
for what reason. I didn't want him to share a taxi with me back
to the Co-op. It was not because he didn't know where Afer
was. It was because I was going to have to lose him before I
dipped into my room, where trusting Duallo waited. I told
Bags I'd had a work-related appointment before I ran into him.
Bags did not have me on his mind.

He knocked past the bicycles and grunted the whole way
up to the fifth floor. He could yell. Afer and his girlfriend both
came, undressed, into the hall. Clearly, that wasn't news to Bags,
but I was turned on. The young Germans on our floor had
plastered homemade nonsense posters everywhere and scrib-
bled with Magic Marker when off their heads.

"Why would you do me like this?" He was yelling at Afer. "Go home."

"Where's that at?"

The house leader was beside us in no time. We'd have to respect the rules. Afer's girlfriend did not want Bags inside and the café was closed. Bags refused to leave and he would not be quiet either. The hall was icy. I just stood there, wondering what had happened between them. The house leader frowned at the posters. Everything was messed up, Bags repeated while we waited for Afer to get dressed. They went out after the house leader had blocked their exit and been firm with them again. Duallo was in my room, unaware, on his earphones. The stove he'd kept lit was wonderful.

I thought it was because love on Dad's scale was hard, but it was probably because mine was the higher make-believe. I could not project a future for us, what we would do or go on doing. Duallo let me rest his head on my chest for a second, that blossomy smell coming up from his skin, his thick cap of hair. I let him down every day, because I thought of him as African, not European. I felt in him the touch of his grandmother's Ngala, the creator of the world. But it was easier to spot what was going wrong than it was to admit how hard I was trying to stay with the feeling, to make it real.

If it doesn't go away, it multiplies in some fashion, spreads in some biological manner, becomes overarching context, the lid you no longer see it's so prevalent in the sky of your head. But my desires were contradicted by my circumstances. Besides, the parent gets hurt; the lover finds himself doing hard time. It is not possible that an unconditional love does not show the scars as it ages, become less quick in the joints, a more costly show to run. The parent or the lover has no choice but to pass on some of his or her costs to the loved one, unspecified amounts deducted without warning from the loved one's freedom account, which is therefore perpetually in danger of falling into arrears.

Where I lived, how I sat around were not conducive to adult life. Duallo smoked about once a month. I couldn't. I liked his books and I liked the untouched blue pouch of cigarette tobacco spilling out onto the tray on the floor next to that futon beginning to split that I hadn't thrown out. I knew not to tell him too much.

I'd heard that there was a price, and I couldn't wait for the exquisite piercings. I would have talked to anyone about my fear of the pain, except everyone would say that I must have known that it was the pain I'd been after all along. My inability to relax into being with Duallo was just excitement, anticipation of the blow. I'm about to get hurt. I'm about to come. I wanted to say that that wasn't me.

•

Frederick Douglass said that slaveholders were most anxious for free black men to leave the country, but he wanted these slaveholders to know that he was not disposed to leave, that he had been with them, was still with them, and would be with them to the end.

•

They settled in to see *Out of Rosenheim*. Father Paul had seen it before and loved it. I didn't like the way Hayden detached me from Father Paul and Duallo, who seemed happy enough to hear that hilltop Austrian accent. I wasn't really paying attention to what Hayden was saying about a crate of antique army gear, a present for Cello. He said something about that little black boy in the film putting the accent on the second note of every bar in the Bach piece that he was shown practicing throughout the film and then repeated the Cello story.

They were supposed to play four hands, but of course she changed her mind, so Hayden was there when a shipper from Oxfordshire announced himself. Two men brought up in the elevator and unpacked for her two teak folding chairs, a teak games table, ivory-handle cutlery for two, two brass traveling candlesticks, two round leather cases lined with cork, two hinged sandwich cases, a leather cigarette case, and a decanter set.

Hayden was saying how at first Cello was unimpressed by Dram's way of telling her that he and she would be leaving the children and getting away to Sri Lanka for New Year's. But then the British military campaign furniture turned out to be a birthday present from Rosen-Montag, only just now reaching her.

"Child, I thought she was going to scream. 'Help me hide this, Ethel. Ricky will be home any minute.'"

I was not going to laugh with him at her expense. After all, she wasn't the one encouraging her hot boyfriend to befriend my hot boyfriend and he wasn't the friend I could tell what a mess I was. Nevertheless, she couldn't have a drama going on, not in the middle of mine. Hayden said she left the invoice and Rosen-Montag's innuendo-free message—he peeked—on top of the games table. I'd been right in my suspicion that he'd been fishing, that he wasn't sure.

Mom practically told me to mind my own business when I asked if Cello had said anything to her about how things were with Dram. He hadn't come back to the café and that was for the best, lonely though I still was, and eager as I was to be a gender Uncle Tom, the kind of gay man to sell out a straight woman to her straight man in the name of male solidarity.

"You'll miss the beautiful sunsets, but you'll always have turnips," Dad said when I couldn't get a date to my junior prom.

•

I was not going to Chicago for Christmas and Duallo wasn't going to Paris. Though he wanted to go away with me, I was struggling to trust the Isherwood promises that Berlin was keeping with me. I sure as hell was not going to accept the mountains with Hayden and Father Paul and his parents and grandmother and sister and brother-in-law and little nephew. I made Duallo coffee and brought up Greece or Tunisia. Moscow was not the answer I was expecting. I'd never gone anywhere from Berlin, except back to Chicago.

Bags came in not long after Lotte. I wasn't used to seeing him in the morning, dark, wide, and tense. He was staying in his painter friend's storage closet on Moritzplatz. His old lady had put him out. There was no stove, but he needed to be alone. Anywhere else he could have crashed would have been a story. Eventually she would get over his having been in detention. He had got over it.

Duallo and I never made a fuss of goodbye. *Plus tard*, he'd say, and reach for his book bag. *Plus tard*, I'd answer, cool as all get-out.

Afer had a gig in Amsterdam. Lotte, over by the window, wasn't talking yet. Bags downed his coffee. It was not about the child. As far as I could tell, Afer's girlfriend left the child with its grandmother and clothes she'd lost interest in. I didn't ask how much he'd seen of his baby daughter. I understood what it was to be a black man doing the best he could, even though it was my fondness for dubbed thrillers that filled in the information I could not hear through the walls on the fifth floor.

Because it was cold and silent, the kind of Berlin morning when you realized just how far from where you came from and on your own you were deep down, I got Bags to tell me most of the story. They'd not picked him up with the keys on him. He'd flushed the luggage claim slip. Nothing had felt right that day and he didn't go for the car at the Frankfurt airport. But they must have been waiting for him, because they picked him up anyway when he left the terminal. They detained him and lost him for some time on purpose before they questioned him about drug smuggling and former or current U.S. Army personnel.

Things had not been cool with Afer, because his people had lost money. Neither of us named Odell and Zippi. When they cut Bags loose, he had to get out of the country for a while. He headed upstairs to have his argument with Afer's girlfriend.

I hadn't seen a thriller since I met Duallo. I took him to the art cinema and to hear jazz and the opera, because I wanted him to have a certain impression of the culture I was into. He was into David Bowie.

"I used to be."

"Essaie une autre fois."

·

We'd been in Schöneberg at a hip agency, finishing up on getting our visas for Moscow. Everything had been nail-biting and I remembered why I never went anywhere. But Duallo paid close attention to what was said. Then we ran into Bags and Afer at Europa Center buying traveler's checks as well. Bags said that everybody was tightening up on how to get the fuck out of Dodge.

I wouldn't let Duallo walk to the Techno Institut. The three of us escorted him to a taxi rank and I went with Bags and Afer to the ChiChi. It was a tradition. I was getting out of Dodge. I had our tickets in my breast pocket.

I also had a letter. It had come two days before. I was carrying it around. I never got letters. I never wrote letters. Alma warned me that she never wrote letters. This letter had been forwarded to me. Mom had my address, but she'd sent this letter in care of Cello. That was Dram's handwriting on the outer envelope. I'd not noticed it on the mail table. I never looked at the mail table. Mom had stopped forwarding my alumni newsletter and subscription renewal notices because I'd moved around so much.

The letter in my breast pocket came from Manfred, written from his *Schloss*. He said he wasn't sure where I was. He said he had been back. Had I not also returned to Lessingsdorf before the legions of destruction reached the village? We could be proud of the conversions, and why not accept what had become of Rosen-Montag's fantasy on a mud pile? So that *had* been his Deux Chevaux. His letter began, "My Darling Doughnut . . ."—our old joke, the literal translation of Kennedy's famous line about his being a Berliner.

Zippi hugged us. Odell gave us the black man's nod and pointed the remote. The ChiChi was a smoky murmur. It was going to be hard to find somewhere in Berlin where people were not talking about the Pan Am bombing over Lockerbie. The attack brought people in the ChiChi closer together and while they bonded I did not smoke or toke or drink. I'd not seen footage of the crash debris before. I was nervous that some real feeling might get up and menace me in my cage, my isolation.

Around midnight, Odell wanted to show off his new automobile, a 1933 Mercedes sedan with places for tires on either side of the engine. This one had no spare tires. It was in hilariously battered shape. A hole in the rear floor let winter swoosh along with us. Odell gave us a foul-smelling-gasoline ride to Potsdamerplatz. Zippi's dark eye makeup ran with anger when he left her. Big Dash stood at her side, fanning.

I didn't lose it too much when the three of them talked openly about a good deal coming that they wanted to get in on with these Yugoslavs. They knew me as a fool who threw money around. Bags rested a sexy hand on my shoulder. AA cautions us not to people-please, not to say yes to people just to get them to like us. He said they weren't talking about any crazy Russians. They themselves were not crazy. I decided that they bought traveler's checks for lots of reasons. I liked being taken for a ride, but I had not in the hours I'd been with them said much and that felt like power.

Duallo wasn't back yet, because the message was still taped to my door, a message from Cello for me to call Solomon. Urgent.

Solomon and Francesca were already in Chicago with Mom. Dad had had a heart attack.

NINE

The prisoner, a revolutionary who loved pensive weather, said in a letter written in December 1917, her third Christmas under lock and key, that she lay awake at night, pondering why it was that she was in a state of joyful intoxication. She had no cause to be, entombed in the silence of her cell, her mattress hard as stone. The gravel beneath the guard's boots made a hopeless sound, she said.

Yet her heart beat with joy, as though she were moving in sunshine across a meadow. Enveloped in the manifold wrappings of unfreedom, she said she still smiled at life. The darkness of night was beautiful, if she looked at it in the right way. Even the heavy tread of the guard was a song to life, if she let herself have the ears to hear it.

Wagons of bloodstained tunics arrived in the prison courtyard for the women to mend and send back to the army. One day a wagon appeared, drawn by buffaloes instead of horses. They were trophies from Rumania, to be worked to death. A soldier beat them with the butt end of his whip. While the wagon was unloaded, the beasts stood still. She looked into the eyes of the buffalo that was bleeding, the expression in its eyes like that of a child who has been thrashed but does not know why or how to escape the ill-treatment.

She was freezing and she said that spring was the only thing she never got tired of. A Jewess who spoke Polish, not Yiddish, when growing up, denied magna cum laude in Zurich because that was considered too much for a girl, she shared in her letter to her friend the inexhaustible bliss of remembering the wind through the rocks on Corsica or the gloaming at Whitsuntide in her garden in Berlin. She asked about the berry picking in Steglitz, her South End of town.

She'd called them on the telephone at ten in the morning once to come to the Botanical Garden to hear the nightingale. She understood, as her mother believed King Solomon did also, the language of birds, the shades of meanings conveyed by their different tones. She hoped to die in the service of her principles, but her true self belonged more to her tomtits than it did to her comrades. As much as she loved birdsong, she did not look to nature as a refuge. She suffered at its cruelties. Meanwhile, the disappearance of songbirds in Germany because of the destruction of their habitats made her think of the vanquished Red Indians in North America.

The worse the news, the more tranquil she became, hearing the throaty rooks in the evening, observing them full of grave importance on their homeward path. Surrounded by brick, she liked to recall her love for the songs of Hugo Wolf and how they had laughed in the Café Fürstenhof the morning Karl was arrested. The sky was so interesting. She said people ought not to fret about morality. If they paid attention to the sublime indifference of the sky they could not fail to do good.

·

There was no drama. The morning I landed at Tegel, Duallo had been back in classes for a while, in the beaver skin hat that— he said he couldn't wait to tell me how—became his in Moscow, in what was called Little Harlem, the few blocks where black youth were tolerated near Patrice Lumumba University.

The house leader, who had survived a coup, was firm with

me about my emergency, Co-op rules, Duallo's access to my room, his having guests. Incredibly, the leader handed me written criticism from other Co-op members. The Germans, I couldn't wait to say to Bags. I segregated myself, he summarized for me, and did not help in any political action or hunger strike in support of South Africa. I especially minded criticism of my handling of the café. They wanted to say that I was too friendly, that I did not respect the Berlin style of not giving a shit who had just entered the establishment. Instead, they said that I put my personal life ahead of cleaning the place or keeping track of what needed to be ordered.

And before I could explode, he embraced me and said to the wall behind my shoulder that they were relieved my father had recovered. Duallo had kept them informed. The house leader shook my hand and said yes, and that was the delicate matter. He did not believe Duallo had made an accurate account of his use of the café telephone. The last bill was historic.

I was on Duallo's side. The young Germans from the fifth floor who were covering my shift had friends in Iceland, I pointed out. He said that the calls in question were mostly to Paris, Austria, and the USA, not Reykjavik. I'd never seen an itemized phone bill in West Berlin. I said I would make good any sum immediately, indignant as I was for Duallo's honor and his right to benefit as my boyfriend from my Co-op membership. I was also thinking of the generous supply of prepaid phone cards I'd left him.

The first thing I had to do once I'd taken my bags upstairs was to return and pick up the café phone. I'd promised Mom I would call as soon as I got back. The stairs were cold and lined with extra junk, and my room was like that of a boy who's used to having either his mother or the help to clean up, someone who simply hasn't noticed the zoo, someone confident from experience that someone else will come along who won't accept it and the zoo will be flushed out. German clean was something I could achieve. The stove in my room had not been emptied in some time.

To look down at your father in his hospital bed sets off a wavering inside you. Your footing becomes insecure and you have to make an effort to keep your balance. Everyone has been dreading your arrival because of your history of inappropriate, inopportune displays, but that inclination leaves you once his face has confirmed for you your place in the great chain of being—soon enough after his. The grimace lets you know that you have been a weight. The momentary imbalance by the hospital bedside was you learning in an instant how to stand on your own, and it was uncomfortable at first, like any correction of posture.

He was the wrong color and texture and temperature. Solomon and Francesca were standing on one side of him, I was at the foot of the bed, and Mom was seated on the other side, stroking his hand as machines chirruped. He was asleep a lot of the time. Then he would come to and float for too long, ending on, "You went into labor with Jed when we were out at *Peyton Place.*"

"No, it was *Beginning of the End*. They were going to nuke Chicago."

"What a downer for everyone. We used to call you Bugs."

And we'd crack up, mostly because there was nothing else to do, perched around my father's sad allotment of hospital bed, plastic tray, and synthetic curtain.

Solomon had come to O'Hare to get me, leaving Francesca with Mom at the Med Center. He said Mom was very shaken up, just from having heard Dad fall in the kitchen. Imagine if he'd had his heart attack in the basement. But then she is never someplace else, somewhere he isn't, not anymore. Maybe when we were kids, back when women didn't express themselves and she did. I could tell that Solomon was getting a lot from Francesca's memories of her American Studies electives. He'd said

nothing about praying for Dad. Mom would have been relieved. Our names didn't come from the Bible; they came from
Black Reconstruction.

On my way out of the terminal, I saw a white guy in shirt
and tie waiting in line at a newsstand. The young cashier was
so busy she didn't see him look around and then just wander
off with the magazine and nuts, called after by no one. From
the escalator a few yards back, I'd seen as I descended a black
kid in a baseball cap snatch the plastic cup of tips from the
counter of a doughnut concession. Solomon would not have
believed me, so I didn't bother.

•

It was never less than wondrous that he consented. I'd just
pulled off the condom, making it snap, when they knocked. If
they weren't going to wait down in the café, then I was certainly going to take my time getting dressed before I let Duallo
unlock the door. He said it would be unfriendly to send them
away. He'd run out of his mother's blossomy lotion. It was my
first night back.

Hayden and Father Paul had looked after Duallo while I was
away, and now there was a gay café in Kreuzberg, on Oranienstrasse, where he was comfortable. He liked that there weren't
just bar stools, there were sofas, too. Hayden had been too
modest in front of me about his French and Duallo and Father
Paul had built up more German between them. I couldn't help
myself and I kept my voice to a low register because Hayden was
in the vicinity. But West Berlin was mine to give.

I took the four of us to an elegant Italian restaurant in
Schöneberg, on a side street of leather bars and back rooms
smelling of poppers. The three of them had tall white beers and
I a small coffee in a crowded gay bar not far away. It was loud
with hits from ten years before. I bopped through the noise
and didn't join in the conversation. It was enough that while
Duallo listened he now and then let my hand seek his.

I'd not been by the Mercedes-Benz star as yet. Hayden found it ridiculous that I paid obeisance to a corporate emblem, to a company that had a far from blameless war record. I asked him what German company didn't and knowing what we knew, why then had we come to Berlin. That was a ritual I should have confessed to Duallo when we were alone.

I led the way to the ChiChi. There'd been a Budapesterstrasse, a Budapest Street, over in what was now East Berlin that they'd changed the name of, to Friedrich Ebert Street, in honor of the first president of the Weimar Republic. But nobody wanted to offend Hungary, so a stretch of the Ku'damm was renamed Budapest Street.

Hayden told me to get them out of Mr. Rogers's neighborhood and in front of several drinks. It was cold.

Ebert ordered the suppression of the Spartacist uprising. Rosa Luxemburg stepped onto the podium on November 9, 1918, the day after she walked out of prison, and never saw another spring.

It was late, but I could hear the alcoholics screaming on the other side of the door, the sign that the bar was peaking, riding that night wave. Zippi and Odell were making out, making up for whatever quarrel they'd had earlier. They acknowledged Big Dash's applause. Afer gave his girlfriend a peck and Bags lit his old lady's cigarette for her, she who seldom left her Schöneberg. You are leaving the American sector. Dishes of little heart-shaped chocolates in different-colored tinfoil had been placed around the smoky, twinkling bar.

Zippi shrugged like she didn't know what he was talking about when show-off Hayden said that the Jewish Valentine's Day was in the summer, was it not.

And that was *my* fifty-mark note on the bar, luxurious though Hayden looked in his sweater. But we were all wearing beautiful sweaters. I saw Duallo look at himself in his present in the mirror behind the bottles. It had turned back into a great day.

Zippi went on tiptoe to give me kisses on both cheeks and a smile that said she was glad I'd figured out that these things didn't have to be complicated. She had a special smile for Duallo, and one for Father Paul, too, and the wrinkles at the edges of her eyes, emerging from pitch-dark eyeliner, affected me somehow.

I didn't go into the kitchen with Bags, his old lady, and Zippi, because Hayden wouldn't, he who never touched the stuff and made Father Paul say that he, too, was happy with his tall white beer that Manfred had also liked.

And when they came back to the bar, giggling and terribly pleased with themselves, I realized that that evening was the first time I'd touched Duallo in public since the day we met. I rubbed his back and he swayed. He conversed with Bags's old lady, who was pretty funny in her angry German confrontational way, while I stood over him, big-chested and prepared to retire the legends I'd twisted myself over about the romance of pain and the agony that was true love. It didn't have to be that way to be real.

Hayden could have got a light from the person he bummed the cigarette from, but he had to come back over and lean between Duallo and Bags's old lady and borrow her lighter, letting his left hand rest on the very patch of beautiful black boy back where I'd just had my right hand.

◆

For Mom, the catastrophic-enough event was followed by several aftershocks of the heart, among them her apparent humiliation at having to make her peace with us—Solomon, Francesca, and me—because we'd be all she had should anything ever happen to Dad for good. She said some people are alone even though they're married, but she hadn't been one of them. Dad was her soul mate and if Francesca was that for Solomon, then

she as a mother could not ask for more of her daughter-in-law.
Or of anyone I chose to care about, she added.

•

"This is your home," Mom would say to Rhonda and Ronald
when they came through the door again with empty Flint-
stones lunch boxes and their crayons in one of their mother's
discarded traveling cases. Cello sometimes broke down when
she finished her practice for the evening. Mom would sit next
to her in the kitchen.

Aunt Loretta's family considered itself much too good for
Uncle Ralston and she agreed. She never took in her grandchildren, though she had all those bedrooms. Her husband was
too deep into himself as well to offer them anything. He
didn't want them underfoot, for all his dreams of a great black
dynasty bursting forth from his deadness. It was bad enough
that often he had to throw out his own son. Old Man Shay
complained about the cost of his grandchildren's education.

When Dad knew whom Aunt Gloria was really trying to
get away from and why he didn't help her, I didn't ask.

•

Dad's favorite thing was to remember Uncle Ralston's inani-
ties. The EKG machine blinked and he was entertained by our
versions of family meetings on South Parkway. It was a hoot
how much Uncle Ralston disliked Mexicans, Vietnamese, Indians, any new group. To him, race in America was a story between white and black, and anything else was yet more change
for the worse.

"What a bummer for everyone," Dad said, fiddling his paper
hospital bracelet.

Mom said that during the World's Fair of 1893, one black
woman hated Aunt Jemima so much she went on a two-month
rampage, brutally assaulting white men at night.

■

Bags's old lady smoked Rothmans Menthols, and I bummed one. Just like that.

"When did you again?" Duallo breathed. He broke away from my kiss. That was going too far, though we were at the ChiChi, where a cellulite-smacking contest was taking place among some crones at Odell's end of the bar. I didn't look to see what Hayden might have seen.

They'd been dancing for two days, Zippi sighed.

■

In the hospital corridor, Solomon said if I was going to be related to him, then I had to lose the beard. The kid brother, I let him drop me at a barber's. I hadn't realized how shaggy I'd got. A black barbershop in Chicago was the place to go if you wanted to continue to taste ashes from the presidential election.

A haircut was not easy for a black man to find in Berlin. It was roulette. From shop to shop, the same short guy in a white jacket with the same scissors would hunch his shoulders, as if to say he had no idea what to do with you. Then you'd find someone who was willing to give it a shot, so long as you understood that he—one time it was she—had never cut black hair before.

The barbers who frowned you out the door without speaking were kinsmen of the old woman who said on the street to a friend of Bags's old lady, a white girl with her brown baby in her arms, "At least if it were a dog it could be put down." They still lived in Berlin, those types, sitting behind you upstairs on the bus.

Of course I had done the simple thing of asking another black man where he had his hair cut. Duallo ignored my hint that I hang out with him the next time he was seeing his friend who had the girlfriend who had clippers and hooked everybody up, even cut designs into their hair. That was his black Frenchman's Africa life. Hayden sent me to his Kreuzberg barber. You had to holler up at his window or phone from a pub. A creamy German guy with *Angel on the Rock* curls sat you at his cluttered mirror, his bed unmade no matter the hour, his box of clippers and attachments lost, his room filthy with the sticky sweet aroma of just-fucked ass.

Whatever had happened in the meeting with Dad's cardiologist, by the time I got back to the hospital cafeteria with my beard merely trimmed, Mom said she had decided that she would be fine whenever that was going to be required of her, so we never had to fear that she would become a problem for us ever. She'd watched her mother live alone her whole life and she knew how to do it, what it looked like, and maybe her mother hadn't been wrong with her all-or-nothing, love-me-or-leave-me attitude.

Upstairs, Solomon batted away the hand I was protecting my face with. "Who are you trying to be?"

"Let your reading advance your facial hair," Dad, awake, rasped from his side of the room.

■

I thought the noise in the ChiChi was the reason we couldn't hear what was being said on the television news report. But Odell said it was CNN, not just a new station, but a new concept, uninterrupted news footage from around the world, day and night. There was no audio commentary. A ticker tape of captions concerning "The Rushdie Affair" ran along the bottom of the large screen.

Bags returned and said, yes, that book that made fun of that piece of ayatollah who took our people hostage. They had just put a price on the writer's head. From where I stood, I could see images of fires and mobs, but I wasn't sure if they were pictures from Islamabad or Bradford, England.

The bar was wild with St. Valentine's Day. Odell stood like Neptune in his stormy sea, entranced by his Schaub television. We'd never seen a picture that clear, he informed everyone. It was because of that satellite dish, which he could have installed himself. A few people would get up, stand next to Odell, watch for a while, and then resume their places. Zippi liked him preoccupied. I was not going to leave Duallo, who was happy listening to Bags's old lady explain that although she was glad the Soviet Union hadn't won last year, she was truly sick of the Dutch thinking they had the greatest captain in the world.

Father Paul snatched Duallo's beaver skin hat from where he'd tucked it at his feet, not trusting the rack by the door. He was outside with it, Duallo behind him, and something happened in my stomach when Hayden, grinning, chased after them.

I was stuck: either the cool father staying inside or running in the cold. When I at last decided to go out and put a stop to the game, they were coming back in. The cold on their clothes was an affront, an experience I did not share. Duallo petted his hat. It was a cat and made purring noises. Father Paul did it, too.

Hayden said that Duallo was proud of that hat because he won it arm wrestling in Moscow.

That story Duallo should have told me when we were alone.

■

Mom refused to take in Ralston Jr. and Aunt Gloria. Cello and her brother and sister knew the drill and were on their way upstairs. Dad told Solomon to go back to bed, too, but since he'd turned twelve Solomon was allowed to give Dad an incredulous you're-joking face, and Dad would let his little man get away with everything.

Aunt Gloria looked so pathetic, her wig in curlers, heading back into the night with her suitcase. Dad took her and Ralston Jr. both to South Parkway and left Uncle Ralston no choice. While Uncle Ralston was putting the chain on the front door, Dad used his keys to unlock the back door. Aunt Loretta hardly left her room once her mad son and unhappy daughter-in-law turned up. Dad got a succession of janitors to move in. Mrs. Williams cooked and the asylum was complete. Ralston Jr. and Aunt Gloria lived mostly with his parents for the next twenty years.

Mom was strict about not discussing in front of Cello, Rhonda, or Ronald what we knew would upset them. But the morning after they'd come, smelling of smoke and hysteria, clutching pillowcases of beloved, petty possessions, nobody had to say anything to me. I could read minds that breakfast.

"So you're sure Ralston set fire to the apartment on purpose," Francesca said, standing by Dad's bed.

Mom and Dad exchanged a look and began to play thumbs.

I explained to her that the riot in Newark that summer excited Ralston Jr. Solomon asked me what made me think I could say that, given that I was ten years old in the Summer of Love. He and his bride were healthy and camera-ready. I wanted to lie, to bring in the perverse, to say that Ralston Jr. used to beat off to the *CBS Evening News*, that Solomon hadn't been at the *Eagle* those miserable summers. But I was officially as well fucked as my older brother and dropped my voice to say, "Think about it."

■

The last syllable was scarcely out of his mouth when his dearest little friend got up and chose Ascyltus as his lover. Thunderstruck by this verdict, he fell on the bed. He would have laid violent hands on himself, like an executioner, if he hadn't begrudged his rival that victory.

.

They were disappointed in my books, Duallo and Uwe. To which era did I belong? I looked over my shoulder in the Co-op bookstore when I was reading Fanon's case study from 1932 about the woman from Madagascar who only wanted a relationship with a white man. I had not wanted to be in West Berlin with those sorts of books and questions.

Maybe that was why I really lost it in a house meeting about the bookstore selling Eldridge Cleaver's *Soul on Ice*, which to them was a classic from the black American revolution of the 1960s but to me had nasty things to say about gay black men wanting to have babies by white men and the rape of white women as Cleaver's personal retribution for the Vietnam War.

One woman framed the argument that Cleaver was not, as an oppressed man, an evolved man. I shot Afer a look that he didn't want to acknowledge but couldn't help but agree with. And this was the woman who, I heard, had decreed that she would not allow the Co-op to stock the memoirs of working-class-traitor terrorists or waifs who hung around Bahnhof Zoo, overdosed, survived, and then starred in films about their self-destruction.

I didn't hear Lucky rise to introduce his motion. He wanted to address the subject of blasphemy and that book.

The house leader said we had no copies to sell and no plans to order copies from the London publishers. The Co-op would wait for the German translation.

The mother of his children went back to her oven. A few others made to leave the crowded café. I had to laugh at Co-op members like Afer, who enjoyed telling the stray customers we got in that part of town at that hour that we were closed.

Lucky had tried some of us already, deploring news of book-store bombings in California while saying that it was very human that faith, when insulted, moved the faithful to act in defense of faith. I hadn't thought of Lucky as Muslim or in the least observant. He hadn't kept Ramadan last year, as far as I could tell.

I told Lucky that maybe I hadn't made a motion, but I still had the floor. The house leader backed me up.

A girl with red pigtails who could repair any bicycle brought to her said that we were not the Bundestag. She wore black boots, even in summer, had them on the back of the chair in front of her, but most emphatically was not a lesbian. I stayed clear of her. Alma told me that a while back she gave Alma a black eye when Alma said that the redhead's boyfriend was petit bourgeois, not proletarian, because his family had a butcher's shop. The redhead was saying that every time they called for a free discussion, the house leader appointed him-self police of that discussion.

I made a motion that the one copy in the original English by Eldridge Cleaver that was on sale be withdrawn and the house leader by way of restatement yelled it out for me. Duallo wasn't present, but I thought I should be doing my own yell-ing. I opened my arms wide, like Frederick Douglass, and in-toned that Cleaver once had a beautiful wife but he had become a Mormon and a Republican, signs that he had been a fraud in waiting, and Koh-op Hah-ee had to leave him behind, in the wet dust, as had his wife.

I felt some amazed eyes on me. Sometimes the house leader translated what he thought the English-shy among them had not understood fully. I waited.

Yao stood and raised his arm, stepping forward. The house leader acknowledged him. The redhead barked that he should just talk and forget recognition.

Yao asked me to have the patience to let him point out to

me that *Soul on Ice* was first published twenty years ago. He could verify for me that twenty years was a long time, because he had not seen his mother, had not been back to Ghana, in twenty years. He was reluctant to say such things to me, but we were brothers in intellectual progressiveness, which he had understood the Co-op to consider among its foundation principles. Therefore, he had to ask if Europe did not do funny things to the black man.

I'd been depressed on the fourth anniversary of my having gone into rehab. I was sober except for the return of menthol cigarettes and lukewarm coffee. In the café, I had poured the occasional late morning glass of white wine for Lotte and still not asked for its new phone number.

But I knew that after the house meeting I would be back in the kitchen with Afer and some others, then upstairs with Afer and his girlfriend, then in my room, with me, my menthol, and little mouse droppings of hash, waiting for Duallo, whom I'd not seen in three days. I'd not been to the AA meeting in Dahlem since we met.

How else, Yao continued, could I, a black man, want to ban a book written by another black man. He moved closer and was breathing hard, struggling, I feared, with his own question of identity, whether he was a healer or a basher. I didn't know how to stand. Yao placed his hands on his back and talked to me with his chin.

I did understand, did I not, that I was saying such things in Berlin, where in living memory books had been burned. Maybe an American, even an unwanted black-skinned American, held on to being an American, because for the American that rainy day always came. But for him, and for many of his brothers, their presence in West Berlin was a political solution in which the tragic personal destinies that had brought them to this city could be overcome.

I withdrew my motion. Yao got handshakes as he took his

seat, his tribal stool. My face was hot. What year of grammar school or high school had I not metaphorically pissed myself in front of the entire class. To be back in school, with those feelings, as though I'd been beamed, made me consider that maybe the AA Big Book, which I looked down on because it was not great literature, knew more than I did about alcoholism and drug addiction.

Lucky said that the arrogance of Europe belittled the beliefs of millions. I hadn't assigned religious feelings to anyone I lived with. I thought I saw homesickness in Lucky's insistence on bringing up a subject that people were allergic to, that and maybe weariness with his invisibility in West Berlin.

After the Seven Years' War, Frederick the Great, big in queer history, thought of building a mosque to encourage Turks to move to his capital, Lotte once told me. She was surprised I'd never been to Sanssouci.

Yao got to his feet again. First, Cleaver. Second, Rushdie, which he had not yet had the privilege to read. He couldn't get anyone he knew in England to mail *The Satanic Verses* to him. In Brussels they shot the one imam who respected where we lived, on a continent that should know better. The National People's Army killed its own people who tried to get over to where we were.

Members applauded and adjourned themselves. The cups were mine. Sugar and honey had been spilled everywhere. I tidied up Uwe's copies of *Afro Look*, a magazine for black Germans. No one had signed up to go with his group to a conference in Frankfurt on minorities and immigrants in the Federal Republic. This was a collective that preferred to concentrate on its war with the German Democratic Republic and much of "the international Spartacist tendency" over Liebknecht's and Luxemburg's legacy. I should have aced that part of my interview, thanks to Manfred's tirades, but the sound of his voice in my head had made me struggle.

Lucky walked out. He scooted his chair up before he left, but he definitely walked out without a word to any of us.

"Right on," I said like a fool to Yao and extended my fist for a dap, for him to tap the top of my fist with the bottom of his.

He contemplated my hand for a few seconds and then knuckled me harder on my shoulder than he needed to. Smiling.

■

Security procedures had been stepped up at the airport on the way out of Berlin and probably would be even more so at the airport when I left Chicago. Solomon and Francesca had to get back. That was understood. They had high-powered jobs, a real life together, and there was the problem that neither of them liked Greenwich Village. They'd made a mistake.

They assumed that I had nothing urgent to get back to. No one asked. I didn't say. Almost two months had gone by before Duallo at the café and I on the phone in the front hallway managed to have a conversation.

Moscow was the most exciting city he had ever been to and he wanted to go to Beijing next. He loved the statue of Pushkin and was glad he had no packs of cigarettes to give people. He had the correct pink vouchers and a view of the Kremlin, but lunch and coffee were impossible to find. Not to speak Russian tired him quickly. Two black students spoke French to him when it was clear he was not American.

Mom gave no sign after I hung up that she heard me tell Duallo I would wire funds. I was a problem solver. Dad hadn't liked the setup on the second floor and to install him in the basement had been a strain. He was the only thing we had to move and he simply walked down two flights and got into bed. I was the strain, the intruder in their basement. They had everything down there—stereo, double hot plate, refrigerator-freezer. I could see his workbench of model planes in the back room. Mom's poster-making Magic Markers would have been to the left of the door.

It was clear I was in the way, but Mom said I could be of use. I walked to the pharmacy. Mom knew that Dad wouldn't have let me touch the car. Perhaps she wanted to have a different conversation from the one we had when I came back with Dad's medicine. His prognosis was good. She told me to sit with her a minute. It was the end of his pancakes, her grill pan, their Belgian waffles.

"She's left it too long to get back with it now . . ." Mom started. She could only have been talking about Cello. Mom said that in getting the basement ready for Dad, she'd found her dissertation on Florence Beatrice Price. Mom met Mrs. Price once, when she was a music/music education student. Mom said she'd nearly fainted, to meet a black woman who wrote symphonies.

Cello had a gift for composition. Her teachers said so. It was not too late for her; she loved music so much. Mrs. Price made Mom realize how important it was to make a contribution to what you loved.

Mom had kept me from getting back to my life in Berlin in order to have a conversation about what the future held for Cello, the thirty-six-year-old mother of four who had only written music for school and had not tried to play in public for more than a decade, not since her Bicentennial Disaster, which was the reason they had fallen out with each other for so long.

Mom had said, "Your father has never been fifty-eight years old before either. It's new for him, too."

Mom said maybe I could talk to her about composition. I may not have thought so, but Cello respected my opinion.

I made no comment about the hot tub, gas heater, and pumping system they had in an alcove off the laundry room. It was like being surprised, after we left home, that they'd tried to have a fondue party, years after fondue had gone out of fashion.

Mom said that the Spirituals were not Gospel music. When Dad sat upstairs to listen to Mom play arrangements of Spirituals, I knew it was safe to leave them.

■

"With Father Paul?"
"Paul. *Cela ne l'amuse pas.*"

·

Hayden Birge was at work on an opera, *Wittgenstein in Love.* But his love story wasn't about Ludwig Wittgenstein and David Pinsent, Wittgenstein's Cambridge friend who died in World War I. They'd ended up on opposite sides. No, Hayden's gay opera was about the philosopher's brother, Rudi Wittgenstein. Three of the five Wittgenstein brothers were to commit suicide. In 1904, Rudi Wittgenstein, in his early twenties, drank milk he'd poisoned himself, in the middle of a gay bar in Berlin, in despair over a hustler, according to Hayden's plot.

·

Dram was in Dortmund. Konrad, Hildegard, and Maximilian were asleep, but Otto, a very serious boy, was still up. He said he remembered me. He'd reached the age at which he understood that he could not repeat everything he heard his parents say. He looked at me an uncomfortably long time and then went away with purposeful strides.

"*Carnaval*," Hayden called from the study with Cello's Bösendorfer.

"Schumann," Cello said and lit a scented candle, a thing I'd never seen her do, just as she never wore pants.

"Schumann. Difficult." He came back, Canova-shaped, an African American artist abroad, the kind of black man white people threw themselves on.

"No, but it's big. It's not big like the Brahms Paganini vari-ations. It feels good to play it. It's like listening to a set of vir-tuosic waltzes." And men of all races would kill for her.

I had sworn not to mention Hayden's opera in front of Cello, but I did. She gave me a look that said I was one of the glorious underbidders in life and went to check on Otto. They had a new nanny, a Russian, a fat friend of their cleaning lady's, Hayden had said, but she didn't live with them.

Hayden turned his nose up at the menthol I suavely held out to him. He crossed his legs and said I might have noticed that he was on his own, too. He said he knew where Duallo was and I didn't. Father Paul took Duallo to techno bars, but mostly he let Duallo find nirvana between his Tom of Finland cheeks.

"They found some voodoo butter and your boy started banging my boy. I even joined in once. I thought you should know."

I'd not touched Duallo in public, because I thought that would have violated his African sense of propriety. I was in no condition to handle cleverness and scorn.

I slapped that So-and-so so hard. Dad and Mom both said So-and-so when they didn't want to say either Nigger or Motherfucker.

I could see Hayden's tongue touch blood in the corner of a beautiful lip. "Bullshit." He stood and didn't let me see him cock his arm.

There were those spots telling me I was about to black out, one of which quickly became Duallo.

But it was not Duallo. I'd stayed away too long and lost him.

·

It was time. Duallo was returning to his friends at his branch of Paris Tech, where evidently he was some sort of young black hope. His mother cried when they talked, he said. He was not going for another few days, but he carefully collected his things from around my room, our room, and placed them in his duffel bag.

I'd not confronted him about Father Paul, but how could he not know I knew. I felt that I deserved extra points for my Berlin cool about the whole matter, having done the royal thing of slapping the messenger. But he did not want me to see him off at Bahnhof Zoo. He wanted us to make our farewells then and there. I pressed on him the gifts he was not putting into his duffel bag. He unpacked his book bag and took the CD player from the socket where he had been recharging it. I told him to come back for the racing bicycle. If he didn't want me to ship it, then he could take it on the train.

I was impressed by the grace and unhurriedness of his movements. He declined the two small speakers attached to the portable CD player I'd got for myself, careful not to make it better than what I had given him. He omitted to give me the time of his departure. He was perfectly composed. He would not let the kiss linger. He'd thrown out some time ago his gray shirt of little white fish leaping in the same direction. Downstairs, he let me call a taxi from the café. I'd been naked with this beautiful, gleaming boy and he with me.

One morning not long afterward, Duallo's racing bicycle was no longer in the entrance hall. He'd grown up and left town.

■

A model airplane friend of Dad's had taken him to the park to fly their model airplanes. Mom said she understood why Florence Beatrice Price, Mary Lou Williams, and Margaret Whatchamacallit Bonds ended up writing religious music. There was far too much out there for it to be just us. She said she was not aware of a particular reason she should not sometimes use only black women as examples, but I did not have to worry about her ever walking on pews.

She'd found the score of Cello's first piece of music, a clean presentation copy she'd been given. Cello was sixteen when she wrote it. The piece, for piano, was very ambitious. She'd had theory, including species counterpoint. Mom had never heard Cello play it. She said she hated to think how devout Bach probably was.

I meandered around on the other side of Zoo Station, but I couldn't get any of the loitering Turkish boys to respond. I gave up and went toward the ChiChi, singing the theme song of *Cheers* to myself.

I was singing as I stepped into the bar and raised my voice, and none of the cocktail hour crowd joined in. Zippi was setting up a white wine on the bar.

I stood where I was and said that there had been a misunderstanding. The miniature lights blazed as I pried Satan off my back. Zippi said it was just that the last time she heard me sing, I was stinking.

"West Germany pays West Africa to take its garbage," Afer said. "You will go to sea."

I was not used to Afer's style of camaraderie. He and Bags never asked me for a drink. I asked them to accept drinks from me.

"You are inviting me?" Bags crooned prissily, satirically. He'd said it in German. It had been some time since I'd cared whether someone was speaking German to me, counted up my mistakes. I'd given up, knowing what I knew in junior high school, that I was only going to be so good at German and that Tadzio was not my type.

Odell's vintage car was falling apart and he let the three of us out along the Landwehrkanal. I liked Bags taking command, lining up Afer and me behind him, moving us quietly under the trees. The real trouble was far ahead, and not wanting to get trapped, Bags led us off to the side the first chance he got. We hurried along the Wall, dropping down at Marienenplatz, and at Oranienstrasse enrolled ourselves in the mayhem, the singing, whistling, and bright camera lights.

The anticapitalist, antipolice anarchist marches had long been over, and the streets were jammed. We ambled along behind huge groups also seeking that flash point. Scores of police in visors mingled among us. I could see boys waving flares from rooftops. We walked so much Afer bought beers. Darkness fell. Bags had a joint—not hash, but marijuana. I was in Berlin, living May Day, inhaling the carbon dioxide from hundreds of cigarettes and hundreds of white boys.

The battle, when it came, was between the German police in black gear and Turkish youth in jeans, their faces wrapped in notorious scarves. The air went acrid from burning cars, from fires in the direction of Lausitzerplatz. In the tense quiet, I could hear stones raining down on pavement. A sudden warning "*Hupp!*" from someone, and Bags almost knocked me over, turning me to run from Turkish boys stretching at full speed in our direction. They swarmed past us, running from the bulls.

The thing was to keep moving, to get around the next corner, to fly past doorways, and not to get trapped between the police and the vans they maybe intended to drive stone throwers toward. And not to get involved in the barricade and bonfire making either. I let Bags turn me twice more. The police had no batons. They were not to be provoked. But word was going around that some crowds had attacked police. I started wondering how to get away.

We got into a taxi. I had to turn myself inside out to get a look at the full orange moon. Hope of my youth, where were you all this time?

Back at the Co-op, Alma was at the top of the stairs. "Dueling comes next."

■

When I was copping weak, stepped-on coke in the block down the street from the *Eagle*, Cello's daughter, Hildegard, was an infant Cello had brought back to show Mom and her dying grandmother. Cello wanted to brandish her happiness in front of women who used to feel sorry for her and the grandmother who had barely acknowledged her existence.

Cello insisted that the hospice room be disinfected before she brought her children for their black grandmother to bless. Mrs. Williams went over and supervised the extra cleaning by a furious nurse's aide. Cello reported how much it meant to her to have the chance to tell her grandmother how she'd made her feel all those years, she who had a disconcerting way of looking through her own mother, leaving her to her sister. Cello's deposition lasted for more than two hours. Aunt Loretta couldn't talk anymore. She had to lie there and take it. She was a beetle on her back and if Mrs. Williams was an ant pulling off her legs, then Cello was the meadowlark that cracked her in its beak.

■

It was Whitsuntide and Rosen-Montag had received the Schopenhauer Medal of Freedom, awarded by the institute endowed by Dram's father. In the newspaper photograph, Rosen-Montag stands between the director and the director's astonished wife, a lamb in the instant the fatal jolt is administered. Rosen-Montag is bare-chested under his fitted dinner jacket. It was a cinch he wasn't wearing underwear or socks either.

And then the next night the two of them showed up at the

café, Cello and Dram. Lucky had resigned from the Co-op. He claimed a post office box was the only thing he needed. Allah is with those who restrain themselves. He had so little to storm out with. I nearly offered him the Schwinn I'd lost interest in, though winter had got on the train out of Dodge.

Yao looked at my impeccably groomed guests and excused himself. They'd been to a private evening at the Philharmonic. Dram spoke. I owed Hayden an apology. I'd been thinking only of myself. Duallo had come to mean something to them, too.

I thought I deserved admiration I wasn't getting for my indifference to whatever treaty of promiscuity Hayden and Father Paul had signed during the international emergency of a sexually transmitted disease.

Cello was smoking; her dangerous hair wandered in a fog and on the other side of it we might happen upon the remains of a recent battlefield. West Berlin was a city where the necessities had to be imported: food, clothes, coal, but not beer. I got up when I felt like it and filled an order or two. Some Co-op members went behind the bar to help themselves. One of those spring evenings in Berlin had happened and the sounds we could hear in our isolated corner of cloud were those of transportation, cars and a bus somewhere.

Dram said that to lure a horse, I mustn't chase it.

I cursed like Odell when I came back from plunging the toilet. It was my party. Hayden, Father Paul, and I were not feeling the same and everyone knew it. Cello and Dram weren't there to commiserate with me. They had come to smile at me. They'd come to expel me from the thirty-thousand-feet club. They'd known it from the get-go: I could not fuck in their league. I got them drunk and offered to call a taxi. Dram could come back for the Mercedes.

I'd never known Cello to drink in order to blot herself out. Back in the bad times, I would have dwelled on her pride, her capacity for duplicity. I would have felt sophisticated analyzing her actions. But I was through fixating on the slave mistress and slave master instead of on myself. If Dram said he was cool to drive, who was I to argue that there was no traffic at that time of night.

•

"It's not eating. It's called quality control," Dad said.

•

The days were getting longer. In the Tiergarten, the chestnut trees were black while the sky behind them resumed that glazed blue of Nabokov's evenings. In the bushes someone played a plaintive sax. I could hear an artificial waterfall and smell the wet cement. I wanted the middle-aged black man with the middle-aged white woman whom I passed to know that I approved. I smiled at the cute black girl holding hands with the white boy whom I came across next. I was in favor of things working out for others.

The first thing I did when I got back to my room was to light a cigarette. Then I took off my shoes. Often I threw away my socks. I noticed the coffee things on the table where I'd left them the day before, intending to clean up when I got back that night. The milk was sour, my half-finished cup had gone filmy. My room made me a detective on a case, surveying how the missing person had left things.

Brown and sweaty in Central Europe, I dug in the *Schrebergärten* as though to find clues. I sat with a book in the café; I went upstairs and opened a book across my stomach. I came back to the café, usually rinsing and then taking Lotte's place when she left for the day. The nearest shops were some distance and she liked to get to them when people were going home from work, just to be among them, to remember that she was alive because she knew how to steal, pick pockets.

"Ah, the sweet Berlin air," she said. "You should have been here in 1937."

From Lotte's table, I could see the green fender with the white splotch. I crossed the street to make sure it was Manfred's Deux Chevaux parked behind the brewery. In no time, I was losing it on the other side of the building, bursting into the architecture firm on the ground floor, answering their German in English and they my German in English. Manfred, yes. A guy in a blue shirt said he bought that rickshaw from him the last time Manfred was in Berlin with his guru, N. I. Rosen-Montag.

•

I took the giant train that was passing like a chapter of history through Berlin, stopping at Bahnhof Zoo long enough to pick me up. The train was thick with black youth sleeping since Moscow and every compartment was full. I sat up in a seat the whole way to Paris. I was still young enough for the point of travel to be what I was willing to put myself through.

But I was also older. I tried to check into a fancy hotel that didn't want me. One of the reasons I lived in bohemia was that I was allowed to. The second fancy hotel let me have a small room. The trip had been so uncomfortable I deserved a nice hotel. I also wanted to make the right impression on Duallo when he came over.

He didn't come over. "*Il n'est pas ici,*" female voices at two numbers informed.

His *école* was somewhere in the north of Paris. Then I wandered through Saint-Denis. I returned to his suburb in the morning. I went up and down a market of stalls and tables, but noticed only the huge number of leather belts for sale.

I'd read about the Basilica of Saint-Denis, the oldest Gothic structure in Europe. Berlin could never have had anything like this. The Gothic cathedral was a twelfth-century rebuilding of one of Charlemagne's churches. Inside, centuries of kings and

queens. I imagined their slabs of maiden marble white leapfrog-
ging around the ambulatory. The white basilica had two towers
until lightning zapped one of them, but it seemed to be crouch-
ing on both elbows nevertheless.

The doors opened and without warning three columns of
black people started into the forecourt. The basilica was big,
the numbers of black parishioners who kept emerging said so.
Some had on the immigrant's version of Sunday best; some
women wore bright pagnes under sweaters draped across their
shoulders. The handful of priests stood out, white and white-
haired. Children stalked their own shadows between the stripes
cast by the railings. The congregation was still leaving the
basilica as those ahead spread into the street and farther market stalls, young men, too, leading a Catholic army. They were
all black, not a European war veteran among them. Out of
feudal portals, on the site of martyrdom, late twentieth-century
France was going off to lunch at *mamamuso*'s or headed to *ca-
bines* to make transcontinental calls.

I couldn't face the train and made for Charles de Gaulle. I
was a scruffy black man with little luggage asking for a one-
way ticket.

I was not paying attention. There was a mop-haired boy
in the street as the tanks rolled by.

I was so into myself that it was a day or two before I caught
up with what was happening in China. I'd not understood what
Alma and the others were talking about, but I'd not asked either.

What had been the problem? We both liked Menzel and
Fab 5 Freddy.

◼

We were downtown, looking at Christmas lights, and Dad
said Jehovah knew not to promise that parking would be any
better in the Heavenly City.

It made us nervous to go anywhere together as a family.

∎

I'd been stoned constantly since my birthday. I hung on long enough to talk to Dad and Mom. Solomon had even called— more of Francesca's influence. Then I hung up and blew my brains out on that rare commodity in Europe, marijuana. Bags was loosening me up for an Irish air cargo deal. It was working. East Germans were taking chances, escaping across the Hungarian border into Austria, and suddenly Bags indicated a willingness to have sex with my mouth again, just like that.

I turned him down. His calculation moved me. I said I'd stake him. I regretted both decisions immediately. But that was why I was in West Berlin, to make stupid decisions. I was starring in a romance or a thriller, but at the same time I could get up and turn it off at any moment. I was in control. Lament was just a social key. Some things were expected, such as being blue on the anniversary of meeting him.

If I put down my mask I could admit that I'd got what I wanted—footsteps full of meaning: b) I'd stayed away too long and lost him and a) I threw him onto my futon and spent the rest of the night trying to lose my fears.

The music of blue went well with being stoned. Odell was keeping it Curtis Mayfield/Marvin Gaye. Huey Newton's murder settled heavily over the ChiChi. The black men weren't going to give him up just because his shit had gone wrong. For them, he had been the Man when they needed him to be. Violence is not the issue, policies are, one session man said, as though quoting a line from a song.

"He was fine," Big Dash fanned. "That man was so fine."

Bags hovered close to me. Instead of letting me drop him off, he convinced me to come upstairs and hang with him and his amused old lady a hot minute. They were getting the marijuana in all the way from Washington State. I was too aroused to stay any longer.

•

There was the city of Jopp, but it was called Jaffa, after one of Noah's sons, Japhet, who founded it. And some men said that it was the oldest city in the world, for it was founded before Noah's flood.

I couldn't see how anyone ever believed what Mandeville said. It was clear to me he had never gone anywhere he claimed. Yao accepted my suggestion that the bookstore have a discount shelf, and Mandeville was my first donation. Then I got ruthless and really purged my shelves.

•

Poles and French-speaking Africans with suitcases were still turning up at the city's borders. Bags spread his arms at the Polish flea market behind the State Library, around the corner from Potsdamerplatz. He said whatever we were doing, we weren't selling Gucci shit, like the Senegalese brothers in Italy, or grandma's drawers, as these Polish families were forced to. The area looked like a refugee camp; the items for sale on blankets or on top of suitcases or just in the dirt were hopeless.

Clothes of every description, assorted bric-a-brac, radios, classical records, and not every participant would make eye contact. One man sat resolutely over his book, a large selection of toys at his plastic shoes. They'd been coming for months, the Poles, every weekend, released by Solidarity to scrabble around West Berlin because the few marks they could come up with were many zlotys back in Poland.

The sort of Germans I didn't know—people who, say, got up in the morning to go work at the facility where the Federal Republic printed its money—complained about the noise and the stench of the Poles in the neighborhood. Some Co-op members were confused by their failure to find representatives of the heroic people whom they could sponsor in Berlin.

One astute girl figured out that the Polish guys haggling

with Turkish guys over stuff unseen were Catholic, not lefties, and the Café Rosa had someone new in it at any hour of the day. The flea market commerce had become more organized and I sometimes saw at Bahnhof Zoo crews of men with duffel bags of goods for resale.

Bags said he knew an African guy with a dry-cleaning shop on Hermannplatz who had a basement full of ivory. He said he didn't like him and you could be sure he was paying off the authorities. Only fools would talk about the machine guns for sale at the Anhalter Bahnhof.

He and his old lady didn't share the same taste in films. He did his business while she went to the black-and-white French classics. One acquaintance he pointed out in the ChiChi he said did a brisk business knocking off Mercedes cars, driving them to the West, and then shipping them to the Arab world. He'd go into a Mercedes showroom somewhere, pretend he needed a new alarm system, learn how it worked, and then use that information on the street.

Bags said everybody in Berlin talked too much and all junk shops were fronts. He took me to a dirty shop off Kantstrasse. The black American proprietor was commie and crazy. He cackled at the end of every sentence. His toupee made him look like a Motown nostalgia act. He said he survived on the S and M paraphernalia he made in the back. He also sold hash, so openly that Bags said when we went back to the ChiChi that he'd wanted me to meet that a-hole because he was sure he was an informer.

Bags asked me if he should get a tattoo for his other arm and I said no, which was what his old lady had said. He didn't know why she liked performance art. He locked an arm around my neck and said I needed to get my 'fro shaped. He knew where to send me. He said African students who came over from East Berlin to shop were routinely thrown in jail and deported, not back to East Germany, but to Africa.

Odell was going through a phase, too. He played "Fight the Power" incessantly. His jazzmen protested.

Bags said just because I had refused to notice it, that didn't mean that clerks weren't watching me, too, to make sure I wasn't stealing anything. If I wasn't thinking I was special, then maybe I had made the mistake of thinking Berlin was.

•

Lotte said that even had she known who Marian Anderson was, she would not have gone to her concert in Berlin in 1934, young and starving as she, he, was then in her life of living by the church bells.

Josephine Baker was another story. Lotte knew who she was, but had been too young. Then, after the war, well, she just didn't. There was no point in her saying she'd try to come back for Alma's evening of improvised music down in ZFB. She said she'd reached the age where the arrival of midnight sent her into a tailspin if she wasn't sitting in her own chair.

Liebknecht was not Rosa's lover, Alma said, shocked. Rosa had her own lover; she would not have taken the man of a friend. She was not that kind of woman. Alma had sung at a special memorial in Zurich back in January. She wanted to write to Margarethe von Trotta and she never wrote letters. I'd not seen much of her, because Uwe followed her barefoot everywhere and was shirtless when in her rooms.

In the candlelight of the closed café, Co-op members were drinking up the stock. It had been Yao's shift, which was the only reason he had an audience. I'd heard that at first they were glad to have the wisdom of an exile from the 1960s generation. But every encounter with him was the same and after a while they didn't encourage him when he got on to his late-night subject: Africans had it worse than black Americans in West Berlin, in spite of government benefits.

He managed to be morally superior about the fatwa, too.

The Co-op didn't contest the justice of his position in relation
to their history, but once they'd acknowledged that being
German disqualified them from human feeling they clammed
up. He was at the same time telling some Co-op members that
as rebels they had a father complex about the state.

Alma said Austria had much to answer for, so it might as
well succor East Germans.

.

Outside, different kinds of lights divided in the distance. Someone in the café was remembering the Democracy Wall and it
took no time for someone else to bring up "the German
Autumn." That was the year to have been in Berlin, 1977.
Berlin was really the free city Berlin in those days. "You should
have been here in 1977."

.

Alma was gone again, on her autumn music tour, taking Uwe
with her. Lotte grieved alone in her window. My marijuana thing
had calmed down. I couldn't believe how much money I'd been
spending, including an idiotic investment in Bags. I'd slashed
at the amount of time I had to do jack with my footsteps in
Europe.

Cello forgot that Solomon no longer lived in San Francisco.
He hadn't been in the earthquake on CNN. She said she might
as well have a coffee while I was making it. Shawls and sweaters
settled around her. It meant something when she, a lady, took
a seat at a bar. Cello and I would always make up, I thought.
She didn't want a cigarette. She struck her breast and coughed,
as if to show how horrible.

Her hair was extraordinarily restless, milling from her forehead, tumbling over her formidable huntress cups. She asked
for the phone. The light caught a glistening behind her narrow
glasses. She pushed the phone away and covered herself with

her hair. Cello didn't have any friends either, not really. Where
was Hayden?

"*Was gibt's?*"

"*Wir sind verliebt. Nevin und Ich.*"

I hadn't thought to inspect her pupils.

Cello said she wanted to tell Mom, but couldn't yet. She was
leaving Dram for Rosen-Montag. She called him Nevin.

TEN

It is by this means that we remember Carthage and all the other places we have been.

·

I went around to what I knew was the right building and encountered trash on the run from the trash right behind it. A fiery bearded guy bundled up in orange dragged ahead of him long bags of what he'd been able to trap. Neither he nor the terrible smell stopped me. I was prepared to meet her remains in plastic. Nobody in the café had seen her in two weeks. One of the unlucky fisherman's nets broke and his catch of rotted matter dropped under his hurrying feet.

Another guy in orange spoke through a blue mask. The police had had to break in. A neighbor unlocked her door and shrieked in Turkish. The odor was not just two weeks old. This is what survival had led to—an avalanche of garbage. It was the most trashed place I'd ever been in. Handprints on the doorframes said where someone had made her way to bed. But the bed had disappeared, along with any table. One grubby, stained easy chair was semi-clear. She must have lived and slept in that chair.

We were standing in an accumulation of years. This was Lotte, she who doused herself every day with violet water. Whoever it was, the person ate takeaway and never threw out the containers. Plastic bags, paper bags, cardboard food containers, tin food containers, wax wrapping paper, hair-spray cans fenced in by trench works of newspaper. To finish the inventory of squalor were empty wine bottles. They were in plastic laundry baskets, lined up along the floor, nesting atop ratty, plump plastic garbage bags, on wall shelves, on their sides along the newspaper hedges.

The orange guy said that it was unbelievable how people lived, unbelievable. He pushed with a wide broom at stuck-together notepads. In the café, we didn't know Lotte's legal name.

.

In any early twentieth-century U.S. census, the mother of Christian philosophy would have been described as colored. For me, Saint Monica comes off in Saint Augustine's *Confessions* as unpleasant in her obsession to rescue her son from his lust, Roman writers, the Manichee, Milan, whatever it was he was into that kept him from being what she considered a good Catholic. Party killers come into their own in a disaster, and it was Saint Monica who, when her ship was in danger, put heart into the crew, promising them that they would safely land because she had had a vision of her son saved from error.

She held out, did not get out of her son's ear until every article of her vision had been satisfied. Little else could be expected of a parent who, as a child, was watched over by an old woman who wouldn't let her drink water between meals. Her son's chains were broken and he asked what kind of evil he had not done. Saint Monica defied the emperor's mother, then died as she was about to embark with her prize for home. Her grandson Adeodatus wailed. Saint Monica had had a drinking problem. Prayer was her AA. Still, other women couldn't understand why Saint Augustine's father hadn't beaten her, his mother, dead and hidden away from his sight.

·

It was in the vulgar press, as Cello referred to tabloid newspapers like *Freitag Inserenten*. Rosen-Montag's estranged wife tracked them to the hushed restaurant of a chic hotel by the Landwehrkanal and nearly connected with Cello's eye when she lunged to sock her. Rosen-Montag was quicker, sweeping Cello to safety in the manager's office. The hotel physician and the head of security were summoned. First Cello wanted the woman ejected from the premises so that they could dine in peace. Then she wanted her detained so that they could leave by a side door.

I recognized the picture of Cello, taken at the memorial for the victims of the La Belle disco bombing three years before. She looked amazing, her wide black hat and majestic hair framing her downcast bearing.

I did not say that she seemed proud to have been covered in the junkyard press, only because I hadn't had the time. The afternoon when I was brought in on her side, an innocent photograph had appeared in a respectable morning newspaper of Dram at a hunt in Grünewald, of all places, attired in red.

He expected her to accept his affairs, his custom of sleeping with school friends' sisters and wives. She did not want to tell me any of that. I never felt more sorry for her. She was in a black-and-white knit suit, like someone dressed for a grand jury appearance, and she sat on her hair. "As we know, the mad are completely dishonest," she said.

She was without her instruments and she was without her children and who was sufficiently intimate with her to ask if she was aware of this. She was mistress of a pink and black satin-covered sofa in a fussy suite at the Hotel Kempinski. I knew what Rosen-Montag thought of the Ku'damm version of the venerable hotel, but he made it not my place to think that she was near her children. Cello of the incredible posture sat back tall against the sofa, fighting her disliked body's need to be hunched over and hugging her elbows. She had learned to ride, for Dram, but horses bored her, as did bicycles, all buses, most trains, and anything slow, she once said.

I stood when I heard his voice in the carpeted corridor. Looking only at Cello, his intensity lighting the space around her, a fully suited Rosen-Montag, flanked by three stony-faced members of his entourage, followed by competent board-member-looking guys or attorneys. If there was going to be a drawn-out battle with his second wife over his copyrights and intellectual property, they knew who would prevail. If they were ever going to have to tell him that his second wife had committed suicide, they knew what their faces should show.

He had something he had to tell a flushed and trembling Cello and bent over the coffee table for her hands. His abdominal muscles pulled her to her feet.

I nearly burst into tears at the little-girl steps that her resistance to him made her take. The extra faces around him went somber for this genuine Helen in his life.

I could see her mouth of subdued lipstick form the question, What? and in her stretched face the hottest fright at what he was about to tell her. Her knees folded, her shining hair no comfort. Rosen-Montag did not need help. He walked her down the corridor. I heard her sad little cry of surprise.

It didn't sound as though Dram had killed the children. I stood around with the staff. We weren't speaking. Rosen-Montag took a long time coming back. He'd got her to lie down. His people disappeared into the deluxe corridor and I was alone with him for the second time in my life. We didn't sit. He didn't seem manic. In order not to call him Nevin, I called him nothing.

I could tell from my own reaction that I had not expected

him to have them on his mind. Dram, he said, was making it as hard for them as he could. For the moment, they took turns being with the children, she by day, he by night, but Dram would not let her see them alone or take them out of the apartment or let the man who would be their new *abba* accompany her. Rosen-Montag wanted her to rest before it was again her turn to put the children to bed. The youngest wasn't sleeping.

I was going to have to wait to ask after Manfred. Rosen-Montag walked me to the door. He appreciated my not telling her and he was just as glad that I hadn't known. He'd been keeping it from Cello. Finally, he'd had to tell her. Vladimir Horowitz, entirely beloved, was dead.

I told Francesca what was going on, who told Mom. What exploded between Mom and Cello that could not be taken back I did not find out. She and Cello never spoke again.

•

I didn't know when I got on the S-Bahn that November night that I had had my last conversation with my European cousin. I also didn't know what had been happening down the street, although a while back Co-op members had returned one night dejected because trains to Leipzig had been stopped.

Bags said he heard that East Germany's top dog complained to the Soviet leader that his car had no brakes and the Soviet leader told him that didn't matter because the only direction possible for him was downhill. I knew things were weird enough in East Germany and Prague for me to wonder more than I had why Bags was sending me across the border at Friedrichstrasse. I'd done unexplained currency-smuggling favors for him as casually as I'd done drugs.

I had no trouble at the station checkpoint, though the East German border police had new detection equipment the size of an iron lung. I was on my invincible American way down Unter den Linden in a taxi, a gaseous plastic Trabant, a make of the East German state auto company. I was thinking that I had to take things down a notch, known to security at the Palast Hotel as I imagined I was. I'd got across the border with newspapers I'd forgot I had on me on my first trip for Bags, and I offered them to the barman. He stashed them sharply, as he did the envelope of West German marks I'd carried to the men's room in my boot.

Again, I ordered a cocktail and brazenly didn't touch it. Jay, or J., Bags's contact, took the architectural drawings and said something about the books that were not available in the German Democratic Republic. He said that he sent his grandmother shopping for rap records when she visited West Germany.

The Palast was tawdry in its East Bloc magnificence. Tiers of bronze or copper panels made the hotel front blind, an echo of the bronze-like mirrors that covered the unfortunate People's Parliament building across Unter den Linden not far away, late Soviet Modernism of the 1970s, pretentious and off-target, buildings that inspired compassion for the lives that produced them. Lurking across the Spree was a prickly, blackened dome, the indestructible Baroque Revival monstrosity of the early twentieth-century Berlin Cathedral, which I'd never seen the inside of.

It was too cold to walk back to Friedrichstrasse and would soon be too late for the last train. Already J. or Jay was someone I would not see again, a contact in a network Bags was about to lose but would find easier to reconstruct than he expected. Half a million people had massed on the Alexanderplatz the day the pianist Cello most revered died, and I heard in the café that when the government resigned, dancing would be permitted at East German demonstrations.

I'd walked down Unter den Linden some weeks before, from the forced fun of the Palast enjoyed by very few, past the tall gates of the university where W.E.B. Du Bois had been a doctoral candidate during the rule of the last kaiser. In those days, I paid attention to the long arc of his alienation—black nationalism, Stalinism, Ghana, death. But once upon a time he could read Goethe and still go to bed happy every night.

The Neue Wache, that lucid Doric temple by Friedrich Schinkel, had become a shrine, a place of architectural pilgrimage. It was kept empty, except for an eternal flame marking the tomb of an unknown soldier. Usually, shifts of two handsome sentries did duty in the portico. On this night I found an army in front of Schinkel's guardhouse, a rehearsal for the fortieth anniversary of the founding of the German Democratic Republic.

The mournful band music and the parade of soldiers and sailors in the klieg lights were a country's funeral for itself. Two older soldiers and a young one watched from the sidelines behind me. The young one had such beautiful cider eyes under his gray helmet, with such an expression of canine suspicion in them, that I had to walk back and look at him again.

East Berlin was so underlit that I could make out the Little Dipper. It suited many like me that the unreal city was surrounded by a society with an inferiority complex. Manfred said that Rosa Luxemburg would have been as nasty as any of them had she gained power. Such people were at their best in the opposition.

The old dream's yearning had crept comfortably back into my heart. I'd not come to Berlin to be noble and gay. I wasn't there to get down with history either. I was there to let go in the shadow of either a Teuton or a Tartar thug. My hour, was it coming? I called to it: it's time, it's time.

·

"The Wall is gone." She flew back to her car. She'd been on the café phone with the rumor to a friend at a television station. I dropped the milk that I'd hiked to the gas station to buy, the only reason I was at the front door when the redhead Co-op member's sister screeched to a halt and grabbed her and the butcher's son.

It was nothing to drive fast in West Berlin, insanely, though people on the opposite corner would lecture you, the foreign pedestrian, if you crossed toward them against a red light. The redhead's sister had to reverse twice, she was so unsure which turn led where. We met heavy traffic under Speer's lamps in the Tiergarten. Dozens of incredulous others were leaving their automobiles. We took off.

I ran in the direction of the Brandenburg Gate. There weren't that many people yet. Some were walking on the Wall, bathed in light from the West, but British soldiers pulled them down. We booed. I tried to listen to what one soldier said on his walkie-talkie. The soldiers formed a line in front of the Wall. Then suddenly they withdrew. Two guys were left on the Wall. One looked like a beefy worker, the other a kid. From the eastern sector came a long shower of water, then two feeble streams. The kid drew cheers from the growing crowd when he sat down and opened an umbrella. The water hit and spun his umbrella. The worker stood with his back to the East and let the water cannon drench him. The water couldn't move him, much less knock him off, as he raised his fist to the agitated crowd.

Police, or maybe they were soldiers, idled along the sides, occasionally stepping forward to prevent someone from trying to climb up. Periodically the sweeping water pushed us back, more because it was so cold than from any force it had. People darted through puddles, chanting, "Away with the Wall," and photographers also rushed about. The observation platforms were packed. Now I couldn't see where the crowd behind me ended. Most eyes were fixed on the two men on the Wall, who were by now standing together, arm in arm, huddled against the water. I couldn't tell what was going to happen. The police did not seem clear in their minds either, other than to keep calm when they intercepted some excited person.

I saw that behind the Reichstag people were being hauled up and there were no police to stop them. I ran to the edge and raised my hands. I was lifted up and set down on the Berlin

Wall. It was at its thickest at the Brandenburg Gate. The surface was wide enough to lie across. More people were coming up. I walked toward the lights at the middle of the Wall, but it became so bright I couldn't tell where I was putting my feet. The wet made me think they'd reactivate the water. The lights turned the Wall pink and the people shiny as they ran back and forth, each person seeming to talk to himself or herself as in a dream.

The way down looked long. I expected a hard fall, but guys lowered me like a sack. I saw a woman stop in front of the white crosses behind the Reichstag. She put her hands on her cheeks. On one side, the black Spree. On the other, thin trees failing to contain a three-quarter moon. There were cyclist shapes in the dirt path and the red tips of cigarettes everywhere. The S-Bahn to Friedrichstrasse glowed orange in the night, like a UFO. Across No Man's Land, I heard chants of mass impudence.

The bullet holes in the Invalidenstrasse bridge had been filled in ages ago, but I had the time to count them. It took so long to get across and through the gates into East Berlin. People leaving West Berlin pressed against people leaving East Berlin, and on either side they passed through a gauntlet of applause. Grown men pounded on the hoods of Trabis or passed bottles up to long-coated border guards, the hated Vopos. One looked away, as if ashamed his side had lost. My dear Marcellinus, false gods cannot save a city.

I mounted a ledge next to a group of guards who waved back to people colliding with joy. I saw two women hug each other and pass on. Clap and whistle, and the occupiers would be gone. I couldn't imagine what this meant to those going in one direction, those coming out the other. I felt alone and in the way. I'd not tried to hug anyone.

In East Berlin, state-owned hotels were ominously quiet. I'd chosen to walk south from the checkpoint and approach the Brandenburg Gate from the eastern side. It took far longer than I had thought. But that was the way it usually was: me trying to get to the noise, to where the party was going on.

The Russian embassy on Unter den Linden was dark, but the one guard waved to me. It was three o'clock in the morning and the Brandenburg Gate was alive. East German police stood around, expressionless. I offered my arm to a woman and we passed through the gate. We backed up and promenaded under the quadriga one more time, stepping lively. She blew me a kiss, but I was still alone. The moon had moved higher, changing from Alpine white to Prussian yellow.

The outlines of hundreds of people showed against the lights at the Wall. For a moment I thought the water had been turned back on, but that was champagne flowing. I made a step with my hands and hoisted people up. Then I was pulled up. It was crowded, crazy with faces wandering back and forth. A festival was going on in the awakened square: people in a state of elation and disbelief. I sat, turned around, and was helped down into the sudden friendliness, the sudden youth of the West Berlin police.

•

It was odd to see East German cars parked everywhere and sometimes people in full sail in their nightclothes. Maybe not every white person I saw was German, but it felt like it. Afer and his girlfriend were kissing at a little table and the ChiChi was hosting a riot.

Big Dash was screaming: "Do you like black beer!"

The bar screamed in the awful smoke: "Yes!"

"Do you like Fassbinder!"

"Yes!" That could have been another black beer for some who were present, still smoking their terrible brand of tobacco.

"We are one planet!"

"We are one people!" the Germans screamed in correction, many in stonewashed jeans.

"Let's hear it for the monks of Neuzeller!" Big Dash also asked everyone to give it up for the Holy Roman Empire.

No one had any idea what he was trying to connect with anymore, but a huge black American comedian of some kind was what an East German might have expected to find in a little bar in the forbidden half of his capital, not far from the notorious Zoo Station and the blue windows of the twenty-four-hour porn theaters and the winking casinos. Maybe some of them had never seen a television picture with the crisp definition of Odell's, but it did not seem a surprise to East Germans in the way that it was to West Germans that they could speak their mother tongue to non-Germans.

Bags told me I had it wrong, as usual. They all thought we were GIs. He liked to cross his leg behind his other leg and kick me in the hollow of my knee. They also thought every black man in the ChiChi was a hustler, he added. How could they have, with Odell in charge. People over from the deserted German Democratic Republic drank for free, but Odell wasn't asking for identification. Therefore, his regulars kept in circulation a brandy snifter for donations to Odell's spontaneity.

Odell assumed that everyone at his party had in common victories in Europe over totalitarianism and authoritarianism, if not Berlin. In 1937 or 1938, when Der Grosser Stern was moved from the Platz der Republik to the Tiergarten, it was made even taller, so that little Goebbels, that horny toad, could not, as they said then, reach Victory's skirts. For us, that pantomime never got old, but they said no, they'd never heard that, and some faces maybe said they were thinking it was typically American to bring all that up again, especially at an unprecedented time like this. Odell poured.

He was more popular in the privacy of the kitchen, where session musicians were coming out to one another as patriots.

"I feel U.S.-grade American. Job well done."

They hadn't tensed up at my presence and they'd even

scooted over for me against a counter. Bags wouldn't let me get in on the fat joint that two musicians passed between themselves. He just reached out and put my arm down. From the way he shook his head I understood that there was something in that joint I didn't want to mess with. He said West Berlin was finished because the first thing that would happen was that the city would get regulated and what were they going to do with us, the irregulars.

"Moses, you can split. We're good now. Here, take this atom bomb with you."

Zippi was losing it. Her makeup had run completely. She looked like she had a spider tattoo on her face. She and a large woman were head-to-head over the bar. Zippi gripped the woman by her henna-soaked hair and the woman had her fingers in Zipporah's dyed black scalp. They were sobbing and understanding each other, sobbing and understanding. She had fallen out with her family not over her black lover, but because she came back to Berlin, where her family had moved to from Polish Prussia in 1910. Why was she telling strangers things she'd never told me?

My bitch of a white wine date from back-when recoiled from Big Dash's dancing a jig with her. "Am I Aunt Wanda from Uganda? She I am not."

"You say kosmonaut, I say astronaut," Big Dash belted out to two East German youths trying to help each other get to the men's room in time.

I couldn't take any more. The emissions from sputtering Trabi and Wartburg engines seemed to have become visible and were floating waist-high in the streets.

·

West Berlin had been up all night, crying, honking. Café Rosa hadn't closed. Smoke was awake, a thick band extending from ceiling to shoulder level. A radio station was interviewing thrilled brother after thrilled brother. At the same time, Stevie Wonder was singing, "They say that heaven is ten zillion light years away," and there he was, with guys from the architects' collective, that white boy in all his masculine glamor. "Jed." The god of Weimar culture pulled me down by my arms. "Jed, *Mensch*." My forehead scraped his buttons.

He drank all day long and we smoked all day long. We saw an East German family in a supermarket count the varieties of marmalade. We eavesdropped on East Germans giving one another directions and telling one another where they'd been. We smoked in front of a school on the Bundesallee with three Turkish boys. They blew into their hands or kept them tucked in their armpits. They said East German teens had beaten up a friend of theirs behind Bahnhof Zoo, warning him that from now on it was their station.

We found Trabants parked on sidewalks and locked his new BMW next to a big Russian Lada. We bought beer and *bouletten* for some men in Manfred's pub so that they wouldn't drink up their one hundred West German marks of Welcome Money. We took the U-Bahn to Kochstrasse and walked into an East Berlin of plastic bags and new down coats. At the Friedrichstrasse station, the line of people trying to leave stretched down the stairs and into the street. We went through the unguarded diplomatic exit and up to the platform. As we went over the river, a little boy with a Bon Jovi haircut said to East Berlin, "Adios."

It took a long time to get off the Freedom Train, to get down the stairs at the station, to get into the street. Stores were giving away food; some people carried big boxes of appliances. There were people everywhere, but no taxis. We talked our way in the cold back to the Co-op. The East German brand of stonewashed jeans was heartbreaking. A unified Germany was only acceptable in the context of a unified Europe. We passed out on the old futon.

Fate left us fully clothed, though Manfred got up in the night, and when he came back, he turned out the light and pulled off his boots. He groped for my right Doc Marten. He fell to a disgraceful pillow on his back, hands above his flattened hair. I waited for his toe to brush my instep, for him to cradle me to him. I waited until he sat up in the weak light, hair standing. I made coffee down the hall. I had no milk. He lit the stove, his back in his seaman's sweater carved with power and beauty.

They drilled a hole in the Wall at Potsdamerplatz. The Polish flea market had gone on as usual. The Poles had nothing, but at least they were Poles, whereas the East Germans had always been made to feel like second-class Germans, Manfred said, he who still had not really been to East Berlin.

The fortress island was overrun and my footsteps had taken me along the top of the Berlin Wall. History had freed Manfred and I'd never seen Yao so quiet. Alma and Uwe phoned from Basel. Dad called and when I called him back Mom told me not to do anything dangerous. I called Solomon myself, and it was not like him to say that I must not forget that the Germans did not like blacks and Jews.

It was a miracle, people said, as if the cobblestones had, indeed, yielded oysters, just as in Heine's poem. Something like Rhine wine washed through the gutters as emerald bottles rolled in the cold under the dancing, the *chassez-dechassez* of the very drunk. White boys in sad shoes tried to be cool at the Mercedes showroom.

"I think we shall have to send them all back, no?" the house leader said low to Yao.

After a visit to the Polish flea market's chess players, a film in Café Rosa on The Doors, another on Jimi Hendrix, and hours of tall white beers, Manfred bear-galloped on all fours onto the futon, stretching a pair of my sweatpants and winter socks. He filled and reshaped a sweatshirt and shook his clean hair from his eyes. I fished in a drawer, pretending to have just remembered something, and handed him his Zippo lighter. It was out of fluid, but he was glad to have it back. We talked about my meeting him and Rosen-Montag in Japan. We'd shared nights in German history that he'd scorched the autobahn not to miss. I could tell how much it meant to Manfred, because he turned the joint around in his teeth so that the fire was in his mouth, leaned over, closed his eyes, and sent a gust of marijuana-and-non-menthol-tobacco smoke toward my parted lips.

·

They cut the Wall at Potsdamerplatz like a loaf and artfully set the three sliced sections to one side, an open door, the pieces leaning, historic relics. Souvenir hunters, mostly Americans, worked along the Wall with hammers and chisels, some perhaps manufactured by Schuzburg Tools. East German soldiers and West Berlin police managed crowd control together. New people filed between red rails into my world. The East Bloc way of life had arrived: long lines for everything.

A great summer of the head, the postwar era, swept to its end. Playgrounds were preparing to rust behind empty barracks. It was too late for me to try for what I was never going to be, and I never bothered to work out what I would do with myself if found. Tourists poured from distant birches, coming from the future of skyscrapers and magnetic trains, and girls disappeared into the future, with plastic bags of pineapples and cosmetics, days and days of them, and then it snowed.

I missed the unification of Germany ceremonies at the Brandenburg Gate the following year, because I was in a graveyard blinking rapidly as two large coffins were lowered into the cookie-cutter earth. A prince of a man had spun out of control, killing himself and the woman he loved, who was buckled in beside him, setting off in those horrified to survive them a seeping away of life, a deterioration of soul.

•

"Under the spreading chestnut tree, I sold you, and you sold me."

•

On his twenty-fifth birthday, in 1893, Du Bois went to Potsdam for coffee and saw a pretty girl. He had candlelight in his room on the Schöneberger Ufer. The Landwehrkanal crept below him and he wrote to himself that he was a strong man, glad to be alive, rejoicing as a strong man. He'd trimmed his beard and mustache in the fashion of the crippled kaiser's and learned about Wagner. He said that the Chicago Exposition had a lot of art and not the loan of a single masterpiece from Europe.

But he knew all about the Sorrow Songs, he thought of them what Frederick Douglass knew of them, and they took him home to Negro-hating America, where the great man, Douglass, died as Du Bois was putting down his cane and taking off his German gloves. Nobody knew then that Douglass had had a German mistress for twenty-five years. Who knew that Douglass wrote poetry, he who never saw his mother's face by daylight.

When Douglass married a younger woman, this mistress, a journalist, Jewish, a refined woman, swallowed cyanide in Paris. I have sometimes wondered what Mom would have said about that.

•

So far from his Jamaica, Claude McKay had been warned in 1923 by friends in Moscow not to go back to Berlin because France was using black troops to occupy the Ruhr. Some German Americans were hysterical about the jungle threat to the white women of the precious Ruhr.

Berlin was inflation-sick and hostile, but not toward him.

The Wandervögel, German youths who were supposed to sling knapsacks over their shoulders and make harmonies in the forests, roamed the streets. McKay met a friend from his Greenwich Village days, Baroness von Freytag-Loringhoven, the poet who dressed like a parakeet and talked Dada with the leaves. She was selling newspapers, reduced to German homespun, a pitiful Frau. He asked his rich American boy to give her some dollars. The white boy liked McKay's poetry and kept him drunk. Gentlemen liked McKay; McKay liked sailors and the guts of banjos. He wrote sonnet after sonnet in Berlin and didn't know he had syphilis.

•

Berlin was the place where European powers got together in 1884 to divide Africa among themselves and that's why Du Bois opens his operatic novel, *Dark Princess*, in the German capital. It is 1923 and because his medical school in New York won't permit the protagonist to take obstetrics where he might touch white women, he, an accomplished black student, storms off to Berlin. He's seen white women smoke, but never a colored one, and he pours out his heart to an Indian princess over tea in the Tiergarten, having saved her from the advances of a white American boy in a café on Unter den Linden. He knocked the guy down.

A few years and some misadventures later, the black student is a popular state legislator from Chicago about to win the nomination for Congress, his idealism wiped away by big-interest politics. But reunited with the princess, he renounces political office and abandons his scheming wife. Don't let black Chicago think you're down and out because of one man, a cigar-chomping ward boss tells the cast-off wife.

The liberated black politician and his princess put on knickerbockers and pick up knapsacks and hold hands in Jackson Park. By the waters of Lake Michigan, she recites from the

Rig Veda. She reveals that she rejected an English suitor whom London approved of and went on a grand tour of the Darker World, the world that was and is to be again, from China to Egypt. A Japanese baron turns out to be the prime minister of the Darker World. In Berlin, at a conference of Turks and Arabs, the black American was considered a slave, a half-man, not fit to be part of the new world order of Dark People raised up, and she came over to see for herself.

They part. He works as a laborer, digging the Chicago subway. She is with his mother in Virginia, where he writes to her of the innocent sandy dust and gas pipes of the city. She quotes the Buddha. He goes home to find that she has borne him a son, the Messenger and Messiah to all the Darker Worlds.

•

Claude McKay died in Chicago, twenty-five years after he left his American in Berlin. He was young, or not much younger than Dad was, and a Catholic, like Marcus Garvey.

•

My presence hurt them. They had a silent denouement. They were too decent not to be ashamed of the hurt my presence made them ever more conscious of. The longer the intervals between my visits, the more café time abroad I found on deposit. Ronald said openly that he wished it had been me, but Mom and Dad just became more recessive, because of what had happened to them through the actions of their elder son one early morning on the Long Island Expressway, and the hurt of no children for Solomon and Francesca to leave behind.

•

I don't know anyone I knew twenty-five years ago. I went to a couple of goodbye parties way back there. One bald brother didn't want to say what a commie he'd been over there in East

Berlin with his big apartment, but he'd written for newspapers and he'd had a radio show. He made a big deal about needing to get back Stateside. Still paranoid after all those years, he was ditching his formerly state-controlled girlfriend in the process. I am one of the black American leftovers who sit by themselves. We nod to one another, my fellow old heads and I, a veteran session musician, a widowed engineer, that second-rate Beat poet, now a celebrity because of his age, and low-frequency me. I have their general outlines and they pieces of mine. We exchanged them a few years ago, but since the engineer's German wife died, we have not added to the kitty of information. They don't come in as regularly as I do, a fat guy again. To gain weight is to become neutered. Yet the crew of dealers I manage in Hasenheide Park is scared of me.

I never tried to belong. I stayed in the great head with the unratified deeds, a phrase I always took to mean the things we do in the dark. I just wanted to be left alone. I was. I have been, my slowed footsteps a perfunctory but familiar chorus. During the worst of the antiforeigner attacks, the neo-Nazis never messed with American-looking blacks, not even at four in the morning. I was still bleary-eyed in Powell's Bookstore basement with the deutsche taschenbuch verlag editions I couldn't really read.

I kept moving. Armies withdrew, but I didn't go anywhere. I became the kind of unexplained American in Berlin who only met people in public. I gave up a long time ago looking either for the brewery or for the polished steel line marking the Wall's old course through the profound disappointment of what Potsdamerplatz became. Who knew that the East Bloc was broke or that on her mother's side Cello had three cousins in two state penitentiaries. She'd never been threatened by my presence, but there I was, hanging on, like the flu.

I know I'm supposed to sound sorry. But am I? I eat alone at Christmas. I close the door and don't have to swing it for anyone, not even for myself. Big Dash used to sing a Blues, "Empty Pants." It is not that I am too old for a young man's idea of freedom, which would somehow justify the sitting, the uninterrupted days of false expectations. It's that my rendezvous with machines is drawing nearer and I am not brave.

Schöneberg has cafés full of one beautiful mixed-race girl after another. I sometimes wonder which one is Bags's daughter by Afer's girlfriend. A certain place is one of the oldest and dreariest of local pubs and therefore fashionable among the young who smoke.

Everyone loves that recording of Ella Fitzgerald forgetting in concert in Berlin the English words to "Mack the Knife." Tell me tell me tell me could that boy do something right . . .

•

In all these seasons, I have seen her only once, and that already a while back, in what people still called the new Café Einstein, though by then it had been on the Linden for more than ten years. I'd been sitting there for at least twenty minutes, not noticing the music, when a waiter carried past me the sort of frothy-looking coffee with milk that I wasn't having at the time. The imposing brown woman upright on a banquette was none other than Cello, able to fit into her vintage Agnes B. Berlin was in its bleak winter period, cold, deserted, damp, with pig dishes in many kitchen pots.

She was right out there, in the open, not hidden behind the newspaper racks. She would have had it shaved before she'd ever cut it. I could tell from her hairstyle just how crazy she was: it was pinned up into several thick, tight, glossy Spartan braids. A family of black lizards was riding on her head. The bartender smiled over the bar and down the long wall. The iPod behind him was suddenly playing something other than mellow pop, something that made me want to pay attention to the way people were looking at one another. It was Joe Williams singing

"It's the Talk of the Town." The black wall of her sunglasses in the winter light gave her an advantage over everything she looked like she was ignoring. Her three divorces, campaigns of mutually assured destruction, told village Berlin of damage I'd known nothing about. But time had gone by. I wasn't sure how many people cared about her overdose. No one was smoking.

She and Mom didn't laugh at the old white lady back in Hyde Park who used to welcome audiences to the Harper Theater wearing an evening gown. The old dear was not from the artists' colonies that Dad managed to scare Mom into having little to do with. Cello, Ruthanne, curtsied to the woman, mesmerized by French and Italian films Mom didn't care that she was much too young for. The woman was someone Cello responded to, her movie theater one place where Cello would go. Curtsying made her happy; the foreign languages made her happy. Mom did what she didn't like to do, dress up, and helped Cello step into yet more taffeta in order to continue the rebuilding of the destroyed fat girl, her brilliant black Rapunzel who'd vomited over herself backstage and couldn't go on.

She sat alone, expecting no one. I stayed where I was. I had to. Our stories allowed for nothing else. I was sure she spotted me, from the way she started and reached for her jeweled throat. The waiter took away the coffee and brought her tea. He poured. She didn't touch it. Her hands were shaking. Cello, the fat girl who butterflied into that ravishing woman, the young black artist who adored playing like a demon Rachmaninoff's Third Piano Concerto but couldn't with a spotlight on her, though Mom had put together an Olympic training team of therapist, yoga instructor, trusted former teacher, and dietician.

I didn't care that she'd been right. There was no there where I came from anymore. I'd lost what there had been somehow, and not through not paying attention, busy as I was, wishing myself into a café scene without end, into a bygone era on loop, repeating and repeating in the museum emptiness. To put off grief, I offered my book of moonlight to the Spree. I thought to escape my Chicago River, domestic waters flavored by dead rats. I must have believed that it would be there always, ready to reverse current with me. Mistaken, I disappeared, blotchy and drug-trim, another lexicographer of desire and ruin.

The statue of Saint Maurice in the Gothic Cathedral of Magdeburg was my idea of Black Power. The look of him, helmeted, mailed, thirteenth century, and black. But I never much liked the story of this longtime patron saint, the Theban soldier of the Roman Empire. He got along with the pagan power structure, but when ordered to ravage a Christian town, he refused, his Christian legion was twice decimated, and then finally all were slaughtered. Europe brought people from Africa as slaves and the church had no problem with that and Europe made sure one of the wise men in the paintings was always black as coal.

•

I stayed behind, in Isherwood's last days in Berlin, as he put them down in the final journal entry of his novel. I used to carry Isherwood around with me. I'd skip class for the day and go from the bar on North Wells Street to the bar on Woodlawn, lost in the daydream of being the rootless stranger in Berlin who seduced tough German boys.

At the end of his novel, Isherwood makes a tour of the dives before the police close them. In a communist bar near the Zoo, a whitewashed cellar of students at long wooden tables, he finds a beautiful boy in leather shorts and a Russian blouse wholly unaware of the torture he will face under the Nazis. History is not a game, Isherwood warns us—and himself, angry at the loss of the city where he could be what he most wanted. It was clear to me what he wanted from his portrait of Otto, who, in real life as Heinz, I read at Powell's Bookstore, had nice legs. Isherwood explained in a memoir that he felt he had to chill how gay he was sounding in his novel by making Otto's legs unattractive.

I'd read Isherwood's novel so often I had no trouble inserting myself into its scene. I am the negro boxer—small *n* of the British 1930s—whom Isherwood sees at the far end of Potsdamerstrasse, working at a fairground, in an attraction of fixed boxing and wrestling matches. I take my turn knocking guys out and getting knocked out. And I, the black boxer in his stance, am going to meet Otto's brother, Lothar, a smoldering Nazi whose bed Isherwood was given when he moved in with the working-class Nowaks. I am going to guide him to the light and we will never age.

·

I knew that one day I would get too old to move those boxes of books, but I could not give them up. They held my undying love. I looked back and saw myself standing in the rain with a suitcase. The *salaat al-mahgreb* drifted from an innermost courtyard. Rise up with your bad self one last time, O splendid Susan Sontag. She told me home is the place where there is someone who does not wish you any pain.